BLOODSHED ON THE BOARDS

JUDY LEIGH

Boldwood

First published in Great Britain in 2024 by Boldwood Books Ltd.

Copyright © Judy Leigh, 2024

Cover Design by Rachel Lawston

Cover Illustration: Rachel Lawston

The moral right of Judy Leigh to be identified as the author of this work has been asserted in accordance with the Copyright, Designs and Patents Act 1988.

All rights reserved. No part of this book may be reproduced in any form or by any electronic or mechanical means, including information storage and retrieval systems, without written permission from the author, except for the use of brief quotations in a book review.

This book is a work of fiction and, except in the case of historical fact, any resemblance to actual persons, living or dead, is purely coincidental.

Every effort has been made to obtain the necessary permissions with reference to copyright material, both illustrative and quoted. We apologise for any omissions in this respect and will be pleased to make the appropriate acknowledgements in any future edition.

A CIP catalogue record for this book is available from the British Library.

Paperback ISBN 978-1-83751-468-7

Large Print ISBN 978-1-83751-469-4

Hardback ISBN 978-1-83751-467-0

Ebook ISBN 978-1-83751-470-0

Kindle ISBN 978-1-83751-471-7

Audio CD ISBN 978-1-83751-462-5

MP3 CD ISBN 978-1-83751-463-2

Digital audio download ISBN 978-1-83751-466-3

Boldwood Books Ltd
23 Bowerdean Street
London SW6 3TN
www.boldwoodbooks.com

To my mum, who will never know that I'm an author.

It may be possible to gild pure gold, but who can make a mother more beautiful?

— MAHATMA GANDHI

The Spriggan Travelling Theatre Company presents

The Return of the Cornish King

Cast

Uther Pendragon – Daniel Kitto
Igraine – Mackenzie Fuller
Guinevere – Ingrid Ström
Merlin – Musa Omari
Morgan le Fay – Mackenzie Fuller
Lancelot – Rupert Bradley
Arthur – Ben D'Arcy
The Mermaid of Seal Bay – To be played by a local actor under the age of ten

Directed by Daniel Kitto
Lighting by Jesse Miles

With Thanks to Our Sponsors

Korrik Clay
Daniel Kitto

For whatever we lose (like a you or a me), it's always our self we find in the sea.

— E.E. CUMMINGS

GLOSSARY

Ansom, ansum – Nice, handsome, good.

Backalong – In previous times, a while ago.

Bleddy – Local pronunciation of 'bloody' as an emphasising adjective.

Dreckly – At some point in the future; soon, but not immediately.

Emmet – A tourist. It actually means an ant.

Giss on! – Stop talking rubbish!

A gurt licker – A large object.

Heller – Lively, troublesome child.

Jumping – Angry.

Maid – Any girl or woman, often used as a form of address.

My bewty – My beauty, a term of affection. Bewty can also be substituted with ansom.

Oggy – Pasty (from Cornish language *hogen*).

Proper – Satisfactory, good.

Tuss – An obnoxious person.

1

Morwenna Mutton stared up at the blue sky over Seal Bay. The spattered clouds reminded her of dollops of clotted cream. Or the mottled paint on her bathroom wall. The ocean lifted her, lapping against her wetsuit, spattering her face. It felt good to be alive, floating on her back – springtime was here, the earth was warming. But the sea was as cold as ever.

'I'm getting out now – I'm f-freezing...' Louise shouted from a licking wave somewhere beyond Morwenna's toes. Morwenna rolled over, thrashed her arms and blinked the water from her eyes. 'You go. I'll be with you dreckly.'

She kicked furiously, bobbing above the sea level, and wondered what to do with herself this Saturday evening. It was a toss-up between spending time with a good book or visiting family. But Tamsin was taking Elowen to her friend Britney's for a sleepover before watching Netflix with a friend and splashing out on a takeaway and a bottle of wine. Morwenna reminded herself that her daughter needed time off: Elowen was a handful at six and a half – she knew her own mind, that one.

As Lamorna often said, she was a typical Mutton maid, which meant that she was a feisty individual, inclined to obstinacy.

Poor Lamorna. She'd been feeling a bit low lately, although she'd never admit it. Morwenna's mother was eighty-two now, living by herself in the middle terrace in Tregenna Gardens, where she had a lovely view of Seal Bay from her bedroom window, but not much else to cheer her up. Other than family and the people she spoke to on the way to the corner shop. Morwenna texted her mum that later, she'd walk over – it would take twenty minutes – and they'd watch a DVD, something with Brad Pitt in it or George Clooney. They were Lamorna's favourites. Her obsession with handsome men was as bad as it had always been. No, she'd become worse in her old age, Morwenna thought. Definitely worse.

She swam towards the beach where Louise stood wrapped in a towel, quaking, trying to dry her hair. Morwenna ran across the sand to join her, helping herself to a flask of hot tea, her skin gooseflesh beneath the wetsuit.

'It's been a long week. Thank goodness the rain's finally stopped.' Louise groaned. 'I'm making *penne alla vodka* tonight to cheer us up. Steve's fed up with driving halfway round the county with a lorry-load of fish.'

'I thought he enjoyed his job.' Morwenna tugged off her swim cap and her fountain of silver hair tumbled out.

'He used to. The roads are busier, roadworks everywhere on the A30 and beyond. Besides which, Steve gets a nosebleed if he goes north of the Tamar bridge nowadays. Middle-age syndrome,' Louise joked. A thought came to her. 'Do you want to come over? We've got wine.'

'I'm going up to see Mum.'

'How is Lamorna?'

'Wicked as ever. She won't come swimming, although she always threatens to. It would do her good though,' Morwenna said, sipping hot tea. 'Are you coming tomorrow? I love our Sunday-morning swims.'

Louise nodded. 'I've put up posters in the library to advertise the SWANs. We'll get a better take-up now spring's arrived. People are keener when the weather's warm.'

'Swans…' Morwenna smiled at the image of herself, Louise, the Grundy sisters, Donald Stewart from the library and young PC Jane Choy standing at the edge of the sea, their arms flapping around freezing bodies. Swans was far too elegant a term for a group of locals who floundered in the water once a week like clumsy ducks. Louise was determined to expand membership, but the same six people met every Sunday morning, despite her asking everyone who walked into the library if they'd come. People were deterred by the icy water and the cold Cornish winds. But Morwenna loved it; swimming in the ocean was her favourite thing, almost.

Her mind drifted to Ruan Pascoe, her ex, who lived across the road at number nine Harbour Cottages, with the sea-green door. He'd be in The Smugglers' Inn tonight with the rest of the Seal Bay fishermen.

'Seal Bay Wild Aquatic Natation,' Louise said, interrupting her thoughts. 'It's not perfect, but who is?'

'Not me, that's for sure,' Morwenna agreed. Something caught her eye and she turned to stare. Further up the beach, people were unloading large objects from a four-by-four pickup and trailer, setting up a marquee. She narrowed her eyes to see better. 'That must be the travelling theatre company putting up their tent.'

'They have posters all over Seal Bay – they open on Tuesday. They're The Spriggan Travelling Theatre Company,' Louise said.

Morwenna knew – she'd seen the advertising. 'That's proper Cornish – a Spriggan is an evil spirit that takes the form of a wizened old man.'

'A wizened old man?' Louise smiled. 'That's a shame. I was

looking forward to seeing some buff young actors. Don't tell Steve though.'

'They're doing the Cornish version of King Arthur.'

'Maybe we'll get to see some hunky knights of the Round Table, then?'

'Maybe.' Morwenna rubbed her skin with a towel. 'Last spring, The Midnight Washerwomen brought their show here. Did you see them? Three feisty Cornish women singing, rapping, dancing their way through a poem of "Tristram and Iseult", playing all the roles. It was really good – they took it to the Edinburgh Fringe.'

'I missed it. My mum used to tell me about the midnight washerwomen though. Apparently, if you saw them, they wrapped you in their wet sheets and your arms fell off. I was scared to death.'

'They're small, dressed in green and have webbed feet. I had nightmares about them when I was Elowen's age.' Morwenna shivered beneath the drying robe, tugging on stripy leggings over damp flesh. 'They'd be a perfect match for the Spriggans.'

'I've never heard of The Spriggan Travelling Theatre Company. That's a huge trailer they've got,' Louise said. 'I'll get myself a ticket for Tuesday. Steve's not really keen.'

'Come with me,' Morwenna offered. She was dressed now, strapping her cycle helmet on, gazing towards her electric bike padlocked by the sea wall. 'I might just stop for a chat with them on the way home.'

'Here's Steve now.' Louise grabbed her bag, pointing to where a blue car was slowing down. She hugged Morwenna quickly. 'I'll see you tomorrow – and on Monday at the library. It's all work and no play for me...'

'Enjoy your *penne alla vodka*,' Morwenna called as Louise clambered in the car. She sauntered towards her new bicycle as if she had all the time in the world, admiring the red frame with matching wheels and saddle. She'd been given it last autumn by

Pam Truscott and her family after she'd solved the case of her husband Alex's murder. She'd heard Pam was wintering abroad – it was what rich widows did, according to Susan and Barb Grundy at the pop-up knitting shop. Morwenna recalled the exact moment she'd become involved in the crime last October, on the beach at Tamsin's engagement party. Of course, the engagement hadn't lasted. Morwenna hadn't seen that coming. But then, she wasn't the best sleuth in the world. She was just an amateur with a sense of fairness, who wanted to make things right for people, that was all.

Having the electric bicycle made the roads in Seal Bay so much easier to manage. In her youth she'd cycled everywhere, but the hills were tough now she was sixty-two – her legs and lungs ached as she struggled up to number four Harbour Cottages. The motor that kicked in as she pedalled was a lifesaver. But she was blessed with being full of beans – that was what counted. And her family. She shoved her bag, stuffed with damp clothes, phone and keys, in the basket at the front, flung a leg over and was on her way.

Morwenna cycled as far as the pickup that was parked by the sea wall. There was a trailer behind it, with a name painted on the side in green and yellow – The Spriggan Travelling Theatre Company – and a design of a grotesque green face, pointed ears, and wild leafy hair. Two people were laying a canvas on the beach, placing long poles on the sand. The wind ruffled their clothes. A smallish man in jeans and a bomber jacket, curls over his collar, lifted a heavy wooden box from the trailer. Morwenna caught his eye and waved a hand in greeting. 'All right?'

The man put his box back and stood up straight, rubbing an aching muscle in his back. 'All right.'

'It's good to have the theatre in town,' Morwenna remarked. 'I've never seen you lot before.'

'We've been touring for years – we do Europe every autumn,'

the man said. 'Europeans love anything Cornish. But this tour's exclusively south-west.'

'Oh, we're honoured.'

'Have you got your ticket, maid?' the man asked, and Morwenna noticed the Cornish burr.

'Not yet. You're local, then?'

'Me? Penzance, born and bred. There aren't many proper Cornish people in our company though. The director was born right here in Seal Bay, mind, but you can't have everything.' The man raised an eyebrow enigmatically and Morwenna wondered what he meant. 'We opened the show in Penzance last week. It went down well.'

'The King Arthur story.' Morwenna examined his face and decided he probably wasn't the lead. 'Are you one of the actors?'

'Me? Giss on.' The man laughed as if she had said something hilarious. 'But you're right, it's all hands on deck in this company – we muck in. I'm the technician, general dogsbody. I put scenery up and take it down, deal with the special effects, music, lighting.'

'Impressive,' Morwenna said, and she meant it.

'Nah.' The man shrugged as if he was humble but Morwenna noticed the pride in his face. 'I'm just jack of all trades here.'

Morwenna couldn't help it: the name Jack still made her prickle. Jack Greenwood had been her daughter's fiancé until last October. He'd been a disastrous choice. She pushed the memory away – it was best forgotten. 'How many actors do you have?'

'Six, if you count our silly old tuss of a director. He'd worm his way into someone else's grave, that man. Seven, if you count the extra one we're recruiting while we're here...'

'Oh?' Morwenna patted her hair in jest, preening. 'Recruiting, eh?'

'You'd be a bit old for the role, I reckon.' The man realised what he'd said and clapped a hand over his mouth. 'No offence meant.'

'None taken,' Morwenna replied. The technician was probably approaching forty himself. She offered a cheeky smile. 'Is the play any good?'

'"A tale of sorcery, secrets, bloodshed, betrayal and passion",' the technician quoted. 'And I'm behind the scenes every night, doing all the hard work while the actors show off out front.' He held out a hand. 'I'm Jesse Miles.'

Morwenna shook it. 'Morwenna Mutton. I work in the town library most mornings – and the Proper Ansom Tearoom is our family business.'

'That's good to know.' Jesse Miles beamed. 'I like a nice pasty. We're staying in a local B & B, The Blue Dolphin Guest House. Do you know it?'

'I do. A friend of mine owns it, Carole Taylor. My granddaughter goes to school with her little one, Britney. You'll be fine there. Carole will do you a proper Cornish breakfast,' Morwenna said, conscious that she'd been standing still for a while and was getting cold. It was time to go home for a shower.

'Sounds good.' Jesse raised an eyebrow. 'I love a Cornish breakfast – especially with hog pudding on the side. But two of our cast are fussy eaters. Guinevere only eats paleo, whatever that means, and Merlin's a vegan.' He shook his head, disapproving. 'Anyway, I hope you'll be there on the opening night. We're expecting a good turnout. It's a two-week run – our last night is 4 May – then we're off to Padstow.'

'I'm looking forward to it.'

Jesse picked up the box again. 'Nice to have met you, Morwenna.'

'Likewise,' Morwenna said cheerily. She put one foot on the pedal. 'See you around.'

'Duw genes.' Jesse called out the Cornish phrase for goodbye and winked. Then he was off towards the beach where others were

erecting a marquee, the canvas flapping in the breeze. Morwenna rode away, negotiating traffic towards the hill that led home.

She puffed up the gradient, passing houses on both sides. Morwenna believed that exercise kept her young – that and a good night's sleep. She'd spend an hour round her mother's later, and be back home in bed by half ten. She liked her sleep. Although even now, almost two years after she split up with Ruan, she couldn't get used to the coldness of an empty bed. She blamed herself. The car crash, she called it. A series of arguments that left a wreckage. She still liked Ruan though. And some. He was fond of her too. But she wouldn't look back, not now.

An engine rumbled, an aggressive snarling. Behind, an open-top car hovered close to her back wheel, the driver revving impatiently. Then a horn blared a loud warning. Morwenna felt her bike wobble as a yellow sports car drove too close, almost knocking her into a hedge as it roared away, dark smoke chugging from the exhaust. She noted the occupants: the driver was an older man, broad-shouldered, wearing a cloth cap, a scarf, and in the passenger seat there was a young woman with billowing auburn hair. They were gone in a flash of yellow and the growl of an engine, up the hill and round the bend, before Morwenna could yell 'Road hog!' or any other words that sprang to her lips.

She took a gulp of air – it was full of petrol fumes – and pushed her way to the top of the hill, feeling the electric motor kick in. She rounded a corner into Harbour Cottages, stopping outside number four. She glanced across the road to number nine, wondering if Ruan was home. He was probably in the snug at The Smugglers, a pint in his hand. She could imagine one of his friends from the trawler saying, 'That fish you caught today was a gurt licker,' and Ruan replying with a modest smile, 'Giss on! It was just a tiddler…'

More than anything, Morwenna missed his company, the way he was so calm while she went full pelt at everything. That was the problem, she thought with a sad smile – they were incompatible. Now she was being sentimental about the past. She put it down to all the rain they'd had in the last two weeks – it was usually wet in April in Seal Bay; it made everyone properly melancholy. Thank goodness spring was here.

Morwenna opened the door to number four, pushed the red bike into the hall and shivered. What she really needed was a hot shower. It was time to feed Brenda, who'd be asleep on the bed. She needed to text Lamorna, pop over for a couple of hours and walk back. She planned to be fast asleep by eleven.

Suddenly, she felt tired. 'I've let that man in the sports car get to me,' Morwenna muttered aloud. 'I could have fallen on my backside in someone's privet hedge – but I'm here and I'm all right.'

She took to the stairs stoically. The sports car had annoyed her – it had been lurid and loud. Worse, it had been driven recklessly, the driver showing off – a mid-life crisis of a car, belonging to an ageing boy racer with more money than sense.

Morwenna decided it wasn't right for her to judge. She hadn't fallen off. Everything was fine. She stood in the bathroom, peeling off her clothes, and turned on the hot water, watching the steam rise.

She'd never seen the yellow sports car in Seal Bay before though. She wondered whose it was.

2

An hour later, Morwenna was hurrying towards Tregenna Gardens wearing striped leggings and a purple velvet coat, her hair still damp. She had a DVD under one arm and a bottle of Prosecco in the other hand. She was already imagining her mother's cheery face at the door, the ringed fingers pulling her inside, a barrage of questions about Tamsin and Elowen before she grabbed two flute glasses and *Legends of the Fall*. But as she turned the corner, Morwenna stopped in disbelief – the bright yellow sports car was parked outside Lamorna's little terraced house.

She approached it as she might a dangerous sleeping dog. Or like a sleuth, looking for clues. The emblem on the front was Vauxhall; at the back, a silver badge proclaimed it a VX220 Turbo. She'd never seen one until it had overtaken her too closely – the headlights were shaped like angry eyes. The car, she decided, might be one of those racy things men thought might impress women, a 'babe magnet.' She wandered around to the back. There was a scuff mark on the left-hand side, a series of deep scratches, white beneath the yellow paint. Morwenna imagined what sort of person would drive the car – she'd seen the man in it already, but she asked herself what he was *like* – and, more interestingly, why he'd parked outside her mother's house.

She knocked at the door tentatively. Lamorna appeared almost instantly in a white flowery dress that looked as if it had been rescued from the sixties. She wore a red flower in her hair, bare feet with crimson-painted toenails. She grasped Morwenna's hand and tugged her inside. 'Come in – come in. There's someone I want you to meet.'

Lamorna hauled Morwenna through the hall, seemingly oblivious of her usual hip pain, into the lounge. A man was sitting on the sofa, one arm stretched casually across the back, a tumbler in his other hand. He was probably Lamorna's age – early eighties – although his hair was brown, grey at the sides, and he sported a jaunty moustache. He wore a tweed jacket and trousers; his long legs were crossed. His cloth cap was on the table. Morwenna was assessing him already – it was the man she'd seen in the yellow car, minus the young woman. He had twinkling blue eyes – he was self-assured, with a deliberate air of confidence. She knew him from somewhere. She tried to imagine him younger.

Lamorna sat beside the man and patted his knee. 'You remember my Morwenna?'

'Of course – how could I forget?' The man had a deep gravelly voice that many might have thought sexy. He spoke slowly and deliberately to an imaginary full room, as if performing. 'You were a gangly youngster when I last saw you.'

Morwenna frowned – she'd never been gangly. 'When was that?'

'She couldn't have been more than eight or nine.' Lamorna turned her most seductive gaze on the man. 'You remember Daniel, Morwenna? The actor?'

'Daniel Kitto.' Morwenna said – it was all falling into place. She put her hands on her hips. 'You nearly knocked me off my bike earlier.'

'I remember.' Daniel chuckled as if it amused him. 'I was momentarily distracted, seeing a well-rounded bottom on a bicycle – perhaps I came in a little too close for comfort.'

'Are you with the theatre company?' Morwenna ignored his comment and flourished the Prosecco and DVD.

'Spriggan? I own it.' Daniel stretched his body across the sofa as if he owned that as well.

'They're doing the Cornish King Arthur.' Morwenna added, 'We should go to see it, Mum.'

'I've brought some complimentary tickets – four of them, to be precise.' Daniel smiled smugly. 'It's been a long time since I was in Seal Bay. It's good to be back.'

'So – you've been touring Europe?' Morwenna remembered the technician's words on the beach.

'The wide world.' Daniel made a grandiose gesture, raising his little finger, still acting. 'But wherever we may roam, the heart still yearns for home…'

Lamorna snuggled next to him, smiling as if she'd won first prize. 'Daniel's taking me to dinner tomorrow night.'

'In that car?' Morwenna couldn't think of anything else to say.

'Lamorna is in safe hands,' Daniel purred. 'I'm a young eighty-two. I keep myself toned and fit. I do yoga, t'ai chi, I'm teetotal – and I still tread the boards, would you believe?'

'I would,' Morwenna said. He looked like a man who took pride in himself. One who'd never give up acting, even after retirement. She noticed the way her mother's eyes gleamed.

'Daniel and I go way back,' Lamorna said proudly. 'Do you remember he used to come round all the time? It was when you were doing Shakespeare, Daniel.'

'At the Theatre Royal in Plymouth. I was playing Macbeth.'

'He was very good.'

'So good I was offered the role in London.'

The smile left Lamorna's face. 'And you left me.'

'We lost touch,' Daniel said, by way of an excuse.

Lamorna was momentarily dejected. 'The next thing I heard, you'd come back to Seal Bay for the summer and you'd taken up with someone else.'

'That would have been in the early seventies perhaps?' Daniel lifted her hand, kissing it gallantly. 'I always knew what I'd missed, Lamorna. The chance to spend my days with a woman of your ilk, someone warm, kind and affectionate – with lasting charm and beauty.' He kissed her fingers again.

Lamorna fluttered her eyelashes. 'You always were a flatterer.'

'So, you're here for two weeks, Daniel?' Morwenna said, trying to bring some perspective to the conversation. 'Then he'll be off to Padstow, Mum. The show must go on.'

'I suppose you'll have to go?' Lamorna was momentarily saddened, then Daniel took her hand in both of his, as if warming it.

'*The Return of the Cornish King* is my swansong. This will be my last tour. It's the right time for me to retire. My career has been illustrious, but even the best of actors must one day hang up his codpiece.'

'You're selling the company?' Morwenna asked.

'No – I'm abandoning it, I'm afraid. When we started Spriggan, I pledged all my money in a rash moment of thespian ardour. As things stand, they'd get everything if I shuffled off my mortal coil. I'm afraid I upset the applecart when I changed my mind. One or two of the cast were quite vocal. I have something else I want to spend my money on now. But that's a secret between me and my solicitor...'

Lamorna patted the sofa on the other side of her. 'Come and sit down, let's open that bottle of Prosecco.' She looked keenly at Daniel. 'Will you have a glass with us?'

'Ne'er a drop shall touch my lips,' Daniel replied dramatically. 'Besides which, I'm driving.'

'The yellow VX220 Turbo?' Morwenna said. 'It's an unusual car.'

'It has style and pace and good looks.' Daniel tapped his chest as if the words applied to him. 'I must take you for a ride, Morwenna.'

Lamorna grasped his hand in both of hers. 'I can't wait until we go to dinner.'

Morwenna glanced at the tumbler in his hand. 'Can I refill your glass, Daniel?'

'That would be splendid. Cold water, please.' He held out the glass. 'It's lovely to see you again, Morwenna. Lamorna says you are a grandmother – there are four generations of delightful Mutton women now.'

Lamorna agreed. 'Oh, you must meet Tamsin – she's twenty-eight and very beautiful – she runs our tearoom now – and her little one, Elowen, six and a half, so full of beans.'

'Is the child confident and pretty? Can she act?' Daniel asked.

Morwenna returned from the kitchen, offering a glass of water. 'That's an odd question.'

'Only...' Daniel crossed his legs emphatically and took a thirsty sip, '...in each town we play, we recruit a child to be the mermaid. She will only appear at the beginning of the play, dressed in a swimsuit and a tail, sitting behind a wooden board painted like waves. She has to say...' Daniel assumed a measured, childish voice '..."Welcome to Cornwall, to the home of King Arthur. Tonight, we present a tale of sorcery, secrets, bloodshed, betrayal and passion..."'

Morwenna met her mother's eyes. 'Oh, Elowen could do that.'

'She'd love it, Daniel,' Lamorna breathed.

'The audition is tomorrow afternoon. We always invite all the local children in every venue we play. Ingrid – our lovely Inga, who plays Guinevere – runs the children's audition. Bring your little one down, or ask her mother to bring her – Tamsin, was it?' Daniel arched an eyebrow.

Morwenna put the DVD on the table. 'I don't suppose you'll be wanting Brad Pitt now, Mum?'

'Oh, who needs Brad?' Daniel stretched an arm around the back of the sofa, to encompass Lamorna's shoulders. 'Tonight, you have Daniel Kitto – he's the real deal.'

Morwenna was still wearing the purple coat. 'I might get off home, Mum. I'll leave you to it.'

'Not at all,' Daniel insisted. 'I must depart soon. I believe in a good night's sleep – at least, when I'm alone in bed.' He arched an eyebrow again and Morwenna was tempted to make a gesture, fingers pointing down her throat. She noticed how her mother's eyes glimmered with delight.

'I'll just stay a little longer.' Daniel winked. 'Then I'll give you a lift home, Morwenna – in the Turbo.'

'And have a cup of tea and a biscuit before you go.' Lamorna was on her feet. 'I want you to get to know Daniel properly, Morwenna. Especially as he's coming back here to live. I do hope the pair of you will get on famously now Daniel and I are...' her expression was too eager, '...reunited.'

'Early days, but, yes, Seal Bay is where I want to live, where I'll be finally laid to rest near the place I was born, not far from the whisper of the ocean.' Daniel tapped the seat beside him. 'I'd love a cup of good Cornish tea, Lamorna. And while you're in the kitchen, your charming daughter and I will become reacquainted. It's been too many years. Let me tell you about the lonely life of an actor, the comedy, the tragedy of each new day. I have trodden the boards since my youth, you know – every role from Dick Whittington to

Dick Tracy. Oh, and I must tell you about the time we toured Kent and I played Lear on the White Cliffs of Dover in a snowstorm...'

* * *

The cup of tea lasted for an hour and a half, along with Daniel Kitto's monologues. Morwenna was squashed at the edge of the sofa, her legs full of pins and needles, while a rapt Lamorna listened as he narrated them through his performance of six Shakespeares, three Becketts, two Greek tragedies, *Cats* the musical and *The Mousetrap*. Daniel certainly had enjoyed the most incredible career.

Then Lamorna said hopefully, 'Do you regret not marrying, Daniel?'

He paused for a moment, his eyes wistful. 'Romantic opportunities were lost in the mad dash for success and fame.' He sighed. Morwenna thought he was acting again. 'A family, that's so important when one is ageing and alone. You have it all, Lamorna, your three Mutton maids.'

'Oh, I do,' Lamorna agreed. 'Family is everything – and love, of course.'

'And you are beautiful as ever.' Daniel was enjoying his own debonair performance. He raised an arm as if centre stage.

> *'Love's not Time's fool, though rosy lips and cheeks*
> *Within his bending sickle's compass come;*
> *Love alters not with his brief hours and weeks,*
> *But bears it out even to the edge of doom.'*

Lamorna caught her breath, transfixed. 'How gorgeous. Did you just make that up?'

'Shakespeare's sonnet number 116 – we have copies in the library,' Morwenna said.

'Oh, you work in a library? How marvellous!' Daniel exclaimed, as if no one had ever worked in a library before.

'Just mornings,' Morwenna said, stretching aching legs. 'Daniel, I'm off home now. Is your offer of a lift still good?'

'Of course. A gentleman's word...' Daniel stood up and Lamorna did the same, grabbing his arm.

'Must you go so soon?'

Daniel brought her fingers to his lips. '"Parting is such sweet sorrow... That I shall say good night till it be morrow."'

'Then I look forward to dinner,' Lamorna breathed.

'I'm wild swimming bright and early tomorrow, Daniel.' Morwenna faced him mischievously. 'If you'd like to try out your fitness with the SWANs.'

'I have occasional cramps,' Daniel said. 'It might be wise to refrain.'

'And it's too bleddy cold.' Lamorna shivered. She'd never ventured further than the water's edge.

'Early morning rehearsal for me, after a spot of yoga and a bowl of muesli, I'm afraid,' Daniel said. 'Perfection is an actor's perpetual quest.' He led the way to the door. 'But my heart will not rest until tomorrow evening when I see you again, sweet Lamorna.'

'Me too.' Lamorna reached up to peck his cheek.

'My house is only ten minutes away in the car.' Morwenna looked at the VX220 Turbo dubiously.

'Less than five, the way I drive,' Daniel said roguishly and waved a set of keys.

* * *

Daniel insisted on taking the scenic route through Seal Bay, roaring along the seafront too loudly, given that it was past nine thirty and most of Seal Bay had settled in for the night, apart from a few fishermen who were still inside the taverns or loitering on the street. The sea was black, the moon reflecting gold threads on inky waves. Daniel turned the car away from the town and accelerated up the hills, arriving outside Morwenna's house in Harbour Cottages with a flourishing rumble of his engine. He switched it off 'Well, here we are.'

'Thanks, Daniel.' Morwenna unclipped the seat belt. The wind penetrated the threads of her velvet coat and she shivered. Her ears were cold and her hair was rearranged across her face.

'My pleasure.' Daniel said the word pleasure as if it were the only thing that mattered. 'It's been so good to catch up after all these years.' He offered a mischievous smile. 'Especially since I'll be seeing a lot more of your mother.' Again, the raised eyebrow, the innuendo.

'Well, I hope you'll enjoy living in Seal Bay.' Morwenna felt for the door handle. But Daniel wanted to talk.

'Indeed. I will settle here now. It's been a long and lonely life. As Brando said, "an actor is at most a poet and at least an entertainer." We suffer for our art…'

'Well, I wish you a happy retirement.' Morwenna pushed the car door open.

'You're in a minority, I fear,' Daniel said dramatically.

He had Morwenna's full attention now. 'Why's that?'

'When I announced to the cast when we opened at Penzance that this was our last tour, that I'd be no longer funding Spriggan, they weren't pleased. They need my financial input as well as our sponsor and what we make at the box office.'

'Can't they manage by themselves?'

'Alas, no.' Daniel said theatrically. 'I made money on property in the sixties and seventies – I was in London, right time, right place. So, Spriggan Travelling Theatre has been a pet project of mine for the last few years, a labour of love. But now I have other things to consider and – they are, for the most part, a troupe of ham actors with very little initiative.'

'So that's the end of Spriggan?'

'I'm afraid it is. But most of them dislike me anyway – oh, the jealousy that exists amongst actors, you'd scarcely believe it, Morwenna. "I could a tale unfold…"'

Morwenna wondered if he was angling after another cup of tea. 'Well, I must go, Daniel – and you'll be needing your beauty sleep. Thanks for the lift.'

'My pleasure,' he said again. 'And don't forget – bring that granddaughter down for the audition – and her glamorous young mother.'

'Right. I'll text Tam and tell her about it.' Morwenna closed the door with a clunk. She pushed her hands in her pockets to warm up and felt the cold metal of her door keys. Daniel and his VX220 Turbo snarled away loudly in a cloud of smoke and she turned to go.

The upstairs curtains of number nine were open and a figure in silhouette was watching her. It was Ruan, making sure she was home safely. She turned away and walked inside; he could make what he liked of the yellow sports car.

3

Morwenna and PC Jane Choy were the only SWANs who made it for the Sunday morning swim. Louise texted that she had drunk too much wine with the *penne alla vodka* and couldn't get out of bed. Donald Stewart from the library messaged that he was immersed in a book about the paranormal and would give swimming a miss. Barb Grundy and her sister Susan didn't text at all. Morwenna and Jane stood in their wetsuits, stuffing their hair into swimming caps.

'It's been a week of endless paperwork,' Jane grumbled. 'And Rick doesn't get any easier to work with.'

'Why – what's he been up to?' Morwenna thought briefly of DI Tremayne. He wasn't the most agreeable man in the force.

'He's had me on long shifts – I've been called out three times this week to deal with disturbances.' Jane pulled a wry face. 'Spring's coming – I always expect to be busy in the run-up to summer. The bay's starting to buzz with tourists and mostly they are great, but one or two make for an interesting life. Now the theatre's in town, it pulls in the locals and what do some of the locals like to do?'

'Watch the show?' Morwenna tried.

'Drink too much. I had to disperse a paralytic hen party on Friday – it wasn't pretty,' Jane said. 'Mind you, last night was quiet for a Saturday. We only had one episode of antisocial behaviour.'

'What happened?'

'I was in a patrol vehicle with another officer who stopped the youngster. We told him to go home quietly, and he said he was desperate for the loo and he peed against the front tyre. Of course, that's breaking the law, but I knew how to deal with the kid. I stuck him in the car and gave him a lift home. His mother gave him a right earful.' Jane shrugged – it was routine. 'He's been caught a few times, D & D, peeing in the road, too much beer in his belly. We call him Wee Willie Winkie back at the nick. He's only eighteen. He's going through a difficult patch.'

'Anyone I know?'

'You know the family. Nice people. I won't say anything else.' Jane gazed towards the choppy waves. 'It looks freezing this morning.'

'I'll race you.' Morwenna was getting cold beneath the wetsuit.

They were about to make a run for it when they noticed a woman jogging towards them, waving an arm. She was dressed in dark clothes, a long coat, a beanie and a stout pair of boots. She shouted something that sounded like, 'Wait up.'

Morwenna jumped up and down to keep warm. 'Hello.'

'Are you off for a swim?' The woman had a lilting accent, probably Scottish, Morwenna thought. She was somewhere in between her own age and Jane's; forties probably.

'We are,' Morwenna said. It was fairly obvious.

'In the sea?' the woman asked again.

Jane nodded. Morwenna shivered and was tempted to say, no – we always dress like this when we're out for a stroll, but instead she said, 'Do you want to join us? You'd be very welcome.'

'Yes, please – I've no cozzie with me right now, but next time you go in…' The woman met her eyes. 'I'm Mackenzie Fuller. Kenzie. I'm one of the actors.' She pointed down the beach towards the marquee as if that would explain everything.

'We swim every Sunday,' Jane explained.

'Not every day?'

'I'm often here,' Morwenna said. 'You're staying at Carole's guest house, The Blue Dolphin?'

'Yes, I am,' Kenzie replied. 'The whole cast is.'

'Then I'll leave you a message next time I go,' Morwenna promised. 'It'll be during the week, if you have time.'

'I'll make time. I love a swim. An actor needs to keep herself fit. I'd better get off – we're rehearsing. I'm already late.' Kenzie winked. 'Not that I care. Our director can go to hell. I'll be seeing you.' She turned back to the marquee.

Jane watched Kenzie go, shaking her head. 'The poor director. She clearly doesn't have much time for her boss.'

'I've met him, Daniel Kitto,' Morwenna said. 'He was at my mum's last night. She had a bit of a fling with him when I was young. He's aged well.' She gave a short laugh. 'Haven't we all?'

'I'm doing my best…' Jane gazed towards the lapping waves.

'Let's get in,' Morwenna suggested. 'Before the wind changes and we freeze to death.'

They ran towards the rolling surf and dived in, squealing.

* * *

An hour later, they were sitting in the Proper Ansom Tearoom cupping a hot drink between their palms. The customers were trickling in. The tearoom opened on Sunday mornings now spring was here. It was good to see the tearoom filling up after the quiet season. Tamsin was busy serving teas, collecting dishes, chatting to people in her usual chirpy way. Elowen was telling her grandmother and Jane about the terrible dilemmas of being six and a half.

'I had a sleepover so Mummy could get drunk with her friend Becca from the shop next door. Carole bought me and Britney takeaway pizza because she didn't have time to cook with all the guests she's got. It was 'ansom. We took the whole box to bed with us and Britney got tomato sauce all over the duvet.' She was clutching a purple-faced knitted dog toy; she took Oggy Two everywhere. 'My mummy never gets me takeaways. She says we have to eat proper home-made food. It's not fair.' Elowen pulled a face to show just how unfair it was.

'Home-made's much better.' Morwenna sipped her tea gratefully. She was still cold.

'No, it's boring, Grandma. Mummy's boring too. She keeps telling me she has to open the tearoom and it's Sunday, for goodness' sake. I want to go to the beach. And she won't let me have a dog now Oggy's gone.'

'Oh?' Morwenna was suddenly more interested. Elowen hadn't stopped talking about her invisible dog for months. 'Where's Oggy gone to?'

'He left. I told him it was OK to go back to the made-up dogs' home. He was bored with being invisible. He wanted to be a real dog.' She wiped her nose on her sleeve. 'It's not fair. You've got Brenda now. She's the cleverest cat in the world. Why can't I have a dog?'

'Maybe when you're older.'

'That's years away, Grandma.' Elowen stuck out a lip. 'Grandad would get me a dog if I asked him. Grandad loves me. He's the best grandad.'

'You need to be patient.' Morwenna reached out a hand and patted the purple toy. 'You have Oggy Two.'

Elowen ignored her and turned to Jane. 'Can I have one of your police dogs?'

Jane made a sympathetic face. 'All our dogs are very busy, Elowen. They help us to fight crime and protect people.'

'My great-grandma says the police are bleddy useless – she said most of them couldn't catch a cold.' Elowen sniffed, then wiped her nose again. 'I'm getting a dog when I'm seven. I told Mummy I need one because I'm an only child. I heard Britney's mummy say it's a shame I'm an only child and it will make me spoiled. And this afternoon I'm going to go to the theatre to be a mermaid with a real tail. Mummy told me.'

'I texted your mum earlier to tell her about it. You're off to an audition.' Morwenna was about to explain, but Elowen wandered away to the counter, declaring loudly that she needed a Labrador this afternoon or she'd be spoiled. Tamsin ruffled her daughter's hair affectionately and gave her an apple instead. Elowen put it back on the counter, disgusted, and it rolled away. Morwenna met Jane's eyes and mouthed, 'She's a character.'

Jane winked. 'She's a survivor, bless her... She's doing all right after what happened last autumn.'

'She's growing up fast and developing a real attitude. I can't believe the difference in her since October.' Morwenna looked around, changing the subject. 'It's busy in here. That's good to see.'

'It is – it seems we're amongst professionals.' Jane indicated a nearby table where two men were talking animatedly over mugs of coffee. Morwenna listened for a moment and heard the words '...final scene fell completely flat...', '...and the costumes don't even fit properly...', '...letting things run down to absolute basics...', 'after all, I'm Lancelot, I'm supposed to be a romantic hero, for God's sake, and I have to wear something that amounts to a piece of sacking... and it's so itchy...', '...complete shambles to work with a man so unprofessional, and he's a cheapskate...'

Morwenna smiled. 'Actors,' she muttered.

'King Arthur's a famous Cornish myth. I'll be there on the opening night,' Jane said. 'I think Rick's going too – he's taking Sally and the boys.'

'He has a social life?' Morwenna suppressed a laugh. 'Bless him, the Seal Bay police force will grind to a halt if he's not in the office.'

She looked up. The tearoom was still busy. Elowen was demanding something to eat, wanting to get changed into her best clothes. She was excited – the auditions were being held at three. Morwenna needed to get home early, shower, feed Brenda and come back to watch. She turned to Jane. 'I'd better get a wriggle on. Same time next week?'

'Wouldn't miss it.' Jane gave her a hug.

Morwenna waved to Tamsin, called a quick, 'See you dreckly,' and was making her way towards the red bicycle chained outside.

* * *

At ten past three, Morwenna stretched her legs in an uncomfortable seat in the front row, inside the marquee. Lamorna was on one side and Tamsin on the other, Carole Taylor and Rosie Buvač just behind them. Morwenna was puzzled as she hugged Oggy Two on her knee. 'I thought when people had auditions, the candidates were called up one at a time?'

'It's a funny business, if you ask me,' Lamorna agreed.

They watched an auburn-haired woman, slim in a long black dress, crouching amid twelve huddled children, all girls apart from Billy Crocker and another boy Morwenna didn't recognise. She introduced herself. 'You can call me Inga Ström.' She smiled. 'What can I call you – in turn?'

'Elowen Pascoe.'

'Maya Buvač.'

'Britney Taylor.'

'Billy Big Willy,' Billy joked, and all the other children gave a roar of laughter.

Inga listened with interest, then she said, 'Can you find a space in the performance area? Stand up straight. Concentrate. Now, I want you to mime for me that you are swimming in deep water.'

'Just like my grandma does,' Elowen said.

'She's a show-off,' Billy grunted.

'I can swim,' Britney said. 'Like a real-life mermaid.'

The children began to move their arms energetically.

'Now imagine you are a mermaid, and you dive deep, deep into the depths of the sea. You are happy underwater. You have spent your whole life there. Imagine you have a crown – you put it on your head… You are regal, powerful,' Inga said as the children mimed furiously, their faces tight with concentration. 'You see a giant octopus – he's your friend – go and shake hands with him… and a whale that spouts water… You swim with the whale – you own the water.'

Morwenna watched as Billy rolled on his back, spitting furiously in the air. Britney lay on her stomach and thrashed her arms like a crab. Elowen moved in slow motion like a dancer, and Maya twirled as if underwater. Morwenna understood. The auditions had already singled out the mermaid qualities in some of the children without them being under any pressure.

She whispered to Tamsin, 'She's very clever, Inga – she has them in the palm of her hand.'

'She's incredible,' Tamsin agreed, her eyes on her daughter, tears of pride shining.

Lamorna stared around. 'I thought Daniel might be here – his car's parked outside.'

'Are you looking forward to having dinner with him, Mum?'

'I can't wait.' Lamorna placed a hand over her heart. 'He's such a gentleman. I always had a soft spot for him.'

'Take it day by day,' Morwenna said kindly.

'I don't have time to hang about.' Lamorna opened wide eyes. 'I'm eighty-two.'

'Just...' Morwenna wondered what to say – don't pin your hopes on him? Don't get hurt? 'Just have a good time.'

'I will,' Lamorna said. The children were now hypnotising imaginary sailors, calling them with long movements of their arms. Billy was doing his silliest impression of a zombie.

'Elowen's good, Tam,' Morwenna whispered.

'She's a perfect mermaid,' Tamsin said and Morwenna wished Ruan had been there to see his talented granddaughter.

Then Inga said, 'Right, take five, lie down. You are mermaids floating in the water on your backs, basking in the warm sunshine. Nothing moves except the occasional flick of a tail.'

All was suddenly quiet as the children lay down. Carole, blonde-haired and round-faced like her daughter, leaned forward and pressed Morwenna's shoulder. 'Britney's set her heart on being the mermaid. We have the actors staying with us at the guest house so she may be in with a chance.'

'What are they like, the other actors?' Lamorna whispered.

Carole fanned herself with her hand. 'Oh, they're lovely, especially Inga and the young men. The Scottish woman, Kenzie, is a bit full of herself. Daniel is charming.'

'He is,' Lamorna agreed wholeheartedly.

'He's taking his sports car to Vic to get it repaired tomorrow. Vic says he's very well off – money's no object.'

'Oh, that's good to know.' Lamorna clasped her hands.

Morwenna turned to chat to Rosie Buvač. 'Little Maya's very graceful.'

'So's Elowen. I hope Maya gets the role though. It would cheer us all up at home.'

'Why? Is Milan all right?' Morwenna was concerned.

'Oh, he's fine. Tommy's started work with him on the boats – I thought what with him being the eldest of six, he'd be responsible. He wanted to be an electrician, but he couldn't get an apprenticeship. He's got all the BTECs from school, but there were no placements to be had. I'm not sure he's going to stick with the fishing – he hates it. He's hard to get up mornings.'

'The fishermen will look after him.' Morwenna imagined Milan, a gentle giant, his hand proudly on his son's shoulder. And Ruan would keep an eye on the youngster. 'He'll be fine.'

Rosie exhaled. 'I hope so. Oh – look.'

She pointed and Lamorna said, 'It's Daniel.'

Daniel Kitto had taken position centre stage, where Inga gazed at him adoringly and the children copied. He spoke in his deep husky voice. 'That was charming. Thank you, children. And now I have decided who will play our mermaid for the next two weeks...'

The children caught their breaths, waiting. Daniel adjusted a dicky bow at his throat, a professional movement. 'I'm Daniel, the owner of the company – and I play Uther Pendragon...'

'Are you a real dragon?' Billy called out. Daniel ignored him.

'The life of an actor is not easy. It demands discipline, focus, sacrifice.' For a moment he seemed to catch Lamorna's eyes and he smiled. The other actors had gathered behind him on the stage area. 'Meet my cast. When you come to the show on Tuesday night, you'll know them as Arthur, Guinevere, Lancelot, Morgan le Fay, Merlin...' He waved a hand towards a small man who had taken his place behind all the others. Morwenna recognised Jesse Miles. 'And here is my overworked technician, who is responsible for the lighting, the music, the special effects.' He raised an eyebrow. 'He creates fireworks and bangs; he organises the false daggers we use on stage in one of the scenes.'

'Do you have proper daggers that kill people?' Billy shouted. 'Will there be blood all over the floorboards?'

Carole Taylor's face clouded. She raised her voice. 'That's not a suitable subject for six-year-olds. Britney will have nightmares.'

'I agree,' Tamsin whispered, her face protective as she glanced towards Elowen, who seemed engrossed in Daniel's words.

'Not at all – the stage daggers are perfectly safe. They have retractable blades so no one is hurt. We do use fake blood though.' Daniel was in his element. 'Houdini said, "A magician is only an actor – an actor pretending to be a magician."'

A child called out, 'Who's Houdini?'

Daniel swept his gaze across the raised seating, smiling at the parents and family members. 'So, for my decision. I have watched Inga's wonderful work with the children and I have decided on one mermaid and one understudy. They will both play the role, the understudy on Wednesdays and Fridays, the mermaid on Tuesdays, Thursdays and Saturdays of each week. They will be on first, so it's possible to get them home straight after their performance and in bed, although we'd obviously prefer them to be available for the final bow on the last night when the curtain falls. So, congratulations to – Elowen Pascoe, first mermaid, and Maya Buvač, second mermaid and understudy. We like to have a backup actor in case something problematic occurs, in which case, Billy Crocker will be asked to step up. I will talk to your parents and we'll get the rehearsals in place as soon as possible.'

Tamsin clapped her hands with pleasure. Rosie Buvač reached out and squeezed Morwenna's shoulder, sharing her delight.

Carole frowned. 'That can't be right. Britney was far better.' She stood up and marched over to Daniel just as the children came rushing over.

Elowen threw herself into Tamsin's arms. 'I'm a mermaid, Mummy.'

'That's wonderful.'

'So can I have a dog now?'

'No, Elowen.' Tamsin met her mother's eyes. 'Always the same thing.'

'One day, perhaps...' Morwenna said, pushing Oggy Two into Elowen's arms. She heard Carole Taylor arguing with Daniel Kitto. Carole muttered the word 'favouritism' and Daniel replied something about build being an important factor in his decision and Britney was a little hefty for a mermaid. Carole turned on her heel, grabbing Britney by the hand, and tugged her away.

Morwenna watched as Jesse, the technician, sidled over to Daniel, hovering awkwardly. 'Can I have a quick word, boss? It's important. I can't pay—'

'I'm busy. Do try again when I have more time on my hands,' Daniel said uninterestedly as he turned on his heel and walked away, leaving Jesse open-mouthed.

Morwenna shook her head: Daniel Kitto was a strange man. He had absolutely no idea how to win friends and influence people. She wondered how he managed to direct a cast of actors with so little tact and patience.

4

On Monday morning, Morwenna sat at the table eating porridge as Brenda pestered her for a spoonful. Brenda had an appetite. The scrap of a cat she'd found in the library six months ago had filled out, and now Brenda was a solid chunk who'd eat anything. Worse, she was a thief, and naughty with it. Brenda sprang on the table at every opportunity. Morwenna decided that she ought to train her to stay on the floor, but it was so nice to see her, paws in the air, asking for food. It was wrong to reward adorable begging, but Brenda knew how to manipulate her human pet. She'd raise a paw, cock her head on one side, and if Morwenna hadn't offered up a morsel at that point, she'd swipe it with a claw.

Morwenna chewed as Brenda lurched towards the bowl, her little nostrils sniffing milk. Morwenna ruffled her fur – the cat was good company and there was no one in the house to complain about her antisocial behaviour. Not that Ruan would have complained – he'd have been more indulgent with the cat than she was. Morwenna pushed the unfinished porridge towards Brenda and let her snaffle the scraps, her pink tongue scraping the sides of the bowl. She placed a palm on the cat's back, tickling the fur at the base of her tail.

'I'm off to the library now, Bren, then I'll do a shift in the tearoom. Make sure you're in when I get back and don't bring me any presents through the cat flap. I might bring you a bit of fish.'

Brenda's purr became louder and Morwenna stroked her again. 'I wonder how Mum's date went last night. She hasn't had one in years. I hope she's not putting all her eggs in one basket.'

At the mention of the word egg, Brenda flopped over and stuck her paws in the air. Morwenna smiled, reached for her purple velvet coat and a beret and made for the hall.

As she cycled down the hill into Seal Bay towards the library, Morwenna was still smiling. It was a glorious spring day, the bay gleaming below like a silver bowl. She felt her spirits soar. She whizzed past the pop-up shop where Susan and Barb Grundy sat at the window, knitting to raise money for the Lifeboats Institution. She raised a hand but for once they didn't see her. Susan was leaning forward, her mouth moving ten to the dozen – the Grundy sisters were giving someone in Seal Bay a hard time. Morwenna knew they loved to gossip, but their hearts were full of kindness.

She slowed down outside Seal Bay library; a Victorian red-brick building with a heavy wooden door that gaped open to welcome visitors. Hurriedly, she pushed the bike inside, leaning it against a wall in the corridor. The faint scent of books was already in her nostrils. Louise was at the counter, immersed in a book, two mugs of tea beside her. Morwenna took one gratefully. 'What are you reading?'

'This is about the history of Seal Bay.'

'We have a few more on the shelves: *The Maritime History of Seal Bay*, *Tales of the Bay* or *Cornish Histories*?'

'I ordered a new one, just published. It's called *Hidden Secrets of Seal Bay*. It's by a Cornish writer, Pawly Yelland. It's fascinating.'

'Oh?'

'I've just been reading about Pengellen Manor, on Pettarock Head. Did you know it was built between 1540 and 1545 to protect Seal Bay against invasion from the French and the Spanish? It says here, "The house was originally called Chi an Mor, the house by the sea. The Pengellen family changed the name – they've lived in Pengellen Manor since the sixteenth century... some of the family were distinguished, others less so..."' Louise looked up from the book, her eyes round. 'What do you think that means?'

'All families have secrets, I suppose,' Morwenna said.

'Yes – listen – "Smuggling and piracy were a way of life for many of Cornwall's great seafaring families, among them the Pengellens, who acquired the house in the late fifteen hundreds. Despite the family's notoriety, the Crown turned a blind eye to such activities in return for Cornish support in times of invasion."'

'Exciting stuff,' Morwenna agreed. 'I can't imagine the current Pengellens being smugglers.'

'Oh, I don't know.' Louise's imagination was running riot. 'Julian Pengellen has a big house in London – maybe he runs a drugs ring, maybe his minions smuggle cocaine from South America.'

'He's a banker, something to do with venture capitalism, whatever that means,' Morwenna said. 'It must be nice to have a house on the Embankment and a weekend retreat in Seal Bay.'

'Pengellen Manor is much more than a weekend retreat,' Louise replied. 'It's a beautiful home. Have you ever been in there?'

'A few times. They had a big bash for the millennium.'

'That was over twenty years ago.'

Morwenna was surprised – those twenty years had rushed by. 'I often see Pippa Pengellen in town. She supports the local community.'

'Their son's only ever in Seal Bay when the sun shines. He likes the surf. I've heard Tristan is a playboy.'

'I suppose having a city job and not being married by the time you're thirty makes you a playboy.' Morwenna finished her tea. 'It's quiet in here this morning.'

Louise was still engrossed in the book. 'I was searching for stuff on Lady Elizabeth. I hoped Pawly Yelland would shine some light on her ghost haunting the library. The Pengellen family built Seal Bay library, you know – she was always in here reading, Lady Elizabeth, in Victorian times, Lady Elizabeth, in Victorian times.'

'There's a library in the manor house, isn't there? This one was built for the common people.' Morwenna leaned forward. 'Where did she die?'

'At Pengellen Manor. Her husband broke her heart and she took poison all alone, but her spirit returns here each night. It's the only place she feels safe.'

'Do you really think she's still here?' Morwenna asked.

'You know I do,' Louise insisted. 'I often feel her presence.'

'Or perhaps it's just the cold breeze that blows straight off the sea, through the front door and into the library.' Morwenna raised an eyebrow.

'It might be her,' Louise said just as footsteps sounded in the corridor. She jumped slightly as a young, handsome man wearing a dark jacket walked in briskly. He wore a beanie hat over short dreadlocks and leaned easily against the counter.

'Do you have anything on Saxon potions and remedies?'

Louise glanced towards Morwenna. 'We have *English Medieval Remedies... Eat Like a Saxon...* or *Divination and Wortcunning in Early England.*'

'Or we have *Saxon Sorcery and Runes,*' Morwenna added.

The man said, 'Can I see them all?'

Louise frowned, unsure. 'You're not a member.'

'Does that matter?'

Louise folded her arms. 'I'm afraid you can't borrow books unless you're a member.' She beamed hopefully. 'You could join.'

'I'm only here for two weeks. I'm an actor,' the man replied with a cheeky wiggle of his eyebrows.

'You could get a temporary membership,' Louise suggested.

'Or you could just sit here and read them,' Morwenna offered.

'I'll do that, then.'

'I'll get them for you.' Louise was already off, browsing through shelves.

Morwenna asked, 'What role are you playing in *The Return of the Cornish King*?'

'Merlin,' the young man said. 'I'm always on the lookout for ways to improve my character. I thought I'd have a look at the sort of spells and potions Merlin might whip up in a moment's madness.'

'I'm looking forward to seeing the play. My granddaughter's playing a mermaid.' Morwenna examined the young man's face; there was something troubled in his expression. 'Aren't you rehearsing?'

'We have the morning off. The others are taking a walk on the beach. I didn't fancy it.'

'Oh?'

The man shrugged. 'The rest of the cast have been in the company for a while. I'm the newbie.' He met her eyes. 'The director drafted me in last November when the previous Omfra the Piskie got peritonitis and left. I get all the clowning roles now.'

'You must enjoy it,' Morwenna said. 'Merlin must be fun to play.'

'Oh, definitely – spells and potions and being a bit of a baddie. I can pretend to kill someone I don't like just by mixing a few ingredients.' The young man's face lit up. 'I'm never happier than when I'm on stage, only...'

'Only what?'

'Well...' The young man scratched his head thoughtfully. 'The director can be very critical.'

'Really?' Morwenna was thinking of Daniel Kitto's date with Lamorna. 'Isn't he nice?'

'Put it this way, he's not my favourite person on the planet.' The actor shook his head, clearly keen not to say too much.

Louise arrived with a stack of books.

'Here you are. You can browse to your heart's content.'

'Thanks. I'm Musa, by the way. I hope you enjoy the play. It should be a great show.'

'I'm sure we'll love it,' Morwenna said.

Musa turned to go and Louise called, 'I'm getting a ticket too. It's not violent though, is it? All those knights of the Round Table, battling with swords?'

'It's a family show – *The Return of the Cornish King*,' Musa explained. 'No one's sure if King Arthur ever existed or if the Cornish or the Welsh should claim him, but we spin a good yarn. Passion, power and spells.'

'Sounds great,' Morwenna said encouragingly.

'Uther Pendragon will get what's coming to him though – wait and see.' Musa clutched the books, spreading them out at a table, sitting down. 'Thanks for these.'

'It's a pleasure,' Louise said, lifting her empty cup. She turned to Morwenna. 'Fancy a refill?'

* * *

Musa was still leafing through the books of spells and potions when Donald Stewart arrived to take over from Morwenna. She waved a cheery goodbye, grabbed her bike and cycled across town to the seafront, where the Proper Ansom Tearoom stood, gleaming blue

Bloodshed on the Boards 37

and white in the spring sunshine. The door was marked: Open. Welcome. *Kernow a'gas dynnergh*.

Morwenna only spoke a little Cornish, but she knew the words for welcome to Cornwall. The phrase she used the most was *Yeghes da!* She often said it as she was holding up a glass of wine or something stronger. She pushed the door open and saw Tamsin, her hair in a swinging ponytail, weaving between customers carrying a tray. The tables were filling; the tearoom was busy. Morwenna was about to put on her apron when she noticed Lamorna sitting by the window, waving her over. 'I'll have another tea and a scone, please, waitress.' Lamorna winked. 'And be quick about it.'

Morwenna was glad to see her mother. She placed the items on the table as Lamorna grabbed her wrist with ringed fingers. 'You got a minute? I want to tell you all about the date.'

Morwenna perched on the end of the chair. 'I need to help Tam with the customers but giss on – how did it go?'

'It was heaven.' Lamorna rolled her eyes in a fake swoon. 'We went out in that beautiful yellow car to a fish restaurant up the coast and I drank sparkling wine. He was so attentive and nice. He had on a beautiful grey silk suit and a cravat. He looked just like Laurence Oliver. And we had such a good time.'

Morwenna was delighted for her mother. 'So, he's a nice man?'

'Oh, he's wonderful. We talked and talked in the restaurant, then he drove up to the clifftop overlooking Pettarock Bay and it was so romantic – we talked some more, about the past and missed opportunities. He wished we'd stayed in touch. We were gazing across the ocean until past midnight. And he's so sweet. He's busy tonight – I expect they are getting ready for the play – but he's going to take me out tomorrow after the performance. I mean, they won't pack up until ten, but he's suggested we get fish and chips and he'll buy champagne – he doesn't drink, of course – and we'll drive to the other side of Seal Bay and look at the moon together. Oh, Morwenna...' Lamorna's lip trembled. 'Do you think this can be it, at last? Have I waited eighty-two years to find the man of my dreams?'

'Who knows, Mum? Let me know after the next date. It's exciting, though.' Morwenna squeezed her hand. 'I'd better go and help Tam.'

'Come back dreckly.' Lamorna fake-swooned again. 'I want to tell you everything he said to me. Oh, it was bliss – I can't wait for tomorrow.'

'As soon as I can, Mum.' Morwenna's face shone with affection. She rushed to the counter and began to pour tea from a large pot, leaving Lamorna holding her mug to her lips in a dream.

5

On Tuesday lunchtime, Morwenna decided to go for a swim before she started work at the tearoom. It was the perfect day for it – bright sunshine, sharp sea breeze. The ocean was rough as corrugated iron, waves rolling along the sand, spraying surf. Jane Choy was working; everyone else was busy, but Morwenna messaged Carole at The Blue Dolphin Guest House, asking her to invite Kenzie along for a swim. By half past twelve, she was nowhere to be seen. Morwenna wrapped her arms around herself in her wetsuit and decided she'd go in alone.

She stuffed her cascading hair into an orange cap, ran furiously across the sand and plunged into the waves. Every time she swam in the sea, she felt as if it was for the first time: the initial shock of the cold, the clutch to the heart. Then came the calm, the moment she rolled on her back and was held in the sea's arms, cradled, staring at the sky. It was a special time when she was truly alone: her mind cleared and she felt at one with nature.

Morwenna bobbed in the water, kicking her legs, stretching her arms. She loved Seal Bay. She loved her strong, feisty daughter, her adorable grandchild. She was devoted to her mum, who was healthy, happy and ready to embark on a new romance. Her family being well and safe counted for everything, and Morwenna felt blessed. She had her home, good friends, her cat. She was contented. And Ruan was loyal and supportive. Morwenna stopped her thoughts there; she wouldn't let them roam down the Ruan road. The past hurt; the future was better left alone, like a covered wound. It would heal in time.

She plunged beneath the surface and when she emerged from the depths, she heard someone calling. At first she thought it was the water buffeting her swimming cap. No, a voice was yelling her name and someone was swimming towards her. She blinked, taking in the woman in the blue swimsuit, no cap, her dark curls dripping. Her face was calm, laughter lines around the eyes, an intensely blue gaze. Then Morwenna recalled the last time she'd seen her, and she called out a greeting. 'You came – I'm so glad you got my message.'

'Sorry I'm late,' Kenzie spluttered in the water. 'I got kept back for a telling-off.'

Morwenna pulled a quizzical face. 'Kept back?'

'Our evil director – nothing new,' Kenzie said. 'Oh, I love swimming – so tinglingly cold, like fish gnawing at your flesh. I haven't swum in the sea for ages.'

'You're from Scotland?' Morwenna said.

'Aberdeen. It's beautiful – I miss it. I've been on the road with Spriggan for almost five years now. We've been all over the UK and Europe.' She ducked under the water and came up again, her face shining. 'I suppose it's a blessing in disguise, this will be our last tour.'

'Oh?' Morwenna kicked hard in the water. 'What will you do?'

'Find something else. I left my last job because of the sexist actor who was my ex-partner. Now I've been stuck with that misogynist from the ark for the last few years. It'll be good to try pastures new.'

'Daniel Kitto?' Morwenna asked.

'You've met him?' Kenzie curled her lip. 'All I can say about him is it's a pleasure to be playing Morgan le Fay opposite his Uther Pendragon. It's not acting when I tell him that I wish him dead.'

Morwenna studied her face for signs that she was joking. 'You hate him that much?'

'Yes, I do – but those are lines from the script.' Kenzie struck out to sea with powerful arms and Morwenna followed her.

'You're a strong swimmer.'

'So are you,' Kenzie said. 'Are you the organiser of the swimming group?'

'Not really.' Morwenna shook water from her face. 'We meet whenever we get the chance.' She opted to change the subject. 'How's life in Seal Bay?'

'Great. The cast get on OK, mostly – we played football on the beach this morning and had a walk. The guest house is comfortable and the food's good. Carole and her husband are real characters.'

'They are.' Morwenna was happy to let Kenzie talk.

'Vic treats her like a skivvy and Carole grumbles all the time. But she's really kind – she can't do enough for us.'

'She's a good person.' Morwenna recalled how kind Carole was, often bringing Elowen from school, letting her stay for sleepovers. 'She's a typical Cornish maid with a warm heart.'

Kenzie said, 'Are there seals in Seal Bay?'

'Yes – we see them a lot, all year round. It's lovely to swim with them,' Morwenna replied. 'And sometimes, when it's really warm, they climb onto the rocks to sunbathe.'

'Cool.' Kenzie's teeth were chattering. 'I'm so glad I came for a swim.'

'Any time.'

'It's been good – a chance to relax after the stress of rehearsals.' Kenzie gazed towards the shore.

'We'd best get back,' Morwenna suggested and pushed towards the beach, Kenzie just behind her.

They stood on the sand wrapped in towels, trembling, and Kenzie said, 'Is your granddaughter playing the mermaid?'

'Elowen, yes, and Maya Buvač is doing it too.'

'Carole's not too pleased her daughter didn't get a role,' Kenzie said. 'Daniel handled that badly too. Rude, if you ask me.'

'Britney's lovely.' Morwenna peeled off her wetsuit, revealing a damp swimsuit below.

Kenzie nodded. 'Well, it's our big opening night tonight. Will you be there?'

'I wouldn't miss it – the whole of Seal Bay will be watching, I'm sure.'

Kenzie shivered. 'I'll see you then. I'm going to jog back to the B & B and grab a shower. Thanks for inviting me.'

'You're welcome any time,' Morwenna said, watching Kenzie shuffle into ankle boots and scamper off across the sand. She glanced towards her bicycle. She'd cycle home, have a quick shower herself and be back in time to join Tamsin for the afternoon teas.

* * *

That evening, Morwenna sat on the front row of the tiered seating inside the marquee, clutching her complimentary ticket, waiting for the show to start. She shuffled sand below her boots as Lamorna threaded an arm through hers. 'I can't wait.'

Morwenna studied the set. The scenery was basic but effective: painted wood, a series of flats depicting the sea, a night sky, a castle in the distance, placed in front of a black backdrop. Tamsin was backstage with Elowen, helping her into a spangly, scaly costume, and was probably now chewing her nails, anxious about her daughter's performance. Morwenna wondered if her granddaughter was nervous. She doubted it. Elowen would be clutching Oggy Two in the wings as if there was no pressure at all. Becca Hawkins, Tamsin's friend who'd just taken over The Celtic Knot gift shop next door to the tearoom, was sitting next to Morwenna chewing sweets. Becca pushed a hand through her short white-blonde hair and held out a bag of fudge. Morwenna accepted a square and Lamorna did the same.

Next to Becca, some seats were still unoccupied: the whole of the front row had been reserved for people with complimentary tickets. At the end of the row, a woman was reading the programme. She was small, fair, a few years younger than Morwenna, wearing a heavy coat, clutching a large handbag. Morwenna knew her name was Gill and that she worked for Vic Taylor at the car showroom. She was the receptionist there, but she turned her hand to being a saleswoman when Vic was busy. Carole said that Vic called Gill his Girl Friday, and that he couldn't manage without her. Carole had been miffed by the remark – she helped Vic out at the garage herself from time to time, but Vic had never told her that she was indispensable. Carole felt undervalued. Morwenna reminded herself to pay her a compliment when she saw her to cheer her up.

At the front of the stage, Jesse Miles was busy arranging electrical wires. He noticed Morwenna and gave her a wave. She waved back, then she felt a tap on her shoulder; Louise smiled from the seat behind her. Rosie and Maya Buvač were in the row behind Louise – the whole family had tickets for the following evening to see Maya perform. Morwenna gazed around. Damien Woon from the boatyard had arrived with his new partner, Beverley, her hair piled high in a silk scarf. Morwenna thought of her prolific paintings of nudes, and wondered if she had painted Damien yet.

She noticed that Susan and Barb Grundy were in the centre row – they'd both brought their knitting and were crunching on a family-sized bag of crisps. Rick Tremayne, his wife, Sally, and their teenage boys, Benjamin and Jonathan, were sitting together at the back. Rick looked bored already. Several seats below, Jane Choy waved her programme. She was sitting alone. Morwenna gestured for her to join them, but she signalled that she was fine.

Loud laughter burst suddenly from the back row. Morwenna noticed Julian and Pippa Pengellen from the manor house, expensively dressed, talking to an elegant woman who was probably Morwenna's age, perhaps a bit younger. Morwenna studied her – she'd seen her somewhere around Seal Bay, but she wasn't sure who she was. She had smooth blonde hair in a bob, blue-framed glasses, a fitted black and white check suit. As she talked to the Pengellens in a booming voice, she seemed oblivious of those around her.

'Who's that?' Morwenna asked Becca. 'The woman talking to the Pengellens?'

Becca shrugged. 'Anna Carlyon. She's something to do with Korrik Clay. She comes into the gift shop and buys the most expensive things. She's got great taste.' She went back to her bag of fudge.

Then Carole Taylor appeared at Morwenna's shoulder, her hand clutching Britney's small one. She hissed, 'Is Elowen all right? Is she nervous?'

'She's fine.' Morwenna took in Carole's neat pale coat and said, 'You look nice.'

Carole brightened for a moment then she said, 'Vic never notices. I asked him to come and he said he'd rather stay home with the telly.' She glanced down at Britney anxiously. 'To tell the truth I'm still jumping. That director made me so angry yesterday, what he said about Britney.'

Morwenna ruffled Britney's fair hair. 'You're a poppet, Britney. Pay no attention to silly comments.'

Britney piped up. 'Daddy says if I'm hefty it's because I get it from Mum.'

Carole's face flushed. 'I might just go backstage at the end of the play and give him the sharp edge of my tongue. People like him shouldn't be allowed to work with children.'

Morwenna lowered her voice as she glanced at Lamorna, but she was too busy gazing at a photo of Daniel in the programme. 'Pay him no mind, Carole – he's wrong.'

'Exactly – he's just a silly tuss.' Carole said. 'The rest of the company are lovely. It's a pleasure to have them at The Blue Dolphin.'

'Especially Musa.' Britney giggled. 'Mummy thinks he's handsome.'

'I only said that he has lovely manners.' Carole's blush deepened. 'Oh, never mind. We'll catch up afterwards. We'd better sit down, Britney.'

'Enjoy,' Morwenna said, watching Carole tug Britney to seats several rows behind. She heard Carole's voice mutter a greeting, 'All right, Ruan?' and Morwenna couldn't help looking as Ruan Pascoe hurried down towards the front row and squeezed next to Lamorna. He winked in Morwenna's direction.

'So, our little heller Elowen's a mermaid now?'

'She is,' Lamorna said excitedly. Morwenna glanced across at Ruan, who looked fresh from the shower, lithe and handsome in jeans and a jacket, his eyes fixed on the stage. Then the lights dimmed and music began to play through large speakers: tinkling harps, resonant rebecs.

A spotlight came up on a dark-haired girl in a spangly costume sitting on a wooden rock, a swishing fish's tail containing her legs. Elowen was brushing her hair with a comb, singing a little song. She turned to the audience and, with the knowing expression of someone five times her age, she said, 'Welcome to Cornwall, the home of King Arthur. Our tale is the ancient story of kings and knights, a tale of sorcery, secrets, bloodshed, betrayal and passion...'

She paused dramatically. 'The Spriggan Travelling Theatre Company warmly welcomes you to the special Cornish version of... *The Return of the Cornish King.*'

The mermaid then dived behind the wooden rock onto a soft gym mat, hidden from view behind the scenery. Merlin rushed on stage, appearing to haul her from the water as if by magic and carry her off in his arms as the audience clapped. Ruan leaned towards Morwenna and whispered, 'She's good. And she did well to learn all that lot – it's a proper mouthful.'

'She's bright,' Lamorna said. 'She'll end up on the stage.'

'It wouldn't surprise me,' Morwenna agreed with a quick glance at Ruan, whose face shone with pride. Then actors rushed into the performance area, shouting something about a boy who had just pulled a sword from a stone.

Throughout the play, Morwenna was conscious of Ruan, intently watching the play. Once he caught her eye and smiled. Lamorna didn't notice – she was waiting for Daniel to appear on stage. Morwenna forced herself to concentrate on the play.

It was clear that Mackenzie Fuller was gifted. She was utterly convincing as Igraine, Uther Pendragon's wife, who died in the first scene in her husband's arms. She wore a blonde wig, gazing at Daniel Kitto, her eyes filled with love. Morwenna thought it was hilarious, given how much she hated him. And as the scheming Morgan le Fay, Kenzie excelled, thoroughly evil and vengeful. Musa Omari was a mischievous Merlin, leaping around the stage, and the audience took him into their hearts. Inga was humble, dutiful, devoted to Arthur. But Morwenna was not convinced about the other two actors, the ones she'd seen talking together at the tearoom. Ben D'Arcy, as Arthur, boomed loudly, hamming everything up. Passionate, volatile, he wrung a different emotion out of every line. And Rupert Bradley's character was far too bland, devoid of any likeability. He spoke his lines as if he were reading them from a book.

The play was drawing to a close. Uther Pendragon was centre stage – where else would Daniel Kitto be? Morwenna watched her mother, leaning forward excitedly, knuckles clenched as he delivered a monologue in his rich resonant voice: he, Uther, was King of Cornwall and Arthur, his son, brought up in secret by Merlin, would be crowned King of all England, Guinevere his queen, and Cornwall was safe again now that Arthur was reunited with his family. Merlin offered to cast a spell against all evil and suddenly, there was a bright flash and a bang. The audience jumped as one. Morwenna glanced over to the wings where Jesse Miles had set off a pyrotechnic. Then Kenzie was on stage, a seething Morgan le Fay, cloak whirling, a dagger in her hand. She swore that Arthur would never be king and launched herself at him. Arthur leaped back and the heroic Uther Pendragon filled his space, taking the dagger blow in the chest.

Morgan le Fay stared from father to son, then she hissed, 'You are a loathsome man, Uther, and I have wished you dead for many years. Now I turn to your son, Arthur. May you all be cursed hereafter.'

Daniel Kitto fell to his knees and an arc of fake blood sprayed dramatically into the air, pooling on the stage. His wound spread in a rose across his chest, bright against the white shirt. It looked real and some of the audience gasped. A small voice in the audience murmured, 'Look at all that blood...'

Daniel rolled his eyes and tottered forward, grasping Arthur, ready for his final soliloquy. 'I die – leaving behind all I love, my country, my son Arthur, my heir... I go to meet my queen Igraine in the afterlife. But I have given you the best part of me, O Cornweal, home of my ancestors...' His voice became weak. 'I will depart now with the promise that I will always... always...' He fell to his knees, an arm extended. The audience held their breath. '...always love...' Then he was still.

He didn't move.

There was a moment on the stage where no one budged. The actors were transfixed. Then they looked from one to the other: clearly, Daniel hadn't finished his speech. Then Inga was behind him, her fingers on his neck feeling for a pulse. She tried again, a third time. 'His heart has stopped beating. He is truly...'

She paused. Her fingers went to his pulse; she rolled him over, listened to his chest. Her voice rose in panic. 'There's no heartbeat... None at all. He's dead.'

6

There was mayhem in the theatre, people scurrying for the exit, others loitering, gawping, talking excitedly. Jane Choy was crouching down on the stage with Rick Tremayne, checking Daniel's pulse, calling for the defibrillator. Then paramedics rushed in and kneeled next to Daniel. The actors asked the audience to go home, and Jane Choy repeated their request emphatically, but stragglers stayed to watch the body as it was lifted onto a wheeled trolley and covered. Morwenna heard Rick Tremayne say, 'Heart attack? Are you sure? And how old was he? OK, I'll leave you to it.'

Lamorna was in tears; Ruan held her in his arms as she sobbed. He said, 'Can I bring her back to yours for a while?'

Morwenna nodded. 'Of course – I'll just catch up with Tam backstage and say goodbye. I want to see how Elowen is, after what happened. I won't be a minute, Mum.'

Lamorna dissolved into fresh tears. Morwenna left Ruan consoling her and went to look for Elowen.

The small area behind the set was crowded, the actors talking loudly, perhaps less concerned than they should have been given poor Daniel's recent death. Ben and Rupert were whispering together in a remote corner. Kenzie was eating chocolate. Inga had lit a cigarette. Jesse Miles was clearing up, whistling as he unplugged electrics, tidying away sound equipment. Morwenna watched as Tamsin helped a mystified Elowen into her coat. She heard the little girl say, 'Mummy, what happened to Daniel?' Morwenna stood back – she'd let them have a few minutes together. She thought about what had happened: Daniel might have had a heart attack. The police had accepted the paramedics' professional opinion. But Morwenna's instinct told her something was wrong. A quick look around wouldn't hurt...

There were several curtained dressing areas inside the marquee. Morwenna peeped behind one. It was unoccupied, thankfully, a women's dressing room, crammed with costumes, wigs, make-up, bags. The next one was empty too, the curtain already pulled back – Morwenna could see it was the area designated for the men. Morwenna peered into a third area, where a small table had been rigged. She saw her reflection in a huge ornate looking-glass; there was a grey silk suit with a cravat on a hanger. Daniel had probably left it there ready for his date with Lamorna. It was his private dressing room.

Morwenna glanced over her shoulder quickly, and slipped behind the curtain, tugging it closed. She had no idea what was driving her, but she couldn't resist having a look around.

Daniel wasn't tidy. He'd left lots of things on the table: make-up, his car keys, a pungent aftershave – Morwenna sniffed the bottle. There was a gold St Christopher on a chain, an expensive-looking watch with a thick metal strap, silver and bronze. She scanned the table for other items: a fat leather wallet, dark brown, the initials DK embossed on it. Blue notes were protruding, a huge wad of them. Quickly, she opened it. There must be three hundred pounds at least in there, and bank cards. She was suddenly filled with sadness – these items belonged to a man who was dead now. Respectfully, she closed the wallet.

A bottle caught her eye, unlabelled, medicine perhaps. A mobile phone, pristine in its gold case. And there was a small book with a pen attached. She picked it up and flicked through. It was a five-year diary in which he'd been making brief notes. Her eyes fell on a small silver-framed photograph, a woman with light curly hair, a tentative smile. Morwenna thought the photo was old – judging by the photographic quality and the clothes, it must have been taken around the sixties. She wondered who it was – a sister? A friend? An actor he'd worked with and admired? Morwenna looked at the woman's face, shy eyes, an awkward smile, as if unsure of her own happiness, and wondered why Daniel had kept her photograph.

In a flash, Morwenna pocketed the diary, the photo and the bottle of medicine. She had no idea why. But it wasn't a crime scene – she wasn't completely breaking the law. After all, she intended to return the items once she'd looked at them properly. As she whirled from the makeshift dressing room checking no one had seen her, she realised that she was working on instinct. She couldn't explain it. It made no real sense, but the items were in her pockets and she was on her way to hug Tamsin and Elowen, smiling, saying, 'You were a brilliant mermaid, my lovely,' for all she was worth.

* * *

Lamorna clutched a glass of brandy, which she downed in two gulps. Ruan was hunched next to her on the squashy sofa as she gripped his hand in hers, her face streaked with tears. 'I can't believe he's gone...' She dabbed her eyes with a screwed-up tissue. 'We'd just found each other and now – this has happened.' She dissolved into fresh sobs.

Morwenna was in the kitchen, filling three mugs with tea. Brenda left the cat basket, following her, yowling for biscuits. She received a small handful of treats for her trouble and stayed, purring and nibbling from her bowl. Morwenna brought the tea tray into the sitting room, placing it on the table, before sitting on the other side of Lamorna, who snatched her hand desperately.

'Mum?'

Lamorna squeezed her eyes closed. 'He was such a nice man. The first time we met, years ago, I thought it was too good to be true. But he was coming back to live in Seal Bay. He was going to leave the theatre behind.'

Ruan said gently, 'He died on the stage. That might have been the way he wanted to go.'

'No, he'd have wanted to die in my arms, happy – in ten years' time.' Lamorna snuffled. 'We sat on the clifftop in his car on Sunday night and he talked about it. He said this year he'd discovered new things about himself and it made him want to come home. He'd finished with the theatre. He said he was truly happy – he'd found what he wanted in life.'

'Meaning he'd met you again,' Morwenna murmured.

'And something else – there was another reason he wanted to turn his back on the theatre. He didn't say what it was.' Lamorna met her daughter's eyes. 'It's not fair.'

'I'm sorry, Mum.' Morwenna kissed her mother's forehead. Brenda was back on Morwenna's knee, butting affectionately. Biscuits were still on her agenda.

Lamorna shuddered. 'I can't believe he had a heart attack. He'd seen a doctor just before Christmas for his annual health check and he'd been told he was remarkable for his age. He didn't drink or smoke, he kept himself fit, he had a dose of tonic every day, for goodness' sake.'

'It's unlucky, Mum.' Morwenna squeezed her hand, thinking of the bottle in the pocket of her coat. 'Stay with me here tonight. We can sit up for an hour or two if you need to – the spare bed's made up.'

'I'd like to stay, thanks,' Lamorna said gratefully. 'Oh, I can't believe he's gone.'

'Does he have any family?' Ruan asked.

'No one in the world. The theatre was his family. Then – he changed his mind.'

'Why, Mum? Do you know?' Morwenna was already beginning to feel suspicious. 'Had he fallen out with the other actors?'

'They hated him – especially since he was going to stop funding the theatre.' Lamorna stared as if stunned. 'But it doesn't matter now.'

'Who will arrange for his funeral? And who'll sort out his will?' Ruan asked, ever practical.

'I suppose one of the people at Spriggan,' Lamorna said. 'Most of them couldn't care less. He only had me.' Fresh tears sprang to her eyes. 'We didn't have long together.'

'Drink your tea, Mum.'

'Can I have some brandy in it?' Lamorna closed her eyes. 'No, it's not good to drink sadness away.' Her hand shook. 'I thought my life was on the up. What have I got to look forward to now?'

Morwenna snuggled closer. 'You have us. Me, Tam, Elowen.'

'And I'm always here for you,' Ruan said kindly.

Lamorna sighed. 'You and Morwenna are my rocks.'

Ruan glanced at Morwenna to see how she'd react. She said, 'We are, Mum.'

He gave her another look, this time a sad one, and she turned away.

'We watch out for each other,' Ruan said.

Morwenna felt the familiar warmth of affection. It was always the same: she regretted some aspects of life without him.

'Perhaps I need a lie-down now?' Lamorna whispered.

'There are clean pyjamas in my wardrobe, top shelf. And a new toothbrush in the bathroom. You go on up.'

'Thanks, my lovely.' Lamorna draped her hands around Morwenna's shoulder. 'You're a good maid. I wouldn't manage without you.'

'Get some sleep, Mum – and if you can't, come into my room and tuck up with me and Brenda.' Morwenna gazed down at the cat, who was asleep now. She watched sadly as Lamorna padded upstairs.

Ruan said quietly, 'It's a shame.'

'It is, bless her,' Morwenna replied. 'She wears her heart on her sleeve. Puts her eggs in one basket.' She paused. She and Ruan were talking in clichés again.

'It was bad luck, though, the poor fella dying like that.'

'I'm not so sure it was bad luck.'

Ruan read her expression instantly. 'What's on your mind?'

'Something doesn't feel right.'

He pressed her hand then realised and took his away. 'The paramedics said it was natural causes. The police won't be interested.'

'That doesn't mean there's nothing wrong.' Morwenna thought of the items she'd taken from Daniel's dressing room. Borrowed.

'It was a heart attack, Morwenna. He was in his eighties.'

'I know. But... his doctor told him he was fine just a short time ago. And the timing's interesting. He was going to come back to Seal Bay, to change his life, pull money from the theatre. Then, magically, he dies. I bet that means the theatre benefits now. Doesn't that strike you as odd?'

'So what are you thinking?' Ruan moved closer. 'That someone at the theatre bumped him off?'

'I don't know.' Morwenna's mouth twisted in a grimace. 'But I'll find out.'

'I met a few of the actors. They've been into The Smugglers' Inn a couple of times. The one who played the witch was telling everyone how much she hated her director.'

'Kenzie, yes. I don't think Daniel was well liked. Maybe that's why he wanted to close the company down.'

Ruan smiled affectionately. 'Are you sleuthing again?'

'I just want to... check things out. Make sure.'

'I'll help,' Ruan said a little too quickly.

'Thanks, Ruan.' Morwenna shifted in her seat and Brenda changed position, settling down again. 'I think I'll pay them a call tomorrow. I know exactly what I'll say – and what I want to find out...'

* * *

The following day, Morwenna left the library after her morning shift, cycling past Susan and Barb's pop-up shop. They were doing good business; several customers were visible through the window, most likely talking about Daniel Kitto dying on stage. Morwenna hoped they were buying lots of knitted items while they were nattering. The Lifeboats would benefit. She continued on to Busy B's florist, buying a bouquet of carnations from Beattie Harris, whom she had known since primary school. With them safely stowed in the basket of her bike, she rode along the seafront to the marquee. She hoped she'd catch the actors having lunch. She had rehearsed in her mind what she'd say.

She secured the bike against the railings next to Daniel's yellow car. As she walked around it, she paused. The scratches on the left-hand side of the car had been filled in and sprayed perfectly. The bouquet in her hands, Morwenna wandered inside the marquee. She could hear voices. She paused by the tiered seating, unseen.

The actors were having a meeting. Inga was talking, a catch in her voice. She was clearly upset.

'So – I think he would have liked us to – to carry on...'

'I agree – we shouldn't call off any of the performances.' Rupert Bradley spoke up. 'Daniel lived for this company. It would honour his memory. I can double up, play Uther Pendragon. The show must go on.'

'But shouldn't we just cancel tonight – one night – out of respect?' It was Musa, the actor who had played Merlin.

'That would be dishonest – we all want to be on stage,' Kenzie said emphatically. 'I vote we just keep going. After all, Spriggan isn't going to close now.'

'It looks that way –Daniel told me he'd leave everything to the company.' Inga wiped a tear from her eyes.

'The thing is though,' Ben, who played Arthur, pointed out, 'he would have spent his money on a home in Seal Bay and lived off it for his retirement. He can't do that now – sadly,' he added as an afterthought. 'So, we can use the funds to keep Spriggan going with a clear conscience. It makes sense, right?'

'Right,' Inga said. 'I think his solicitor is called Walters or Waters. I'll find out and call them. I'm arranging for someone to come up from the funeral director's this afternoon. We ought to be the ones to sort it. Daniel had no family, after all.'

'I suppose it's fair that we do that for him,' Rupert agreed. 'In a way, Spriggan was his family.'

Musa sounded sad. 'The poor man had no one else. It's the least we can do.'

'When should we have the funeral?' Kenzie asked. 'Can we arrange it for after 4 May? That's the night we close in Seal Bay.'

'I'll ask the solicitor if I can organise it... after all, I was probably closest to him,' Inga said.

'And I'll help,' Ben offered, taking her hand.

Inga muttered, 'Thanks, Ben,' and withdrew it quickly.

'Rupert and I have put all his things in boxes, for storage,' Jesse said. 'What will happen to them?'

'We'll think about that later,' Inga replied.

'But if we inherit the theatre, then all his stuff belongs to us,' Jesse said eagerly.

It was at this point that Morwenna took a step forward. She'd heard enough to start her investigations. She gave a light cough and held out the bunch of carnations. 'Hello. I brought these... to put on the stage. I'm so sorry about Daniel... and I just wanted to ask about Elowen, and what the arrangements are for her next performance...'

7

The actors finished their meeting and set up the performance space for a short rehearsal. Now that Rupert was playing both Lancelot and Uther Pendragon, he needed to practise. Morwenna thought he was probably the weakest actor. It was between him – he had little skill and presence – and Ben, who played a histrionic Arthur, hamming up every moment. Perhaps he'd be great in Shakespeare – or pantomime?

Morwenna gave the flowers to Inga, who had tears on her face as she told Morwenna that it would be ideal if Elowen could continue as the mermaid as planned, alternating each night with Maya. Billy Crocker would be available in the background in a special merman costume in case either Elowen or Maya were not able to perform; his family would be recompensed with free tickets.

As the actors prepared for a run-through, Morwenna placed herself next to Jesse, who was winding cables around his arm. She spoke quietly. 'It must be very tough for you all – after what happened to Daniel.'

'Oh, it is,' Jesse agreed wholeheartedly. 'He'll be missed, although Spriggan is saved and for that we can be thankful.'

'That's good news, then?' Morwenna asked.

'For the theatre company, yes. We'd have folded otherwise. Daniel paid for everything. We only got a few thousand a year from our sponsor. That wouldn't keep us going.'

'Who's the sponsor? Anyone I've heard of?'

'Korrik Clay out in St Mengleth. The china clay company. They've been a sponsor for a couple of years.'

'What does that entail?' Morwenna had seen the Korrik Clay lorries on the roads – she'd inhaled their fumes on her bicycle many times: St Mengleth was five miles away.

Jesse shrugged. 'The woman who sponsors us bungs us money in exchange for Korrik's name on the programme. A bit of local advertising.' He gave a cynical groan. 'She probably claims tax relief on it.'

Morwenna edged her way into the next question. 'I wonder who will get his car. I mean – it's rare, isn't it? You don't see many of them about.'

'I'm hoping it'll come to me. I don't expect anyone else wants it. Maybe I can buy it – who knows?'

'It would suit you – the racy image,' Morwenna said encouragingly.

'It would.' Jesse pushed back his shoulders. 'Everyone would see me coming for miles.'

'It's a lovely car – has it been done up recently?'

'How do you mean?' Jesse was little defensive.

'I thought it had a scrape on one side?'

'Oh, that.' Jesse bridled a little. 'Daniel had it fixed.'

'It looks in perfect condition now,' Morwenna said.

'Carole's husband, Vic, did it in the repair shop. He's very quick.'

'Well—' Morwenna indicated the cast, who were in position, rehearsing, 'I shouldn't keep you.' She wondered if she should ask about Daniel's belongings. Jesse said he'd put them in boxes. She wondered if he'd noticed anything missing – she'd keep quiet for now.

Jesse nodded. 'Well, good to see you again, maid. *Duw genes.*'

He turned to watch the cast, then he moved to a spotlight, fiddling with the coloured gel filter. Morwenna decided she'd leave via the back of the marquee and wandered into the dressing area. No one had noticed her. She smiled to herself – the invisibility of a woman in her sixties was useful sometimes...

The cubicle that had been Daniel's dressing room was open, the curtain drawn back and the mirror exactly where it had been. The table was empty – Daniel's belongings had been moved. Morwenna scanned the space; in one corner several cardboard boxes had been stacked, a grey silk suit folded on the top. She felt suddenly sad for Daniel, and for Lamorna, whom she'd left asleep beneath a crumpled duvet in the spare room earlier. Then she realised that she was running late. It was almost one o'clock – Morwenna would be needed in the tearoom, and she'd better get a wriggle on. She hurried outside.

* * *

It was a busy afternoon. Morwenna and Tamsin had no time to talk as they rushed from table to table, bringing full trays and taking away empty mugs and plates. Just after three o'clock, the custom started to dwindle. Carole came in with Britney and Elowen, and sat down with a huff, watching the two girls and Oggy Two drinking sparkling water and nibbling biscuits at an empty table, chatting happily. Then she accepted the mug of tea Morwenna offered and said, 'If you ask me, it serves him right.'

Morwenna knew where the conversation was going. 'Daniel Kitto?'

'He was full of himself, a poseur. And he had no right to say what he did about Britney.'

'It's in the past,' Morwenna said soothingly. 'And the way he died was sad.'

'I suppose it was. He was very polite at the guest house.' Carole thought for a moment. 'I wonder what will happen to that awful noisy car?'

'Didn't Vic repair it?'

'He did. Vic liked Daniel – he visited the garage a couple of times. He said he'd move down here for good, sell the sports car and buy something brand new. He'd picked out a nice BMW or something similar and they don't come cheap.'

'He was going to get a new car?'

'He was. Oh, he and Vic got on like a house on fire. He called round the showroom a few times for a chat. Vic's proper jumping that he missed a good sale... and of course that the poor bloke died.'

'Mmm.' Morwenna was thinking. 'So Daniel was serious about settling in Seal Bay?'

'Yep. Britney, don't climb on the chairs...'

'Can you sit down properly, Elowen?' Morwenna gazed at the two girls, crouched over the table, playing with the condiments. 'They are both as bad as each other. Tam...' She called to her daughter, who was wiping surfaces. 'I'll get on now, if it's all right. There's something I need to do.'

'OK,' Tamsin called back. 'You'll want to check on Grandma, I suppose. Give her my love. I'm doing ratatouille tonight – just so you know what you're missing. Becca from next door is joining us.'

'Ratty-twee is like sick,' Elowen piped up. 'Can I have a pasty, Mummy? And a dog?'

'You'll have what you're given,' Tamsin said firmly and Elowen shrugged.

'I'll see you all later,' Morwenna called. 'Take care.'

She didn't hear Carole's muffled reply. She was outside the tearoom, throwing a leg over the bicycle, on her way. She pedalled through town and came to a halt outside Walters and Moffatt solicitors. She knew Sheena, the secretary, well. She locked the bike outside and pushed the door.

Sheena Mercer was on the phone in reception. She looked up over dark-framed glasses and indicated that she wouldn't be long. Morwenna gazed around. The three seats were unoccupied; there was a grey blind at the window, a potted plant, a water dispenser. Sheena put the phone down crisply, offering her full attention. 'Morwenna – how *are* you? It's been a while...'

'I'm all right. You? Jim?'

'Ah, we're both good. Same old. We're looking forward to the summer. We're off to Corfu.'

'That's nice.'

'How's your Tamsin? And the little one?'

'All good.' Morwenna took a breath. 'I'm after a favour, Sheena.'

'Oh?'

'My mum had taken up with Daniel Kitto. The one who died...'

'I heard. Not about your mum – about Mr Kitto.'

'Was he a client of Andrew Walters?'

'He was, but you know I can't divulge anything personal. I've already written to his beneficiaries.'

'He told Mum he was going to change his will though.' Morwenna offered a puzzled face. 'Mum said he had an appointment this week with Andrew to discuss it... before... you know...'

'He did. I know he wanted to amend his will. Of course, it's too late.'

'It is. The money goes to Spriggan Travelling Theatre now, I suppose?'

Sheena half nodded, then looked guilty. 'I can't say. It's confidential.'

'Right. I'll be on my way. Give my best to Jim.'

'I will.' The phone began to ring and Sheena said, 'That will be someone else wanting to know about Mr Kitto's will, I'll bet. We've had a woman on the phone twice, asking questions, but of course I can't tell her anything. The phone's been red hot – all sorts of people are coming out of the woodwork claiming to have been his best friend.'

Morwenna unlocked the bike and pedalled down the street, around the corner. She rode through town; it was quarter to five. She wondered if her mother would still be at number four Harbour Cottages or if she'd gone back to Tregenna Gardens. She ought to catch up with her. She paused and tugged her phone from her pocket, texting Lamorna quickly.

Where are you mum?

She didn't have long to wait for an answer:

im at your house putting pasties in the oven.

Morwenna replied that she was hungry. Then she was on her way. She cycled back along the seafront, gazing at the thrashing tide, feeling the breeze buffet her face. The tearoom would be closing soon, the theatre opening its doors for the second showing of *The Return of the Cornish King*. It was Maya Buvač's turn as mermaid tonight. Morwenna wondered about the decision to hold a performance so soon after Daniel's demise. Was it respect, irreverence or cool professionalism? She assumed Daniel would have bought into the 'the show must go on' axiom.

A car hovered behind her, driving close to her mudguard. She slowed down and the car drew up beside her; a silver E-type Jaguar. The engine idled and Morwenna recognised the two occupants immediately. The driver was a handsome silver-haired man, probably in his early sixties, and his sister, a little younger, blonde, very tanned, wearing sunglasses. Morwenna was suddenly conscious that her hair was windblown, her cheeks were flushed and she probably smelled of sweat. She offered a broad grin in compensation. 'Hello, Pam – how are you? Hi, Barnaby.'

'Good to see you, Morwenna. I'm fine, thanks.' Pam Truscott took off the sunglasses and smiled. 'How are you? How's the bike?'

'Good thanks. I'm enjoying the hills much more now I have the electric boost. It was very kind of you.'

'The least we could do after...' Pam waved a hand, dismissing the awful occurrences of last autumn. 'I'm just back from Barbados. Barnaby brought me home from the airport.'

Barnaby smiled with perfect teeth. 'It was just what Pam needed, to be away for the winter, to try to put what happened behind her.'

'I bet.' Morwenna recalled how Alex Truscott had been found dead on the beach. What happened afterwards had affected her family badly too. Of course, they'd soldiered on.

'Simon's still in Barbados,' Pam explained. 'He's working in a beach bar. It's good for him. He has some growing up to do.'

Morwenna remembered Simon, Pam's son, how he had been devastated after his father's death. 'Are you all on your own in Mirador?' She asked.

'I am,' Pam murmured stoically.

'I pop down from London when I can,' Barnaby said smoothly. 'That reminds me – I think I owe you dinner, Morwenna. Didn't I promise?'

'You might've...' Morwenna remembered it well.

'What are you doing tomorrow evening?'

'Oh – nothing much...'

Pam smiled. 'Barnaby – why don't you take the *Pammy* – have dinner on the boat? Damien's made a superb job of it – you could give her a whirl.'

'How does that sound?' Barnaby met Morwenna's eyes with his dazzling blue ones. 'I'll pick you up at six, we can drive to Woon's boatyard and set sail? I'll cook you something – do you like pollock?'

'Yes, lovely,' Morwenna mumbled, thinking that Ruan would probably have caught the pollock that Barnaby would be sautéing in lemon garlic butter.

'See you at six. Harbour Cottages, isn't it?' Barnaby smiled again and waved a hand. Pam replaced her sunglasses and the Jaguar glided away.

Morwenna stared after them, wondering what had just happened. Tomorrow evening she was going out on a boat, having dinner with Barnaby Stone, the singing plastic surgeon. She could hardly believe it – she didn't see herself as his type.

8

Morwenna and Lamorna sat at the small table in the living room, huddled over pasties and mushy peas. Lamorna's eyes were red with crying but she hadn't lost her appetite. She forked huge chunks of pastry into her mouth as she sobbed. 'I still can't get my head around it, Morwenna. This time yesterday I was looking forward to our next date and...'

Morwenna reached across the table to squeeze her hand. 'Why don't you stay here again tonight, Mum?'

'I don't want to be a burden... I ought to go home, do a bit of ironing, go down the corner shop and try to get back to normal.' She shovelled another hunk of pasty. 'It's not as if we'd been together for long, Daniel and me.' Tears fell, a pale stream of mascara, and she wiped it away. 'I'd just hoped beyond hope that...'

'You're grieving – stay tonight. Besides—' Morwenna broke off a morsel of pasty, cooling it by waving it in the air as Brenda jumped on the table and gulped it down, 'I have some stuff I want to show you... to do with Daniel.'

'Oh?' Lamorna stopped eating. 'What might that be?'

'Last night, in the confusion of everything, I had a wander backstage and a couple of things caught my attention so – I picked them up.'

'What things?'

'Daniel's things, from his dressing room.' Morwenna waited for her mother to reprimand her for stealing. She might be sixty-two but Lamorna could still tell her off. 'I borrowed them.'

Instead, she said, 'Giss on! I can't wait to see.'

'The thing is, Mum – they might be clues. I'm not sure Daniel died of a heart attack, even if the paramedics think he did. I think someone might have had it in for him.'

'I'm bleddy sure of it – he told me how awkward some of those actors could be, always cadging and wheedling.' Lamorna met her eyes. 'Finish your food and let's have a gander.'

Half an hour later, they were sitting on the squashy sofa. Morwenna produced the diary and turned to the dates Daniel had written against.

Tuesday 23 April: opening night, Seal Bay.
Thursday 25 April: Andrew W, 10 a.m. Change will.

Morwenna was not surprised. 'So, he was seeing the solicitor to update his will.'

Lamorna stared, interested. 'Leaving Spriggan in the lurch. The timing is right. It had to be one of them who killed him.'

Morwenna flicked back. Daniel wasn't a great diarist – he'd inserted a few appointments: haircut, dentist, doctor. On Monday 22 April he'd written:

Taylor Maid, a.m.

'Vic's car place – he's spelled Made wrongly,' Morwenna noted. 'And... look.' She pointed to Sunday 21 April. He'd put:

Lamorna. 7 a.m.

He'd drawn a heart after the entry. Lamorna's eyes filled with tears. 'That heart means so much.' She sniffed. 'But none of it proves that someone killed him.'

'I'll go through everything again when I get time,' Morwenna said. 'What about this picture?' She produced the photo of the young woman and Lamorna took it, holding it close to her face.

'No, that's no one I know. Hang on – oh, I don't know – it could be someone Daniel knew from touring.'

'Let's have a closer look.' Morwenna unclipped the frame. She took out the photo and turned it over. Daniel had written:

Diane. Seal Bay, 1971.

Lamorna examined it, staring at the face. Then she shook her head. 'No bells are ringing. Diane? She could be anyone.'

'But it's probably a local person, we know that – I'm assuming Diane was from Seal Bay, or the photo was taken in Seal Bay – and Daniel would have been around thirty years old in 1971. Diane looks in her twenties here – she must be in her seventies now.'

'Who would have hated him enough to harm him?' Lamorna brought her knuckles to her mouth. 'We don't have a clue.'

'What about this?' Morwenna produced the bottle.

'That's his special health tonic – I saw him taking it when we were in the fish restaurant,' Lamorna said.

'Look at the container.' Morwenna shook the bottle. There was just a little left. 'There's no label, no make, no ingredients.'

'So – it could be anything at all? Medicine for an ailment? Liquid Viagra?' Lamorna suggested.

Brenda leaped on Morwenna's knee, sniffed the bottle and sprang away disgustedly, rushing to the kitchen for her bowl.

'Brenda doesn't like the smell. Cats' sense of smell is fourteen times better than humans' – I read it in the library. Perhaps I need to take a closer look,' Morwenna said thoughtfully. 'Leave this with me...'

* * *

The following morning, Morwenna hurried into the library to find Louise with her feet up, reading. Morwenna said, 'I'm on tea duties, then?'

'Oh, my goodness, I forgot what the time was – this book is so gripping.' Louise hugged it. 'It's Pawly Yelland's *Hidden Secrets of Seal Bay*. It came yesterday, last thing. I can't put it down.'

'What's so interesting?'

'Oh, all sorts. Fishing tragedies off the coast – smugglers. Listen to this... "In the eighteenth century, the tax on tea rose to 110 per cent, and prices went sky high on salt, candles, leather, beer, soap. The tax burden on the ordinary population was enormous. The people of Seal Bay had no issue with turning to smuggling to support their families. Cornish smugglers were usually fishermen and impoverished labourers..."'

Morwenna was fascinated. 'We still have poor fishermen and labourers – not enough has changed, has it?'

'But Pawly Yelland draws you in. This is wonderful stuff.'

'I'll read it after you, then,' Morwenna said. 'And does he mention our ghost?'

'There's a whole chapter on the Victorian Pengellens later – I haven't got to the ghost yet.'

On the mention of the word 'ghost', the outer door banged. Morwenna already had a smile on her face as Susan and Barb Grundy waltzed in.

'All right, ladies – what can I do for you?'

'Oh, we don't want a book,' Susan said.

'We're too busy knitting to read,' Barb added.

'I've got the perfect solution.' Morwenna beamed. 'Audiobooks – listen while you work.'

'Right,' Susan said. 'Get us a couple of those audiobooks, then, Louise. We like good crime stories, lots of blood and guts – and a bit of passion.'

Barb took over. 'We came to see you, Morwenna. We wanted to ask you about that poor actor that died.'

'You were on the front row so you must have got a good view of it,' Susan said, her voice full of sympathy. 'It was a terrible shame. Do you reckon it was a heart attack?'

'That was the official line,' Morwenna observed.

'But you don't think so – I can see it in your face, maid,' Barb said.

'Are you sleuthing again?' Susan was delighted. 'Can we help?'

'Oh, it was a heart attack, surely,' Louise insisted, handing over two crime-fiction audiobooks. 'You'll love these two – they are proper good listens.'

'But we have to keep our options open about the poor actor, don't we?' Barb asked.

'So, to that end,' Susan added, stuffing the audiobooks in her bag, 'we're going to the marquee just before the performance later on – we're taking some knitted stuff to sell on behalf of the Lifeboats.'

'And we'll have a good look round for you.' Barb raised an eyebrow complicitly.

'And let you know what we find,' Susan said smugly.

'That's good.' Morwenna leaned over the counter. 'Thanks, ladies.'

'I reckon Guinevere killed him,' Barb said, folding her arms.

'Why? She's lovely.' Louise picked up her Pawly Yelland book.

'We saw her in his car, that yellow babe magnet...' Susan said.

'We probably need a bit more evidence,' Morwenna said. 'I'll be in the shop soon. Summer's coming – I fancy a light knitted cardigan for after swimming.'

'All the colours of the rainbow?' Susan suggested. 'I'll knit you one.'

'What about the Cornish flag all over – white cross, black background?' Barb suggested.

'Both?' Susan was a keen businesswoman. 'It's for a good cause.'

'All right,' Morwenna said. 'But don't rush – I'll have to save up.'

* * *

When her morning shift finished, Morwenna cycled to the tearoom, deep in thought. Daniel Kitto was uppermost in her mind, but she was also anxious about the date with Barnaby Stone. She wasn't sure why – she was trying to work out how she felt. It was Elowen's turn as mermaid tonight. Morwenna thought that she ought to be there, given what had happened at her previous performance. Even more importantly, she should be spending time with Lamorna – her mum needed company, and here she was swanning off on a date.

She wondered if that was why she felt guilty. She needed a swim in the sea to compose her thoughts – she'd text Jane to ask if she was free around five o'clock.

As she cycled past the shops, she saw Jesse Miles standing outside a bank and she braked. 'Jesse... hi.'

He was just about to use the cash machine. He turned round, his face a little guilty. 'Morwenna.'

'I'm going swimming later – can you tell Kenzie she's welcome to join me at five?' Morwenna stared at Jesse's hands. He was holding Daniel Kitto's dark brown wallet, which was embossed with his initials. There were only a few blue notes in it now – Jesse was gripping a bank card. He looked furtive.

Morwenna had to ask. 'DK? Isn't that Daniel's wallet?'

Jesse shoved it in his back pocket and turned with a false smile. 'It is. He always sent me to get money for him when he was busy. I know his PIN number.'

'But—' Morwenna wondered how to state the obvious. 'He won't be needing money now.'

Jesse forced a laugh. 'He owed me a few quid. I mean, he's not here – I know it's not respectful, but the guys need to buy a few things for the show – and the solicitor will close the account soon anyway.'

'I see.' Morwenna didn't believe a word of it. 'Jesse, can I ask you something?'

'Oh, of course – ask away.' He was glad to change the subject.

'Daniel was fit for his age, wasn't he?'

'Very fit,' Jesse agreed wholeheartedly. 'He did t'ai chi, took a special tonic.'

'What sort?'

'Oh, expensive stuff. He got it from one of the actors.'

'Who?'

Jesse seemed happy to talk. 'Ben D'Arcy. He's a black belt in something – aikido, I think. He's very into body building, he's ripped and toned.' Jesse patted his chest. 'A bit too much, if you ask me, he's obsessed with it. I think he wants to impress someone.' He sniggered. 'It's not working though.'

'Oh?' Morwenna tried again. 'I might get some of his special tonic. Does he sell it?'

'I'm sure he would. He swears by it – it's free from cyanocobalamin, whatever that means. Musa would be able to tell you.'

'I'll talk to Ben,' Morwenna said, taking in his words. 'I'm keeping you from your cash machine. Don't forget to tell Kenzie – swimming at five?'

'Will do.' Jesse pulled Daniel's wallet from his pocket. 'Morwenna – don't say anything about...' He looked momentarily embarrassed. 'You know, I don't want to seem – disrespectful.'

'Right,' Morwenna said, neither agreeing nor disagreeing. 'I'll see you, Jesse.'

She turned the bike, pedalling into a line of traffic. Jesse called after her. '*Duw genes.* Hey – I might come swimming with you. I'll bring my thermals.'

She heard him laughing as she cycled through green traffic lights. As she took the road for the seafront and the tearoom, she asked herself who might have killed Daniel. She had two suspects now – at least.

* * *

Hours later, she was swimming in the sea. Jane Choy had finished her shift and they were both treading water, catching up on each other's news. Jane said, 'Business is quiet at the nick today.'

'Quiet?'

'As the grave. That's how I like it.'

'You have no interest in the Daniel Kitto case?'

Jane splashed her arms. 'There is no case, Morwenna – he died of natural causes.' She studied her friend's face. 'What's going on?'

'Just a feeling. More than a feeling. I think the police are wrong – I think you've missed something.'

Jane raised her eyebrows. 'Tell me.'

'Unofficially?' Morwenna joked. 'I can smell a rat. Lots of people hated him.'

'Most coppers hate Rick Tremayne but we haven't bumped him off yet,' Jane said.

'I know, Jane, but a few things don't add up. I was having a look through his belongings.'

'I don't think you should be telling me this.' Jane raised an eyebrow.

'I've got the message.' Morwenna winked. 'I'm just working on a few leads.' She plunged beneath the water, enjoying the feeling of exhilaration as she bobbed back up. 'I'll keep you in the loop though – I'm sure it wasn't an ordinary heart attack. There are too many people who wanted Daniel dead...'

Jane pointed at a swimmer who was pushing towards them. 'We have company.'

'Oh, that's Kenzie – she's one of the actors.' Morwenna called out. 'Hi, Kenzie – glad you could make it.'

'Sorry I'm late.' Kenzie joined them, wearing a swimsuit and no hat. Morwenna thought of her own wetsuit and thick cap and admired her pluck. 'We had a Spriggan meeting.'

'Oh?' Morwenna noticed Jane's sudden interest.

Kenzie said matter-of-factly, 'Daniel left all his money to the company. That's what we were discussing.'

'He had no family?' Morwenna wanted to keep her talking.

'No,' Kenzie said. 'He didn't have any friends either. He was fairly universally disliked.'

'Who'll get his car?' Morwenna asked.

'Oh, Inga, probably – she was his little pet and he was minted.'

'In what way was she his pet?' Jane asked.

'He took her everywhere in that car.' Kenzie splashed her arms. 'He didn't really like the rest of us. He used Jesse as a skivvy, he made misogynist remarks to me and he was jealous of Musa because he was so popular with audiences.' Kenzie shrugged her shoulders in the water. 'But he's gone now and Spriggan are back in business.' She looked around. 'No seals around today?'

'I'm sure we'll see some before long,' Morwenna said. 'Shall we have another five minutes in the water and then call it a day?'

'Absolutely.' Jane flapped her arms. 'I'm getting cold.'

'I'm just warming up,' Kenzie said. 'The swim will set me up for the night. I'm raring to go. I'll do the show later and then go down The Smugglers' Inn. I'm getting quite fond of the place.'

'It's a proper fishermen's pub,' Morwenna explained.

'Isn't it just,' Kenzie said enigmatically. 'They are a nice bunch of blokes, and I'm developing a bit of a liking for one of them in particular,' she said. 'Most men have a soft spot for an actress. We're irresistible.'

Jane glanced at Morwenna anxiously. 'And which fisherman in particular do you have the hots for?'

'That would be telling.' Kenzie rolled her eyes. 'But I've always had a thing about rugged older men. I'd better get a move on – I'll be seeing you.' She plunged beneath the surface, swimming back to shore.

Jane met Morwenna's eyes quizzically. Morwenna dived beneath the waves and let her thoughts clear. She needed to rush home, change and get ready for the date with Barnaby. She was running late.

But it was not Barnaby who was on her mind right now. She was thinking of a certain fisherman who often joined his friends in The Smugglers last thing at night and what he might be doing later…

9

Morwenna sat in the Jaguar next to Barnaby. She was wearing a tube dress that was at least twenty years old, and a light wrap. She carried a knitted bag she'd bought from Susan and Barb, in the shape of a chicken, complete with red comb. Her hair shone although it was still damp – it had taken her fifteen minutes to shower and change. Barnaby looked cool in chinos and a blazer. He smelled of something smoky, a spicy cologne, and he seemed calm and assured. Morwenna's heart was thumping. She hadn't been on a date in years – the last time she'd worn the dress was months ago when Ruan had cooked bao buns and she'd drunk too much wine. She reminded herself not to drink too much this evening – she needed her wits about her.

They drove to Woon's boatyard where the *Pammy* was moored. Another vehicle had been parked by one of the outhouses and Morwenna shuddered – she hadn't been to Woon's since the dreadful incident last October. It stayed fleetingly with her, the moment of terror – she'd come so close to tragedy. She glanced at the twenty-five-foot sailing boat, now painted cream, sea blue just below the water line, the name *Pammy* in blue scroll. Barnaby rushed round to Morwenna's door, offering a hand as she stepped out precariously. The breeze blew in her face immediately, lifting her silver hair. Her shoes had high heels – she hadn't worn them in years and she wished she'd worn trainers to clamber onto the boat.

Barnaby said, 'Here she is, the *Pammy*. What do you think?'

'She looks good,' Morwenna said, wishing she'd brought a coat.

'I made a good job of her,' a rough voice said and Morwenna turned to see Damien Woon emerging from his office, a woman wearing a vibrant-coloured dress just behind him.

Damien laughed, that rough friendly guffaw between men. He was hefty and powerful, with low brows and a huge beard. 'Hello, Barnaby. So the time has come for the *Pammy*'s first outing. I hope you'll like what we've done.' He nodded to Morwenna by way of greeting.

'I'm sure I will,' Barnaby said smoothly.

'You're having dinner on the boat, then?' Damien said.

'I'm cooking pollock and I've brought wine.' Barnaby lifted a cool box from the boot. He offered Morwenna a charming smile. 'I'm well organised. There's a fridge below deck, all the mod cons.'

'You're a lucky lady.' Damien's partner gripped his arm possessively as she spoke to Morwenna. 'I can't wait for the summer. Damien and I are going sailing every day.'

Damien gave her an affectionate look. 'I've a boatyard to run, Bev.'

'How are you, Beverley?' Morwenna asked. 'How's the painting going?'

Beverley gazed at Damien with adoring eyes. 'He's the perfect subject, if that's what you mean.'

Damien looked momentarily baffled. 'Well, we'd better get on home, things to do.'

'Always,' Beverley said, snuggling closer to him. 'Enjoy your meal, Morwenna. I was amazed it was you Barnaby was taking out though. I wouldn't have put you two together.'

'Life's full of surprises,' Morwenna said with a wave.

Barnaby stepped from the quay onto the boat and held out a hand. 'Welcome aboard, Morwenna.'

An hour later, they were out in the ocean and Morwenna was glad to be below deck. She was cold: her ears, bones and skin were freezing. Barnaby poured wine into two glasses then delved into the cool bag, bringing out salad ingredients, a large white fish, lemons and cream. He smiled. 'You're my guest – put your feet up.'

'I can help you.'

'I won't hear of it. Relax, drink your wine. It's a nice claret – Reserve du Château Mouton 2001.'

Morwenna took a mouthful. It was certainly smooth. So was Barnaby, in a roll-top sweater – the blazer was off now – and he was chopping garlic like a pro, arranging salad in a wooden bowl. He pressed a button on a CD player and mellow jazz began to play. Morwenna felt momentarily out of her depth and wondered whether it might have been better to meet him at The Smugglers for a drink.

She swallowed more wine and reminded herself to slow down. Conversation was the best way forward. 'So, Barnaby – what do you do in London exactly? I mean, I know you're a surgeon.'

'I'm very busy. I do breast enlargement, rhinoplasty, liposuction, abdominoplasty and hair transplants.' He paused, thinking. 'I ought to retire soon. It would be nice to keep the flat in Islington and buy a place in Cornwall.'

Morwenna crossed her arms over her chest, sucking in her stomach. Perhaps Barnaby saw all women as potential patients in need of reconstruction. She wondered what to say next. She thought of something banal, just chit-chat.

'I've heard that you sing while you work.' She smiled. 'Aren't you the singing surgeon?'

'I'm famous for it – I know all the latest pop songs. I keep the radio on and my clients enjoy it – it relaxes them.'

'Do you like the Cornish way of life best, or London?'

'Oh, both, equally,' Barnaby enthused. 'Look at us now – dinner on a boat in the middle of an ocean, then next week I'm going to a West End show and dinner in a Michelin-starred restaurant.'

Morwenna couldn't imagine it – Barnaby's lifestyle was very different from her own. She said, 'I'll probably be cycling to the library.'

'I can't tell you how much I admire that,' Barnaby said, sliding white fish into a frying pan, and grinding black pepper. 'Not to mention how clever you were with what happened to Pam – and Alex.'

'It was a bad time all around.' Morwenna didn't want to be reminded.

'It was – but you were so brave. Everyone respects you.' Barnaby spoke over sizzling fish. 'I was telling some of my friends about it the other night over cocktails.'

A light came on in Morwenna's mind. 'Are your friends all surgeons?'

'Some – I have a big social group. There are journalists, politicians...'

'Do you know any chemists?' Morwenna asked quickly. 'I need one.'

'Don't you have chemists in Seal Bay?' Barnaby looked puzzled.

'No, not that kind of chemist – I mean someone who can find out what's in things...'

'Ah, I think you mean a pharmacologist. No, I don't know any of those – but I do have a hair-replacement client who is a biochemist.

He works at a big research lab, so he might be able to help.' Barnaby turned to look over his shoulder. 'What do you need?'

She delved into the chicken bag and brought out the bottle she'd taken from the dressing room. 'I'd love to know what this is. It's supposed to be some sort of health tonic but...' She couldn't tell Barnaby the truth, not yet. 'I found it in the back of my cabinet and the label's come off. I think it's still OK but I want to be sure. Could you ask your client to check?'

'Can't you throw it away and buy more?'

'I could if I knew exactly what it was. You'd be doing me a huge favour.' Morwenna held the bottle out.

'All right – it's a strange request, but I'm driving up to London tomorrow. I'll ask him to take a look – it might be interesting to find out how much is tonic and how much is sugar or placebo.' Barnaby slipped the bottle in a pocket. 'Now the pollock is ready, the salad's dressed – shall we dive in?'

He placed a plate in front of her, the fish perfectly cooked in a lemon sauce. Morwenna eased herself back in her chair and felt her mood lift.

* * *

It was just after eleven as Barnaby drove her home. She relaxed into the leather of the passenger seat, her uncomfortable shoes off. It had been a lovely evening filled with easy conversation. She wondered if there was a spark between her and Barnaby. He was attractive, certainly, but in terms of their characters and life experiences, they were poles apart.

Barnaby spoke as if reading her thoughts. 'Have you had a nice time tonight?'

'I have,' she admitted. 'The pollock was lovely.'

'Everything was lovely,' Barnaby said, glancing at her, then his eyes were back on the road. 'It's good to be out in the *Pammy* again. You're a lover of the sea, aren't you?'

'It's my second home.' Morwenna smiled. 'I like swimming in the ocean all year round.'

'I should try it,' Barnaby said and Morwenna wasn't sure if he was angling for an invitation. 'Do you use a wetsuit?'

'In the winter.' They were driving along the seafront now. 'I have an ordinary costume for the warmer months. I must admit, I cling to the wetsuit as long as I can.'

'I'm sure swimming is very beneficial,' Barnaby said.

'I think so.' They were passing The Smugglers' Inn. The door was flung wide and people were leaving. Morwenna caught a glimpse of a woman, long hair flying, and a man with his arm around her. She was sure it was Kenzie Fuller. And the man was familiar – she couldn't be sure, but she felt her heart lurch. The Jaguar flashed by, passing the tearoom – the lights were on upstairs. Morwenna could imagine Elowen asleep in her yellow bedroom, Oggy Two in her arms, Tamsin and Becca-from-next-door sharing hot chocolate in front of the TV. On the other side of the road, the theatre marquee was in shadow, the name Spriggan obscured, the bright lights extinguished. A solitary figure moved on the beach, the end of a cigarette glowing. Daniel's yellow car was still parked by the tent.

Barnaby drove uphill, accelerating easily past houses and around the corner towards Harbour Cottages, before slowing down. Morwenna couldn't help glancing over at number nine. The house was in darkness. He brought the car to a halt outside number four and turned to her with a perfect smile.

'Thanks for a delightful evening, Morwenna.'

'It was lovely.' She didn't move, but her fingers clutched the chicken bag, the other hand resting on the door handle. She slid her shoes on, ready to go.

'We must do it again when I'm next back from London.'

'We must,' Morwenna said, although she wasn't sure how she felt about a second date.

'There's a restaurant I want to try in St Mengleth. The Marine Room. Have you heard of it?'

Morwenna shook her head – she seldom ate out, and when she did it was usually in Seal Bay.

Barnaby leaned over. 'We'll go there. What do you think?'

'Sounds great.'

'So – does Pam have your mobile number?'

'I think so, yes.'

'Would you mind if I asked her for it?'

'No – help yourself.'

'Then that's sorted.' Barnaby looked pleased with himself. He moved back to his seat, settling. 'Well, it's been delightful. You're fascinating company.'

'Thank you.' Morwenna wasn't sure quite how or why she would fascinate a man like Barnaby. 'It's been fun.'

'It has. I don't think I've ever met anyone like you.'

'I'm unique,' Morwenna admitted with a flourish. 'Well, thanks for dinner.'

Barnaby leaned over quickly and kissed her cheek. 'Thank *you*,' he murmured. 'Until next time.'

Morwenna wriggled out of the car into the cold air and waved as Barnaby drove away, taking the corners at speed. She walked up to her front door slowly. She still wasn't sure if she wanted to date again. It was all too new and felt too complicated.

As soon as she was inside the house, Brenda rubbed against her ankles.

'Biscuits?' Morwenna said indulgently. 'Come on, then. I'll get you some treats and then I'll go up.'

Minutes later she was sitting up in bed, Brenda at her feet

purring furiously. Morwenna was leafing through Daniel's five-year diary.

'I wonder if he had any plans for next week…'

She turned the pages. There was his appointment with the solicitor on Thursday 25 April, 10 a.m. today. Nothing for the following days – 26th, 27th, 28th. She turned the page and noticed something had been written on the page for Wednesday 1 May.

Flowers.

It was followed by a tick. Had he ordered flowers for someone, or was that the nickname of a person or a place? Morwenna flicked back through the pages for clues – recurrent names. There were a lot of entries for plays being performed – they'd done several runs of *The Mermaid of Zennor*, *Bolster the Giant*, *The Legend of Tom Bawcock* and a play for children, *When Omfra the Piskie Lost His Laugh*.

She frowned as she looked back through his diary; on 8 April, he'd scrawled:

the idiot scraped my car!!

Morwenna looked at the entry again – so the damage had been done by someone else? And he'd scribbled something on 6 February:

Telephone call confirms – I have D in SB!!!!

Morwenna assumed SB was Seal Bay and 'D' could be anything – date, dinner, a dry run? Drugs? Why the excitement, the exclamation marks? She turned to the back of the diary. There were various telephone numbers – Inga Ström, Jesse Miles, Rupert Bradley,

Andrew Walters the solicitor, various garages, guest houses, Carole Taylor. Other numbers without names. There was a mobile number for Will C, which had been crossed out, interestingly. Morwenna considered the reasons why he'd do that. There was also Lamorna's mobile number – the last entry. The sight of it made Morwenna feel sad. And there was a number: 1571. She'd have to think about that one – a door or a flat number, maybe in the USA, a PIN, a map reference? Wasn't it the BT Call Minder number?

The next page was confusing: it was all small squares for calculations. Daniel had written a series of initials, dates, numbers:

Payments and balance, R. 2:4: 2,000. 14:4: 1,800. 2:4: 1,400.

She had no idea what that meant.

She picked up her phone and texted Lamorna a quick check that she was all right. There was a message from Tamsin – Elowen had been impressive as the mermaid that evening. The audience had given her a standing ovation and, on the way home, she'd asked for a dog again. Morwenna replied with a smile emoji and that she'd see them tomorrow. Lamorna's text pinged in. She was in bed and they'd catch up soon.

Morwenna glanced through her bedroom window. The street lights were still on – it wasn't quite midnight.

There was a movement outside and she glanced through the window. A solitary figure was wandering along the road at a steady pace, hands in pockets. It was Ruan. He was late coming back from The Smugglers. Something about his rolling gait made him look pleased with himself. No, she was reading too much into it.

Morwenna recalled glimpsing the two figures leaving the pub: a man with his arm around a woman. The woman was almost definitely Kenzie Fuller.

Morwenna wondered again if the man had been Ruan.

10

Morwenna rose early and took the road to the seafront, pedalling furiously in hooped leggings and a patchwork velvet jacket past the tearoom and the marquee, past The Blue Dolphin Guest House, towards Taylor Made Motors. She was furious with herself, and it made her speed increase with each rotation. She had no right to question Ruan's private life. If he'd left the pub with Kenzie that was his affair, perhaps literally. After all, she'd just had a date with Barnaby. She was being unfair. She needed to let it go.

She arrived at Vic's car showroom. It wasn't yet nine but someone might be there – she wanted to fill in the blanks about the yellow car. She locked her bike outside the glass window with the word 'Reception' printed in gold lettering. A small fair-haired woman was inside, a keyboard in front of her. Morwenna waltzed inside. 'Hello – Gill, isn't it? I was looking for Vic.'

'We're not open.' Gill glanced down briefly at her name badge and then at Morwenna. 'Vic's not in yet. He'll be a bit late today. Carole's busy with a few guests and he's taken the little one to school. He'll be here dreckly.' She studied Morwenna's face. 'You work at the library, don't you? Maureen Mutton?'

'Morwenna, but yes.' Morwenna smiled. 'So – can I wait for Vic?'

'He won't be long,' Gill said, her tone one of efficiency rather than warmth. 'Was there anything I can help with?'

'I just wanted to ask Vic about a car.'

'Are you thinking of buying one?'

Morwenna thought that was a ridiculous idea. 'No, I wanted to ask him about Daniel Kitto's VX220 Turbo.'

'What about it?' There was a defensive edge to Gill's voice now. She seemed suddenly less amenable.

'He brought it in here to get a scratch removed.'

'And?'

'I wondered if you knew who'd scratched it.'

'I can't divulge a customer's private information.'

'Oh, it's just – Mum asked me if I knew. She was going out with Daniel, you see. She thought a lot of him, and she – she accidentally bashed the side of it with her shopping trolley. It upset her a lot, what happened to him. And she loved being driven around in that car. It would put her mind at rest to know that she didn't do the damage.'

'She's not the only one who's shocked by what happened. I was there when he had the heart attack.' There was a vertical line between Gill's eyebrows. 'It was so upsetting. But from what I hear, most of the people on stage wouldn't have cared less.'

'Don't you think the cast were upset?' Morwenna asked.

'They were a selfish bunch, by all accounts.' Gill put a hand over her mouth. A thought seemed to pass through her mind. 'You were asking about his car. It wasn't your mum who bashed it, it was one of the cast members who scraped it in a hedge – they drove it without his permission too, and more than once. If you ask me, those actors took advantage of Daniel's good nature.'

Morwenna thought she'd push her luck: Gill was suddenly

happier to talk. 'They'll get everything, won't they? All his money and belongings?'

'That's got nothing to do with me.' Gill folded her arms. 'Bunch of vultures, all of them.'

'Mum was devastated,' Morwenna persisted. 'I think she was falling for him in a big way. And he was coming home to live in Seal Bay.'

Morwenna was surprised to see that Gill had tears in her eyes – she was clearly moved. 'But he never made it, did he?' She took a breath. 'Now, if you'll excuse me, I have a lot to do.'

'Yes, thanks – sorry.' Morwenna turned to go as Gill began to type furiously on her laptop. Morwenna wondered if she'd touched a nerve.

She hadn't expected such a strong reaction.

* * *

Morwenna knew she'd be late for the library, but she rode towards the Spriggan marquee anyway. She paused to gaze at the tent, the wooden header board with the name Spriggan in lights. The place was deserted, but Daniel's yellow car was still parked outside. She stared beyond at the beach, the glittering sea. Where should she go next with her investigations? So many people said that Daniel had enemies in the company. But did any of them dislike him enough to kill him? And how would they have done it? She was sure the tonic held the answer... and the diary.

'Hello.' A light voice called from the beach and a young woman in a pale silk gown strolled towards her, a cigarette clamped between her fingers. Morwenna recognised Inga Ström, dressed in costume.

'Hello. You were a great Guinevere.'

'Thanks. You're Elowen's grandma?' Inga said with a smile. 'She's a brilliant little mermaid, one of the best we've had.'

'Thanks.' Morwenna noticed how Inga's hazel eyes shone, brown mixed with amber and green. '*The Return of the Cornish King* is a real triumph.'

'Oh, thank you,' Inga agreed. 'We made the right decision to keep going.'

'I suppose it saves cancelling tickets,' Morwenna said.

Inga eyed her suspiciously for a moment, as if she might be being critical. Then she said, 'It's what Daniel would have wanted.'

Morwenna nodded in agreement. 'When's the funeral?'

'I've organised it for 6 May. We finish on the 4th. We'll pack up, say goodbye to him and move on to Padstow.'

'You'll miss him,' Morwenna suggested.

'I will, so much. We were close.' Inga met her eyes. 'He was close to your mother too? Lamorna?'

'They met up again after a long time, yes.'

'He was a wonderful man.' Inga sucked on her cigarette. 'Kind, generous, protective. We meant the world to each other.' She ground the butt beneath her slipper. 'He was like a father to me, an uncle.'

'I expect the whole cast thought the world of him.' Morwenna tried a leading question.

'They didn't. I'm sure you'll have picked that up. Kenzie doesn't care who knows how much she hated him. Don't you and Kenzie go swimming together?'

'We have, a couple of times.'

'Look.' Inga put her mouth close to Morwenna's ear. 'Let me give you some advice.'

'Advice?'

'A few people in the company have noticed you asking questions. Jesse Miles told everyone yesterday that you were asking about the will.'

'I don't think I said anything out of turn,' Morwenna countered.

'I'd advise you to keep your distance.' Inga's eyes narrowed. 'Daniel's gone now. We're all sad. But that's the end of it.'

'I didn't mean to offend anyone.'

'I'm not offended.' Inga brightened. 'But Jesse has a mean side. He can be a nasty piece of work. He stirs up trouble just for fun. Daniel could have told you about the awful things he's done, but it's too late now.'

'Right.' Morwenna placed a foot on the pedal. 'I ought to be getting off to work.'

'Me too – no peace.' Inga smiled, friendly again. 'And I'm sure you'll be around for Elowen's performances. As I say, she has bags of talent, that one.'

'Thanks,' Morwenna called, but Inga was hurrying back to the marquee, her long dress swishing. Morwenna frowned, confused, and set off for the library. She was definitely late now.

* * *

Louise had two mugs of tea ready. She held out a book. 'It's all yours now, Morwenna. You won't be disappointed.'

Morwenna took the copy of Pawly Yelland's *Hidden Secrets of Seal Bay*. The cover was a grainy photo of the seafront, probably taken around the fifties. The tearoom looked jaded, dated – she wondered who'd owned it then, before her mother took it over in the nineties. 'Thanks Louise – I'll enjoy this.'

'The chapter on the Victorian Pengellens is inspirational but he only mentions the library once.' Louise was clearly a little disappointed. 'I thought he might have written more about our ghost.'

'You should suggest he calls in and we can show him the evidence.'

'Oh, what a great idea... the door that creaks, the books that move.'

'Well, the moving books are probably me being careless.'

'I'll find a contact email address and invite him. Do you think he'll come?'

'All writers love libraries – I don't see why not.' Morwenna sipped her tea.

On cue, as always seemed to happen when Lady Elizabeth was the subject of conversation, the door groaned. Morwenna greeted Musa with a smile as he wandered in. 'Hello. What can I do for you?'

He said, 'I've heard there's a book called *Poisons and Spells in Merlin's Realm*, by T. P. Grayson. Have you got it?'

'Hmmm. I don't think so, but I can order it for you.' Morwenna tapped on the laptop keys in front of her. 'There – Truro library has it. I can get it by Tuesday but I'm afraid this time you really will have to join.'

'How do I do that?'

'Just fill in a form online. Give Carole's address and your home one.'

'I'll put my parents' address in Handsworth. I'm sort of in between homes at the moment.' He smiled. 'Thank you.'

Morwenna studied his twinkling eyes, the short locks sticking out of a beanie. 'Are you interested in spells?'

'It's research,' he explained. 'I love playing Merlin.'

'You do it brilliantly,' Morwenna said honestly. 'I thought you were great in the show.'

'You're Elowen's gran? She's a lovely kid.' Musa had a charming smile. 'And thanks – that means a lot. Most of the cast are formally trained. My dad wouldn't let me do an acting degree

– I had to follow the family business with my brother. But here I am.'

'Here you are,' Louise repeated with a smile to Morwenna. Then she added, 'You wouldn't like to come wild swimming with us on Sunday morning, would you?'

'Not for me – it's far too cold.' Musa shook his head, leaving quickly.

Morwenna gave a ridiculously exaggerated cough. Louise met her eyes and muttered, 'What? I only asked...'

* * *

In the tearoom, the lunchtime rush was frantic; Morwenna had no time for anything but work. But by three twenty, there were only two customers remaining, hunched over a pot of tea. Tamsin said, 'Time for a cuppa?'

Morwenna sank down at a table, her legs aching, and pulled out her phone. There was a message from Barnaby, which she read carefully.

My client has had your tonic tested. It contains arsenic. What's going on?

She texted back.

Will explain later. Sorry to have misled you that it was mine. Might it have been enough to kill someone?

She scratched her head, lost in thought. There was a gentle pressure on her shoulder and she accepted the steaming mug gratefully. Tamsin plonked down beside her and said, 'You look tired, Mum.'

'Do I?'

Morwenna wondered if it was the date with Barnaby that had made her tired. Or the business with Lamorna and Daniel. Or the strain of sleuthing. All of them. She said, 'Elowen will be in any time.'

'Grandma's picking her up – they are going for an ice cream because it's Friday. She's not on stage tonight.'

'Right.'

'I wanted to ask you – how do you feel about having Elowen tomorrow afternoon? Becca and I were thinking of shutting up early, going into Truro shopping and out for a drink until late.'

'That's great. You deserve a break. Elowen can spend time with Brenda, stay for tea, then I'll take her to the theatre for her performance and she can sleep over…'

'Perfect but – er – Dad suggested taking her to Hippity Hoppers. She loves the trampolines there.'

Morwenna bridled. 'What – are both of us taking her?'

'She'd love that.' Tamsin met her eyes. 'She has two grandparents, Mum.'

'You're right.' Morwenna sighed. 'Elowen comes first. I'll pick her up at two thirty.'

'Dad said he'd drive you down to the trampoline park.'

'Did he?' Morwenna relented. 'All right.'

She was about to add 'whatever' but the door clanged open and two of the Spriggan company came in, clearly a little the worse for wear. One of them carried an open bottle of champagne. Morwenna recognised Rupert, who'd played Lancelot and was now playing Daniel Kitto's role as well, and Ben, who was Arthur, wearing a faded denim jacket. They plonked themselves down at a table near the window. Ben gazed out to sea as Rupert waved an arm towards Tamsin. 'Come and join us for a glass of champers – what do you say, gorgeous?'

'I'm busy,' Tamsin countered as she sipped tea. She clearly wasn't.

'Two coffees – coffees and your best cakes,' Rupert yelled. 'And don't spare the expense.'

'Make mine black coffee – and strong,' Ben added.

'Two black coffees – and a Cornish cream tea, served up by a semi-naked filly with a low moral compass,' Rupert said.

Morwenna heaved herself to her feet. 'You'll have to settle for me.'

She heard Rupert groan. He said too loudly, 'What's wrong with the fit one? Why can't she serve us?'

The word 'fit' gave Morwenna an idea. She poured two treacle coffees into mugs and approached the table.

'Isn't there any music in this place?' Ben muttered. 'What a dive.'

'Here are your coffees.' Morwenna faked a wobble and plonked the mugs on the table, spilling a little. She'd show them she had acting talent too. 'Oh, I've gone all dizzy,' she said, bending her knees.

'You should have got the young one to serve us, Grannie,' Rupert admonished.

'Sit down.' Ben offered her a seat next to him. 'Are you all right?'

'Light-headed.' Morwenna panted to prove her point. 'It happens sometimes. What I really need is a good healthy tonic. I've heard that there are things you can get – capsules, miracle water or something. You can't get it at the chemist though.'

'Are you all right?'

'I work too hard, and I pedal my bike everywhere. I'm overdoing things.' Morwenna groaned, fanning herself with her hand. 'I need antioxidants. Essential fatty acids. Brazilian acai berries...' She was grasping for anything she'd ever heard of. 'Cruciferous vegetables. Superfoods.'

'I might be able to help,' Ben said.

'Here we go.' Rupert rolled his eyes. 'He never misses a sales opportunity.'

'Oh, could you? I'd be so grateful.' Morwenna gave him her most winning look.

'I'm a black belt in aikido and I've used the same tonic for years. It works for me. You can't get it on the high street... It's my cousin's business.'

'He's on commission.' Rupert swigged champagne from the bottle.

'So, do you have any on you now?' Morwenna asked. 'I'm sure I'd feel a lot better.'

'Oh, you'd feel the difference almost immediately,' Ben assured her emphatically. 'I'll bring you some round tomorrow morning. It's twenty quid for a month's supply...'

'Bargain.' Morwenna heaved herself upright. 'Thanks so much. Cream tea, was it?'

'I'm on it, Mum,' Tamsin said, moving to the kitchen. Morwenna smiled slyly. She'd get her hands on another batch of the tonic to double-check her theory.

Her phone pinged. Barnaby had replied.

Yes. Enough to kill someone over several days. I need to know what's going on.

She replied.

Don't worry. Will tell you next time, over dinner...

The door chimed as it opened and Elowen came in, gripping Lamorna's hand, Oggy Two in the other, blue ice cream around her mouth. She rushed straight to Morwenna and transferred some of it to her lips. Bubble-gum flavour. Elowen hugged her.

'Hello, Grandma. How's Brr-brrr-Brrrenda?'

'Purring and eating biscuits, just as she always does. How are you, my bewty?' Morwenna asked.

Elowen said, 'I'd be better if I could have a dog. I want a Labrador. I'd call it Oggy.'

As Tamsin placed a cream tea on the table between the actors, Rupert grabbed her wrist. 'Buy the little poppet a doggie, darling.'

Tamsin gave him an icy stare. 'Hands off.'

'Watch your manners, son, or go outside and cool down.' Lamorna snorted disgustedly. 'Have a scone and sit quietly. Some of us know how to behave in a public place.'

Rupert turned back to the almost-empty bottle, his face sullen. 'I thought the Cornish people were supposed to be friendly. Why don't you all celebrate with us? Guess what – we own a theatre company. We all had letters from the solicitor, saying that the company is ours. Sort of ours, as good as. In a manner of speaking. Isn't that the best news?' He raised the bottle and tipped it over his mouth, froth pouring down his chin.

'Can I have some of that fizzy lemonade, Grandma?' Elowen piped up.

But Morwenna didn't hear: her head was full of theatre companies and arsenic.

11

On Saturday afternoon, the rain came down; good honest Cornish rain, splashing against the windows from grey-washed skies. Morwenna gazed out into the road, staring at the puddles, the gurgling gutters. A lone seagull landed on the gatepost of number nine. Ruan's van was outside, water dripping off the roof. He'd be round in ten minutes, bang on time – Morwenna was ready, but she didn't feel like going out. Of course, it would be good to spend time with Elowen, but she'd be leaping on a trampoline, hyperactive and excited with all her friends, and Morwenna would have to make small talk with Ruan. She was already weary. It had been a long week.

Tamsin had messaged to say that 'the fit actor and his obnoxious friend' had been into the teashop first thing and dropped off some of the special tonic – she'd paid him twenty pounds. Apparently, the obnoxious one had asked her out to dinner and she'd refused him without any further comment. Morwenna was delighted to get her hands on another sample of tonic – she hoped Barnaby's friend could test and compare them. She didn't expect her bottle to be contaminated, but what if it was? In her imagination, Ben was a psychopath who wanted to kill older people, like the GP they called Dr Death who had made all the headlines years ago.

Then a thought came to her: what had Jesse said about the tonic? 'It's free from cyanocobalamin, whatever that means. Musa would be able to tell you.'

Musa. It was just a hunch, but she wanted to check it. She rushed to her laptop and typed a name and a location into Google: Musa Omari, Handsworth. It wasn't a common name – she might find out something interesting. His face came up, the broadest of grins, huge blue false ears, an elf's costume. Morwenna read the first lines of a newspaper article.

> Local actor Musa Omari is a hit as the mischievous fairy in When Omfra the Piskie Lost His Laugh. The Spriggan Travelling Theatre visits primary schools in Birmingham.

It was dated last December.

Morwenna tried again. Musa had said something about his training. She recalled his words. 'My dad wouldn't let me do an acting degree – I had to follow the family business with my brother.' She typed in Omari and Sons, Handsworth. Then a map came up, a website. P. J. Omari and sons, Pharmacist.

Pharmacist. Of course.

Morwenna let the thought sink in. So that had been his profession before he'd become an actor. It explained the type of books he borrowed, his interest in poisons and spells…

There was a crisp knock at the door. Ruan. She'd have to put all the sleuthing behind her for the time being and concentrate on her granddaughter. She'd make sure Elowen had a nice day, at least. That was her priority, above everything else.

An hour later, Morwenna and Ruan stood side by side in

Hippity Hoppers, in a huge hall full of trampolines of various sizes, a coffee bar, a ball pit, and countless noisy children. They each clutched a cardboard cup of coffee, watching Elowen, who was bouncing with her friends, being supervised by eager assistants in green tracksuits who shouted out instructions. Ruan wasn't saying much; he'd hardly spoken since they arrived other than to ask her if she wanted a coffee. Morwenna's reply had been a monosyllabic grunt.

She noticed Elowen was still hugging the knitted dog as she bounced; her face shone with happiness. Morwenna smiled. 'I think she's doing all right, our Elowen. She still takes Oggy Two everywhere though.'

'She's growing up so fast.'

'She is.'

Morwenna closed her eyes; it was platitude time again. She said, 'I'm taking her to her show tonight and then back to my house to stay over.'

'We could go for something to eat first. A pizza.'

'I don't know, Ruan.'

'It would save you cooking.'

'Maybe.'

There was silence for a while, then they spoke at the same time. Ruan asked, 'How's Lamorna?'

And Morwenna said, 'This rain's depressing.'

They looked at each other properly for the first time that day and their eyes held. Ruan said, 'Damien said he saw you at the boatyard.'

'He did,' Morwenna agreed. So that was what was on his mind.

Ruan's voice was expressionless. 'With Pam Truscott's brother, Barnaby. The surgeon.'

'Yes, he cooked dinner.'

'On the *Pammy*?'

'That's right.' Morwenna took a breath. 'It's not illegal.' She wondered why she'd said that – it sounded hostile.

'No, it's not illegal.' Ruan hadn't touched his cardboard coffee. He was quiet for a while, then he said, 'Is that the first time you've been out with him?'

'Yes.'

'Will you see him again?'

Morwenna felt suddenly irritated. 'What's it got to do with you, Ruan?' The anger was replaced immediately with sadness. She wished she hadn't been so rude. She hadn't intended it. In truth, she wasn't sure what she felt.

'It's got nothing to do with me.' Ruan looked away. 'Nothing at all.'

Silence filled the space between them. Then she said, 'We drove back past The Smugglers just as they were turning out. I saw Kenzie Fuller with a man – he had his arm round her.' She turned to face him. 'Was it you?'

'I walked her back to the B & B.' Ruan didn't deny it. 'She was a bit the worse for wear.'

'That was gentlemanly of you,' Morwenna said and immediately regretted it – she sounded sarcastic and she hadn't meant to. In fact, she could imagine him being kind to someone who had drunk too much. He was like that.

Ruan said nothing for a bit and then he said, 'It was.'

'I mean – you can see who you like.' Morwenna took a deep breath. 'We're not together.'

'No.'

'And I can see who I like.'

'Right.'

Morwenna dropped the half-finished coffee cup in the bin and went back to watching Elowen. She said, 'That little maid is our priority.'

'She is,' Ruan agreed. 'And Tam.'

'And Tam.'

Ruan threw his coffee away. He'd hardly touched it. He pushed his hands into his jeans pockets. 'It's a shame though.'

'What is?' Morwenna knew exactly what he was talking about.

'Us, splitting up. We were good once.'

'Ah,' Morwenna exhaled. 'We were.'

Elowen waved and Ruan waved back. Morwenna called, 'Are you all right?'

She shouted back, 'Proper job,' and continued bouncing.

'Remember when Tam was her age?' Ruan said quietly.

'They were good times, Ruan.' Morwenna sighed. 'I can't deny that.'

She knew exactly what he'd say next – he'd say that those were the best of days. She knew he regretted the way they'd split up. Morwenna still thought of it as a car crash – they'd argued too much, hit a bump and over they went.

Her phone buzzed and she tugged it out of her pocket. 'It's a message – from Mum.'

'Is Lamorna all right?' Ruan was immediately concerned.

'No, not really.' Morwenna held up her phone, her face confused. 'She's asking us if we can go round to hers right away. She's had a bit of a shock.'

'What's happened?'

'She says she's just had a strange text.' Morwenna shook her head, mystified. 'From Daniel Kitto.'

* * *

They arrived at Tregenna Gardens to find Lamorna in the kitchen, holding out her phone as if it had burned her fingers. Her mouth was open. 'He's messaged me – Daniel – from the grave.'

Morwenna threw an arm round her mother. 'It's his phone, Mum. Not him. What does it say?'

Lamorna shook her head and handed her phone over. 'You read it.' She glanced at Elowen, who was hugging Oggy Two.

Morwenna read the text.

WARNING. Stop digging around or you'll regret it.

'It's sent to you, but it's for me,' Morwenna said.

'Who's it from?' Lamorna was confused.

'From whoever has Daniel's phone. Last time I saw it, it was on top of his things in the dressing room – in a gold case. Someone's clearly using it, and your number is in there.'

'I don't get it.' Lamorna frowned. 'Why send me a warning for you?'

'Mum, when you were with Daniel, did he ever complain of any symptoms? Did he say he felt unwell at any time?'

'He was very healthy.'

'But did he mention anything – you know, feeling under the weather, headaches, that sort of thing?'

'He said he had a tummy ache when we went to the fish restaurant – and he had this funny cramp thing in his fingers. Why?'

Morwenna glanced at Ruan. 'Can you take Elowen into the living room and get her to watch some TV?'

'Right.' He met her eyes and nodded. 'Come on, maid, let's see what's on the telly.'

Morwenna waited until they had gone, then she tugged out her phone.

'What are you up to?' Lamorna asked.

'I'm googling arsenic – right – so, side effects – here we are – nausea, vomiting, cramps, diarrhoea.'

'Daniel and I didn't discuss diarrhoea.'

'Mum, I think he may have had arsenic poisoning – hang on.'

'What are you doing now?'

Morwenna spoke as her thumb moved. 'Can arsenic poison cause a heart att—? Yes, here we are: arsenic-induced myocardial infarction in particular can be a significant cause of mortality.'

'What does that mean?'

Morwenna took a breath. 'It means, Mum, that Daniel's heart attack might have been caused by arsenic poisoning through the health tonic he took. I think it might have been tampered with.'

'I knew it. I knew he didn't have a proper heart attack. He was so fit.' Lamorna's lip trembled and her eyes filled with tears. 'Who'd do that to him? He was a lovely man.'

'He got a health tonic from Ben D'Arcy. I'm going to find out if it's tonic or not. I bought some from him – it's in my bag now,' Morwenna said excitedly.

'But there might not be any arsenic in your bottle, Morwenna. It won't be in all the bottles.'

'No, but... if someone is sending you a threatening message on Daniel's phone for me, then they just might take the opportunity to try to do to me what they did to Daniel.'

'That's a bit far-fetched...' Lamorna pulled a face. 'This sleuthing business has gone to your head.'

'But I need to rule it out – what if someone did put arsenic in my tonic, Mum? And if not Ben, then who?'

'Do you think one of the actors killed him?' Lamorna asked.

'I'm trying to work out who would have the opportunity, or the motive. The actors stood to gain the theatre. The solicitor has written to them all. Two of them were in the tearoom this afternoon drinking champagne, celebrating.'

Lamorna pressed her lips together. 'Daniel said some of the cast didn't like him. The lad who played Lancelot was always arguing about everything – jumped-up little tuss, that Rupert has a very a high opinion of himself. The technician owed Daniel money. And the dark-haired woman – something funny was going on there, if you ask me. They fell out over something big and she hated his guts.'

'Can you remember anything Daniel said about it, Mum?'

'I can't.' She put a hand to her head. 'It's still all fuzzy.'

'Of course – just see what comes back to you in time. It might be useful.' Morwenna glanced towards the door. Ruan was there, watching.

'Elowen's tucked up on the sofa, watching cartoons.' He looked concerned. 'We ought to feed her and get her to her show.'

'Oh.' Lamorna moved towards the fridge. 'I'll get us all a nice salad – would that be all right? I've got a tin of tuna in the cupboard and a few cold potatoes.'

''Ansom,' Morwenna said. 'Thanks, Mum.'

'It'll give me something to do.'

As Lamorna began to bustle around, Ruan moved closer to Morwenna. 'What are you thinking?'

'Someone killed Daniel, Ruan.'

He placed a gentle hand on her shoulder. 'Should you tell the police?'

She looked at him as if he was being ridiculous. 'Rick Tremayne?'

'Jane Choy. She's a friend.'

'I might – we're going swimming tomorrow I'll mention it.'

'Shouldn't the police arrest whoever it is? I mean, that phone message was a threat.'

'It was. But you know how it works – I don't expect you can arrest someone because they message you on a dead man's phone.'

'But the police can test the bottle of tonic.'

'Maybe,' Morwenna agreed. 'I just want to work a few more

things out for myself first. I want to talk to someone at the theatre when we drop Elowen off.'

'I'll come with you,' Ruan said.

'Please yourself.' Morwenna stopped herself and offered a warm smile. 'No, that's kind, Ruan. Thanks.'

His face was concerned. 'I know you too well. Once you get involved with this sleuthing business, you'll forget about your own safety, and that worries me.'

'I'll be fine,' she reassured him. 'It's Mum I'm concerned about.' Her voice was low. 'She's still in shock. What happened to Daniel upset her and now she's getting texts from his phone.'

'It was a threat,' Ruan reminded her.

'It may be just hot air,' Morwenna said. 'I'm not going to take it seriously. Now – let's help Mum make salad, get our Elowen down to Spriggan and into her mermaid costume.' She was thoughtful. 'Then there are some things I need to find out.'

12

Morwenna and Elowen arrived backstage and she helped her into her costume and applied the glittery make-up. Elowen was bouncing up and down, asking Musa if she could take Oggy Two on stage and if mermaids had pets. Musa showed her how to make clown faces, happy, sad, mischievous – each time he slid a hand up and down across his face, there was another grotesque expression. Elowen copied perfectly. Morwenna went back to Ruan, who was watching from the wings. She stood next to him, waiting for the lights to go down. She said, 'This experience is so good for Elowen. I can see her ending up on the stage.'

Ruan smiled. 'I wouldn't be surprised. There's a lot of the Mutton maid in her.'

'What's that supposed to mean?' Morwenna asked; she knew it was a compliment.

'Tam's like me, a Pascoe – steady, she takes her time with things.'

'Not with men,' Morwenna disagreed. 'She came back from that holiday pregnant with Elowen. She didn't take her time with that. Or moving in with Jack Greenwood.'

Ruan sighed. 'We give our hearts away, we Pascoes. Tam made a bad choice twice, that's all.'

Morwenna was about to tell Ruan that he'd only made a bad choice once. But it hadn't been. It had been wonderful at first: they'd had Tamsin, brought her up; they'd been happy. Then two years ago, they'd hit a rut.

Morwenna changed the subject. 'Are you going down The Smugglers when Elowen's finished?'

'I'll drop you both off first.'

'Oh...'

So, he was off down the pub. Kenzie would be there too, later. Of course she would. Morwenna imagined her chattering to Ruan at the bar, all smiles and compliments. She said nothing.

Ruan looked at his hands; large fisherman's hands. 'The lads are keeping an eye on young Tommy Buvač. He's hit a bit of a rough patch.'

'Why? I thought he'd started fishing.'

'He has. He's not a natural. He looks washed out in the mornings and he's sick a lot on board. Milan's giving him space to find his sea legs. But he takes his pay down The Smugglers and drinks it away. We're all hoping it's a phase – he's just a kid.'

'I remember Rosie saying something – and Jane Choy. How long has he been on the boats?'

'A month, two. He gets a lot of stick from the lads, teasing and stuff. He's not like Milan, a gentle giant – he takes it to heart. Then he's in the pub evenings, sinking beers.'

'That's a shame,' Morwenna said.

The lights started to fade and a spotlight came up centre stage, a little mermaid with long dark hair and a flipping tail, pulling clown faces at the audience. Then Elowen said in her loudest, clearest voice, 'Welcome to Cornwall, the home of King Arthur...'

Morwenna turned to Ruan, who was looking at her. She smiled and a familiar warmth passed between them.

Elowen was carried off stage by Musa and deposited next to Morwenna with a grin. The show was under way. Morwenna whispered to Elowen, 'Just take the tail off, pull some leggings on and your coat, and we'll take you home. I'm going to take a look around for a minute.'

'Right. I'll be here,' Ruan said. The audience could be heard gasping. Morgan le Fay was making evil magic. Morwenna moved nimbly into the backstage area behind the flats. Elowen was whispering in Ruan's ear as he held up her coat. Morwenna decided she'd take a look around while she had the chance. No one had noticed her: the actors who weren't on stage were chattering, warming up, drinking water from bottles.

There was no one in the male dressing area. She slid behind the curtain and looked around. Clothes were laid out on benches, on hangers. There was a mirror, a few chairs, a rail crammed with costumes, another curtain. She moved to the discarded clothes – everyone was wearing their stage dress – and slipped her hand into jeans pockets, jacket pockets. She was searching for a phone in a gold case. If she found Daniel's mobile, it would be clear who was threatening her. She checked Ben D'Arcy's faded denim jacket, left alongside his phone, some keys and a bottle of tonic. She checked Musa's dark jacket and found a set of keys. There were several phones on a shelf: one with a black case, a silver one, one top-of-the-range, bright zany colours. But none of them were Daniel's. Then she heard voices and looked around frantically for somewhere to hide. The curtain rail! Morwenna dived behind it, crouching between the rows of velvet, net, silk, coarse calico and fur. Her face was filled with yellow feathers from a duck costume. Her nose itched; she was inhaling dust. She took a steady breath to calm her racing pulse.

Two men were inside the dressing room, deep in conversation as they changed costumes. She gazed out from behind the duck costume at a pair of red boxer shorts, long muscular legs.

'I couldn't believe it, seeing the Carlyon woman's name on the letter.' The voice was Ben D'Arcy's. Morwenna peeped through the feathers. He was pulling on a different tunic, a fur-edged cloak, as he spoke in a low whisper to Jesse Miles.

'I thought Korrik Clay was just in it for the advertising. But Anna's the trustee – Kitto's put her in charge. Still, Spriggan's as good as our company now he's out of the way.'

Morwenna frowned. Anna Carlyon's name was familiar. Of course – she'd seen her at the opening night of the play. Becca had told her that she was connected with Korrik Clay...

Ben shook his head. 'Only while we work here.' He sounded dubious. 'We're just employees.'

'What about his money?' Jesse asked. 'The assets will be sold; Kitto's flat in London, his car.'

'It will all come to the company in time – the solicitor will sort it,' Ben said. 'Our future's guaranteed as long as we keep our jobs.'

'And as long as that Korrik woman doesn't interfere.'

'Of course – Daniel's will is watertight.'

'And when a man dies, anything he's owed dies with him, doesn't it? And if not, nobody knows about it,' Jesse said.

'You mean the personal loans...' Ben whispered.

Jesse nodded. 'Fancy a pint down the pub? I'm buying.'

'When did you last buy drinks?' Ben joked, astonished. 'You're always skint.'

'I was paying Kitto back for the prang I had.'

'He wasn't amused, you taking his pride and joy.'

'I don't care.' Jesse shook his head. 'I don't have any money worries now. I'm flush.'

'So's Rupert.' Ben lowered his voice. 'Apparently, he owed the old man thousands.'

'Did he?' Jesse sounded surprised.

Morwenna leaned forward to listen and held her breath. She hoped she wouldn't sneeze. The feathers were scratching her face and dust from the costumes' years of use filled her nose.

'Yes, drinking, gambling, living it up – Rupert likes the high life and, on an actor's wage, he just accumulated debt. He borrowed all the time. Daniel was a soft touch when it came to a sob story.'

'Rupert'll be glad that's off his shoulders. Me too. Kitto was always on my case,' Jesse admitted. 'Anyway, the sad git's gone now. Let's celebrate. Like I said, drinks are on me.'

'We have plenty to be pleased about,' Ben sneered and the pair of them walked away.

Morwenna paused for a moment to make sure, then she crawled from behind the costume rail and scratched her nose. She stood still, thinking, letting it all sink in.

Then she was moving quickly. Hoping that no one had seen her, she slid from behind the curtain and walked easily towards Elowen and Ruan.

'Well, we should be getting Elowen home,' Morwenna muttered.

'I like staying with you, Grandma, so Mummy can get pissed with her friend Becca next door. I want to sleep with Brenda on my bed,' Elowen said in one breath.

'We can do without the bad language.' Morwenna frowned. 'You're getting a bit too uppity, Elowen. It's time we got you to bed.'

'But can't I watch the rest of the play?'

'Home,' Morwenna said firmly.

Ruan was studying his mobile. He said, 'Have you seen what's on your phone?'

'No.' Morwenna shook her head. 'Why?'

'Lamorna's sent us both a message. She's had another...' he glanced at Elowen and chose his words carefully '...another strange text.'

Morwenna pulled out her phone and checked messages. One was from Lamorna saying she was going to forward what had been sent to her from Daniel's phone. The second simply said:

Rodenticides are toxic to cats and can cause bleeding, kidney failure, seizures and death.

Morwenna caught her breath. 'Ruan – can we go home? I need to check on Brenda.' She turned to Elowen, an excuse already on her lips. 'We don't want her to get lonely, do we?'

* * *

Ruan drove up the hill and they stopped abruptly outside number four. Morwenna rushed inside and gazed around. She'd expected to find a scattering of doctored Dreamies on the welcome mat, a plump cat slumped next to it, but everything was normal. Morwenna tugged Elowen into the lounge and turned on the small TV. 'You sit here a moment, my bewty – your grandad will make you hot chocolate.' She mouthed to Ruan: I'll check upstairs.

Ruan disappeared into the kitchen and Morwenna thumped up the stairs two at a time. As she turned the corner into her bedroom, she saw Brenda stretched out on the bed. She was quickly by her side, stroking her fur, and was relieved to hear a rhythmic purring. Brenda opened one green eye.

'Thank goodness,' Morwenna breathed, then she yelled, 'Brenda's asleep on my bed, Ruan.'

He called back. 'The hot chocolate's ready. Then we'd better get Elowen into her pyjamas.' She reached the living room. Two steaming cups had been placed on coasters. Morwenna was disappointed. 'Aren't you having one?'

'I was going to have a pint.'

'Oh?'

'I'll stay if you need me.'

'No, we'll be fine.' Morwenna felt her phone buzz in her pocket and glanced at a text anxiously. 'Mum's had another message. She's just forwarding it now.'

Ruan tugged his phone from his jeans and they both stared at the screen:

The cat was lucky. But what about Elowen? Or Tamsin?

Ruan met her eyes. They both glanced towards Elowen, who was drinking hot chocolate, a half-circle above her top lip. Morwenna said, 'How are you feeling, sweetheart?'

'A bit tired.' Elowen looked up. 'Can I sleep in your bed with you, Grandma? Mummy lets me sometimes. I get bad dreams...'

'Of course you can – yes, you tuck up with me and Brenda.' Morwenna shared a look with Ruan, remembering the episode last autumn after Alex Truscott was murdered. Elowen had recovered from the trauma, but there was bound to be residual hurt.

'I'll be off, then,' Ruan muttered. 'I'll make last orders.'

'Right,' Morwenna said. 'Can you sort out Elowen's breakfast tomorrow morning while I go for a swim?'

'Tam's opening the tearoom first thing on Sundays now – I'll see if she can rustle us all up some beans on toast,' Ruan offered.

'Can I have scrambledy eggs, Grandad?' Elowen said, her eyes still on the screen, and Morwenna's heart expanded as she thought of the phone message again. No one was going to harm her family. She was even more determined than ever to find out who was behind the threats, who had killed Daniel.

She followed Ruan to the door. 'I'll see you first thing.'

Ruan frowned. 'Whoever sent Lamorna the text knew you had a cat...'

'I was wondering about that...'

'Right,' he replied and stepped into the shadows. Morwenna thought it might not just be a pint of beer that was tempting him to The Smugglers. She locked the door, drawing the bolt across, and went back to sit next to Elowen.

'Have you finished your hot chocolate?'

'Two more minutes, Grandma?'

'Just two then. Brenda will be getting lonely.'

Morwenna watched as Elowen took another gulp of her drink. She was remembering the conversation she'd overheard behind the costume rail. Jesse and Ben had sounded surprised that Anna Carlyon was named as trustee in Daniel's will. She picked up her phone and typed 'china clay' into Google. Jesse had said Korrik was a china clay company, but Morwenna wasn't really sure what china clay was, so perhaps that was the place to start. Anna Carlyon had been in the audience at the opening night. Morwenna recalled her booming, confident voice when she'd spoken to the Pengellens, as if she were a celebrity guest. Fleetingly, she wondered why she was interested in theatre.

Morwenna read carefully: '...negative environmental impacts such as: ecological and agricultural imbalances, erosion, silting of rivers.' '...China clay hides in your toothpaste, your paper, your car tyres and even your cosmetics...'

She made her search specific – Korrik Clay: 'Korrik Clay at St Mengleth... the Cornish word korrik means elf – we started small but now we are a worldwide company...' She read on... 'English porcelain industry began with the 1745 discovery of kaolinite... Company owner, William Carlyon...'

Morwenna typed the name William Carlyon. Several photos

immediately popped up. One was of a distinguished-looking man with a moustache, smiling eyes, and, beneath, the words Korrik Clay, one of the few remaining working mines, producing Cornish kaolin. There were several more of a smart-looking woman with a blonde bob. 'Anna Carlyon donates funds to local hedgehog conservation.'

Morwenna remembered the blue-framed glasses, the elegant check suit, the easy confidence. So Anna Carlyon would have been made the trustee of Spriggan by Daniel Kitto two years ago...

But what connected Anna and Daniel? She needed to find out.

13

Morwenna stood on Seal Bay beach, blinking in the bright sunlight, wearing her rainbow swimming costume and orange cap. She was surrounded by the other five SWANs. The waves glittered silver in the distance. Everyone had turned up for the Sunday morning swim, but she was the only one not wearing a wetsuit. She'd been brave – and foolish, she thought as she trembled, her skin gooseflesh in the sea breeze. Susan and Barb Grundy were in matching navy-blue wetsuits, Louise's was black, as was Donald's, but he had sporty orange stripes across the arms. Jane Choy was lean in a grey wetsuit, which she told everyone was 100 per cent Ultraflex neoprene with a double seal neck closure. The one thing they all had in common was that they were eyeing the rushing waves, counting down to the moment they'd run towards them. Morwenna was considering telling Jane about the threatening messages from Daniel's phone, but she decided she'd wait until she had more evidence about the second sample of tonic. It was an outside chance that her bottle would have arsenic in it, but if it did, she'd be fairly sure about who had killed Daniel.

Louise was animated, chatting to Donald about the ghost. 'I've invited Pawly. He hasn't replied yet, but I thought he'd like to research the circumstances of Lady Elizabeth's death. I told him the library was her sanctuary.'

Susan grunted. 'And that actor died on the stage last week. We are murder central in Seal Bay.'

'Don't forget Alex Truscott, stabbed a few yards from where we are standing right now,' Barb said gloomily.

'I wonder who's next,' Susan added.

'Lady Elizabeth's husband broke her heart and she took poison in 1859,' Louise explained.

'It must have been a terrible end for the poor woman,' Jane commented.

'Cyanide, strychnine and arsenic,' Donald intoned. 'They were murderers' poisons of choice in those days.'

Jane met Morwenna's eyes. Her voice was low. 'Anything to report?'

'Soon,' Morwenna said. She pointed towards a figure rushing towards them; a coat and black beanie over a red swimsuit. 'Hello, Kenzie. You made it.'

'Only just,' Kenzie said. 'It was a heavy night in the pub.'

'Oh, where did you go?' Louise asked.

'The Smugglers. That reminds me – Morwenna, I owe you a huge apology.' Kenzie's expression was one of exaggerated regret. 'I should have made the connection and I didn't. Ruan Pascoe, Elowen Pascoe, Elowen's your granddaughter. I just think of you as a Mutton.' Everyone's attention was on Kenzie, but she spoke directly to Morwenna. 'I didn't realise – Ruan's your *ex*.'

Morwenna made a sad face. 'Ex is about the size of it.'

'It's just – oh, I hope you don't mind...' Kenzie said, as if she was embarrassed. 'Do you?'

'Mind what?' Susan turned to Barb.

'What's she got to mind about?' Barb was interested.

'We get on so well, Ruan and I – we have so much in common. We shared a few drinks together again last night – it's getting to be a bit of a regular thing.'

'You can drink with who you like,' Morwenna replied quickly in an attempt to disguise the awkwardness. Louise was staring at her.

'He's just incredibly attractive. He's walked me back to the B & B twice now, and I was thinking we might just – you know – but I wanted to check first that you'd be OK with it all.' Kenzie was making a meal of it. 'I mean, if you still have feelings for him, if it would upset you, then I'll back off now – while we both still can.'

'Ruan and I split up two years ago,' Morwenna said quietly. 'He's a good person. He deserves some happiness.'

'Oh, if you're sure, then I won't hold back. A travelling actor's life allows little time for romance but, as you say, Ruan's quite a catch.' She raised an eyebrow. 'Which is funny, with him being a fisherman, that would make me the catch, wouldn't it?'

'We should get in the water before we freeze to death.' Louise grunted, glancing at Morwenna.

'And there are already enough deaths in Seal Bay,' Barb announced.

'Are you OK?' Jane spoke quietly as she placed a hand on Morwenna's shoulder.

'I'm fine – thanks, Jane,' Morwenna said gratefully. 'Louise is right – we should dive in.' She forced a smile. 'I'll race you to the sea.'

'If you're sure.' Jane hesitated. Everyone else was already running ahead. 'I mean, I know you and Ruan are still close.'

'It's up to him – and her,' Morwenna said grimly. 'If they like each other, then, as far as I'm concerned, they can knock themselves out.' With that, she started to run towards the freezing waves for all she was worth. She needed to surround herself with icy water, to compose her thoughts.

* * *

Two hours later, she was sitting opposite Ruan and Elowen, munching baked beans, sipping tea. It was quiet in the tearoom, so Tamsin joined them briefly. 'Penny for your thoughts, Mum?'

'Just enjoying the hot food,' Morwenna said. 'It was freezing cold in the water. Thanks for looking after her, Ruan.'

'You're a star, Dad,' Tamsin said.

'I got scrambledy eggs,' Elowen said proudly to Oggy Two, who was on her knee.

'What are you up to today?' Tamsin asked Ruan.

'I was going to put wood preserver on the shed,' Ruan replied.

Morwenna snorted lightly. 'Nothing more interesting to do than that?' She raised an eyebrow.

Tamsin was perplexed. 'What are you up to, Mum?'

'I'm taking the bike to St Mengleth for a look around. I'd like to find out more about Korrik Clay.'

'That's five miles away.' Tamsin groaned.

'It's an electric bike – I won't peg out.' Morwenna's tone was decidedly prickly. She tried again. 'What I mean is, it will be fun.'

'I couldn't bike anywhere today.' Tamsin put a hand to her head. 'Becca and I had a great time last night, but it involved a few gins.'

'Mummy, can I have a few gins?' Elowen asked.

Ruan said, 'Scrambledy egg's much nicer...'

'Dad, you could take Mum to St Mengleth.' Tamsin made a cheeky face. 'It might be more fun than painting the shed. You could get lunch somewhere.' She made a hopeful face.

'Your dad might be looking forward to doing up the shed,' Morwenna began.

'No, it's a nice day for a drive, and I know exactly where Korrik's depot is.' Ruan leaned across the table. 'Is this a sleuthing escapade?'

'It might be.'

He said, 'Then I'd better come along.'

'You can please yourself, Ruan.' That bristling tone again. Morwenna softened. 'That's very kind of you. Thanks.'

Tamsin made a face that meant her parents were behaving like children and they should stop it. She said, 'When I close up at lunchtime, Elowen and I might go down to the beach.'

'Can we get a pizza, Mummy? Britney's mum always gets her pizzas.'

'We could get a takeaway brought to the flat maybe?'

'Maybe make your own from scratch?' Morwenna interrupted. She wondered if takeaways might be in danger of being tampered with. The phone messages had made her overly cautious. Ruan's glance told her he understood what she was thinking.

He said, 'Shall we get going? The sun's shining. We'll take a drive around St Mengleth and maybe afterwards, we can get a bite to eat?'

'OK.' Morwenna was perplexed. Sunday was Ruan's day off. Why hadn't he chosen to spend it with Kenzie? She'd certainly made it sound as if they were both smitten. She pushed her plate away. 'Thanks, Ruan. That would be nice.'

* * *

They drove to St Mengleth along the coastal path overlooking the sea. The sky was wide, filled with clouds. Ruan said, 'I love springtime. Best time of the year.'

'It's May next week – it's almost summer.'

'Summer's good, as long as it's not too hot. Fishing's better when the weather's mild...'

'Ruan, I want to go to Korrik Clay to look for clues.' Morwenna thought it was time to get to the point. 'Someone murdered Daniel, and I think it's someone from Spriggan, so I want to check out their sponsor.'

'I see.'

'I want to find out who's sending the threats on Daniel's phone,' Morwenna muttered. 'I overheard some of the cast talking yesterday – I hid behind the costume rail.'

Ruan couldn't help the grin. 'You're some maid.'

'They were talking about Daniel's will. They didn't sound pleased that Spriggan has been left in the charge of Anna Carlyon from Korrik Clay. The actors thought they'd be shareholders, but they are just employees.'

'It makes sense financially for the sponsor to be a trustee,' Ruan said simply.

'Do you know anything about Anna Carlyon?' Morwenna asked.

'She's a shrewd businesswoman, I've heard,' Ruan said. 'I suppose Daniel thought the company would be safe in her hands.'

'I wonder why Korrik chose to sponsor the company, though.'

'I've no idea... they're a local business.' Ruan took a breath. 'So – I wanted to tell you – I was in the pub last night.'

'Oh?' Morwenna took a breath.

'Some of the actors from Spriggan were there.'

'Ah.'

'The technician – the one who tells everyone he's from Penzance – was talking to Tommy Buvač, showing off. I couldn't help but hear.'

'Jesse Miles? What did he say?'

'He was trying to impress Tommy with how much Daniel trusted him. He said that he let him drive his car everywhere.'

'The sports car? I heard he'd taken it without asking and pranged the side.'

Ruan turned the sharp bend, past the sign to St Mengleth. 'He said Daniel gave him his bank card, trusted him to withdraw funds for the company. He was even saying his PIN number aloud.'

'What is it?'

'That's a strange question.' Ruan tried to remember. 'It could have been 1571 – or 3571 or 5171. I'm not sure. He was bragging to impress Tommy. Jesse was buying him drinks all night.'

'Isn't 1571 the BT Call Minder?' Morwenna asked.

'I thought it was familiar – why would he choose that though?'

'I've no idea – is that all that happened last night?'

'Pretty much – it was a heavy night for a lot of the cast,' Ruan said. 'Those actors can knock it back.'

'Kenzie too?'

Ruan said, 'She drinks like a fish, that one.'

'Did you take her back to The Blue Dolphin?'

Ruan's gaze was level. 'I saw her safely home.'

'Ah.' Morwenna changed the subject. 'So, we know Jesse is lying. I think he stole Daniel's wallet.'

'That doesn't make him a killer though.'

'We can't rule it out.'

'What else do we have?'

'All the actors had a motive and the means – Ben's bottles of health tonic. Anyone could have spiked them. But I want to find out about Anna Carlyon and her husband, William. She's Spriggan's new trustee. So...' Morwenna frowned. 'What's her connection with Daniel? It might help to sort out who's behind the threats.' Her eyes flashed. 'I'm not having anyone threaten my family.'

'I'm not sure you'll be finding out much today,' Ruan said as he brought the van to a halt outside a tall gate. The huge sign said Korrik Clay. The gate was chained with a large padlock. Everywhere was closed.

'I just hoped I'd be able to get inside for a look around without being seen. I wasn't expecting that big lock.' Morwenna opened the door and wriggled out, rushing towards the sign.

'What are you up to?'

'I'm just looking.' Morwenna peered beyond the gate. Ruan joined her. There were heaps of clay, mountains of the stuff, an abandoned yellow truck with wide wheels, a brick office building. 'Ruan – where do you imagine she lives, Anna Carlyon?'

'Well, not here, that's for sure – the place is so dusty.' Ruan frowned. 'I expect she's not badly off, so somewhere local? What did you say her husband was called?'

'William. I checked his name online,' Morwenna said. 'Let's adjourn to a local hostelry and have some lunch. I've brought Daniel's diary. Let's see what we can find out.'

They sat in a cosy corner of The Cornish Arms in the pretty village of St Mengleth. The pub was busy, customers sitting beneath low beams tucking into Sunday roasts, the smell of cooking heavy in the air. Morwenna and Ruan left their empty plates at the edge of the table as they drank lemonade and pored over the diary.

Ruan said, 'You didn't take all of Daniel's things, I hope?'

'Only the stuff that I thought might help me find out about him. I left everything else. There was a lovely gold St Christopher, an expensive watch.' She was thoughtful. 'I suppose his belongings are in storage. His effects will need to be sold. He had no one to leave them to.'

'That's such a shame,' Ruan said.

Morwenna was flicking through to the last page. 'Look here – the squares show debts that someone owed him. "Payments and balance, R." That must be Rupert. And on 8 April, it says, "the idiot scraped my car!!" Jesse had to pay him back for the repair.'

'Killing someone would cancel out debts,' Ruan said grimly.

'And here's the PIN number on the back page – 1571.'

'Do you think he deliberately picked the BT number so that he'd remember it?' Ruan asked.

'But then why would he need to write it down?'

'People forget things?' Ruan said. 'We all need a reminder.'

'Maybe. Or perhaps it was a new number, one he'd recently chosen.'

'Could be.'

'Ruan – what's your PIN number?'

'The year of Tam's birth. Why?'

'Mine's 1310, Elowen's birthday. A lot of PINs are significant dates. So – what if…?' Morwenna flicked the pages. 'Next week, 1 May. Look – Daniel's written Wednesday 1 May. Flowers, and a tick. That means he's ordered flowers for someone for next Wednesday – 1-5-71? The first of May, '71.'

'Do you think it's Anna Carlyon? Do you think they were having an affair?'

'Not everything's about sex, Ruan,' Morwenna retorted and checked herself. 'Well, I suppose they might be. Flowers for her birthday? Let's see what we can find on her.'

'If she was born in '71, that would make her in her fifties – might that fit?' Ruan suggested.

'I don't know – I suppose it could.' Morwenna was already trawling the Internet. 'Oh – here's an article. Anna Carlyon – wife of William Carlyon. He was born 1962, died just over two years ago of a heart attack. So, Anna's a widow.'

'Perhaps she and Spriggan go back a long way. How long have Korrik sponsored them?'

'Jesse Miles told me – two years.'

'That's interesting.'

'Perhaps Anna was so devastated by her husband's death that she turned to the theatre?' Morwenna was thoughtful. 'Or perhaps Daniel Kitto had a secret he was hiding somewhere? Ruan, I need to find out what it is...'

14
___

Monday morning was hectic in the library. There seemed to be a constant stream of people wanting to borrow gardening books because spring had arrived, and there was little time for a break. At lunchtime, just as Morwenna was tugging on her velvet coat about to leave, Louise announced, 'Oh – Donald's running late. Can you hang on for ten minutes, in case someone comes in and I'm out the back? He won't be long.'

'Tam won't mind,' Morwenna said. 'Mondays aren't the busiest days.'

'Shall we have a cup of tea? I'm gasping.'

'I'll sort it.' Morwenna reached beneath the counter for two mugs, plugging in the kettle.

'Oh, and...' Louise grasped her hand. 'Guess what? I've had an email from Pawly Yelland.'

'The author?'

'He wants to come in and meet me – both of us. To talk about...' Louise lowered her voice '...Lady Elizabeth.'

'Oh?' Morwenna poured hot water into two mugs with the caption *Kernow bys Vyken*, Cornwall for ever.

'I meant to ask.' Louise looked momentarily uncomfortable. 'Is Ruan – you know – going out with Kenzie?'

'I think he knows her,' Morwenna said. 'Not in the biblical sense. She's in The Smugglers a lot.'

'How would you feel if he had a girlfriend?' Louise's eyes bored into hers. 'Honestly?'

'Honestly?' Morwenna wasn't sure. 'I suppose it's up to him.'

'I always thought you two would get back together – anyone can see you're made for each other.'

'Thanks.' Morwenna sipped tea – it was always a comfort to wrap her hands around a warm mug in moments of emotional crisis. 'I expect it would be hard to get used to him being with someone else. He's Tam's dad and Elowen's grandad after all.'

'And your ex,' Louise said meaningfully.

'Ex is the word, though,' Morwenna said resignedly. 'Besides – I can hardly begrudge him a bit of romance. I have a date on Wednesday evening.'

'You do?' Louise moved closer. 'Oh, tell me more.'

Morwenna recalled the text she'd received as soon as she'd arrived in the library. 'Barnaby Stone, Pam Truscott's brother. We're going to The Marine Room for dinner.'

'In St Mengleth? I've heard it's very swanky there.'

'I'll let you know on Thursday morning,' Morwenna said with a wink.

'What does Ruan think of you seeing Barnaby? I've seen him with his sister, in his Jaguar. He's very handsome.'

Morwenna thought that there was little that escaped the people of Seal Bay. 'I don't discuss my private life with Ruan,' she said enigmatically. She knew the answer already: Ruan would be protective and concerned. She changed the subject. 'I haven't a clue what to wear.'

'Oh, something alluring,' Louise breathed. 'I love a good romance.'

'It's just dinner.'

Louise arched a brow. 'Nothing's ever *just* dinner.'

Morwenna opened her mouth to offer a cheeky reply, but Donald had arrived, muttering oaths about the plumber who should have turned up at nine thirty. She thought it wiser to say nothing more about her date with Barnaby for the time being.

* * *

Morwenna was off, cycling through town. She was late for her shift at the tearoom, but she'd already texted apologies. There was another call to make before she reached Tamsin. She passed Susan and Barb's pop-up shop. Barb waved knitting needles through the window, summoning Morwenna inside. Morwenna gestured back – she was in a hurry, but she'd pop in soon for a catch-up chat about sleuthing. She hoped Barb would understand what the wild arm signal meant.

She took a corner at speed and found herself outside Busy B's florist. She needed a quick word with Beattie Harris. Beattie was inside, constructing a beautiful bouquet, her face twisted in concentration.

Morwenna said, 'That's a gorgeous arrangement. Is it for someone's birthday?'

'It's for a local gentleman who's sending his love to a certain lady,' Beattie said coyly. 'Romance is definitely not dead in Seal Bay.'

'And she'll be very lucky to receive such a stunning bouquet,' Morwenna gushed. 'Can I ask a question?'

'You can.' Beattie looked up and smiled.

'Are you sending any birthday bouquets on Wednesday?' She studied Beattie's face carefully.

'I am, but...'

'From Daniel Kitto? The actor who passed away on stage?'

'I can't say,' Beattie replied, but Morwenna knew from her expression that such a bouquet existed.

'Who's it for?' Morwenna asked.

'I can't divulge a customer's purchases.' Beattie smiled, enjoying the fact that she knew something that Morwenna didn't.

'Daniel won't mind,' Morwenna said bluntly.

Beattie seemed a little shocked. 'But the lady might.'

'The lady?' Morwenna arched a brow. 'It's not my mother. Is it?'

'No, it's...' Beattie stopped herself. 'It's a bit of a mystery really. He's never sent this lady a bunch of flowers before, but he used to send them to another lady until a month or two ago. Regular as clockwork, from February to early March, once a week he sent a bunch to the residential home opposite the police station.'

'Autumn Wind?' Morwenna asked. 'What was the woman's name?'

'Oh, I can't say – but he hasn't sent her any for a while. I mean, certainly not for a few weeks before he died.' Beattie shrugged. 'I expect she moved somewhere else.'

Morwenna had an idea. 'Give me a bunch of something cheap.' She tried again. 'A nice bunch of flowers to cheer a room up.'

'I can do you a seasonal posy – carnation spray, dianthus, brassica, rose.'

'Perfect.' Morwenna tugged her purse from her bag. 'Thanks, Beattie. How are the grandchildren?'

'Adam and Naomi are fine. How's your little Elowen?'

'She's good.' Morwenna took the flowers and pushed a note in Beattie's hand. 'Keep the change. Thanks for all your help.'

'What help?' Beattie was baffled. But Morwenna was on her

way, dumping the wrapped flowers in the basket between the handlebars, turning her bicycle towards the police station, throwing a leg across the saddle.

Autumn Wind was a four-storey brick building with many windows. Morwenna wondered how many residents lived there. She quickly locked her bicycle outside and glanced across towards the police station across the road, wondering what case Jane was working on. She promised herself to send her a text, as soon as the results came back from the second batch of tonic.

She knocked on the wooden door and pressed the old bell. Her widest smile was ready as soon as the door opened. A tall woman in a green tunic, black trousers and sturdy shoes stood in front of her. She had sensible short hair and an expressionless face. 'Can I help you?'

'Oh, I hope so – I brought these flowers from Daniel.'

'Daniel who?'

'Daniel Kitto, the actor,' Morwenna said. 'He asked my mother before he passed away if she'd have some flowers delivered to a lady here. He always sends them, every week, and my mum promised, so here I am – the flowers for his lady friend.'

The woman stared at Morwenna, who held the posy out, her face a frozen grin. 'You must mean Diane Bennett? But she's not with us any more. She died a few weeks ago.'

'Oh, I'm so sorry.' Morwenna rearranged her features in an expression of sadness. 'I didn't realise. My mother was so anxious to get it right for Daniel. I expect he forgot to mention the lady had sadly passed.'

The woman was about to close the door. 'I can't help you, I'm afraid.'

'Not at all.' Morwenna pushed the bunch of flowers towards her. 'You've been really helpful, honestly. Please, take these, put them somewhere they can be enjoyed by everyone – in your office, if you like.'

'Oh.' The woman took the flowers. 'That's most kind.'

'No, you do such a great job.' Morwenna beamed and rushed back to the bike, hopping onto the saddle, feeling really pleased with herself. She was late for her shift but she'd work extra hard when she arrived at the tearoom. The truth was, she was bursting with energy – she knew exactly who Daniel had sent flowers to now and whose birthday it was on Wednesday. The missing link was why Daniel sent flowers at all. But she had the means to find out now. She was nearly there.

* * *

The afternoon at the tearoom rushed by. Customers came in dribs and drabs, leaving tables to be cleared and cleaned. Several of the actors came in mid-afternoon, Ben, Rupert and Jesse calling for cups of coffee to be refilled, Rupert flirting with a reluctant Tamsin, who paid him as little attention as possible. Then, at four o'clock, Lamorna brought Elowen in from school and Becca Hawkins, all torn jeans and white-blonde hair, arrived from The Celtic Knot gift shop next door. She hugged Tamsin and shrieked with laughter. The two young women sat together, their heads close, talking. Elowen sipped sparkling water and said, 'Mummy and Becca always talk about the same things. Drinking gin and dancing with boys. It's boring.'

Lamorna ruffled Elowen's hair, then she patted Oggy Two's knitted head. 'What do you think they should talk about?'

'That's easy. They should talk about me having a dog. I wouldn't mind Mummy going out if I had a dog, but I don't want her to get another boyfriend. I don't like it when Mummy has a boyfriend.' She pulled a face.

Lamorna squeezed her eyes shut – she'd opened a floodgate. She gave Morwenna a 'help me' look. Morwenna put an arm around her grandchild.

'Do you like being the mermaid on the stage, Elowen? Is it good fun?'

'Oh yes, and I have another week to go. Miss Parker says that Maya and I can have a gold star for each week we were the mermaids – that's two gold stars. Billy Crocker only gets one star for being the backup mermaid, so he said mermaids are silly and I said mermaids are very strong. He said yes but they have no legs to kick with so I told him they can punch and bite and if he didn't want to find out, he should shut up.'

'That's not nice.' Morwenna stroked Elowen's dark hair. 'Remember what I said about the way of peace and harmony being better than the way of violence?'

'I remember, Grandma.' Elowen stuck a casual finger up her nose. 'But Great-Grandma says that it's not the size of the dog in the fight, it's the size of the fight in the dog, and I asked her what it meant and she said you have to bash someone before they bash you. And I like dogs.'

Lamorna covered her face, peeping guiltily between her fingers. She mouthed, Sorry. There was another peal of laughter from Becca and Tamsin, and Lamorna muttered, 'Do you want me to help you with your homework, Elowen?'

'We have got to do a boring worksheet about safety in the home,' Elowen grumbled.

'Do you need me to help?' Lamorna coaxed. 'I'm good at safety.' She winked at Morwenna. 'Since that chip pan fire.'

'You gave us a shock, Mum.' Morwenna remembered it – it was ten years ago. She'd still been living with Ruan. And Ruan had bought Lamorna a fire banket and an extinguisher after she'd neglected a chip pan and caused a small blaze. She'd never used them, but it put Morwenna's mind at rest. Ruan had always been practical.

Lamorna turned to Morwenna. 'I'll let Tam help with the homework, actually. I don't understand half the big words they use nowadays. We never learned about safety when we were at school.'

'Go and grab an apple,' Morwenna said as Elowen rushed to the counter.

Lamorna was anxious. 'Is Tam going out tonight? She won't start neglecting the little one?'

'Not at all.' Morwenna took her mother's hand. 'She's twenty-eight, Mum. It's natural that she wants a life. Especially after, you know, all that business of thinking about getting married last Christmas and...' Her voice trailed off.

Lamorna shook her head. 'I still can't get over everything that happened back then. Alex Truscott being murdered and the rest of it...'

'Nor can I,' Morwenna said. 'And, you know, Elowen is Tam's first priority. But if I can help her to have some fun, then I will.'

Elowen was back, munching on a green apple. Morwenna noticed she had lost another tooth at the bottom. Tamsin called across, 'It's almost time to pack up now. Mum, do you want to get off home?'

'I don't mind helping.'

'I've promised to help Elowen finish her homework upstairs,' Tamsin said. 'Then Becca and I are going to make pizza. We're going to have a girls' night tonight, me, Elowen and Becca. Why don't you two finish now?'

Lamorna stood up. 'I'll get the bus up to Tregenna Gardens. I'm going to have a night in with the soaps.' She glanced hopefully at Morwenna. 'Can you come round for your tea one night this week?'

'Any night but Wednesday.' Morwenna smiled. 'Text me.'

'Right, that'll be Friday, then.' Lamorna stood at the door. 'Oh, and I've had no texts today from... you-know-who.' She whispered the last bit. 'Are you still looking for the – you-know-what?' Lamorna mouthed the word 'killer'.

'We'll catch up over tea on Friday.' Morwenna winked. She collected her cycle helmet, jacket and bag, calling over her shoulder, 'Right, I'll get my bike and be on my way. I'll see you tomorrow.'

'See you, Mum,' Tamsin called.

'Bye, Grandma,' from Elowen.

As Morwenna left the tearoom, she heard Becca say, 'She's very good for her age, your mum – it must be all that cycling that keeps her fit.'

Morwenna smiled to herself as she rode along the seafront. Being older didn't bother her, nor was she worried about what people said about her long silver hair, her bright clothing, her being single again. Being alive was what counted, and enjoying every moment. She'd go home, feed Brenda, then she'd have a look at Daniel's diary and the photo again. She had some hunches; she'd spend the evening researching.

She whizzed past The Spriggan marquee; it was quiet, although there were a few figures on the beach; none were recognisable. She turned the corner and started to climb. Pedalling hard, she was grateful for the bike's assist motor – it made life so much easier and the gruelling hill-climb home so much more pleasant. Her mind was filled with a jumble of thoughts: her visit to Autumn Wind earlier that afternoon, her date with Barnaby on Wednesday.

It occurred to her that she'd ask Tamsin if she'd like to make a regular thing of Elowen staying over at Harbour Cottages once a week, to enable her to go out with Becca – her daughter needed a social life. Fleetingly, she wondered if Ruan might like to help out.

She was aware of a vehicle pulling up alongside her, an aggressive rumbling motor. In the corner of her eye, she saw a familiar yellow sports car, a driver with a black beanie, and then it swerved deliberately into her, hitting her hard before roaring away. Morwenna was falling sideways, straight down, still attached to the bike. The ground was beneath her, the hard grit of gravel. She felt the vicious bump of the kerb as the helmet crashed against the ground and there was a sharp pain in her elbow.

Her back ached with the impact. She groaned once and closed her eyes as the world around her spun.

The dizziness overcame her and took her away.

15

Moments passed – Morwenna felt dazed. She wasn't sure how long she had been on the ground, but she blinked to clear her vision before sitting up and staring around. Quietly she scanned her body; nothing appeared to be broken. Her face hurt, her chin – her left arm was heavy and the elbow stung. The material of her jacket was torn and damp with coagulating blood. The bicycle was upturned next to her. A car went past, then another.

Rummaging in her pocket, she found her phone and went through a mental list of who to ring. Tamsin was busy with Elowen; Lamorna would be at Tregenna Gardens by now and she'd panic. Louise would have closed the library; she'd be on her way home. Ruan was at sea. She'd phone Jane Choy. She pressed a button and heard an efficient voice. 'Hello?'

'Jane – it's Morwenna. I've been knocked off my bike. Can you come? No, not official – I'm just a bit bruised and wobbly. No, I don't need an ambulance, it's just cuts. Oh, thanks, that's good. Right.'

Slowly, she eased herself to stand, picking up the bike and moving onto the pavement. Another car slid past. Her elbow hurt.

Tentative fingers to her chin came away moist. Then she heard a voice behind her. 'Awright'n aree?'

She turned to see a man wearing baggy trousers, an old shirt and sagging braces, a battered trilby over his thin hair. Morwenna guessed he must have been older than Lamorna by many years. He put his hands on his hips, as if assessing her. His jaw dropped open in a loose smile.

'Yes, I had a tumble,' she said, closing her eyes briefly. 'Someone's coming to help me in a minute.'

'You fell off'n? Giss on, maid!'

Morwenna sighed. 'A car knocked me off.'

'Mygar, tizzardlee on. Driver pastee diddy? Didn't stop?'

'No, he kept going...'

'Wossmarrwiddee? Bike all right?'

'I think I'm fine – the bike seems to be in one piece.'

'T'lltellywot – there's zum bad drivers on these roads these days...'

'There are.' Morwenna's arm tingled. She was still dizzy. She took a few steps tentatively. Everything hurt.

'Nice bike – Costymuchdida?'

'It was a present.' Morwenna was relieved to see a police car approaching. 'Here's my friend.'

The man watched the car come to a halt. He waved a hand towards Jane as she climbed from the car in uniform. 'Awright'n aree, Officer? Maid fell off, outside'n my house.'

'I'll deal with it now, sir,' Jane said crisply. She crouched next to Morwenna. 'What hurts? Do you need an ambulance? Or can I get you home?'

'It's just cuts, I think. What about my bike though?'

Jane looked at the inquisitive man, who was observing her every move, a smile on his face. 'I'm going to leave this bike inside your gate, sir, and lock it up. I'll arrange for someone to collect it later. Now come on, Morwenna – let's get you into the car.'

Morwenna felt herself be guided towards the police car and helped inside. Jane was fumbling with the bike, securing it, then she was next to Morwenna, starting the engine.

'I'm all right, Jane.'

'So – if you were knocked off, I'll have to report it.'

'I'm not 100 per cent sure what happened. Can you just drive me to the Spriggan marquee?'

'No, you need to go home.'

'Jane, I think it was the yellow sports car that hit me – Daniel's. I need to check if it's there, who's missing, if the engine's warm.'

'You need first aid. And the incident will need to be investigated.'

'We ought to check his car now. It will be cool after thirty minutes – we'll know for sure it was his car if the bonnet's warm.'

'Did you recognise the driver?'

'No. They had a hat on – and they had a scarf over their face. Please – Jane, what if someone deliberately knocked me off?'

'Are you telling me that this is a hit and run?'

'No, I'm not.' Morwenna sighed.

'Are you sure it was Daniel Kitto's car?'

'Not completely.'

'Then I'll get you home first, patch you up and then I'll drive down and take a look around.'

Morwenna closed her eyes and gave up. Her head was throbbing.

* * *

Half an hour later, she was sitting on the squashy sofa at home with Brenda. Her elbow was bandaged, there was antiseptic cream on her chin and her feet were raised on a cushion. Jane handed her a mug of tea. 'We need to talk.'

'Officially?'

'I'm in uniform.'

'Then I have no comment,' Morwenna said. Her back ached. Her knee was sore too.

'Let's start from way back,' Jane said slowly. 'You suspect someone killed Daniel Kitto.'

'I do.'

'Who?'

'Someone from Spriggan.'

'How sure are you?'

'About 80 per cent.' Morwenna shrugged. 'I'll be 101 per cent in a few days. I think he was poisoned.'

'Morwenna, if this is true, then it's a police matter.'

'I'll give you all the evidence when I have it. Then you can make the arrest.'

'Why not turn it over to us now?'

'You know why.' Morwenna groaned. 'Rick Tremayne believes Daniel died of natural causes. The only evidence I have at the moment is a dodgy bottle of health tonic, a few mischievous texts from Daniel's phone and a possible but not definite hit-and-run driver in a yellow car that, given how fuzzy my head is now, might have been a Reliant Robin for all I know.'

'So you can't be sure it was Daniel's?'

'I think it was, but look at me – I'm all over the place,' Morwenna said. 'Just give me a few days, Jane. Come swimming with me on Saturday – I'll tell you everything then.'

'It's a good job I trust you,' Jane said. 'We've been through a lot. But can you absolutely promise me two things?'

'Anything.'

'You're not withholding any information that the police should know about?'

'Who knows? I'm in shock...' Morwenna said. It hurt to move her shoulders. 'No. I don't think I have much to go on yet.'

'And – secondly – you aren't at risk? I mean, if someone hit you, then I can pay them a visit – I just need to know who it was.'

'I'm not sure. You could start by going down to the seafront and having a look around the marquee. There might be a dent in the car from bumping me, or scratches...'

'So you're saying it *was* a hit and run?'

'At least I'd know.' Morwenna stretched out a grazed palm and Brenda clambered on her knee.

Jane asked, 'Who can I ring to pick your bike up and come round to sit with you?'

'I'll go on down and get it – I'll be fine.'

'Nonsense. I'll call Ruan. Will he be home yet?'

'Just about,' Morwenna said, snuggling into the comfort of cushions. 'But I'll be all right.' She didn't want to depend on Ruan.

'I'll call him,' Jane insisted. 'Then I'll pop down to the marquee and see what I can find out.'

'Thanks, Jane.'

Morwenna was grateful. Her eyes were closing and she was drowsy. She felt sleep tug at her and she heard Jane say, 'You rest. I'll let myself out. And I'll text you if I come up with anything.'

'Right,' Morwenna said, then she was breathing deeply, falling asleep.

* * *

She woke an hour or so later because someone was rapping lightly at the door. It was hard to sit up; her muscles had stiffened and her joints were sore. She eased herself through the hall, waddling slowly. Ruan was standing on the step, her spare keys in his hand, about to let himself in, his expression concerned. 'I came straight over. Jane said you had an accident.'

'I was knocked off my bike.' Morwenna opened the door and he followed her.

'Your bike's in my van. I picked up some food on the way. Chinese all right?'

'Thanks.' Morwenna glanced at the clock. It was past seven. She wasn't feeling hungry. Her elbow throbbed and her chin was tender. 'You know where everything is.'

'I'm on it,' Ruan called from the kitchen. 'Jane said she brought you back. What happened?'

'The yellow sports car ran into me and I went sprawling.'

Ruan emerged with two plates of something with noodles. 'Are you sure?'

'I think so.'

'You're feeling OK now though?' He sat next to her.

'I'll live.' She tried a mouthful of chow mein but it hurt to chew.

'I phoned Louise and she says you're not to go to the library tomorrow,' Ruan said, ever practical. 'I can take the day off and look after you.'

'Nothing's broken. I'm fine.'

'You shouldn't go to the tearoom either.'

'Who will help Tam?'

'She'll manage. It's a Tuesday, so it won't be too busy. Maybe Lamorna can pop in?'

'You haven't told her I was knocked off the bike?'

'No, I didn't want to worry her. I only phoned Louise. I wanted to check on you first.'

'Thanks,' Morwenna said again. 'I think I'll go for a bob about in the water tomorrow morning. It'll soothe my bruises.'

'Can I give you a lift down to the beach?'

'I'll ride. The bike's fine, isn't it? Just a bit of scraping on the paint?'

'It wouldn't be wise to ride so soon...' Ruan said.

Morwenna turned abruptly and a pain shot through her shoulder. 'When have I been wise?' She forced a smile. 'Ruan, I've found some interesting things out today. You know the woman in Daniel's photo?'

'Diane, 1971?'

'Yes. She died a few weeks ago. She was in Autumn Wind residential home. Daniel used to send her flowers. She was Diane Bennett, I'm sure of it.'

'Meaning?'

'Meaning – oh.' Morwenna felt her phone vibrate in her pocket. She took it out. Ruan did the same thing with his phone that had buzzed simultaneously. 'Mum's messaged on WhatsApp. There's another text from Daniel's phone. It says: "what happened to you today was just an indication of what..."'

'"...will happen if you keep snooping. Only next time will be serious."' Ruan finished the sentence. The same message was on his phone. 'We've got to pass these messages on to Jane. They're evidence.'

'I will, but give me a bit longer. I want to find out who's sending them.' Morwenna's thumb moved. 'Here's a message from Jane. "All seems normal at Spriggan. Car bonnet cool. No scratches or dents. Hope you're feeling better. Don't forget the swim at the weekend, but only if you feel up to it. I need to know everything."' She sat up determinedly. 'Right, I'm definitely paying Spriggan a visit tomorrow. And I know exactly what I want to find out.'

'Let me come with you,' Ruan asked.

'Next time, maybe. Pop round tomorrow night and I'll tell you all about it. But this visit needs just to be me. There's someone I need to talk to, one-to-one.'

* * *

The ride to the library first thing on a bright Tuesday morning was difficult, to say the least. Morwenna's muscles had stiffened and any movement was uncomfortable. Blood still leaked through the bandage from the wound on her elbow. Her chin was so badly grazed it looked like a scratchy goatee beard. She'd looked and felt better. As she locked the bicycle in the corridor outside the library, she heard light voices. Louise and Donald were talking about ghosts again. She heard Louise say, 'Pawly seems such a nice man in his emails. It will be good to meet him to discuss Lady Elizabeth. He's fascinated. He wants to come over here next Monday morning.'

'I'll pop in. I'd like to meet him too—' Donald paused abruptly. He and Louise were staring at Morwenna, who stood in the doorway.

'What are you doing here?' Louise chided. 'I told Ruan to tell you to stay at home.'

'I'm resting.' Morwenna ignored the ache in her spine. 'I'm out for a little spin to loosen up. I've come in for the copy of *Poisons and Spells in Merlin's Realm*, by T. P. Grayson. I'm going to deliver it to Spriggan.'

'Oh, but look at you.' Louise fumbled at the desk. 'Should you be out and about at all?'

'It's a beautiful day. I thought the Seal Bay air would be good for me. Besides, I'll be back tomorrow morning.'

'Here you are – it arrived yesterday.' Louise handed her the book. 'Make sure Musa knows to bring it back before they move on. The actors leave soon and Truro library will be cross with me if I lose a book.'

'Their last night's Saturday. Daniel's funeral is on Monday. They'll pack up then, I expect.'

Donald gave Morwenna a searching look. 'Well, you be careful on that bicycle, young lady. We don't want any more accidents.'

'I will.' Morwenna turned to go, the book under her arm. 'See you tomorrow.'

'I hope so,' Louise called, her voice laced with scepticism. 'Try to avoid getting into any more trouble.'

'Me?' Morwenna shouted back innocently.

Then she was on her way.

16

Morwenna locked her bicycle and helmet against the railings on the seafront and gazed across the beach. She'd have a swim later. First things first – she had a book to deliver. It was in her knitted chicken bag, slouched over her aching shoulder. She walked as normally as possible – which was difficult – towards the Spriggan marquee. Across the bay, the sea looked inviting, turquoise against an azure sky, the surf rolling in, foamy white.

The yellow sports car was parked in its usual place. Morwenna needed to get to the bottom of the mysterious driver's identity. She walked through the entrance as quickly as she could, given her bruises and the stiffness in her joints, and paused by the tiered seating. The actors were sitting in the performance area on chairs in a circle. Morwenna thought they might be performing or warming up, but they seemed to be having a meeting. She slid beneath the raked seating, crawling forwards on the sand. It hurt like mad – the skin on her shoulders and legs was tender with bruises. She closed her eyes, feeling momentarily dizzy. It was painful to move, but she edged forward to a vantage point beneath the second row. She could see the actors perfectly. Feelings seemed to be running high in the meeting; they were leaning forward, their faces serious.

Kenzie shouted, 'Please can we stop mentioning Daniel? It's our company now. We make the decisions.'

'How is it ours? We have to run everything past our new trustee,' Ben said.

'But we talk about it first, right?' Kenzie said furiously. 'And can we stop saying, "Daniel would have done this or that."? He's gone now.'

'But he'd be already deciding on our next play and the venues – it would be scheduled,' Musa said gently. 'There's a template in place for us to do the same. Daniel was a professional and he was organised. It helps to stick to what works.'

'Then, we were a company of six actors including the director. We don't even have a director now,' Rupert said. 'But I've directed before, so it makes sense for me to take it on.'

'Inga's the natural choice,' Ben argued.

'I don't mind,' Inga said quietly.

'Perhaps we can find some new material?' Musa suggested. 'I'll research a few Cornish myths, shall I?'

'Myths?' Kenzie sneered. 'Same old stuff. Can't we leave Daniel's ideas behind and move on?'

'What would you do, Kenzie?' Inga asked.

'Something innovative – a modern tale. We could work on our own Lehrstücke – educational theatre, a lively physical piece we can take into schools. They'd pay reasonably well.'

Morwenna leaned forward. Her head was throbbing now, and her brow was damp with perspiration. She could see the sneer on Rupert's face. 'You mean feminist stuff? Women's rights? Sex education?' He gave a cold laugh. 'What would it be, the story of a poor actress whose mother was jilted by an actor who drove a yellow sports car?'

'Daniel knew how I felt about the way he treated my mum.' Kenzie was furious. 'He gave me the job here because he felt bad about it, although nothing makes up for cruelty and neglect.'

'He was a flirt. He liked women,' Inga said. 'It's no surprise in this profession. Women have to use opportunities, not rail against them.'

'It was more than that,' Kenzie snapped. 'He made promises, then he broke her heart. She was never the same after he left.'

'We should talk about Spriggan,' Musa suggested.

Jesse chimed in. 'Is one technician enough? I could use a hand.'

'That's because you're not very efficient.' Rupert grunted.

'At least I'm not a gambler with a drink problem,' Jesse countered.

'I don't know so much,' Rupert replied.

'Please, everyone.' There was silence for a moment, then Inga continued, 'We don't have to run as a six. We could always put it to the vote and make our company smaller.'

'Last in, first out, Musa,' Rupert jeered. 'That's what Daniel told you, wasn't it?'

'Look,' Musa groaned. 'I'd do anything to keep this job.'

Morwenna edged forward to see a little better. Something buzzed in her bag – her phone. She reached for it quickly to silence it.

Inga said, 'I suggest we break for coffee, guys. We'll resume later. We have a lot of decisions to make.'

'I can tell you now, I'm looking at other options, professional companies, not a bunch of amateurs,' Kenzie said bluntly. 'This place was run by misogynists when Daniel was alive – now it's being run by megalomaniacs.'

'Please yourself,' Rupert said.

'You're entitled to your feelings,' Inga said, and she walked away with Ben in pursuit.

Morwenna froze. Inga and Ben were walking towards the exit, followed by Rupert, who passed them, talking furiously on his phone. Inga hesitated by the tiered seating, a few feet from where she was hiding, to look in her handbag. Morwenna held her breath, conscious of her racing pulse.

Ben placed a hand on Inga's arm. 'Can I buy you coffee at the tearoom?'

'Does it come with conditions?' Inga replied coldly, taking out a packet of cigarettes.

'You know how I feel about you,' Ben said awkwardly. 'I'll do anything...'

'I might like you more if you agreed with my suggestions in meetings,' Inga retorted and swept through the door. Ben followed her and Morwenna scrabbled painfully to the edge of the seating and dusted herself down quickly.

Plastering a smile on her face, she strode forward. The bruises on her legs felt tender and she held onto a rail for support, calling out 'Hello, Musa.'

He was sitting in the performance area, his head in his hands. Jesse was a few paces away, opening a flask of coffee and biting into a sandwich. Musa looked up. 'Hello.'

Morwenna slumped in the seat next to him, wiping her damp forehead. 'I brought your book – *Poisons and Spells in Merlin's Realm*. Louise says can she have it back before you leave, please?'

'Oh, thanks.' Musa took the book and examined Morwenna's face. 'What happened to you?'

'I fell off my bike. I was hit by a banana travelling at high speed.'

She looked for a sign of recognition in Musa's face but he stared, confused. Morwenna heard Jesse laugh, a sarcastic sound. He waved a gesture of recognition, calling, 'Dangerous in charge of a bicycle, are you, maid?'

She spoke quietly. 'Have you got a moment?'

'Of course.' Musa smiled. 'What do you need?'

'Can we go outside into the fresh air?' Morwenna led the way.

They stood in the breeze, facing the sea. She gazed around nervously, to make sure no one was listening.

Musa said, 'So – what can I do for you? Is it about your granddaughter? She's really good...'

'No, it's—' Morwenna was ready. 'I just thought – I know you've read all these books on spells and poisons and I hoped you could give me some advice. I wanted to pick your brain.'

'Oh?'

'I live by myself and I have to say – I'm a bit worried. You see, I have a big rat in my shed and I want to get rid of it. It scares me a bit – I keep thinking it might come into the kitchen. What's the safest thing to use to kill it?'

'Rat poison, I suppose,' Musa said. 'You can buy it over the counter.'

'Wouldn't that be harmful to humans – or pets?' Morwenna scrutinised his expression. 'I have a cat...'

'It would, yes. Rat poison has stuff like bromadiolone in it – then poor rats die from internal bleeding.'

'Could I use arsenic?'

'Arsenic used to be the thing to kill rats, but not now.'

'I don't suppose you can even buy it, can you?' Morwenna said.

'Oh, you can, if you know where to go.'

'And is it harmful to humans?'

'Most certainly.' Musa scratched his locks. 'In the nineteenth century women applied arsenic powder to whiten their faces, as well as to their hair and scalp. It was also used to destroy vermin. But now, it would only be used by pharmaceutical companies, or maybe as agricultural chemicals.'

'It all sounds a bit dangerous.' Morwenna pulled a face. 'Maybe I'll just set Brenda on the rat.'

'Or perhaps call in Rentokil?' Musa suggested.

'Yes, that's a good idea.'

'I'm the worst person to ask. I couldn't kill anything,' Musa said. 'But I hope that helps.'

'It does,' Morwenna said. 'Sorry to keep you from your coffee break.'

'Not at all,' Musa replied happily. 'And thanks for the book.'

'Any time.'

* * *

Morwenna's limbs still ached as she dragged herself in her wetsuit to the water's edge, but once she was lifted in the strong rolling waves, she felt the salt water begin to soothe her body. The pain numbed and, suddenly, she was free and mobile. She swam out, extending her legs, letting her muscles stretch. Not far away, a seal was basking on a rock in the sunshine. Morwenna trod water, enjoying the buoyancy. The seal met her eyes with its limpid ones. Then it slithered in the water with a dull splash. She offered it a calm smile. The round head bobbed, sleek as oil. She could see the white whiskers, the spots on its shoulders, the dark body in shadow beneath the surface. The seal's eyes remained on her for a few moments longer, curious, then it dipped beneath the surface and, flippers like paddles, it dived. Moments later, its head reappeared. It rolled over once, then propelled itself away, cutting a watery line through the sea.

Morwenna felt privileged to have spent time with the seal, but she needed some time to think. She asked herself: who killed Daniel Kitto? Who drove his car? Who would buy arsenic? Who hated him enough to want him dead? She thought about motives and opportunity. There were several candidates...

She had a plan for tomorrow. It was 1 May: Busy B's flowers

would be delivered and it was the perfect opportunity to try out her theory. Then later, she had a date with Barnaby. She'd know what was in Ben's tonic.

Then she'd tell Jane and they'd decide what to do next.

Morwenna swam back, using firm, strong strokes. She was feeling better already. She was thinking about the tearoom, having a toasted sandwich, a cup of tea and a chat with Tamsin. Perhaps she could borrow some concealer – she thought with a smile that she wouldn't look very captivating for the date, her chin grazed and indented with gravel. But it didn't matter; she'd enjoy herself. Besides, Barnaby didn't know it, but he held a vital clue – at least his biochemist client did. She hoped the test on the tonic would tell her something important…

Morwenna stood on the beach, still lost in thought, the sand between her toes. The breeze cut through her wetsuit and she trembled with cold, but it was exhilarating. Her chicken bag was tucked in just behind the sea wall; she dragged out her towel and wrapped herself in it, hauling off the swim cap, letting her hair tumble, wiping salt water from her face. She dabbed the skin around her chin tentatively – it was already beginning to scab over. She snuggled under her dry robe, peeling off layers, rubbing red skin, dragging on her clothes. Then she pulled on her shoes and was on her way.

Her first port of call was going to be The Celtic Knot gift shop, to see Becca. Morwenna wanted a small birthday present for her visit tomorrow, something tasteful but not extravagant. Maybe a scented candle or perfumed bath oil. She strode forward, her movements much easier now than they had been before her swim. Then she saw her bicycle and stopped, hardly believing her eyes. Someone had slashed the tyres. There were huge gaping holes in the rubber, like cuts in flesh. Someone had recognised her bike and left her a warning, she was sure of it.

Then her phone pinged, a forwarded text from Lamorna with a covering text that said simply:

what does this mean?

She read the message from Daniel's phone:

I hope you enjoy the walk home.

Morwenna wondered which of her suspects had deliberately damaged her tyres.

Now she'd have to push the bike to the tearoom and phone the cycle shop in town. She knew Bobby Turpin from Bob's Bikes. He helped out in the primary school sometimes, supplying bicycles for the children to learn on. His dad was a friend of Ruan's too – it was useful living in a small town like Seal Bay. Bobby was kind – he'd pop over and help her out.

That was the whole point, Morwenna decided. She lived in a tight-knit community. Cornish people looked after each other, mostly. And she could rely on friends and neighbours. But someone somewhere was threatening her. They knew that she was onto them. They wanted to frighten her off.

But Morwenna wasn't going to allow them to do that. She was made of tougher stuff. She pushed her bike towards the tearoom, more determined than ever.

17

Louise and Morwenna stopped for elevenses at quarter to twelve. It had been so busy, it had taken until now for Morwenna to ask the question that had been on her mind all morning. 'Do you know anything about William Carlyon?'

'The clay man up at Korrik? Didn't he die last year?'

'Maybe two years ago?' Morwenna remembered. 'What was he like? I don't know much about him.'

'Nor do I. He must have been rich. I expect there was a big wedding – didn't he marry for the second time?'

'I don't know.' Morwenna shook her head. 'Where did he live?'

'No idea.'

'Let's look him up, shall we?' Morwenna moved to the laptop.

'Why the interest?' Louise asked as Morwenna's fingers moved across the keyboard; her left arm was heavy, the elbow still sore inside the bandage.

'Korrik is a sponsor of The Spriggan Travelling Theatre Company. I wonder how much the clay company is involved.'

'What are you doing?'

'Trying to find his address through Companies House – ah,

here. William and Anna Carlyon, Company Directors. He's listed as a former director. Look. She lives in Knave-Go-By. It's a big house just outside Seal Bay, with its own headland.' Morwenna rolled her eyes dreamily as she typed Knave-Go-By and watched a picture flash onto the screen. 'That place is certainly worth a visit.'

'Why would you go there?'

Morwenna put on her innocent face. 'It looks nice – beautiful views – and I expect Ms Carlyon gets very lonely rattling round in such a grand mansion.'

'Let me see...' Louise gazed over her shoulder at the picture of a modern house, panoramic windows set on the headland. 'Oh, that's stunning.'

'Anna and William had a big wedding, you say?' Morwenna tapped the keyboard. 'I wonder if I can find out about it.' She touched a few buttons. 'Perhaps they got married locally – it'd make sense.' She tried again. 'There would be something in the papers.'

There was a noise in the corridor – stamping feet as Susan and Barb Grundy came in. They were holding a large supermarket carrier bag.

'Morwenna – I've been desperate to ask you how things were going with – you know – your investigations about the murdered actor. Then we heard you'd been injured,' Susan said.

'Motor accident,' Barb added. 'Apparently the police were at the scene.'

'Was it deliberate? Are you all right? Didn't you break an arm... or a leg?'

'We heard you'd been knocked down by a hit and run... nearly killed.'

'So we brought you this – it's the first one we've made, but we think they'll sell like hot cakes.' Susan handed over the bag. 'What do you think?'

The sisters both leaned forward, eyes wide, breath held, as

Morwenna opened the bag. They smiled at the same time as she pulled out a black cardigan, knitted in chunky wool, with a large Cornwall white flag on the back.

'Kernow bys Vyken!' they shouted together, each waving a fist in the air.

Morwenna's eyes filled with tears. She murmured, 'Thank you – I love it.'

'We hoped it would keep you warm while you recovered,' Susan said. 'I was up all night working on it. I'm knitting pockets in my cardies now for keys and a phone.'

'And it'll be good on the beach after a swim,' Barb added.

'We'll be there on Sunday.' Susan folded her arms.

'It's our new line in Cornish knits,' Barb decided. 'For the Lifeboats, of course.'

'I'll have one,' Louise said.

'Fifty pounds,' the sisters said together.

'Done.' Louise smiled.

Morwenna tugged the cardigan on. It was large, the sleeves too long and it hung off her shoulders. 'How do I look?'

'Like a proper Cornish maid.' Barb rubbed her hands together.

'Then I'll wear it tonight,' Morwenna said. 'I have a dinner date. It'll look great with some hooped leggings and boots.' A thought came to her. 'By the way – do you know where William Carlyon got married?'

'The clay man who died backalong?' Barb pressed her lips together.

'He married that woman from up north – London, wasn't it?' Susan remembered. 'She was a widow six months later, I reckon. He drank plenty, mind, Will Carlyon. Or so I heard.'

'I expect they got married in London,' Susan said. 'That's definitely where she was from.'

'She's a proper merry widow, Anna Carlyon.'

'Why's that?' Morwenna was interested.

'She drives everywhere in that white BMW looking like butter wouldn't melt – and I expect the money rolls in from the Korrik Clay works and she does just as she likes.'

'In her fancy clothes.'

'The husband she had before Will was a businessman too. I heard he invested in the theatre.'

'Ah.' Morwenna made a mental note. 'So why did she leave him?'

'I don't know,' Susan said.

'I heard he lost a lot of money,' Barb folded her arms. 'Or perhaps he died, I can't remember.'

'I'm sure there will be a way of finding out.' Morwenna smiled. She lifted the sides of the cardigan and did a little twirl. 'I love this. Thanks, Susan, Barb. How much do I owe you?'

'It was meant to be a gift...' Susan's hand was already stretched out.

'For the Lifeboats,' Morwenna suggested.

'Fifty quid all right?' the sisters chorused, their faces shining.

* * *

After her shift at the library, Morwenna rode her bicycle past the tearoom and the marquee, past The Blue Dolphin Guest House towards Taylor Made Motors. It still hurt to pedal the bike: even sitting on the saddle made her bones ache. Her elbow was painful, a ripe shade of plum around the deep cut. But she kept going, turning into the garage past rows of shiny new cars, stopping outside reception. Hurriedly, she padlocked her bike with its new tyres against a set of railings, grabbed her chicken bag and rushed inside. Gill Bennett was nowhere to be seen, but a large bouquet of flowers sat on the reception desk. Next to it was a birthday card with balloons on the front and the words 'Happy Birthday'. Morwenna peeked inside:

To Gill, our Girl Friday, from Vic and family.

Morwenna called, 'Anyone here?'

She waited for a while, gazing around reception. There was a laptop, a large screen, files. No more cards. Then she rang the little bell on the desk, which gave a light ting. Moments later, Gill rushed in, looking flustered. Her fair hair had been neatly cut and she was wearing a smart suit in daffodil yellow. 'Sorry I'm late – Morwenna, isn't it? Hello again. I just took a customer to the showroom to meet Vic.'

'Oh?' Morwenna was making conversation. 'Is someone buying a nice car?'

'It's an Audi A4 estate.' Gill looked puzzled. 'How can I help you?'

Morwenna glanced at the flowers. 'I just wanted to say...' She produced a card and a small tube wrapped in tissue paper. 'Ta-da. Happy birthday.'

'Oh?' The indentation between Gill's brows deepened. 'How did you know?'

'A little birdie told me.' Morwenna indicated the bouquet. 'These are gorgeous flowers. They smell heavenly.'

'Mmm.' Gill's face seemed to close down. She had no intention of saying who they were from. Morwenna waited, and Gill added, 'I'm not used to getting flowers.'

Morwenna leaned forward with a smile and indicated the gift – she had to get Gill on side. 'Do you want to open it?'

Gill fumbled with the card and gazed at the front, which had a colourful line drawing of a theatre with flamboyant red curtains and fireworks, with the words on the front, 'Let's Celebrate – it's your birthday'. Still confused, Gill opened the tissue paper and tugged out a scented candle.

'Thank you.' Gill sniffed the wax.

'It's rosemary and lemon. Rosemary's for remembrance, apparently.' Morwenna glanced at the bouquet.

'Is it?' Gill was suddenly suspicious. She certainly wasn't comfortable with the gesture. 'Thanks, Morwenna – look, this is very kind of you but – what's going on?'

Morwenna breathed in. 'Well, I brought you something else.' She dug deep into her bag, hoping her hunch would pay off.

'Why would you do that? We hardly know each other.' Gill stiffened. She was clearly not used to trusting people. Morwenna handed her a brown paper bag with something flat inside. Gill lifted out the small silver-framed photograph, a woman with light curly hair, a tentative smile, and stared. Her eyes widened with alarm. 'Where did you get this?'

Morwenna avoided giving an honest answer. 'I thought you should have it. It's yours, isn't it?'

Gill nodded. Her face started to crumple. 'It's Mum.'

'Diane, 1971.'

'The year I was born.' Gill's voice was a whisper.

'Daniel was your father?' Morwenna asked gently.

Gill looked shocked. Her eyes shone with tears. Then she said, 'He was.'

'How long have you known?' Morwenna lowered her voice. 'Daniel left it at my mother's by mistake, just before he passed on. He was a great – friend – of my mum's. They talked about the past a lot. The photo was marked for you.' She winced at the implausibility of her fib. It would have to do.

'I only found out about him a few months ago. Mum was very ill – we lived together, and she knew she wasn't going to get better. She'd always told me my father was a great actor. I believed he was someone famous who loved my mother but moved away for his career. He didn't know about me – Mum didn't ever tell him. He left her pregnant here while he went off to act in his plays and meet other women. He was a bit of a ladies' man.'

'He was,' Morwenna agreed, encouraging her to go on.

'When she got very ill, she told me his name – she thought I ought to know before she passed on. So I researched him, found out he was the director of a local company and I emailed him. He was very good – he arranged for Mum to go into Autumn Wind and paid for her care until she died. Then at her funeral, we met for the first time. He took me out to dinner.' The words tumbled from Gill's mouth. 'He was a nice man. I liked him. And he said he wanted to move to Seal Bay, to retire here. He said that now he had a child, it meant the world. He was sorry for all the years he'd wasted. He wanted to come home.'

'He did,' Morwenna said gently.

'And he wanted to get to know me better. On the day before he died, he told me he'd made an appointment with the solicitor to change his will. I was to be his only beneficiary.'

Tears glistened on Gill's face and Morwenna patted her hand. 'I'm sorry.'

'Then he died and that was it. How unlucky am I? I'd been thinking that he and I could have spent time, got to know each other.' She stifled a sob. 'I never had a dad. And I liked him, I truly did.'

Morwenna decided it was better to keep quiet about Daniel's death not being due to natural causes. But now she was even more determined to find out who was behind his murder.

'He sent me these flowers.' Gill lifted the bouquet.

Morwenna pretended she didn't know. 'He clearly thought the world of you.'

'He ordered them the day before he died. The woman at the

florist said when I rang her to ask. It was odd getting flowers from someone who...' Gill touched the cellophane wrapping with light fingers. 'Someone who's gone.'

'It must have been a shock,' Morwenna admitted. 'The photo of your mother is lovely.'

'I'll treasure it.' Gill's face was sad. 'You say Daniel wanted me to have it?'

'He'd kept it with him all these years.' Morwenna said by way of answer. 'He clearly loved your mum.'

'His first love was the theatre though.'

'We can't help who or what we love,' Morwenna said philosophically.

'Mum always said he changed her life. He made her happy for a while and he gave her a child. She was never bitter.'

'She sounds a lovely person.'

'She was,' Gill said. 'Life can be cruel. I lost my mum and now I've lost my dad. The theatre company gets his money and I get nothing. I even phoned the solicitors and asked Walters and Moffatt if I could contest the will. Andrew Walters said it was unlikely I'd get anything.'

'It's not fair,' Morwenna agreed.

Gill's expression had become softer. Her voice was trusting now. 'I saw the play the night he died. I was in the front row.'

Morwenna knew. 'That must have been so awful.'

'It was. People say he died the way he'd have wanted, but that's not true. He wanted to come home and live the rest of his life with me.'

Morwenna had an idea. 'My granddaughter's the mermaid in the play. Why don't you come to the last night's performance? My mum will be there – she was a great friend of Daniel's. She'd love to talk to you about him and the old times.'

'That would be a comfort,' Gill said. She picked up the bouquet and held the flowers next to her cheek. 'Yes, I will.'

'And it would help my mum too,' Morwenna said. She noticed the clock on the wall – it was twenty to two. 'I must dash, Gill. But it will be lovely to see you on Saturday at the play.' She hurried towards the door. 'Happy birthday.'

There was a weak murmur of thanks behind her, a rustle of cellophane. Gill was putting the flowers into water.

Morwenna lifted a leg precariously over her bike, strapping on her helmet, conscious of the ache in her arm and the twinge in her leg muscles, and set off. She passed the showroom with its huge glass windows. Vic was inside in his grey suit, shaking hands with a customer, looking pleased with himself.

Morwenna turned the corner towards the tearoom. She was feeling pleased with herself too.

18

It was almost five o'clock, time to go home. Morwenna had cleared cluttered tables, loaded dirty plates into the dishwasher and swept the floor. Tamsin was checking the day's takings. Lamorna and Elowen were seated by the window reading *There's a Snake in My School!* Morwenna smiled at Lamorna's patience as she helped Elowen with the phonics, encouraging her to read another page. Elowen was staring through the window at the beach, wriggling, bored, asking to go upstairs and play with Oggy Two. Tamsin brought three mugs of tea and a glass of sparkling water to the table and Morwenna plonked herself down with a groan. Tamsin glanced at her mother anxiously. 'Should you be brushing floors two days after you fell off your bicycle?'

'She was knocked off,' Lamorna grunted and Tamsin's eyes moved to Elowen. The six-year-old didn't miss a trick.

'Who knocked you off your bike, Grandma?'

'I fell off because someone came a bit too close. It was my fault. I wasn't concentrating,' Morwenna explained gently.

'In a pig's eye,' Lamorna said beneath her breath.

'What's a pig's eye got to do with falling off a bike, Mummy?' Elowen asked.

'Nothing at all.' Tamsin smiled. 'It's time to go upstairs now. Grandma and Great-Grandma are going home soon.'

Lamorna glanced towards Morwenna. 'You're still coming up for your tea on Friday night, maid?'

'I am.'

'Why not tonight?' Lamorna's face was mischievous. She knew perfectly well why.

'I have a date,' Morwenna said simply.

'With the same man who took you out on the boat?' Lamorna's lip curled. 'The plastic surgeon.'

'Why is he plastic, Mummy?' Elowen asked.

'He's not. He just fixes people's noses,' Tamsin said.

'But noses aren't plastic, they are made of skin.' Elowen's face crumpled in disgust.

'It's from the Greek word *plastikos*, which means "fit for moulding a shape". He changes the shape of people's noses when they don't like what they've got,' Morwenna explained. 'Libraries are brilliant places for finding out information.'

'But can you explain to me why you want to go out with Barnaby Stone?' Lamorna complained.

'He's attractive, good company, rich.' Morwenna was playing the game. 'You went out with Daniel. He was a nice man too.'

'But I didn't have a perfectly good man living across the street,' Lamorna argued.

'She means Dad.' Tamsin glanced at her mother, as if she needed the explanation.

'Grandma, don't you love Grandad any more?' Elowen asked, her brow furrowed.

'Of course I love him,' Morwenna soothed.

'Then why are you going out with a plastic man?' Elowen asked smugly.

'Grandma and Grandad are still friends,' Tamsin explained. 'They just don't live in the same house.'

'Why? That's silly. I live in the same house as you, Mummy, and you love me.'

'It *is* silly,' Lamorna agreed.

Morwenna wasn't sure how to disagree with either of them. 'Well, I'm going to look a right sight on this date with my chin grazed and my arm bandaged.'

'Then don't go.' Lamorna thought she had the perfect solution.

'Or I could lend you some concealer,' Tamsin offered.

'I'll just go as I am,' Morwenna decided. 'He'll have to settle for the real me...'

Lamorna decided to be blunt. She'd always believed in saying things as she saw them. 'I wouldn't have thought you were his type. He's a London surgeon with lots of friends and a posh car and you're just an ordinary Cornish maid who lives in Seal Bay.'

Morwenna had thought the same thing. But it didn't matter – she wasn't investing in a big relationship. She wondered if she ever would. And if she did, would it be someone like Barnaby? It would have to be a special man...

'Mum can date whoever she likes.' Tamsin interrupted her thoughts. 'Anyway, Dad has a girlfriend now—'

'He doesn't!' Lamorna was horrified. 'How come I don't know? What girlfriend?'

'Does Grandad have a girlfriend? Do they kiss and cuddle and all that silly stuff?' Elowen wanted to know. She giggled as if adult relationships were ridiculous. Morwenna examined her hands. Her thumb was grazed; there were still cuts on her palm.

'I think he's going out with Kenzie Fuller,' Tamsin explained. 'She implied as much one night when Elowen was backstage.'

'He's going out with the witch,' Lamorna said meaningfully.

'She's nice,' Elowen piped up. 'She gives me sweeties.'

'Elowen?' Morwenna grabbed her granddaughter's hand urgently. 'Promise me – you mustn't take sweets from anyone in the play. Nor chocolates. Nor drinks. Don't take anything from them.'

'Why not? They aren't strangers. Mummy said don't take anything from strangers. But they are my friends.'

'Why can't...?' Tamsin began, then she noticed the look on Morwenna's face. 'I tell you what, Elowen – if you promise me not to take any food or drink from anyone at the play, I'll buy you a big bar of chocolate at the weekend.'

'And can I have a dog?' Elowen was nobody's fool.

'Let's start with the chocolate.' Tamsin kissed her daughter's forehead. 'Now up you go to the flat and wash your hands and face.'

'But—'

'Go on, there's a good girl.' Tamsin watched her daughter rush towards the door marked 'Private', listening as her feet pounded upstairs. 'What's going on, Mum?'

'It's always best to be safe, not sorry,' Lamorna said. 'Morwenna thinks there might have been some foul play with Daniel. It could be one of the actors. Morwenna reckons he was poisoned.'

'Poisoned?' Tamsin gasped. 'By one of the cast? When were you going to tell me?'

'I didn't want to worry you – but it's better to take no chances,' Morwenna reassured her daughter. 'Just until we're sure.'

'Is she safe at Spriggan?'

'We'll keep an eye on her, Tam. One of us is always backstage.'

Tamsin's eyes flashed. 'I'll watch her every minute.'

'We both will. And—' Morwenna took a breath, 'I ought to tell you, I think Daniel's tonic had arsenic in it. Don't accept anything from anyone at Spriggan that might have been, you know...'

'Contaminated. Spiked.' Lamorna folded her arms. 'If you ask me, Ruan shouldn't go out with the witch actress. She'll poison his beer.'

Tamsin was concerned. 'Will you talk to him, Mum? Tell him to be careful.'

'Ruan can take care of himself,' Morwenna said, but she made a mental note to speak to him, just in case. She turned to Lamorna. 'We'd better go, Mum. I'm running late.'

'Right. For the date. Well, I hope you'll have a lovely time and don't regret going.' Lamorna huffed as she stood up. 'Another night by the TV for me.'

'I'll see you on Friday, Mum. We'll put the world to rights.'

'And you can tell me about the dinner with this Barnaby.'

'I will, every detail.' Morwenna linked arms with her mother, hugging her close. 'I'll walk you to the bus stop and push my bike. I have some news you'll want to hear. Do you remember Daniel's old photo of Diane, 1971, the one I found amongst his things? Well, you'll never guess what I found out about her. Or who her daughter is.'

* * *

Morwenna stood in front of the bedroom mirror. The graze on her chin was garish beneath the too-pale concealer. Her bandaged arm looked wrong poking from the sleeve of the floral dress. She felt awkward. She could hear her mother joking: *Mutton dressed as lamb.* If she wore her hair up, the cuts on her chin seemed to stand out. Her hair down didn't disguise them either. Morwenna's confidence was low when it came to dating. She'd revert to plan A: she'd wear something simple and comfortable.

Ten minutes later, she'd settled for a long black skirt, a glittery top and the Cornish cardigan: it was a talking point. She went back to the mirror and asked herself despondently how she looked. Ruan would have said a million dollars. In truth, she looked all right. She'd compensate for her battle-scarred face with scintillating conversation. She found some perfume that Tamsin had bought her one Christmas and sprayed it everywhere. She checked her chicken bag again. Ben D'Arcy's health tonic was safely stowed with the other things she kept there, her phone, her keys, Daniel's diary. She wasn't feeling remotely hungry. For a moment she wondered why she was going.

The doorbell pinged and Morwenna jumped in surprise: Barnaby was early. She hurried downstairs and opened the front door to see Ruan smiling, his arms folded. He said, 'You look a million dollars…'

'Thanks.' Morwenna wasn't sure what to say next.

'I just popped round to see if you're all right. After the accident.'

'I'm fine thanks, Ruan.' They stood in the doorway staring at each other. He had a dark jacket on with jeans. He smelled of something nice, a warm musky smell.

He said, 'I wondered how you were getting on with the sleuthing.'

'Really well.' Morwenna's face lit up. 'I made some progress today. Did you know Daniel Kitto has a d—' She paused. 'We ought to do this some other time.'

'I'm on my way down to The Smugglers for a quick one.'

'Oh?'

'But I have time.'

'I'm going out, Ruan.'

'Oh?' They stared at each other for a while then Ruan added, 'Anywhere special?'

'The Marine Room in St Mengleth.'

'Ah, that's good. You'll have to let me know if it's a nice place.' He smiled. 'I enjoyed The Cornish Arms last week and helping you with all the sleuthing.'

'Well, the thing is—' Morwenna leaned forward 'I'm working on a couple of leads at the moment. I'd love to tell you about it.'

'I'd like that.'

'Can we catch up tomorrow?'

Morwenna heard the throaty rumble of the E-Type Jaguar before it rounded the corner, the silver metal gleaming beneath the street lights. Barnaby brought the car to a halt outside number four and the window slid down.

'Good evening,' he called, his voice as sexy as the car's growling engine.

'I'll text you tomorrow, then,' Ruan said. He was still standing at the door, watching her. 'Enjoy your meal.'

'We will,' Barnaby replied before Morwenna had a chance to say anything. She rushed back into the house to grab her bag and lock the door. When she returned, Ruan had gone. She slid into the car and Barnaby said, 'Lovely to see you. You smell wonderful.'

She was surprised he could smell her perfume beneath the haze of his spicy cologne. She glanced at him. He was wearing a dark blazer and flannels, a cream shirt. He noticed her face and his jaw dropped.

'My goodness, what happened to you?'

'Oh, my chin's just the tip of the iceberg.' Morwenna indicated the bandaged arm. 'I had a cycling accident.' She saw his face change. 'Don't worry – the bike you and Pam gave me is just fine.'

'And you?' He sounded concerned. 'Were you hurt?'

'I'll get over it.' Morwenna kept her voice light. 'A car drove too close to me, knocked me off.'

'Really? Did you tell the police?'

'Jane knows – that's PC Choy, my friend.' Morwenna said. 'I think I did well to escape with a few bruises and aches. The elbow's the worst thing, but the chin looks pretty horrific.'

'You don't look horrific at all,' Barnaby said smoothly. 'Well, I'm so glad you're all right. Let's have dinner and you can tell me all about it.' He offered her a warm smile.

'Great. I'm looking forward to it,' Morwenna said.

The engine revved loudly and pulled away. Morwenna glanced over her shoulder, across the road. Ruan was watching her from his open doorway, then he disappeared from sight.

19

The Marine Room at St Mengleth was a spectacular place that looked out to the sea, accessed by a spiral staircase, the restaurant light and spacious. It was housed in a high building with three vast panoramic windows, polished oak floors and a glass roof. Guests were already seated at tables, which were fashioned to look like a boat's cabin. The waiters wore jaunty blue and white uniforms and little sailors' hats. They rushed around with trays of porcelain plates and bowls filled with what Morwenna could only describe as nouvelle cuisine. The helpings didn't look very big.

The waiter ushered her and Barnaby to a table for two beside a window. Outside, the sky was tinged pink and grey. Barnaby politely helped her sit, then he took his place. 'I asked for the table with the best view – I thought the sunset might be stunning tonight.'

'It's lovely.' Morwenna meant it. The view over the bay was to die for, an expanse of ocean and sky, waves splashing against rocks below, the broad sweep of sand. She took off her Cornish-flag cardie and Barnaby pointed to the bandage on her elbow.

'Are you sure you're all right?'

'Thanks, I'm on the mend now.'

'I think you're very brave,' Barnaby said. 'Most women I know don't ride bikes up hills and then bounce back after road accidents.' He picked up the menu and lowered his voice. 'I wanted to ask you about the health tonic you asked me to check. I was surprised that there was arsenic in it. I believe you owe me some kind of explanation.'

'I do. I'm sorry I told you a little fib – it wasn't mine at all. Can I tell you all about it later?' Morwenna leaned forward conspiratorially. 'I'd like your opinion, as a matter of fact.'

'Certainly.' Barnaby seemed pleased.

'But first I'd like a glass of wine.' Morwenna gazed up at the tall waiter who was looming at Barnaby's shoulder.

'A soda water please,' Barnaby told the waiter. 'I'm driving.'

'I'll have a large Malbec,' Morwenna said expansively – she had no idea where that came from. She scrutinised the menu. 'And the smoked cod tartlet au gratin to start with, please.'

'I'll have the gravadlax.' Barnaby met her eyes. 'Your French accent is very good.'

Merci, monsieur – j'aime beaucoup parler Français,' Morwenna replied. She didn't mention that she hadn't been to France for several years. Of course, the last time had been with Ruan. They both spoke French reasonably well, but she was rusty nowadays – she needed practice. She added, 'Cornish is descended from the Common Brittonic language, but you know that...'

The tall waiter coughed lightly. Morwenna indicated the menu with an air of sophistication, as if she were used to fine dining. In one breath she said, 'For my main, I'll have herb-crusted salmon.'

Barnaby looked pleased with her choice. 'I'll have the saddle of Welsh lamb.' The waiter moved away discreetly and Barnaby asked, 'What do you think of this place?'

'It's lovely.' Morwenna gazed through the window, where the sun was sinking like a blood orange behind the sea.

'Indeed – we were talking about France. Did you know I have a place there?' Barnaby said. 'A lovely *maison de maître* in the Dordogne. Pam often uses it, Simon too.'

'Is it empty now?'

Barnaby shook his head. 'My ex is there for the next week or so with her husband. It's good for the house to be lived in. We view it as a family property.'

The starter arrived with the drinks. Morwenna glanced at her plate: in the centre was a small delicate pastry filled beautifully with something creamy and pale, leeks, cheese, topped with a few green and burgundy leaves, a smear of balsamic vinegar. It looked too perfect to eat. 'Does your ex live in London?'

'In Sussex. She's a writer. Historical romances.'

'Oh?' Morwenna was interested. 'Would I know of her?'

'She writes under a pen name. But she's Mickie. Michaela,' Barnaby said. 'We get on well nowadays. Our son Dominic and his family use the Dordogne place a lot too. But perhaps...' He studied her reaction. 'I might be able to persuade you to come out at some point?'

Morwenna took a gulp of wine. 'That sounds good.' She'd deal with trips to France with Barnaby later – a long time in the future, if at all. It was too confusing. For now, the wine was making her feel more relaxed than she had been in ages.

She looked towards the window. 'Fabulous,' Morwenna said a little more loudly than she'd intended. 'The sunset is beautiful.'

The sky was melting orange, the sun sinking low into a crinkled sea spattered with crimson and gold.

'That's why I wanted to bring you here.' Barnaby pushed his plate away, half eaten. Morwenna had eaten the whole tart and the vinegar smear. 'You're an interesting woman – there's so much more to you than I first thought.'

'You're absolutely right,' Morwenna agreed. 'I must take you out some time too – they do a great pint and a pasty down The Smugglers.'

'A pint and a pie with the fishermen.' Barnaby chuckled, amused. 'That sounds great fun.'

Morwenna wished she hadn't said it. The waiter was there again, taking plates away, then he was back with more food. She prodded her salmon on the porcelain dish with a fork. The morsel of pink fish was balanced on top of something round and crusty that was made of potatoes. Two asparagus spears perched precariously on top next to the tiniest jug of sauce she'd ever seen. The portions were probably normal sized but, Morwenna thought, they weren't hearty Cornish portions. Lamorna would have asked the waiter to shut the window before it blew away. Barnaby's saddle of lamb lay in a pool of shiny gravy, surrounded by diced vegetables. She thought it looked small, like a mouse's saddle. He was tucking in – it wouldn't take him long.

Morwenna took a mouthful of wine and glanced around. Guests were talking, layers of different voices, seated in twos, in groups, all immaculately dressed. On a table nearby, a man with a grey ponytail was talking to a woman, gesturing earnestly. 'You must see that Pythagoras' political and religious teachings influenced the philosophies of Plato, Aristotle and the west in general?'

The woman frowned, ignoring her plate of food, deep in discussion. 'Yes, but Pythagoras' early life coincided with the flowering of Ionian natural philosophy. He was a contemporary of the historian Hecataeus, who was an incredible influence on him.'

Morwenna thought it must be fascinating to have conversations like that. She and Ruan would have been talking about Tamsin and Elowen, fishing, or the latest news in Seal Bay. She wished she could talk to him about her investigations now, about everything she'd found out from Gill at Taylor Made Motors. Words from Daniel's diary came back to her. *Taylor Maid.* Of course – he'd meant Gill. And *I have D in SB!!!!* A daughter. Poor Daniel.

Barnaby was tucking into the morsel of lamb. Morwenna looked around again and her eyes settled on an elegant woman with a blonde bob. Morwenna stared more than she should have – the woman looked familiar. She wore a fitted cream and navy suit; the previous blue glasses were now black designer frames. She was sitting in front of one of the adjacent windows, talking animatedly to a young man in a dark crumpled jacket. He had a thick thatch of hair folding over his collar, and broad shoulders. Morwenna wondered how he was connected to her.

Anna Carlyon and her friend's heads were close – they were whispering quietly, as if sharing a secret. They seemed well acquainted. Morwenna wondered how she could find out what they were talking about. Then an idea came to her and she was on her feet. She swallowed more wine and grabbed Barnaby's cuff. 'I need a selfie.'

He held up a forkful of meat, chewing. 'Pardon?'

'A selfie.' Morwenna waved her phone to emphasise her point. 'With you. To mark this wonderful evening.'

Barnaby smiled indulgently. 'OK. Let's just finish our food.'

'No – it has to be now. The – the sunset's perfect.' She hauled him to his feet and dragged him to where Anna Carlyon and her guest were seated. She manoeuvred Barnaby so that his back was to the window, raised the phone and they both smiled as she clicked away. 'Nothing so romantic as a sunset. Gorgeous. Lovely…'

Barnaby smiled again for another photo. Morwenna took a third, a fourth. Then she pressed the screen. The selfie became a framed photo of Anna and her guest, sitting opposite. Snap. She had a photo of them both.

'Just one more,' Morwenna cooed. Another snap – she had the man's face framed perfectly. He was young – possibly not much older than thirty – well dressed, clean shaven, heavy brows. She saw him pass something to Anna across the table. A brown envelope. She photographed that too. It might be important.

She turned to Barnaby. 'I'll never forget this sunset. It's marvellous. Thank you so much. Shall we get back to our supper now?'

She hauled him back to their table, sat down and reached for her wine. *'Yeghes da,'* Morwenna purred, raising her glass.

Barnaby gazed in admiration. 'You're a very spontaneous woman...'

'That's me.' Morwenna beamed. 'The salmon is delicious. I'm having such a wonderful time. I can't wait for dessert.'

* * *

The next hour passed in fine conversation and food. Morwenna chose the white-chocolate cheesecake with a mascarpone and raspberry sauce. Barnaby claimed to eat puddings rarely, but he tucked in to the 'floating island'; a thick vanilla and marsala anglaise with soft meringue and almond brittle. Then he insisted on a coffee for himself because he didn't want the evening to end. Her phone, complete with photos, was nestling in her bag, so Morwenna felt free to enjoy herself. She was having a whale of a time. Barnaby was good company; he was regaling her with a tale of strange requests that had been made to him as a plastic surgeon. Apparently, the most frequent demand was to look like Kim Kardashian, the most outrageous being to be given wings like the Angel character in *X-Men*. Only once did Morwenna glance across at Anna Carlyon and her guest. They appeared to be talking a lot and eating little. Morwenna thought about Ruan, what he might be doing at The Smugglers, then she noticed

Barnaby's ice-blue eyes on her and she offered him a rewarding smile.

'It's been a fabulous evening. But it's probably time to go.'

'I can't get you anything else?' Barnaby offered generously. Morwenna shook her head, slithered into her huge cardigan so that she would not hurt her sore elbow, reached for her bag, and Barnaby waved to the waiter for the bill.

On the way out, Morwenna paused by Anna Carlyon's table as if to wait for Barnaby, who was just pocketing his wallet. Barnaby said, 'It's been a wonderful evening.'

'Excuse me – can I just ask you...?' Anna Carlyon twisted round in her seat to look into Morwenna's eyes. Behind her glasses, Anna's gaze was ice. 'I noticed your beautiful cardigan when you were taking all those selfies.' She offered a smile that would chill, showing small teeth. 'Where did you get it?'

'In Seal Bay,' Morwenna said quickly. 'There's a charity shop that supports the Lifeboats.'

'Oh, that's such a tremendous cause.' Anna turned to her companion. 'And I admire the Cornish flag so much. I might pop in and get one for myself.'

'I'm sure they'd be delighted.' Morwenna smiled, with a brief look at Anna's companion. She took in his heavy brows above intense hazel eyes and long lashes, his half-smile, and she was on her way, Barnaby's hand on her back, ushering her towards the door.

He smiled. 'People always respond to your warmth.'

Morwenna wasn't so sure. Anna Carlyon had looked at her with the cold eyes of a snake.

20

Barnaby focused on the headlight beam ahead, the twists and bends on the coastal road leading to Seal Bay. Morwenna was quiet, recalling details of her meeting with Anna Carlyon. They'd never spoken before – Anna's greeting was friendly, complimentary. So why did Morwenna feel that it was a veiled threat? She was overthinking. She thought about the Spriggan actors, going through each suspect's name, motives, opportunity. She couldn't rule out the ones she liked most, or believe the killer was the one she took to least of all. Appearances could be deceptive. She had to rely on logic and deduction, instinct not emotion. But, she decided, it probably had to be one of them and she was weeding them out, one by one.

Barnaby turned to her, a smile flickering on his lips, and placed a hand over hers. Morwenna smiled back, but thoughts of what might come next were already troubling her. When they arrived at Harbour Cottages, what then? Should she invite him in? If so, would they share a cup of tea or a passionate kiss? Or would they just talk as friends, say how much they'd enjoyed the evening before saying a friendly goodbye? Or would they fall into each other's arms on the squashy sofa, causing Brenda to run away in fright? Perhaps it would be wiser to say goodbye in the car, to make an early escape.

Morwenna asked herself if she wanted to kiss Barnaby. She supposed it was the normal thing to do after a lovely evening with a very attractive man. She imagined herself and Barnaby in the car, wrapped in a passionate embrace just as Ruan strolled past, his arm around Kenzie, making for number nine where they'd both spend the night. Morwenna was surprised at how uncomfortable the idea made her. Perhaps that was the whole point – it was time to move forward. A relationship with Barnaby was just what she needed. He was good company and, she had to admit, good-looking. She was conscious of how close they were, their arms touching. He smelled lovely, of nutmeg, warm spice. Morwenna decided she'd play it by ear.

They drove through a quiet Seal Bay, a few cars, just a few pedestrians crossing the road. It was ten thirty. Barnaby turned the corner to Harbour Cottages, past glowing street lamps, and stopped outside number four. There were no lights on at Ruan's. Barnaby leaned over to Morwenna, his eyes gleaming, and put an arm around her. 'Tonight was wonderful.'

'It was.' Morwenna didn't know what else to say.

He moved closer. 'I haven't had such a good time in ages.'

Morwenna felt she had to ask. 'But you live in London. You have a city life and city friends, cocktails, shows.' She recalled her mother's words. 'I'm just a Cornish maid.'

'A fascinating one,' he said. Morwenna believed he meant it.

'I'm not sophisticated or professional.' Morwenna wasn't selling herself well. She wasn't trying to. 'I am who I am.'

'And that's what's so refreshing,' Barnaby agreed. 'My ex-wife, and my previous relationships have always been with women for whom outer show was important. My life's surrounded by superficiality in the industry I work in. Women, men who want to change something about themselves. They appear so rich, so self-assured, but they are not what they seem on the outside. You're someone who has no pretence, no interest in being anyone other than who you are. You ride your bike everywhere; you work in the library, the tearoom, you're furiously loyal to your family.' He touched her arm gently. 'You wear a cardigan with the Cornish flag on it. Do you have any idea how alluring that is?'

'I'm comfortable in my own skin,' Morwenna said. 'I don't want to be in anyone else's.'

'And I like that, Morwenna.' He leaned closely and brushed her lips with his. 'I like it a lot.'

Morwenna inhaled the heady scent of his cologne and closed her eyes. He kissed her again lightly.

She smiled: that wasn't too bad at all. She said, 'I'm not used to fancy restaurants and comfy cars. I've always been more of a pasty and bicycle maid.'

'But you could get used to the lifestyle?' Barnaby asked gently, kissing her again.

'I could,' Morwenna muttered, his lips against hers. Then she remembered. 'Arsenic!'

'Pardon?'

'Arsenic.' She wriggled up in her seat and reached for her bag. Pushing her hand in deeply, she tugged out the bottle of tonic with a flourish. 'Could you ask your client to test this one for me?'

Barnaby watched her, blinking like an owl, confused. 'Another one?'

'Yes – please. You see, if this is arsenic free, then I'll know that Ben D'Arcy isn't the murderer, and if it is filled with arsenic then he probably is, and I'll turn the whole thing over to Jane and she can arrest him.'

'You'll have to start again,' Barnaby said.

Morwenna took his hand. 'Right. So...' She inhaled quickly. 'Daniel took the tonic Ben gave him and he died. You got it tested and there was arsenic present. The police believed Daniel had a heart attack. But now I've had threatening messages from whoever has Daniel's phone – perhaps I might be the new target – so I've given Ben an opportunity to attack me by asking for a tonic too. If this is poisoned, perhaps Ben's the killer.'

'What on earth are you up to?'

'Finding Daniel's murderer.'

'And was that what all the selfie business was about?'

'Of course.' Morwenna tugged out her phone. 'Look.' She showed him the picture of Anna. 'She's a sponsor of The Spriggan Travelling Theatre Company. She owns the clay company in St Mengleth. Who do you suppose the man is? They looked like they were discussing something important.'

'He could be anyone at all,' Barnaby said. 'You have a vivid imagination.'

'I just have an instinctive feeling about it... I have to find out.' Morwenna wasn't deterred.

'You're an incredible woman.' Barnaby wanted more kissing. He wrapped an arm around her.

'But will you test the tonic?' Morwenna insisted, pushing him away. 'Let me know what you find? As soon as you can?'

'Of course, I will. Just for you. But wouldn't you be better to tell the police? After all, if there's arsenic present, it doesn't really tell us who put it there. And if there isn't, well, it doesn't tell us anything at all, I'm afraid. But don't worry,' he added quickly. 'I'll do it for you.' Barnaby accepted the small bottle and tucked it into his blazer pocket.

'It's a lead – perhaps?' Morwenna realised she was clutching at straws. 'What else do I have to go on?'

'Well...' Barnaby pulled her close. 'Now, where were we?'

He kissed her again, this time with the intention of showing her how he felt. His fingers tangled in her hair. She heard him make a low sound of passion. Morwenna realised that they had reached the moment of decision – it was all or nothing now. In a heartbeat, she made her choice and tugged away.

'Thanks for a wonderful evening.' She leaned back from him and offered a wide smile.

He looked confused, a little surprised.

'I'm just suddenly overcome with tiredness – it must be the fall I had from the bike. I feel really sleepy.' She threw her arms around his neck and kissed him eagerly. 'I had a lovely time though.' Her hand moved to the door. 'You'll let me know, won't you – about the arsenic?'

'Of course.'

'I owe you dinner,' Morwenna said as a parting gesture. 'Sometime soon?'

'I'm back in London tomorrow.'

'Next time you're in Seal Bay, I'll take you out.'

Barnaby watched as she clambered from the car, his face unsure. The window rolled down. 'To The Smugglers for a pasty and a pint?'

'Oh, I can do better than that,' Morwenna said mischievously. 'Who knows? I might even cook you something nice at home.' She marvelled at her own words, imagining herself ladling spaghetti bolognese onto two plates before they sat on the squashy sofa with Brenda. 'Well, goodnight – it's been...'

'Lovely,' Barnaby agreed. He started the engine and Morwenna watched as he drove away, waving an arm as he took the corner at speed. Then she sighed. She had no idea how she felt. She liked him. He was sexy, sweet, pleasant. But she wasn't in love with him, and she didn't feel that love loomed large in her priorities – when it had come to the moment of decision to invite him in, she'd rushed away. Perhaps it would take another date with Barnaby for her to relax into the rhythm of a relationship. Perhaps the memory of Ruan was still too raw. Perhaps she wasn't capable of love any more. Or perhaps she was too set in her ways, too independent.

Morwenna ambled towards her front door, tugging out her keys. Brenda was waiting on the welcome mat, purring like a furry little motor. Morwenna glanced around, just in case there were remnants of poisoned Dreamies on the carpet. She found none. Her bicycle was as she'd left it, the helmet across the handlebars, her coats and jackets on the hooks. But she hadn't forgotten the threat sent from Daniel's phone – it still loitered in her mind. She picked up her cat and held her close, feeling the comforting vibrations. She'd go straight to bed and try to sleep.

But Morwenna knew that sleep wouldn't come quickly. She had a lot weighing on her mind. Romance and murder were subjects that were hard to unravel and she didn't have a solution to either, not yet. But she would, soon. It was just a matter of figuring it all out and being patient.

* * *

The next morning, Morwenna woke at five o'clock. She'd had four hours' sleep, but a hot shower brought her round and lifted her mood. Being a sleuth meant talking ideas over with someone, sharing what evidence she had, and she knew who she needed to talk to. She tugged on her clothes, noticing how she moved a little more freely, although her left arm and shoulder were still stiff.

Downstairs, she fed a hungry Brenda, kissed the top of her head and promised to be back soon – she had a particular problem she wanted to work out. It was to do with Anna Carlyon. Was she even a suspect? And what was Morwenna's next move? She picked up a packet of croissants and rushed across the road to number nine.

Ruan would be up but he wouldn't have left for the boat yet, she hoped, as she knocked at the door.

He opened it, lean in faded jeans, his hair damp from the shower, tugging a T-shirt over his torso. Morwenna was reminded of old times. He said, 'It's a bit early. Come in.'

'I brought breakfast.' Morwenna held out the croissants. 'I want to pick your brain.'

He led the way in. The kitchen and living room were open-plan; there was a modern sofa, a bookshelf, a woodburning fire. His home was brighter than number four, which was crammed with Morwenna's clutter and haphazard décor. She noticed photos on the far wall: Ruan holding a huge fish, and several more with Tamsin as a toddler and a teenager. There were a few with Morwenna taken over the last thirty years, one of the two of them together on the beach, their arms around each other. The picture always brought a lump to her throat.

'I'll warm the croissants and make coffee,' Ruan said, bustling around in the kitchen. 'I've got half an hour before I have to get off. What's on your mind?'

'Daniel Kitto.'

'Oh?'

'I wanted to talk a few things over.'

'Right,' Ruan said. 'How was your date?'

'So-so.' Morwenna wasn't sure what to say. 'How was yours?'

'Hardly what you'd call a date,' Ruan murmured. 'The actors were all in The Smugglers. It's funny how drink loosens some people's tongues.'

'Oh?' Morwenna sat down at the table. 'Tell me more.'

'Kenzie,' Ruan said and Morwenna winced a little at his mentioning her name. 'She's a strange one.'

'How's that?'

'It seems Daniel had some sort of relationship with her mum.'

'He had a relationship with everyone's mum. You have to hand it to him, he was popular,' Morwenna said. 'My mum, Kenzie's mum – even Gill Bennett's mum. He was her father, you know.'

'Was he?' Ruan raised an eyebrow – he wasn't surprised. 'Apparently, he left Kenzie's mother under difficult circumstances. She was in the acting profession too. Three months later the poor woman was terminally ill. The two things weren't connected, but Kenzie bears a grudge.'

'So why did she work with him?'

'He was sorry for what happened. He wanted to give her a chance, I guess. She's been with Spriggan for a while – she and Daniel go back a long way.'

'But she hated him with a vengeance. She says he made unacceptable sexist remarks.'

'They are from different generations.' Ruan shook his head. 'What was sadly accepted in Daniel's day is misogyny now. Of course, it was never really right. He made comments that he thought were flattering, you know the sort of thing – and it probably came over as a bit creepy.'

Morwenna understood. 'Do you think she killed him?'

'She hated him enough.' Ruan placed a mug of tea in front of Morwenna along with a plate of croissants.

'Who's your top suspect?'

'I wouldn't rule anyone out,' Ruan said honestly. 'Jesse the techie is bragging to anyone who will listen – he talks constantly about how Daniel relied on him for everything. He's made a friend of Tommy Buvač. They talk in the pub and Jesse buys him drinks. He's waving money about all the time.'

'Ah.'

'Rupert is arrogant – he's made it clear that he wants to be director and influence what happens in the company.'

'How's he going to do that?'

'He thinks the role's his by right of his talent.' Ruan sat down and reached for a pastry. 'Ben's in love with Inga and she won't give him the time of day. She left the bar in floods of tears last night.'

'Why?'

'She misses Daniel. They were very close. His funeral is on Monday. She's had to arrange it.'

'Gill ought to be doing that – she's his daughter.'

'Inga's quite obsessive over his funeral.' Ruan said. 'Musa's a nice chap though – he keeps himself to himself.'

'He used to be a chemist – oh, I'm having the tonic tested. Barnaby thinks it won't tell me much. He's probably right. Anyone could have tampered with it while Ben wasn't looking, or more likely there'll be nothing wrong with it at all...' Morwenna admitted.

'He has a point.'

Morwenna took a breath. 'Are you seeing the – actors – again tonight?'

Ruan seemed ambivalent. 'I said I might go down for a pint. I like to see some of the fishing lads once we're off the trawler. Damien's keeping me up to date about a new boat he's working on.'

'Keep your ear to the ground, Ruan – and keep me posted. It's all useful information.'

'I will.'

'I have another person to add to the mix – Anna Carlyon.'

'The Korrik Clay woman? Because she's Spriggan's sponsor?'

'Yes.' Morwenna said. 'I need to do some digging. But where to start?' She finished her tea. 'I need to give it some thought.'

'We'll talk later,' Ruan suggested.

Morwenna stood up, brushing crumbs from her clothes. 'Yes, and – I think we should all go to the show on Saturday night. It's Elowen's last performance.'

'Definitely,' Ruan agreed.

'It's a date,' Morwenna said and immediately regretted it.

'Do you think you'll find Daniel's killer by then?' Ruan asked.

'I promised Jane I would pass on all my information. She's keen for the police to be involved and I can't keep putting her off.'

'She's only thinking of you.' Ruan walked her to the door. 'You make sure you take no risks.'

'I'll be safe enough,' Morwenna said.

She heard him call after her, 'Thanks for breakfast,' and she waved a hand in acknowledgement.

The sun was rising over the bay, the harbour clustered with silver and mauve clouds. Morwenna sighed. Life was complicated. But every day was filled with new possibilities…

21

Morwenna sprawled out on the sofa in her untidy living room, ready for her morning shift at the library. Still wearing the Cornish cardie, she gazed round at the unwashed cups, the carpet that needed vacuuming. Ruan's place was so tidy in comparison. She had no excuse – she lived by herself. She was responsible for her own squalor. She'd have to tidy up if she was going to invite Barnaby round for dinner. The thought made her smile. They'd had fun at the restaurant. She reached for her phone and thumbed him a message.

Thanks for last night. I had a wonderful time.

It was the least she could do, particularly after she'd bottled out of inviting him in. No, it was up to her to decide when she'd had enough, to lay down boundaries. She had no regrets about calling it a night after a few pleasant kisses.

As she stretched her legs, Morwenna looked through the photos she'd taken. There were some fun ones with Barnaby, both of them smiling, a gorgeous splash of sunset across the bay behind them. They looked like any happy couple enjoying a night out.

The photos of Anna and her companion followed. Barnaby was right. They told her nothing at all. The brown envelope, passed from the man to Anna, caught her eye and she stared at it. Something was written on it but she couldn't make it out. Brenda leaped on her lap and began to knead her knee. Morwenna stroked the soft fur. 'What do you think I should do next, Bren?'

The cat ignored her, crawling up her chest, headbutting her sore chin, pawing the cardigan, catching her claws in the stitches. Morwenna unhooked the paws carefully, kissing the flat top of Brenda's head, between the ears. 'Don't pull the wool, Bren.'

Brenda padded across her chest again and Morwenna lifted her away, kissing her again, then she paused, cat in mid-air. It was a 'Eureka!' moment.

'Brenda, you little beauty! You're right. Yes – that's exactly what I should do.' She hugged the cat, whose purrs became louder. 'You're brilliant – a much better sleuth than me. I ought to ask your opinion more often.'

She rewarded Brenda with a handful of biscuit treats, reached for her chicken bag and her cycling helmet. She stowed a light jacket in the basket at the front and pushed her bicycle towards the path, planning what she would do between her shifts in the library and the tearoom.

* * *

Morwenna spent the morning trying to avoid Louise's questions about the date. Louise followed her round the library as she replaced books on shelves, calling out random questions such as, 'What did you eat?', 'What was the restaurant like?', 'Do you like him, then, the plastic surgeon?' What Louise really wanted to know was if they'd snogged each other's faces off.

Morwenna turned round with an expression of extreme tolerance. 'It was a proper date, Louise, and I might see him again or I might not. He's a gentleman and, yes, we did have one goodnight—' She paused as her phone buzzed. Nowadays her first concern was that Lamorna was forwarding another threat. She exhaled. 'It's from Barnaby. He's back in London. It says, "Lovely to see you. Until next time B".'

'Did he put kisses underneath?' Louise wanted to know.

'No.'

'But that still means he likes you. "Until next time." It still means he'll ask you on another date. Would you go?'

'If he asked me?'

'Yes.'

Morwenna smiled slowly. 'I might ask him.'

'Oh, I love a new romance.' Louise clapped her hands together. 'Will there be wedding bells? A Christmas wedding. How nice!'

'In your dreams,' Morwenna said. She texted back to Barnaby:

I'm looking forward to it

Louise was trying to look over her shoulder. 'Are you sending all your love?'

'Something like that,' Morwenna replied. She had to admit, knowing the contents of the tonic interested her far more at the moment than the singing plastic surgeon. But she liked him. She'd give it time.

* * *

At lunchtime, she cycled to the pop-up knitting shop where Susan and Barb were busy knitting with vibrant red wool. They smiled as Morwenna came in, holding up their needles. Barb said, 'We're making goblin hats.'

'Oh?' Morwenna examined the long woollen shape. 'Is this a commercial venture?'

'It is – we've just come up with the idea after visiting Spriggan,' Susan said. 'We were chatting to that nice actor who plays Merlin and he suggested we sell things for the Lifeboats before and after the show on Saturday. So, Barb and I—'

Barb took over. 'Thought Piskie and Spriggan hats might go down a storm.'

'And a special one for Merlin.' Susan smiled slyly. 'He promised me he'd buy a multicoloured one for twenty pounds.'

'You're sharp businesswomen.'

'And sleuthing assistants,' Barb added. 'So, what can we do to help?'

'Anything you can find out about Spriggan's sponsor, Korrik Clay,' Morwenna beamed. 'And keep your eye on the actors.'

'I don't like the posh one who plays Lancelot.' Susan clamped her lips together. 'He has a high opinion of himself.'

'Plus, he said he didn't believe in giving to charity,' Barb added. 'So, he won't be getting a Spriggan hat made specially for his big head.'

'Talking of charity…' Morwenna indicated the cardigan that she was wearing, with the Cornish flag. 'I don't suppose you have another one of these?'

'Not yet we don't.' Susan shook her head. 'They don't come off the needles quick, big heavy cardies like that.'

'It's just that – if I can sell it for a profit and give you the money – would you make me another, at your leisure?'

'Of course we would,' Barb said. 'You'll start a trend in Seal Bay and everyone will want one. We might have to double the price.'

'Great.' Morwenna was delighted. 'Make my Spriggan hat big and multicoloured please. It will be great to wear after swimming to keep my ears warm.'

'Oh, right.' Susan turned to Barb. 'Here's another idea for you. Swan hats, for the wild swimmers. Big woollen hats in white wool, and for the bobble, a big white head and an orange beak on the top. I reckon the swimmers will love them.'

'It sounds – technical,' Morwenna said, then she was on her way with a cheery wave. Back at the bicycle, she took off the cardigan and folded it neatly, placing it in the basket. She shrugged on the light jacket and glanced towards the road into Seal Bay and the hill beyond. 'Right,' she muttered to herself, feeling just a little nervous. 'Knave-Go-By, let's see what a visit will bring.'

It was a hard three-mile cycle to the headland. Morwenna was grateful for the electric motor in her bicycle, but it was still tough going, the sea breeze buffeting her from one side, flattening the grass. Overhead, clouds scudded by in an azure sky. She saw the house before she arrived there. It was modern with lots of glass to let in the light, perched in acres of grass and an orchard, the huge windows glinting. Below, the sky was the deepest blue, waves crashing against rocks. Morwenna thought it looked an isolated place to live; beautiful, expensive – but lonely. She wondered if the owner was the same.

Knave-Go-By was accessed through tall iron gates, the spikes ending in an arrowhead. Morwenna paused to take in the design, all angles and straight lines with sweeping steps to the front door. There was a conservatory, a roof terrace on the first level; Morwenna could make out patio tables and chairs beyond an attractive guard rail fashioned in metal. To one side, a white BMW was parked on gravel. She pushed her bike towards the house. It was immaculate from the outside: Morwenna felt just a little intimidated. She leaned her bicycle against one of the white walls and collected the Cornish cardigan in her arms. She was tempted to turn back.

But she was here now. Her phone pushed deep into her jacket pocket, she took a breath and began to ascend the steep steps. The front door was set back beneath a wide white porch. Morwenna noted there was one plant outside, a tall palm, but no flowers in baskets or pots, no decorations. The lack of fripperies told her something about the owner. She was a practical woman, or she had no time for peripheral matters. Anna Carlyon had the appearance of a no-nonsense businesswoman; Morwenna recalled the smart bob, the tailored suit. She thought of the young man Anna had dined with at The Marine Room, sitting opposite, passing an envelope. She'd suppose nothing, not yet. She rang the bell, knocked once and waited. Taking a step back, Morwenna gazed up at the panoramic windows for signs of movement. She'd never seen such enormous panes of glass. There appeared to be no one behind them. She rang again.

Minutes later, she was still waiting. Perhaps there was no one at home, although Anna's car was in the drive. Or perhaps she was in the back garden. Morwenna scurried down the steps, the folded cardigan in her arms, and made her way round the back.

She crossed a patio to some French windows. There was no sign of anyone. Morwenna called, 'Hello?' and heard the edginess in her voice. Behind her, the patio gave way to grassland, an orchard, an open field. The patio itself was pristine, with a solid table and six chairs, two luxurious sunbeds, each containing an uncreased linen cushion. Morwenna wondered if anyone ever used them.

A French window was open. Someone must be inside the house and she hoped they were in earshot as she called, 'Hello?' There was no response so she stepped inside to gaze around a comfortable living room.

Morwenna felt her heart beat faster: she shouldn't be trespassing. There was a large leather sofa, perfectly arranged cushions, an open fireplace with a black wood-burner, a mahogany chest with photographs. She approached them nervously. One was a wedding photograph of Anna and, she assumed, Will Carlyon, Anna immaculate in white lace, holding a spray of white roses. The groom had a grey suit and a neat hairstyle. He was expressionless behind his neat moustache. Next to it, there were more photographs of the wedding, others of the couple on various holidays, skiing, sunbathing, sightseeing. Morwenna caught her breath, tugged out her phone and snapped several pictures of the room, the furniture, the photos. She'd look at them properly later. Then, to herald her presence, she called out again, 'Anyone home?'

She crept from the living room into the hall. Steps led down into another room. Morwenna padded down on light feet into the most beautiful, spacious kitchen she'd ever seen. A huge island filled the centre, and all round the walls were marble worktops and blue wooden cabinets. Everything was pristine, as if the place was seldom used. There was a ceramic holder in the window, full of herbs. A tray was set for tea: a teapot, china cups. The fridge was enormous, the range cooker gleamed. It was like being in a showroom. Morwenna took several more photos: a few letters on the worktop, a large brown envelope, a red leather purse, keys.

Behind her, the kitchen opened into a dining room, a long table that would seat twelve people, a panoramic window to the sea beyond. The view was breathtaking, the grassland ending with an abrupt drop to the beach below, the ocean merging with the sky on the horizon. Morwenna tucked the cardigan beneath her arm, pointed her phone and snapped away. She crossed the kitchen silently to a corner door leading into a utility room. Poised on top of a washing machine, benefiting from the light of a wide window, was a lemon plant with several hanging fruits. She angled her phone and pressed the button, taking random photos of cupboards, nooks, corners. She frowned. The house gave few clues about the occupant. She imagined Anna Carlyon rattling round in the enormous building alone. She wondered if it had ever been a family home, how Anna's life had been with Will Carlyon and how things must have changed now she was a widow. Morwenna felt sorry for her. Wondering what to do, she made her way back to the kitchen and caught her breath.

A woman was standing in the doorway, where the steps started, blocking her exit. She was frowning, her hands on her hips, smart in a navy suit. Anna Carlyon took a step forward, one aggressive pace in high heels. Her voice was cold.

'What the hell are you doing in my house? I'm phoning the police.'

22

'I'm so sorry. I did ring the bell but you can't have heard me.' Morwenna offered the biggest smile she could muster. 'I hoped I'd find you. You remember me, don't you?'

'No, I don't.' Anna shook her head. The frown was a permanent fixture between her brows.

'It was in The Marine Room,' Morwenna gushed, determined to find common ground.

Anna didn't move. 'What was?'

'I was there with my – my friend – taking selfies, and you commented about how much you liked my cardigan with the Cornish flag.' Morwenna could hear the desperation in her voice. She shook out her bundle, holding out the knitted cardie.

'I still don't understand.' Anna was unconvinced. 'Why are you in my house?'

'I brought this cardigan for you from the knitting shop. I thought, since you liked it so much, you might want to buy it.' Morwenna could hear how weak the excuse sounded even as she said it.

'Why would you do that?'

'To support the Lifeboats.' Morwenna gave it her best shot. 'I know you sponsor The Spriggan Travelling Theatre Company. My – my family love their version of the King Arthur story. I saw on the programme that Korrik Clay sponsors them and—'

'How did you know where I live?' Anna's eyes were small.

'I'm from Seal Bay. Everyone knows everything. It's well known that you own this beautiful place on the headland.' Morwenna hugged the cardigan. 'I'm sorry. I really didn't mean to intrude.'

Anna took a pace towards her. Her expression softened. 'Can I see it?'

Morwenna handed the cardigan over. Anna shook it out and inspected it. 'It's a bit on the large side.'

'Chunky. That's how you wear them,' Morwenna suggested.

'It would be lovely and warm outside in the winter. Or...' Anna smiled, showing perfect teeth '...it would be really fun in London when I'm visiting family, to fly the Cornish flag, as it were.' She met Morwenna's eyes. 'How much are they selling them for at the knitting shop?'

Morwenna remembered she had promised Susan and Barb a profit. 'Sixty pounds. They are hand-knitted.'

'I'll give you a hundred since it's for a good cause.' Anna's expression was all generosity now. 'I'm so sorry I didn't answer the door. It must have been such a shock when I stormed in here and threatened to ring the police.'

'No, I'm sorry I wandered in,' Morwenna said. 'I was hoping that I'd find you. I didn't mean to trespass.'

'Of course not.' Anna held a hand out. 'I'm Anna.'

Morwenna took the hand in her warm one. It was ice cold. 'Morwenna.'

'Can I offer you tea?' Anna was friendly now. 'It's the least I can do after you kindly brought me a cardigan. And I'll give you the money for your charity.'

'Oh, I don't want to trouble you.' Morwenna took a step backwards.

'It's no trouble,' Anna insisted. 'How did you get here?'

'I have a bicycle.' Morwenna pointed towards the panoramic window. 'It's outside.'

'Then you must be worn out, riding it from Seal Bay. You need to take care of yourself in this bitter wind. Let me at least offer you some refreshment. Come – I insist.' Anna led the way up the stairs, turning into the living room where the French window was open. 'Please, sit. I'll bring tea. Green, Earl Grey or Lapsang?'

'Green.' Morwenna sat precariously on the edge of the leather sofa.

'Right. I'll be back in a jiffy.' Anna smiled before she disappeared to the kitchen.

Morwenna gazed around. Everywhere was tidy, smooth surfaces, not a speck of dust on the photographs. She approached one with a gold frame and picked it up. In the picture, Anna was wearing a hard hat and a boilersuit, holding up an award. Her smile was professional. The background of the picture showed clay pits and a digger. Anna walked in and placed a tray on a small table. Morwenna was still holding the picture. She replaced it quickly and sat down on the leather sofa as if reprimanded.

'I accepted an industry award last year on behalf of my late husband. I met him in London, at a social event. We were introduced…' Anna perched next to Morwenna and handed her a china cup on a saucer. She pushed a small plate with three chocolate biscuits in front of her. 'He passed away not long ago. Poor Will.' Anna lifted a knuckle to her eye. 'It was a shock. We hadn't been married long.'

Morwenna picked up the cup and saucer and stared at the pale liquid. 'I'm sorry to hear that.'

'It was tragic. I miss him so.'

'Did he love the theatre?' Morwenna put the cup down again.

'Will? Oh, not at all. He wasn't interested in anything other than business. I'm the one who has the theatre in my veins.'

'Oh?'

'Absolutely. I've always dabbled. My second husband was an impresario.'

Morwenna feigned ignorance. 'Is that some sort of magician?'

'Oh no,' Anna said. 'He invested money in various theatre and musical enterprises. He was a magician at first, I suppose, of sorts – some of his investments took off.' She gave a half-laugh that sounded cynical.

'Would I have heard of him?' Morwenna asked innocently.

'I doubt it.' Anna wrinkled a delicate nose. 'Xander operated on many levels, but fame wasn't one of them.' Her gaze fell on the teacup and then on Morwenna. 'Your tea's going cold. Drink up. So – let's talk about you, Morwenna. You live in Seal Bay. What do you do with yourself there?'

'I help out in the library.' Morwenna wondered why she felt uncomfortable telling Anna about her personal life. 'I go swimming in the sea a lot.'

'Oh, isn't that dangerous?' Anna shuddered. 'I admire you for doing it. And are you married?'

'Single.'

'But I saw you in the restaurant with a very handsome man.'

'It was a date,' Morwenna said, as if she dated all the time. She noticed Anna's eyes move to her cup again and she felt her phone buzz in her pocket. 'Excuse me – this might be important.'

She opened a text. It was from Barnaby.

The liquid my client checked for you was fine. No traces of arsenic. I'll message you soon to let you know when I'm back in Seal Bay.

Morwenna sighed, disappointed. Barnaby had been right. It had proven nothing – except that Ben probably wasn't trying to kill her. But it still didn't shed any light on who killed Daniel.

Morwenna noticed Anna watching her keenly. 'And is it? Important?'

'I'm afraid so.' Morwenna made a concerned face. 'My grandchild is sick at school. I have to pick her up.'

'Grandchild?' Anna seemed interested.

Morwenna stood up, glad of an excuse to leave Anna and the steaming cup of green tea, which she'd managed not to touch. She wasn't sure if it was just hot water and tea leaves, or if she'd had a lucky escape. And as for the biscuits, who knew what they might be laced with? Morwenna wondered for a moment if she was allowing her imagination to run riot. But she couldn't take any chances. 'I have to go, I'm so sorry.'

'What a pity. But do let me pay you first for the cardigan. That was why you came, wasn't it?' Anna said. She handed Morwenna several folded notes. 'Thank you so much. I'll think of Cornwall every time I wear it.'

'No, thank *you*,' Morwenna said gratefully. 'The ladies in the knitting shop will be so pleased.'

'I do hope we run into each other again soon,' Anna said sweetly. 'It was lovely to meet you, Morwenna.'

'You too.' Morwenna made for the door. She waved over her shoulder as she scurried around the side of the house and back to where she'd left her bicycle. She threw a leg over the saddle and set off towards the tall gates, her heart racing.

For some reason, Anna Carlyon made her feel uncomfortable. She was an independent, rich businesswoman. But, Morwenna thought, as she pedalled furiously down the hill that led to Seal Bay, that wasn't why she felt out of her depth – there was something definitely intimidating about her. She tried to be rational – Anna might be confident, controlling, but it didn't make her a killer. Morwenna wouldn't rule her out, though. Her instinct told her that you could never be too careful.

She thought about her meeting with Anna all the way home. As she cycled, she recalled various snatches of their conversation – she'd suggested that swimming in the sea was dangerous. And her later words echoed back to Morwenna: 'I do hope we run into each other again soon.' Morwenna put thoughts of possible threats from her mind; Anna had been merely making conversation.

As she worked through her busy shift at the tearoom, and all the time she was helping Elowen with her reading, Morwenna found her eyes drifting towards the sea wall and beyond. The ocean was rolling in, the surf splashing, and her thoughts moved to Anna's house, remote, beautiful, filled with memories. Later, she'd have another look at the photos she'd taken and search for clues. Over a cup of tea, Morwenna texted Ruan.

I have things to discuss. Let me know when you have a free five minutes.

Then she texted Barnaby.

Thanks for the information. Looking forward to seeing you next time.

It wasn't a very romantic text but her mind was full of crashing thoughts about Daniel Kitto and the Spriggan theatre. Ben D'Arcy probably wasn't a suspect now – her brain was puzzling for someone else to latch onto.

Tamsin was by her side. 'Can you stay, have some tea with us, Mum? Elowen's in the play again tonight and I'll be backstage. Why don't you come along and keep us company?'

'Thanks, Tam – I'll go home for a quick shower now while you're cooking, and come straight back.' Morwenna pressed her lips together, thinking. Another evening spent watching the actors performing might help her thoughts gel. She needed time when her mind was relaxed so that an idea could pop in and lead to a hunch.

Several hours later, she was sitting in the middle row by herself, watching *The Return of the Cornish King*. Tamsin and Becca were backstage, peeping from the wings. Elowen was cute, warm and funny; her performance as the mermaid received warm and enthusiastic applause from the audience. Each evening her performance was growing and tonight she'd taken to flipping her tail in time with some of her lines. Her plunge into the sea at the end was histrionic, wild arms, thrashing tail and a loud 'Ooooh, the water's bleddy cold.' The audience hooted: Morwenna had often heard Lamorna say exactly the same words in the same manner after she'd poked a toe near the waves. She smiled inwardly; she'd never get her mother in the sea.

The actors were on form too; Kenzie as Igraine was more besotted than ever with Uther and even more malicious as Morgan le Fay. Arthur's heroism boomed to the back of the marquee auditorium and Guinevere batted her lashes perfectly at his every word. Musa was a dynamic Merlin, his physical ability being so much better than everyone else's, but there was a moment where he faltered, as if dizzy, then he shook himself as a dog would shake damp fur and leaped back into his character with more gusto than ever. Even Lancelot had improved; his awkward movements and bland character made him somehow a foil for Arthur's bluster.

The final lights went down, the actors bowed and the audience clapped. Morwenna gazed around for her jacket. She spotted Susan and Barb at the entrance, selling Spriggan hats to the crowd, and she rushed over, pressing the notes Anna had given her into Susan's hand. Barb grabbed her wrist eagerly. 'Hey, we've been doing some sleuthing for you...'

'Oh?' Morwenna was immediately interested.

'Frances Thacker came in this afternoon to buy a tea cosy. You might not know her but her husband works for Korrik Clay – he's been there for thirty years, man and boy. So we asked her if she knew any gossip about Anna Whatsit, the merry widow. Of course, she didn't know much.'

'Except for one thing,' Susan hissed. 'She said that Anna Carlyon got herself introduced to Will – she set her sights on him – and then they got married in London, although Will would have preferred Cornwall. But what Anna wants, Anna gets, it seems. All the workers say so. She said they had a big posh wedding and loads of guests, and her previous name was Driscoll.'

'That's wonderful. Well done.' Morwenna was delighted. 'That gives me something to work on.'

'Seal Bay Sleuths, Inc.,' Barb hissed and Susan tapped her nose knowingly.

'You sold the cardie for a profit, then?' Susan flourished the money.

Morwenna winked. 'Oh yes. Anna was delighted with it.'

Susan opened her mouth to ask another question, but Morwenna felt a hand on her shoulder and she whirled round to look at a young woman with white-blonde hair who was standing breathlessly behind her.

'Becca?'

'Can I ask a big favour, Morwenna? Tam says could you take Elowen back to the tearoom and put her to bed? Only—'

'Of course.' Morwenna agreed before she knew the details.

'The two actors, Rupert and Ben, have asked me and Tam out for a drink.'

Morwenna folded her arms. 'I thought Tam didn't like Rupert.'

'She doesn't. She thinks he's a total prat, but—' Becca lowered her voice. 'I like him. He's a bit of posh and I've always had a soft spot for Hooray Henries.'

'If you're sure...' Morwenna was momentarily protective. 'Does Tam like the other one? Ben?'

'Not really but...' Becca's eyes shone. 'She'll come with me. We were just going to grab a burger and a drink, one hour tops, less, then we'll be back before eleven, I promise.'

Morwenna said, 'It will be my pleasure to take Elowen. You both deserve a bit of down time. But – Becca?'

'Anything...'

Morwenna wondered how to warn her to be careful, not to accept anything from a bottle, eat any secretly contaminated foods. She stopped herself. Tamsin could take care of both of them. 'Just have a lovely time.'

'We will,' Becca gushed. 'Thanks, Morwenna – you're the best. I'll go and tell Tam you said you'd babysit.'

Morwenna watched her rush down the tiered steps, her feet banging on the wood, and she reached for her phone to text Jane Choy. Her thumb moved quickly.

Can you come round to the tearoom asap? There's something we need to discuss.

23

Elowen didn't want to go to bed. She was hyperactive because she'd been on stage. More so because her grandmother was tugging her pyjama top over her head in an attempt to get her into the bathroom.

'Brush your teeth, my lovely, and I'll read you a story.'

'I'm not tired, Grandma. Can we stay up and watch telly?'

'You'll be tired tomorrow when it's time to get up for school, Elowen.'

'Everybody cheered when I said the water was bleddy cold. I was the funniest mermaid they'd ever seen.'

'You were,' Morwenna said. 'But you shouldn't copy Great-Grandma.'

Elowen's eyes danced with mischief. 'Everybody loves her. I like it best when she picks me up at the school gates. She makes people laugh. She's not boring like Britney's mummy.'

'Carole's very kind. She looks after you and lets you stop over.'

Elowen stuck out a bottom lip. 'Britney says she's boring. Where's Grandad? Is he down the pub again. Is he with Kenzie? Kissy-kissy-kissy.'

Morwenna recognised the time-wasting strategy. 'Let's get those teeth cleaned and then we can get you into bed.'

'Can Grandad come round now? I like it when you both take me out. Can we go to Hippity Hoppers on Sunday? Or we could go down the beach.'

'First things first.' Morwenna took Elowen's hand and led her gently into the bathroom. 'Teeth.' She picked up toothpaste, a small pink brush.

Elowen had foam around her mouth. 'Saturday's the last night of the play. Will you be there, Grandma?'

'I will.'

'Then can I eat the chocolate that Kenzie gave me?'

'What chocolate?' Morwenna froze.

'A big chocolate bar. It's in my coat pocket. I didn't eat it yet, just like you said.'

'Was the chocolate in a wrapper?'

'It's got its paper on. It's a big massive bar. Kenzie gave it to me because I'm the best mermaid. I think it's because she likes Grandad a lot,' Elowen said knowingly. 'Can I have my chocolate on Saturday?'

'We'll see. Now wash your face.'

Elowen splashed water on her cheeks from the running tap and waved a towel at her face. 'At least it's not that weird drink in the little bottle. Some of the actors drink it all the time. Ben does and now he's given some to Musa. Musa's my favourite. He's funny.'

'I see.' Morwenna took in her granddaughter's words. 'Come on, poppet, let's get you into bed.'

'I need Oggy Two. I can't sleep without him.'

'I've already put him in the bed. He's fast asleep. We mustn't wake him.' Morwenna was pleased she'd placed the knitted dog under the duvet earlier.

'I'm not tired, though. Can you read me *The Dragon with the Blazing Bottom*? I like that one.'

'All right.'

'Then can you read *Mummy Fairy and Me*?'

'We'll see.' Morwenna had forgotten how difficult six-year-olds could be. They were now in the yellow bedroom, and Elowen slid beneath the colourful duvet, all tigers and toucans. Morwenna sat on the edge of the bed, turning the bedside lamp on. It cast soft shadows of the moon and stars on the wall. She picked up a bright book.

Elowen squeezed her eyes shut. 'I'm not asleep. I'm listening.'

'Right. Let's get you off to sleep.' Morwenna began to read, making her voice slow and soothing. As she suspected, by the time she'd reached the last page, Elowen's face had relaxed, her eyelids had become heavy and her breathing regular. Morwenna slipped through the door on silent feet and downstairs to the tearoom. Jane Choy was sitting outside in a police car, her headlights on. Morwenna beckoned her to come in. She locked the tearoom door, led her upstairs and put the kettle on.

'Thanks, I need a cuppa,' Jane said wearily. 'It's been a long evening.'

'Oh?'

'Nothing much is happening at all out there. All's quiet around Seal Bay. It makes the time go slowly.'

Morwenna pushed a mug of tea in front of her. 'I have some things I need to run past you.'

'Good.' Jane seated herself at the table. 'Fire away. Any lead on the health tonic?'

'No, I got it totally wrong. It seems I'm not much of a sleuth after all,' Morwenna said sadly. 'I thought Ben might be trying to kill me but I was – what did Barnaby say? – barking up the wrong tree.'

'Who can it be, then? One of the other actors?'

'Maybe.' Morwenna recalled Musa on the stage, faltering. He'd looked unwell. 'I have a hunch or two.'

'Do tell.'

'And a wild card. I went round Anna Carlyon's place earlier.'

'She's not involved, surely?'

'I just have this feeling,' Morwenna said. 'You're probably right. I saw her in a restaurant the other day – hang on, I'll show you.' She tugged out her phone. 'What do you think is going on in this picture?'

Jane studied the photo of Anna Carlyon and her guest, and made a soft clucking sound, thinking. 'Just dinner?'

'Look at the brown envelope. Look how secretive they are being.'

'Tenuous, I'd say. People go out for meals all the time and give presents.'

'I just have this feeling about the pair of them, the way they were together felt somehow a bit suspicious... Do you know Anna?' Morwenna asked.

'She's called us out to Knave-Go-By a few times, saying she thought she had intruders. There's never been anyone there. But she lives in a remote spot and she's on her own.'

'Maybe she shouldn't leave doors open,' Morwenna said enigmatically.

Jane went back to the photo. 'I'm ruling her out for now. She's just the theatre company's sponsor, nothing more. Wait a minute.' Jane pressed her fingers against the screen, expanding the picture, scrutinising Anna's companion. 'Where have I seen him before?'

'You know the man?'

'I think so – he rings a bell. I never forget a face. Can I send this to myself and check him out?'

'Of course.'

'You've got nothing on Anna other than this?'

'No.' The fact that she'd married rich men and was a widow counted for nothing. As did the fact that she made Morwenna feel decidedly jumpy.

'I'd focus your energy elsewhere,' Jane said. 'I'm more interested in investigating the potential use of arsenic. Maybe I'll pull Ben D'Arcy in for questioning and ask him why he's selling dodgy tonic. Daniel Kitto is our key. I could talk to the coroner if I thought we had sufficient evidence.'

'Give me until Saturday,' Morwenna asked. 'Please?'

'Why Saturday?'

'It's the actors' last performance of *The Return of the Cornish King* the evening – we're going swimming beforehand. Let's talk about it again then.'

Jane made a 'this isn't strictly how we should be conducting things' face and went back to her tea. 'All right. It's a good job I trust you.'

There was a bump downstairs and Morwenna said, 'Tam's here.' She listened as footsteps hurried up the stairs and Tamsin came in, looking cold and tired. Morwenna asked, 'How was the date?'

Tamsin pulled a face. 'Hardly a date. We all went down The Smugglers and had a shandy and a packet of crisps. We were promised burgers too – cheapskates, these actors.'

Morwenna moved to the kettle and found another mug, throwing in a teabag. 'Tell me all about it.'

'Becca seriously has the hots for Rupert. He's an arrogant arse. The only person he loves is himself. And Ben can only go on and on about Inga and how much she loves Spriggan and not him.' Tamsin yawned. 'I was bored.'

'Drink your tea. Then we'll get off.' Morwenna handed her the mug.

'How was Elowen?'

'She's a little heller,' Morwenna said. 'She didn't want to go to sleep.'

'Dad was down The Smugglers.' Tamsin gazed at Morwenna's face; she was looking for a reaction so Morwenna gave her a smile.

'Were all the actors there?'

'Not Inga. She doesn't really go there since the first time; apparently, she thinks The Smugglers is a dive. Her words. Musa went back to the guest house early. Jesse was in the bar, showing off, buying drinks and behaving like a complete idiot. He was trying to impress Tommy Buvač again, getting him whisky – I heard him talking about the string of women he's conquered and how the secret to a successful sex life is a big motor car.'

Jane pulled a sucking-lemon face. 'It's a shame that's not against the law. I'd arrest him now.'

Tamsin moved in with her final line. 'And Kenzie was sitting next to Dad, all over him as if she owns him. I don't know what he makes of it all. He was talking to Damien and his new squeeze about boats and Kenzie was agreeing with everything he said, gazing at him like Igraine gawps at Uther Pendragon. I wonder if she was still acting.' She gave a laugh. 'If you ask me, the actors are acting all the time. It's hard to know what's performance and what's real with any of them.'

'It sounds like a typical night in The Smugglers,' Morwenna said, wondering why she felt her heart sinking.

Jane finished her tea. 'Well, I'd best be off. Seal Bay will be a hotbed of vice if I don't patrol.'

'Nice to see you, Jane,' Morwenna said. 'I'll be off too.'

'Where's your bike?'

'I left it at home. I walked down.'

'Then I'll give you a lift.' Jane winked. 'I can't have one of our senior citizens wandering on her own up those hills at eleven o'clock at night.'

Morwenna grimaced. 'Thanks.' She turned to Tamsin. 'I'll see you tomorrow afternoon.'

'Don't be late,' Tamsin said. 'I might have to dock your wages – you've been taking a lot of time off sleuthing.'

'I have.' Morwenna smiled. 'And I was thinking I might put my pay up this summer.'

Tamsin hugged her. 'Thanks for looking after Elowen.'

'It's always a pleasure.'

Jane was standing by the door, her cap on. 'We'd better go. The pubs will be turning out. It's my busiest time.'

They walked downstairs together, into the tearoom, which was full of shadows of upturned chairs on tables. Tamsin was behind them with a set of jangling keys, ready to lock up. A figure shuffled along outside, pausing by the window. Morwenna watched as he fiddled with his clothes then stood absolutely still, staring down in concentration. Jane murmured, 'I don't believe it. It's Wee Willie Winkie.'

'Who?' Morwenna asked.

'The phantom Seal Bay tiddler. He comes out of The Smugglers and is taken short on the way home. He often stops for a tinkle. I usually pick him up and give him a ride home.'

Morwenna stepped outside just as a young man in an unzipped anorak, his hood up, rearranged his trousers and met her eyes, his own unfocused.

Jane was behind her. 'That isn't very nice.'

'It's the best I can do, Officer,' the drunken young man said, his face expressionless. He took a wobbly step forward.

'It's an offence, Tommy,' Jane said kindly. 'I have warned you.'

Tommy looked the worse for wear. 'Sorry.'

Morwenna noticed that he was wearing a skimpy T-shirt beneath the anorak. Had she been his mother, she'd have worried that he'd catch his death of cold. She could imagine Rosie Buvač wrapping him up warmly, kissing his cheek. She said, 'Are you all right?'

Tommy stared at her. 'I'm just off home.' He shook his head as if to dispel the drunkenness. 'I just had to go, Officer.'

Morwenna noticed something gleam around his neck, a gold chain. She took a step closer. 'That is a nice St Christopher, Tommy.'

'I bought it. My dad'll go mad…'

'Is it new?'

'I got it in the pub. It cost me a week's wages.' He held out a hand, steadying himself against the wall. 'I bought it to be safe at sea. I hate fishing. The waves make me sick…'

'It's a beautiful piece. Gold.' Morwenna touched the medallion to be sure. She knew where she'd last seen it. 'Who sold you this?'

'Jesse. He said girls like to see a man wearing gold.' Tommy swayed.

'Jesse sold you this?' Morwenna asked as Tommy pitched towards her.

'He was selling things in the pub. A watch, other stuff.' Tommy swayed to the side. 'His wallet was loaded.'

Morwenna held him up and turned to Jane. 'Can we take him home?'

'Of course.' Jane took over professionally. 'Come on, Tommy. I'm going to help you into the back of the car. Morwenna will sit with you – I'm running her home too. This is the Seal Bay Police taxi service tonight,' she joked as she eased him into the back seat. 'What's going on, Morwenna?'

'Let's drop him off at Lister Hill, then we need to go and find Jesse Miles in The Smugglers or at Carole's.' She met Jane's eyes. 'He just sold Tommy Daniel Kitto's St Christopher.'

24

Rosie Buvač was at the gate of forty-two, Lister Hill, looking anxious. She arrived at the police car before Tommy could open the door. She prised him out, her eyes wild, and hugged him. 'He hasn't done anything silly, has he, Officer?'

Jane lowered the window. 'No, don't worry.' She watched as Tommy leant against the car for support. 'He's just had a couple too many down the pub. He's been using the pavement as a urinal again. He needs to be careful – it's indecent exposure. I thought he could use a lift home.'

'Thank you,' Rosie said genuinely. 'I'm so sorry he's troubled you. He never used to be like this. It's since he started on the boats.'

'I hate the boats.' Tommy's voice was muffled.

'Milan will be furious. He got him that job on the trawler in good faith. And now it will be down to me to get you up in the morning, Tommy, and I've got to be at Mirador to do the cleaning for Pam Truscott first thing and... oh, this isn't fair. I have enough to worry about with everything else, and you're coming home the worse for wear every night.'

'Don't worry, Rosie,' Morwenna said kindly. Rosie looked sad. 'Kids go through stages. He'll sort himself out in time.'

'Tommy never used to drink. Now he's spending next week's pay in The Smugglers. Milan's inside with the kiddies – he's been helping Maya practise for her mermaid role with Spriggan. He'll be furious when he sees the state you're in, Tommy. He's asked you before to step up.'

'I don't want to be on the boats. I wanted to be an electrician. It wasn't my fault there were no jobs,' Tommy moaned and Rosie took his arm.

'I'll see if I can get him inside and in the shower before his dad notices.' She glanced at the front window. Milan was staring out, leaning on his arms. Five other faces, from big to small, leaned on the window ledge beside him, all wearing the same expression. They didn't look best pleased.

'Go easy on him,' Jane said. 'He's a good lad. I might be back round to see him tomorrow though – it seems that someone in the pub has been dealing in—'

'Not drugs? Oh, please don't say that.' Rosie was horrified.

'No, but we believe that someone has been selling on stolen goods. The gold St Christopher he's wearing, for instance.' Jane tried a placatory smile. 'Tommy's in no trouble. I just think he might have some important information for us. Get him to bed. He looks like he needs some sleep. I'll pop round in the next day or so for the necklace.'

Tommy was almost snoring, his head on his mother's shoulder. Rosie hugged him and helped him up the steps to the open door. 'Thanks, Officer. I'm very grateful.' She hauled her son though the doorway and closed the door behind him. Jane revved the engine.

'Right, Morwenna. I'll get you home now. Then I'll go to The Smugglers and see if Jesse Miles is still there. And if they are closed, I'll call on Carole at the B & B and pick him up.'

'Can't I come with you?' Morwenna asked, clambering in the front seat enthusiastically.

'No. I'm on my own from this point. Strictly police business,' Jane said firmly, and turned the car, driving down the hill quickly.

'The thing is,' Morwenna said, 'I know the St Christopher was Daniel's. And the watch. It's an expensive-looking one with a thick metal strap, silver and bronze. I saw them in his dressing room. The wallet has his initials on. It stands to reason – whoever took his things also took his phone. The threatening texts sent to my mum from Daniel's phone might have been sent by Jesse.'

'And therefore, if he's sending the threats, then he has good reason to do so. It could have been him who spiked the tonic.' Jane spoke her thoughts aloud. 'I'm bringing him in for questioning.'

'I know he has Daniel's wallet. I've seen him with it, withdrawing money at an ATM. He was telling everyone in The Smugglers that he knows Daniel's PIN number.' Morwenna thought for a moment. When she'd first met Jesse, he'd been overly friendly – by endearing himself to others, he might create opportunities for himself. But was he a killer? She needed to find out.

Jane drove towards the town centre and Morwenna tried again. 'Are you sure I can't come with you? I might be useful.'

'Absolutely not,' Jane said. 'You've helped enough. Let's get you home.'

Morwenna folded her arms, mock sulking; she was interested to hear what Jesse would say, what excuses he might make. She imagined him making up ridiculous reasons for having Daniel's jewellery. Then she saw a car pull out from a side road, turning in the opposite direction, accelerating away. It was a yellow Vauxhall VX220 Turbo. She pointed, yelling, 'That's the car that knocked me over. That's Daniel's car.'

'Morwenna – out,' Jane ordered.

'Let me stay—'

'You can't be in a police vehicle.'

'He's getting away,' Morwenna yelled. 'There's no time. Go, go!'

Jane swerved, turning round in the road, and immediately increased speed. Brakes screeched. Blue lights suddenly flashed around the car. Jane pulled the headlight switch towards her several times and pointed left with her hand, an instruction for the driver to stop as soon as possible. Morwenna heard her say, 'Pull over the vehicle, for God's sake,' as if the driver in front could hear.

The yellow car sped off into the darkness like a bullet; the driver had clearly noticed Jane's instruction and was accelerating away. The yellow car cornered at speed, the tail sliding outwards, out of control. Jane was on the radio, calling for assistance, stating her location, giving the make and number plate of the yellow car. Morwenna was impressed by her eyesight, her calm professionalism and her quick thinking.

They negotiated the roundabout out of Seal Bay. There were a few cars coming in the other direction, a single lorry, but not much else on the roads as the yellow car sped ahead into dark country lanes where trees leaned in on either side of the road like spectators. Jane handled the police car efficiently, edging closer to the tail of the yellow car, her siren screaming, then the Turbo pulled away again. Jane gritted her teeth. 'There's definitely some poke in that car. But he's not the best driver.'

'He?' Morwenna asked.

'Whoever... but I think the driver might just have been drinking.' Jane was concentrating on the chase. 'Hold tight.'

The road stretched ahead in a straight line and she put her foot down hard on the accelerator. The yellow car overtook a small Fiat that pulled to the side of the road dutifully to let Jane pass. Again, she approached the bumper of the yellow car and again, it roared away into the distance. They were approaching a village, a few lights still glowing in houses, the signs on the side of the road proclaiming a 30 mph limit. Morwenna leaned forwards, noticing that the speedometer read 60 mph. Still the yellow car hurtled forward, the rear moving erratically from side to side.

Another corner, then another, a squeal of brakes, and Jane was almost touching the bumper again, then the car increased speed, careering off along a dark country lane. Moments later, Jane was on its tail, edging forward, waving furiously for the driver to pull over. She frowned.

'He's out of control. The lanes are muddy here. He'll have to watch it. Me too.' Jane was talking to herself, steeling herself for a fast bend that followed.

She was right; the sports car was suddenly veering across the road, spinning round until it almost faced her, headlights on, crashing into a hedge, then bouncing back into the middle of the road, the front already dented. Jane braked furiously, stopping against the yellow car's bumper, and leaped out. She tugged open the passenger door, hauling out the terrified driver.

'Jesse Miles, you do not have to say anything, but it may harm your defence if you do not mention when questioned anything which you later rely on in court...'

Morwenna didn't hear the rest of the caution. As she huddled in the passenger seat with the window half open, two police cars came screaming to a halt, then officers running at full pelt. A burly policeman joined Jane, helping her to bundle Jesse into his car; two more began to put road signs up and flashing markers, ready to stop any traffic.

Jesse was shouting as the police officers manhandled him towards the vehicle. 'I didn't do anything wrong. It's my car. Daniel gave it to me. Before he died, he said it was mine if anything happened.' His face was desperate. 'I wouldn't do anything. I was just driving the car because it belongs to me.' Then, in one desperate last attempt, he called out, 'Spriggan's finished, anyway. It's being run by a pack of wolves. I wasn't staying with that lot to go down with a sinking ship.'

Jane slid into the driver's seat. 'Right. The crashed car is an obstruction and the road will be closed for an hour or two. My colleagues will take him to the nick. I'm dealing with you now.'

'Oh?' Morwenna wondered how much trouble she was in. She might have obstructed the police in the line of duty.

Jane was clearly angry. 'You shouldn't have been here. Seriously, I can't take passengers in car chases.'

'I was a witness,' Morwenna tried. 'I didn't want you to miss him.'

Jane gave her a warning look. 'You've compromised my position. It can't happen again. Now I'm running you home.' She sighed wearily. 'It's best we keep your part in this between ourselves.'

* * *

It was past midnight when Morwenna sat in bed, her mind too active to sleep. She wished someone would read something soothing to her, send her into blissful dreams, as she had with Elowen hours ago. The curtains were open, lifting on the night breeze. She gazed out across the harbour, staring at the inky water and the tiny glimmering lights of bobbing boats. Her thoughts moved to Ruan. She hoped he'd be asleep now. There would be an early start tomorrow for the fishermen, Ruan, poor Tommy Buvač, his anxious father. She pictured Ruan waking up in the morning, his skin warm, his hair tousled, moving towards the shower before she called him back to bed, reaching out, sharing kisses. Then in her imagination it was Kenzie enticing him back to her arms, weaving a spell as Morgan le Fay, and Morwenna pushed the image away. The vision of Ruan dissolved and Barnaby was there in his place, handsome and sophisticated in boxer shorts, hurrying back to the duvet, his expression eager.

It was all too confusing.

She turned out the lamp and snuggled down into the warmth. The bed always felt cold nowadays. She rolled over and replayed the car chase with Jane and the Vauxhall VX220 Turbo in her head. Jane had been right – she should not have been there, hurtling round bends in the passenger seat of a police car, the seat belt holding her fast as she jolted and swung this way and that. A nagging feeling of guilt told her that she mustn't take advantage of her friendship with Jane again. She focused on the moment Jesse was arrested; she saw the expression on his face. He'd seemed shocked, terrified even. Surely he'd been the driver of the car that knocked her from her bike on the way home? Her chin was still mottled, her elbow sore. She tried to remember the glimpse she'd had of the driver as the car had flashed past, and saw the black beanie, the figure huddled over the wheel. It could have been him.

She wouldn't worry about it now. Tomorrow she'd apologise to Jane, find out if Jesse had admitted dealing in stolen goods, if he'd been responsible for her bicycle accident. If he'd killed Daniel Kitto by tampering with his health tonic, it would be all over. She could consider the case closed.

Her eyelids were heavy. She was just drifting to the warm place where sleep tugged and dreams were formed from shadows. Her body was limp, relaxed. Then she heard the sound of a phone message.

She lifted the phone from the bedside table and blinked, bleary-eyed. It took a moment for her vision to clear as she stared at the bright screen. It was almost one o'clock. Who'd message her at this time of night?

It was Lamorna. She was sorry to message at this late hour but she'd just received another message from Daniel's phone. Morwenna waited. Then it pinged and she read it, taking in each word, her heartbeat thumping fast.

What will happen next is entirely due to your meddling. You can't say you weren't warned.

25

On Friday morning, Morwenna was working in the library, doing her best to stay busy and keep her mind off her worries. She messaged Jane to say sorry for being a pain and that she was desperate to discuss a text she received late last night. Jane replied quickly that she was about to go into the interview room with Rick Tremayne to question Jesse Miles and would get back to her as soon as possible. Morwenna concentrated on returning books from a trolley, placing them neatly in the right order on shelves. Louise was chattering, very excited about an event she was planning. Morwenna tried to listen, but her thoughts were jumbled. 'Who's coming to the library?'

'Pawly Yelland, the author. Don't you remember? On Monday. I've arranged for him to meet you and Donald to talk about Lady Elizabeth. He's fascinated by her story so I thought we'd ask him if we could have a meet-the-author session soon.'

'Like a séance?'

'No, not like a séance.' Louise put her hands on her hips. 'Are you with us this morning?'

'So people can talk to the ghost of Lizzie?'

'No, they'll talk to Pawly – *the author* – and ask him questions. I thought we could invite people from around Seal Bay, charge five pounds a ticket, get him to bring some books in here and sign them.'

'The books he's already written?'

'Of course I mean the books he's written. How could he sign books he hasn't written yet?' Louise was exasperated. 'I thought we'd make it a cheese and wine soirée, charge the punters, give him the chance to talk about his love of Seal Bay.'

'I thought he was from Redruth.'

'He is, but he loves Seal Bay. It would be a really nice evening and we'd have a fabulous time. What do you think? It could be the first meet-the-author of many.'

'Why not?' Morwenna put the book down and gave Louise her full attention. 'I think that's a lovely idea, Louise.' She gave a larger sigh than she meant to. 'We could all use some fun.'

'Are you still thinking about Daniel Kitto?' Louise asked sympathetically.

'Yes, I suppose so... and other things.' The text message had rattled her. Morwenna desperately wanted to talk to Jane.

'It must be Barnaby on your mind.' Louise made a concerned face. 'Haven't you heard from him?'

'Barnaby? No, it's not him...' Morwenna said. He'd texted her yesterday and she assumed she'd hear something from London before too long. She forced a smile and changed the subject. 'Is it cuppa time?'

'It is,' Louise agreed. 'Oh, and Musa's supposed to be bringing the Merlin book back today.' She glanced at the clock. 'I was hoping to get it to Truro library as soon as I could. Someone else is asking for it. King Arthur's very popular at the moment.'

'Why don't I go and get it from him?' Morwenna saw her chance. 'It's only ten minutes' ride from here to the marquee. I bet the actors are rehearsing. Although I can't imagine what they'll do without a technician.'

'Without a what?' Louise asked, but Morwenna was already on her way.

It was cold outside; the sea breeze filtered through the threads in Morwenna's jacket. She wished she still had the Cornish cardie. Seal Bay was grey as tinfoil, crinkled and cold. She glanced up. The sky hung low as if the clouds were loaded with rain; it would pour down at any minute. Morwenna pedalled faster, turning the corner, pelting towards the Spriggan theatre, her hair flying behind her.

Inside the marquee, there was activity in the performance space. Inga and Ben were talking, their heads close; Rupert was rehearsing his lines, making exaggerated gestures. Kenzie rushed over to greet Morwenna delightedly, as if she hadn't seen her for months. 'Morwenna! Do you want to stay for a cup of tea?'

'No, thanks. I've come to see Musa.'

Kenzie was eating chocolate, pushing a square into her mouth. 'My weakness – well, one of two.' She smiled knowingly and offered the bar. 'Want some?'

Morwenna thought briefly about how, not long ago, accepting a cup of tea or a square of chocolate had been a normal thing. Now she had no idea what might have been added. 'No, thanks – I need to get back to the library as soon as I can.'

Kenzie ignored her; she wanted to talk. 'Did you hear we have no technician? Jesse's been arrested.'

'Oh, has he?' Morwenna feigned ignorance.

'He stole Daniel's car last night and goodness knows what else. Perhaps they'll let him out in time, but if not we'll have to cancel the show.'

'Ah – that would be awful.' Morwenna waited for Kenzie to say more about Jesse, but her mind was elsewhere.

'I was saying to the guys – maybe Ruan could do it.'

'Do what?'

'Be our techie for two nights.'

'Ruan's out on the fishing boat.'

'But what about when he comes back?'

Morwenna frowned. 'How could he do it?'

'He's very capable.' Kenzie rolled her eyes suggestively. 'It's not that difficult to operate the lighting board – not once you get how the system is programmed. And there are a few pyrotechnics. I wondered if he'd come down after work. I could teach him how.'

'He might.' Morwenna had no idea if Ruan would want to be a theatre technician. He could change a plug, wire a light fitting. It sounded a responsible position, and quite specialised. 'Don't you need someone long term?'

Kenzie made a dreamy expression. 'Oh, that would be perfect. He could give up being a fisherman and join Spriggan, come with the four of us full-time on the road.'

'Four?' Morwenna asked. 'You, Rupert, Inga, Ben, Musa – that's five.'

'Oh, Musa will be leaving soon – I think it's on the cards. The others were saying – he's not well. It's such a shame.'

'Not well?'

'He's struggling to make performances. Last night he was sick before he came on stage. He can't stand the rigour of performing every night.'

'Where is he now?'

'Back at Carole's B & B. We're hoping he'll be better for tonight. If not, Inga will have to play Merlin too. Unless…' Kenzie smiled mischievously at the thought. 'Unless Ruan could do it?'

'I know he can turn his hand to most things but—' Morwenna stopped. A thought had come to her. 'You say you need a technician?'

'Desperately.'

'How long would it take three bright men to learn to do the job, all the lights, the effects, for the show?'

'As long as one bright woman?' Kenzie joked.

'I think I have an answer. If I bring three talented men here at... half four? The boat should be back by then. Can they learn to be technicians before the curtain goes up?'

'It's difficult but not impossible,' Kenzie said.

'Leave it with me.' Morwenna flourished an arm. 'The show must go on. Meanwhile, let me pay Musa a visit. I – need his library book.'

'You're a wizard, Morwenna,' Kenzie said.

'I'll see you later – complete with techie volunteers...'

'You're a lifesaver.' Kenzie held out the chocolate. 'Are you sure you won't have some?'

'Ask me when the show's over,' Morwenna called over her shoulder as she rushed to where the bike had been locked by the sea wall.

* * *

The Blue Dolphin Guest House was a pretty white Georgian terraced house with blue window shutters and a sign of a leaping dolphin in navy and aqua. There were vacancies, according to a board in the ground-floor window. Morwenna rapped at the knocker and Carole appeared at the door, her sleeves rolled up, looking exhausted. 'Morwenna?' She was surprised. 'Is everything all right?'

'It's fine.' Morwenna offered her widest smile. 'I'm here on a mission of mercy. I've come to see Musa. He has a library book that we need back today, and he's not well, poor lad.'

'I heard him, when I passed, doing up the rooms this morning. He was, you know...' Carole lowered her voice '...vomiting.'

Morwenna was concerned. 'Can I just pop in for the book?'

'Of course.' Carole looked delighted to have company. 'Have you got time to stay for a cup of tea? Vic went out early this morning. He's doing a great trade in new cars at the moment and his Girl Friday is achieving amazing results, apparently.'

'Oh?' Morwenna was interested.

'Do you know Gill Bennett?'

'A little,' Morwenna said tentatively.

'Well, she's blossoming. Her hair has turned a lighter shade and she's waltzing about in snazzy suits and fawning over the customers to such an extent that they are buying cars like never before. Can you believe it? She used to be so mousy.'

'I bet Vic's pleased that sales are booming – he should give her a bonus.'

'Oh, he will.' Carole looked despondent for a moment. 'You don't think she has the hots for him? I mean – they aren't having an affair, are they?'

'I shouldn't worry, Carole – she's just a great receptionist and a fabulous saleswoman. Maybe she's discovered that she has acting in her blood.'

'Acting?' Carole was mystified. 'Well, I'll get the kettle on. There will be a nice mug of tea and a slice of cake when you come down.'

'Proper job,' Morwenna said. It would be nice to indulge without fear of poisoning. She was about to climb the stairs to the upstairs rooms when a thought occurred to her. 'How come you have vacancies?'

Carole was eager to share information. 'Daniel Kitto's not going to use his room again, is he? And Jesse Miles didn't come back last night. The police came for a snoop and his room is completely empty, so obviously the rumours about him having taken off somewhere are true. And I'm worried about Musa – he doesn't look at all well, poor lamb. He should see a doctor.'

'Right.' Morwenna thought about Carole's words as she climbed the stairs two at a time. She called back, 'What's his room number?'

'Five. Top floor.'

'Thanks, Carole.' She hurried up to the second flight, arriving at a door with a brass number five. She knocked gently and a weak voice answered, 'Yes?'

'It's me, Morwenna Mutton. I've come to collect your library book.'

There was a faint groan and a pause. Then the door opened and Musa stood in his boxer shorts and a creased T-shirt. His forehead was damp with perspiration; his shirt was drenched. There was a little pool of sweat in the small dip below his Adam's apple. He looked dreadful. Morwenna couldn't help the words that came out of her mouth.

'Goodness, you aren't well.'

'I know. I've been feeling a bit off for a few days. It's getting worse.' Musa trudged into his room and flopped down on the bed, leaning forward as if he was dizzy. Morwenna sat beside him. He made a low sound, like an animal in pain. 'I'm not sure I'll make the show tonight. I have serious sickness and – you know – diarrhoea.' He panted lightly. 'I'm sorry – I'll get your book in a minute.'

'Musa – have you been taking that health tonic?'

'Why do you ask?' He raised his head, troubled. 'I'd been a bit tired. Ben gave me a bottle. He swears by it.'

'When did you start taking it?'

'Tuesday evening.'

'That's interesting. How do you get on with the rest of the cast?'

'They seem all right. We work well on stage, that's the important thing.' Musa frowned. 'Where's this going?'

'Last question.' Morwenna took a breath. 'Do you know the symptoms of arsenic poisoning?'

'Vomiting, abdominal pain and diarrhoea.' Musa shook his

head as if clearing his vision. 'Then numbness and tingling, muscle cramping and death.' He turned to her slowly; the penny had dropped. 'Do you think…?'

'Daniel's tonic was laced with arsenic. You should stop taking it – it's slow poison, isn't it?'

'Why would Ben want me dead?'

'Ben? Or another one of the cast? You tell me.'

Musa rubbed his eyes. There were tears there. 'We had a meeting. Someone said we ought to lose one member. Rupert or somebody else joked that it should be me and suddenly the whole thing was serious and I was asked to go when we finished the run of the play. I lost my rag a bit. I said it wasn't right to chuck me out and I'd fight to stay in the company.'

'I think you should go to the doctor's.'

'I'll get a chelating agent, eat lots of fibre,' Musa said. 'I'll feel better in a few days – arsenic comes out through urine.' His hand shook. 'Are you saying someone is trying to kill me? That they killed Daniel?'

'I think so.'

'But that's unbelievable.'

'Someone is using arsenic to poison people, but I don't know exactly why. Can you think of any reason?' Morwenna took his hand to steady it.

'No – other than that people hated Daniel. Rupert, Kenzie – and Jesse, especially. But why give it to me? It makes no sense…'

'Get some rest. Give the hospital a call or try 111,' Morwenna said. 'And do you want to give me the bottle? I'll pass it on to my friend Jane – she's a police officer and she'll be very keen for Forensics to take a look.'

'I will…' Musa met her gaze with serious eyes. 'Thank you.' He reached for a bottle with no label beneath his pillow and pushed it into her hand.

She was tempted to ruffle his hair; he looked so young and vulnerable. 'Get well.'

He pointed to the bedside cabinet. 'The book's there – *Poisons and Spells in Merlin's Realm*.' He gave a faint smile. 'Ironic, isn't it, Merlin getting poisoned? And I come from a family of pharmacists. It's so awful it could be funny.'

'Rest,' Morwenna said again. 'I suppose you won't be able to make tonight's show...'

'I'll get some medication. Whatever it takes...' He offered her a grim look. 'I'm determined I will. I'm not giving up – are you coming along?'

'I'm having tea with my mum at Tregenna Gardens. Otherwise, I'd be there. You rest. And get well soon.'

'I will. Now I know what the problem is, I'll sort it...' Musa said.

Morwenna smiled and closed the door quietly. She felt sorry for him. But there was more investigating to do. And there was a cup of tea and a slice of cake downstairs with her name on it...

26

At lunchtime, Morwenna stood outside Autumn Wind residential home, gripping the handlebars of her bicycle, watching the traffic thunder by on the busy road. Several cars whizzed past, then a Korrik Clay lorry, and for a moment she imagined Anna Carlyon alone in the big house on the headland. The police station was quiet, then the main door opened and Jane came out, sprinting smartly across the road. Morwenna moved through the large gates into the grounds of Autumn Wind, waiting behind a tall oak, and Jane joined her. Morwenna thought of two naughty schoolgirls going for a furtive ciggie at breaktime. She'd never done that as a teenager, but hiding secretly from the keen eyes of Rick Tremayne gave her a delicious feeling.

Jane spoke her thoughts aloud. 'It's best Rick doesn't see us.'

'It is.'

'So, what have you got for me?'

'Musa's been taking Ben's tonic. He's sick.' Morwenna plunged a hand into her bag and held out the bottle. 'Here.'

'I'll get it looked at,' Jane said grimly. 'Do you think it might have been Jesse who tampered with it?'

'It could be,' Morwenna said. 'Musa said Spriggan want him out. There's some closing of ranks going on.'

'We went to The Blue Dolphin this morning. Jesse Miles' room was completely empty. His car was full of stuff. He even had a grey silk suit.'

'Daniel's.'

'And hundreds of pounds in a wallet marked DK. I shouldn't tell you this officially, but you know already.'

'Of course. He was doing a runner. But why?'

'He said the others were getting wise to his activities, selling Daniel's personal things, using his bank cards. Besides, he wanted that car badly, so stealing it and leaving the cast in the lurch was his way of sticking two fingers up.'

'What about the other things? Did he kill Daniel and knock me down?'

'I'm working up to that. We're so busy in there right now. Rick is keen to charge him for theft but I want to find out if there's more. He's weakening under questioning, I'm sure of it.'

'Ah,' Morwenna said.

Jane looked at her suspiciously. 'Ah – what?'

'I received this last night – from Daniel's phone.'

Morwenna handed Jane the phone and she frowned as she read the message. 'There was no phone on Jesse Miles when we searched his things, other than his own.'

'I thought as much. So who sent me this, Jane?'

'We need to find out.' Jane looked anxious. 'It's a serious threat.'

'Definitely,' Morwenna agreed. 'So can we rule Jesse out?'

'Possibly. There's something else that's bothering me.'

'Oh?'

'The photo you sent me. The man in the restaurant with Anna.'

'You know who he is?'

'I haven't had five minutes to think about it. I've just been so busy.' Jane's eyes widened. 'But I know I've seen him somewhere. I can hear his voice in my head. And I have a feeling – I don't know – that I bumped into him years ago. I need to go through a few files when I get a minute, which won't be this afternoon, thanks to Jesse.'

Morwenna chewed her lip. 'So the man in the photo might be important.'

'He might.' Jane's face was serious. 'But this is a police matter now. Once the tonic is checked, there may be a murder enquiry, as well as attempted murder. And there will probably have to be a post-mortem on Daniel Kitto.'

'Right. And is Jesse still a suspect for his murder?'

'We aren't talking murder, not yet. He's sold a few of Daniel's possessions, stolen his car – you know that much. Apparently, he was off to Penzance. He has relatives there.'

'But he's not the killer, is he?'

'I can't discuss it. I have to ask you, Morwenna, to leave this to the police now.'

'And what about the threat sent from Daniel's phone?'

'We'll take it seriously. I can send someone round to check on you later if you like. You remember PC Jim Hobbs? I'll get him to make some inquiries. He'll interview the Spriggan actors if we find arsenic.'

'Don't arouse suspicion,' Morwenna said.

'Jim will certainly be talking to Ben D'Arcy, taking his tonic as evidence. If we're suspicious, they won't be allowed to move on to Padstow.'

'Ah,' Morwenna said. 'Good.'

'So, your work is done,' Jane told Morwenna firmly.

'Is that official?' Morwenna raised an eyebrow.

'It is. No more interfering. Leave it entirely to us now.'

'Then why are we standing here talking about it behind a tree, all cloak and dagger, so Rick won't see us?'

'You have a point,' Jane said with a smile. 'I'll see you tomorrow – strictly for a swim.'

'Make that a swim and a chat,' Morwenna said enigmatically. She pushed her bike towards the gate. 'I'd better be off. I have a shift in the tearoom and I'm late.'

* * *

At four o'clock, as Morwenna was wiping tables in the Proper Ansom Tearoom, the doorbell chimed and Ruan came in, followed by Milan and Tommy Buvač. They were wearing yellow oilskins. Ruan sat down at the clean table, the Buvačs copied him, and Morwenna called, 'Three teas?'

'Proper job.' Ruan leaned on his arm, tired. 'It was a long day on the trawlers. Non-stop, but plenty of fish today, and that's the main thing.'

'It was full-on.' Tommy hung his head as if he was tired or sick or both.

Morwenna placed mugs of tea and slices of cake in front of the fishermen and said, 'Here. These are on the house.'

'Thanking 'ee,' Milan said in his beautiful Cornish-Bosnian accent as he tucked into Victoria sponge. The slice looked small in his large paw. Tommy poked his cake with a knife, looking decidedly the worse for wear.

'So, why did you ask us to come straight here?' Ruan asked. 'Your text was a bit vague. "Come to the tearoom and bring Milan and Tommy – I need you all on a mission of mercy." What mission's this, then?'

'One I think you'll be good at...' Morwenna looked over her shoulder. Tamsin was busy placing cream teas in front of six visitors with warm Midlands accents. She'd be all right on her own for a few minutes. Lamorna would be in with Elowen soon. She'd have collected her from the school gate and they often stopped for ice creams on Friday afternoons – any afternoon, in fact, when Elowen could wheedle a treat from her great grandmother. Morwenna had enough time to put her plan into action. She decided she'd start small, build to the big request.

'So, what are you guys doing tonight?'

'Why do you ask? Are you looking for a date?' Milan guffawed.

'I hope not,' Tommy grunted moodily.

'What do you need?' Ruan asked. 'I'm not doing anything.'

'I'm not allowed out, apparently.' Tommy sniffed. 'Although I'm eighteen. I can do as I like.'

Morwenna met his eyes. 'Did you know Jesse Miles has been arrested?'

'No...' Tommy looked guilty.

'I heard. Damien texted me. Jesse's been selling stolen goods and then he made a getaway in Daniel's car,' Ruan said.

'Ah.' Tommy's fingers moved to the St Christopher around his neck.

'The police will want the chain later,' Morwenna said quietly.

'I paid a week's wages for it...' Tommy groaned.

'Here's a chance to earn more money perhaps?' Morwenna said. 'Spriggan need a technician. Jesse won't be available now.'

Milan frowned. 'What is that to do with us?'

'Apparently, it's simply a matter of running the program on the lighting board, changing a few lights as the play goes on, some music, setting off some pyrotechnics. Not difficult for someone who's savvy. I thought you were interested in these things, Tommy.'

'Eh?' Tommy was perplexed.

Ruan knew how Morwenna's mind worked too well. 'So, Tommy, if your dad and I help you with it tonight, just to get used to all the switches and the sequence of events, maybe you'd be able to do the whole play by yourself for the last night?'

'I can help with that,' Milan rumbled. 'Maya's the mermaid tonight. We can make it a family thing, eh, Tom?' He nudged his son. 'You'll have a chance to show off your land legs without taking them down the pub.'

'So I'll be able to work with the electrics?' Tommy brightened. 'Do you think they'll give me a job?'

Morwenna shook her head. 'We don't know what will happen to Jesse. But it's an opportunity, Tommy. Spriggan can't go on without a technician. I mentioned this afternoon that you might be the man for the gig. And here's your chance. It must be worth a shot.'

'Wow – thanks,' Tommy breathed.

'Will you be there?' Milan asked, his eyes filled with gratitude.

'I'm having dinner with Mum. I'll be at the show tomorrow – you'll be a dab hand by then.'

'You're a star, Morwenna,' Ruan said proudly.

Morwenna said, 'Tommy will be a star too, if he pulls this one off. Come on, boys – drink up and get yourselves down the marquee. I'll buy you all fish and chips. You've only a few hours before the curtain goes up.'

* * *

At six o'clock, Morwenna was sitting on the squashy sofa in her living room, Brenda stretched out full length on her knee. She was looking at the photos on her phone. She ought to leave for Tregenna Gardens soon – she'd promised to be there by half past six. Lamorna would be in the kitchen already, watching the clock, and Morwenna didn't want to be late. But Brenda was settling down, marking time with her paws, pulling at threads on Morwenna's leggings, purring. Morwenna said, 'You don't want me to go out, do you, Bren?'

The cat turned moon eyes on her, as if agreeing. Brenda was

comfortable – she wanted Morwenna to stay where she was. Morwenna went back to checking the photos. She glanced at the fabulous kitchen in Knave-Go-By, the utility room with the lemon tree in a plant pot, the pristine living room. What was she looking for? The place was incredibly tidy – there would be no clues. She went back to the photos in the living room and tried to expand them. She focused on a wedding photo, Anna and Will Carlyon on their special day. There were several other photos, groups of people around the happy couple. Morwenna scratched her head – she couldn't see any of the figures clearly. It was a blur. She went back to the kitchen. There was a beautiful china teapot on a tray, fine porcelain teacups. Of course, Korrik Clay. She zoomed in; there was something next to the tray, but she couldn't make it out. A sugar bowl, perhaps? A jug?

She eased herself back in the sofa. Brenda was like a lead weight now, refusing to move. Morwenna would search Google and see what she could find. She typed in the name Anna Carlyon and lots of photos came up: the one of her wearing a hard hat, receiving an industry award; other articles about her sponsorship of The Spriggan Travelling Theatre Company. There was a newspaper article about Anna and Daniel Kitto. Morwenna read it carefully. It gave details of the new sponsorship, how Anna was delighted to support her old friend, Daniel Kitto, in his travelling company.

Old friend. So they went back a long way.

Morwenna tried to recall her ex-husband's name. Driscoll. She typed in Anna Driscoll. A young face came up, a girl with red hair, someone's Facebook page. The wrong Anna Driscoll. She searched further – what did she say her husband was called? Xander. She searched Xander Driscoll. An article followed. The entrepreneur and impresario, Alexander Driscoll, had attended an opening of *Macbeth* in London eight years ago. The picture showed him with his wife, Anna, impeccable in a smart suit, her hair longer, her face impassive. Morwenna thought she didn't look happy.

She tried again, typing Alexander Driscoll, death, and his obituary flipped onto the screen. Morwenna studied it. He'd died of a heart attack. He was fifty-six. Morwenna scrutinised the dates – it was two years before Anna would have married Will Carlyon.

Morwenna was puzzled. Heart attacks didn't make Anna a killer, they made her unlucky with husbands. She wondered briefly how much of Xander Driscoll's money Anna had inherited. And Xander was her second husband. Morwenna couldn't help wondering who the first one was and what end he came to.

Brenda was asleep. Morwenna glanced at the clock. She'd have to leave soon. She went back to Xander and Anna at the opening night of *Macbeth*. Morwenna researched the theatre, the date, and the cast list came up. She stared hard. Macbeth was played by Daniel Kitto. They clearly had a connection. Morwenna looked at the other actors' names, Lady Macbeth, King Duncan, Banquo, the witches – she'd never heard of any of them. She stopped at that point – the print was small and it was making her eyes ache. She glanced at the clock again.

'You'd better move, Bren. I have to get going.' Morwenna stroked Brenda's ears and the cat opened one lazy eye. 'I ought to have another look at those photos in Anna's house. I can't see the detail.'

Brenda opened both eyes, made a guttural sound of disgust and jumped on the table. 'You can't have biscuits, Bren. You've already had two handfuls today.'

Brenda rubbed her head against Morwenna's laptop, as she often did. Then she sat on it and the screen went blank.

'Oh, you've turned it off, you naughty little...' Morwenna stopped. A huge grin spread on her face. 'Brenda, you beauty. You've given me an idea. Of course. I'll take the laptop up to mum's and upload the pictures. Then I can zoom in,' she said. 'I'd have thought of that immediately if I'd been Tam's age.' She picked Brenda up, nuzzling the furry face. 'Right, I suppose you've been helpful. I'd better give you a treat or two.'

And with that, Brenda approached the yellow box of biscuits and swiped it over with her paw. She looked pleased with herself. In fact, Morwenna was sure she was smiling.

27

Lamorna was desperate for someone to talk to, and Morwenna did her best to concentrate on the conversation as her mother chattered nineteen to the dozen and ladled pasta into bowls. But her mind was on the evening's performance of the play; she wondered how Tommy Buvač was getting on, if Ruan and Milan had been able to teach him the ropes. It was a big deal – if you made a mistake, the whole audience might be plunged into blackout or an explosion might happen too early, during a sensitive, romantic moment. She hoped Musa was feeling better too. She checked her phone for texts, but Ruan was probably busy backstage. Jane hadn't messaged either. Morwenna wasn't surprised: Jane had said firmly that the inquiries were police business now. She'd keep her distance until the sea swim tomorrow.

'...so, I thought I'd wear yellow as that was his favourite and it's a colour of celebration, isn't it?' Lamorna paced the bowls on the table.

'Yellow?'

'For the funeral?'

'Daniel's?'

'Who else?' Lamorna muttered. 'I still think about what he and I could have had. We'd have been company for each other. I mean, I'm lucky to have you and Tam and Elowen – you keep me young – but really, I don't have much else.'

'Mum.' Morwenna reached across the table and grasped her mother's hand. 'I'm sorry, I'm neglecting you.'

'Old age is a lonely time. Old people are just surplus to requirements and waiting for the end. No one really wants to spend time with us because our lives are all in the past.'

Morwenna tried a positive spin. 'What about all the mums at the school gates you talk to? They love to hear your stories about all the boyfriends you've had.'

'*Had* being the operative word, maid.' Lamorna was sad. 'Of course I can tell them about Morrie Edwards, who asked me to marry him eight times, and Harry Woon, who could snog for England, and Freddie Quick, your dad, all the promises and the charm of an alley cat on heat, here today then gone tomorrow.' Lamorna picked up her fork and frowned at the pasta. Tears glinted in her eyes again. 'They're all gone, all passed away. In a bygone era that's forgotten. Daniel's gone too. And that's all that's waiting for me now. My best days are over.' Her voice cracked. 'After Daniel's funeral, the next one will be mine.'

'Don't say that.' Morwenna felt tears prick her eyes. 'You always tell me, we Mutton maids have a strong constitution.'

'It won't keep me going for ever,' Lamorna said sadly. 'And since Daniel died, it's been hard falling asleep at nights. My hip aches something wicked. Then I look at the shadows in the corner and wonder if the grim reaper is there, waiting.'

'Come and stay with me for a bit.'

'I've only got to come back here again, on my own.'

Morwenna gave a deep sigh. 'You could move in and stay, sell this place.'

'If I came to you to live, I'd be wondering every day if I was in the way.'

'You'd never be in the way.'

'You should be back living with Ruan.'

'That boat has sailed.'

'Has it?' Lamorna's eyes glinted. 'Are you taking up with the other one, then? Barnaby?'

Morwenna shook her head. 'I've no idea – it's early days. I'm not sure if we have much in common.'

'I'm fond of Ruan. And he's a good dad to Tam, a good grandad.'

'He is.'

'You don't want to get to my age and be as lonely as I am.' Lamorna forked a piece of pasta and studied it. 'I'm not a good role model. I never have been.'

'You're the best,' Morwenna said, tucking into her food, hoping her mother would copy. 'And we're off to see the play tomorrow. I'm looking forward to it. It should be good. Elowen's final night of being the mermaid.'

'I wouldn't miss it.' Lamorna still hadn't started to eat. 'Who did you say you've got me sitting next to?'

'Gill Bennett, the daughter of the woman in the photograph I took from Daniel's dressing room.'

'She was his girlfriend, Diane Bennett, the one in the photo?'

'She was.' Morwenna wondered if she should tell her mother that Gill was Daniel's daughter. She'd save it for now. Instead, she said, 'I thought you and Gill might have a few things to talk about, some memories to share.'

'I bet she was the one he left me for. Or there might have been a few in between. Daniel was always one for the ladies. I wish I'd known Diane Bennett though,' Lamorna said sadly. 'She died too soon. And you said she was being looked after in Autumn Wind? I don't want to end my days up there.'

'You won't,' Morwenna said determinedly. 'Eat up. This is delicious.' She watched Lamorna take a bite and she continued, 'I'm still looking for the person who poisoned Daniel. I have a few leads. I brought my laptop. After we've eaten, will you give me a hand to look at what I've found? We might solve this one together – for Daniel.'

'I'd like that, yes.' Lamorna took a breath, making a huge effort to perk up. 'When we've finished this pasta, I've got some butterscotch blancmange for afters. I put a glacé cherry on top too. I love a bit of blancmange. It goes down easily and doesn't upset my gut.' Lamorna dug into her pasta. 'Oh, it's so nice having you over for dinner, maid. You cheer me up no end.'

* * *

It was well past nine o'clock. Lamorna had polished off two bowls of butterscotch blancmange and finished Morwenna's. They sat at the table, heads close. Morwenna had uploaded the photos from her phone. Lamorna was wearing a pair of purple reading glasses, squinting at the screen.

'How did you get those pictures up?'

'More luck than judgement,' Morwenna said as she wriggled the mouse. Another row of thumbnail pictures came up on the screen. Morwenna clicked on a photograph of the living room at Knave-Go-By and Lamorna gasped.

'Oh, that's bleddy 'ansom. Look at the leather sofa. I'd love one like that,' she said.

'You should see the kitchen.' Morwenna opened another picture and Lamorna gasped.

'It's like Buckingham Palace. Look at that island. You could park a bus on it.'

'It's a huge house for one person,' Morwenna agreed.

'Oh, but it's beautiful.' Lamorna was staring at the utility room. 'Even the lemon plant looks expensive. All my plants are dwindling weeds. I can't grow anything without killing it.'

'Let's go back and look at her living room.' Morwenna moved the mouse. 'Here, see these photos of Anna and Will's wedding – there's a group one here...' She zoomed in closely, leaning forwards to stare at the guests grouped around the couple in the middle.

Lamorna pointed. 'That's Daniel, at the back, in the cream suit. I'm sure it is.'

'It's quite fuzzy.'

'I'd know the shape of his head anywhere. And those shoulders,' Lamorna said excitedly. 'He was at her wedding.'

'They go back a long way.'

'They must do.'

Morwenna was staring at another of the guests, a person in pale blue in the front row. 'Who's that?'

Lamorna shook her head. 'No idea. Is it male or female?'

Morwenna thought the figure looked familiar. She couldn't get in any closer. Then an idea occurred to her. 'Hang on. I need to check something.' She stared at the screen. 'How can I find out if Xander Driscoll or Anna sponsored Daniel before Spriggan?' She searched for the old production of *Macbeth* again, scrolling down through the cast list, photos of the lead actors, to the bottom of the page. There were adverts for other shows: *Cats*, *Oliver!*, a play by Tennessee Williams. Nothing about sponsors or owners. She scrolled back up – 'the production will be directed by Polly Bell' – and something caught her eye. She paused. Fleance will be played at different performances by members of the RADA Theatre Lab: Rupert Bradley, Ingrid Brownlow, Chantelle Clarke, Ben D'Arcy, and Patrick Yates.

'Oh... that's interesting.' Morwenna turned to Lamorna, her face shining. 'So, they've all known each other a while.'

'Who have?'

'The Spriggan trio, Ben, Inga and Rupert – if Ingrid Brownlow is Inga Ström. She might not be, but Ingrid isn't a common name. I wonder if any of them were at Anna's wedding.'

Morwenna went back to the wedding photo, zooming in on all the fuzzy shapes, staring hard. 'That one in the dark suit could be Ben – who knows? And there's an auburn-haired woman – that could be Inga. She wouldn't have changed much.'

'Perhaps they are all friends.'

Morwenna stared hard at the photo. 'The man with the sharp grey suit – that could be the person Anna was dining with at the restaurant.'

Lamorna said, 'Perhaps he's her toy boy, and she wants to keep it secret?'

'I'm desperate to find a connection, Mum.' Morwenna had to concede that her mother could be right. 'Something that links Anna to the cast and to Daniel's death.'

'It could have been someone you haven't even thought of yet.'

'It might have been one of the Spriggan actors working by themselves. Or perhaps all of them are working together. How can I find out? Come on, photos – tell me something useful.'

'The police will solve it,' Lamorna soothed.

'They might. But the actors move out on Monday. What about the yellow sports car? Who was driving it the night I was knocked off? The driver had a black beanie on, I couldn't see…'

Lamorna was more interested in Anna's house. 'Show me that kitchen again. It's lush. Were you really there, taking photos?'

'I shouldn't have been, but I was sure I'd find something.' Morwenna clicked on the screen and the huge kitchen came to life. She zoomed in. 'Look at the lovely plates and dishes in the cupboards. And the teapot and china mugs on that tray. Hang on a moment. What's that on the counter – letters? Let me enlarge it a bit more. What's this?' She leaned forward, blinking.

'It's a brown envelope,' Lamorna said. Her sight in the purple glasses was better than Morwenna's. 'There's something written on it – it says "Mum"... It must be something from one of her children. There's something else. Is that an A and an S?'

'Initials? Anna... Something?' Morwenna asked.

Lamorna gazed at the clock. 'We've been at this for an hour and a half, more. I'm bushed. Do you want a cuppa?'

'A quick one, then I'll get off,' Morwenna said.

Lamorna's phone pinged and a message came through.

'It's from Daniel's phone again.' Lamorna was suddenly tense, her face pale.

'What does it say?'

'"You were warned"...' Lamorna began. 'What does that mean?'

There was a loud crash, and Morwenna leaped up in alarm as a brick smashed through the window onto the living room carpet. She screamed, high-pitched panic, and then froze. Morwenna backed away, tugging her mother to her feet as a bottle flew through the gap, ablaze. It landed on a tub chair, against a cushion. Morwenna stared, thinking fast; there was liquid in there, a rag. The bottle was tipped on its side, the rag soaking up the petrol, flames leaping, touching the cushion. Morwenna smelled singeing material and knew she had little time to act – if the bottle exploded, there would be an almighty fire and a shower of glass. She dragged her trembling mother to the safety of the kitchen, grabbed the fire blanket from one side of the cooker and tugged it down. Then she was back in the living room, holding the blanket in front of her face, throwing it over the fire on the chair, patting the surface to starve the air and extinguish the flames. She stood back panting, legs shaking, her pulse racing. The chair was charred, the material scorched, and there was a thick smell of petrol in the air.

Morwenna's hand shook as she texted Jane.

We've been attacked. Can you come to Tregenna Gardens?

Lamorna was behind her, wild-eyed. 'It all happened so quickly.' She placed a hand over her heart. 'It's a good job you got me that fire blanket.'

Morwenna approached the window and leaned forwards, looking through. Outside everything was dark; a few lights glimmered from windows. There were no cars; no one outside as far as she could see.

'I have to sit down – I'm all shaky.' Lamorna looked round nervously and moved to the table, sinking onto a chair. 'Do you think I'll be safe here? There won't be any more bricks and bottles, will there? We've used up the fire blanket.'

'Jane will be here any moment. She'll know what to do,' Morwenna said, then she almost jumped out of her skin as someone knocked hard at the door. She rushed to open it, her heart in her mouth, half believing the person who threw the bottle might be there with another.

Ruan was standing outside in the darkness. 'I thought I'd come up and report on how the show went with the new trainee technicians,' he began, then he took in Morwenna's terrified expression. 'What's happened?'

'You'd better come in,' Morwenna said quietly. 'We've just had an arson attack.'

28

Morwenna and Lamorna looked at each other in bewilderment, clutching mugs of tea to calm their nerves. Jane stood opposite in uniform, PC Jim Hobbs at her side. Ruan was boarding up the window. He'd removed the burned tub chair, stowing it in the back of his van. He'd take it to the tip tomorrow unless Jane wanted it. The other evidence, the bottle of petrol, was wrapped inside the fire blanket for her to take away for Forensics.

'Well, it clearly wasn't Jesse Miles,' Jane said grimly. 'He's in custody. We're charging him with theft and driving under the influence, but I don't think he can be held responsible for this attack.'

'We'll find fingerprints hopefully. And we'll examine CCTV footage.' PC Jim glanced at Lamorna. 'It might be wise for you to stay with family for a few days.' He turned to Ruan. 'You say you were at the Spriggan performance this evening. Did you notice anything suspicious?'

'More to the point, were all the cast there when you left?' Morwenna asked. 'Did anyone have time to come up here and throw the brick and the bottle?'

Ruan scratched his head. 'I think Rupert and Ben went straight to the pub. Inga was backstage for a while, then she went on to the guest house. Kenzie was asking everyone to meet her down The Smugglers, and Musa went straight back to Carole's. He wasn't feeling great, although he performed well.'

'Poor Musa – he's not completely better, then. So – who had time to come up here?' Morwenna was puzzled. 'If you were to walk from the marquee, it would take fifteen minutes; none of the actors has a car. Although Daniel's sports car is still parked outside the marquee.'

Ruan said, 'I drove Tommy and Milan home in the van first. That would have been at about quarter past ten. It's quarter to twelve now, and I arrived here just before eleven. Someone would have had time to come up here and get away again.'

'Did you see anyone driving off, Ruan?' Jane asked.

'I didn't see anyone.'

'Well, someone has it in for you, Morwenna,' Jane said grimly. 'Make sure you stay out of this now. I mean it.'

'But we have to find them before they do anything else,' Morwenna replied.

'No,' Jane said firmly. 'This is a police matter.'

Ruan offered, 'Can I stay round tonight and keep an eye on you and Lamorna?'

Lamorna said, 'Oh yes, Ruan – I'd feel so much better if you were there. I'm so glad you got me the fire blanket. I don't know where I'd be without it. Well, I do – I'd be burned to a crisp.'

'Can you pop round for breakfast instead?' Morwenna thought that was a compromise. 'You can check on us then, if you have to. I mean – thanks, Ruan. Yes, let's have breakfast.'

Jim Hobbs agreed with Lamorna. 'It's a good job you had the presence of mind to put the fire out, Morwenna.'

Ruan met her eyes. 'You took a risk there, maid. The whole room could have gone up in flames.'

'Well, at least I saved the fire brigade a visit,' Morwenna said. 'Jane, do you mind if we get off home? I'm really tired. And we're still swimming tomorrow afternoon, aren't we?'

'I'll see you then.' Jane glanced round the room as if to check that everything seemed secure. 'But promise me, absolutely no more sleuthing.'

'As if I would.' Morwenna's eyes gleamed. 'It's all far too dangerous...'

* * *

The next morning, Morwenna woke to someone patting her face. Brenda stuck out a gentle paw and urged her to wake up. She shook herself, bleary-eyed, tugged on a dressing gown and wandered downstairs. Lamorna was already in the kitchen, bustling, boiling a kettle. She scattered a handful of cat biscuits in a bowl and Brenda shovelled them up.

'I couldn't sleep. I'm making breakfast. Ruan will be over in ten minutes.'

Morwenna gave a tired smile. Her hair was unbrushed, her dressing gown crumpled: Ruan had seen it all before. She settled herself at the table as her mother plonked a mug of tea in front of her.

'Here – get this down you.'

'Thanks, Mum.'

'I've been wondering – how did the person who attacked my home know you'd be there?'

'I didn't think to keep it a secret. My bad,' Morwenna said apologetically as she gazed at the laptop she'd left open in front of her, reached out and switched it on. She needed to learn to be more discreet. 'Besides, Elowen's spent time at the marquee – she'll tell everyone everything.'

Brenda leaped on the table and strolled to the laptop, flopping down purposefully on the keyboard. The screen changed. Morwenna lifted a lazy hand and urged the cat to move. Brenda reluctantly took three steps away and stretched out on the table where the sunlight was streaming through the window. A page had come up on the laptop, the cast of *Macbeth* many years ago, with Daniel Kitto in the title role.

Fleance will be played at different performances by members of the RADA Theatre Lab: Rupert Bradley, Ingrid Brownlow, Chantelle Clarke, Ben D'Arcy, and Patrick Yates.

Actors had websites, where they displayed their CV, the range of their skills, their diverse acting experience. She'd start with Inga. Morwenna's fingers typed furiously. Ingrid Brownlow. And there she was, so many bright photos of Inga smiling, auburn hair shining, Inga acting in various roles. Morwenna read the print hurriedly.

Ingrid Brownlow, RADA. Minor roles, soap opera... ITV... Stage roles, *Cat on a Hot Tin Roof*... Nora Helmer in *A Doll's House*... Kattrin in *Mother Courage and her Children*... Role as Lorelei in *Burning Tarmac*, a drama about a dangerous driver who lured men to their deaths. Photos of Inga in her various roles, costumes and poses. Morwenna read on. Inga... joined The Spriggan Travelling Theatre Company... has now adopted her mother's maiden name, Ström.

Morwenna stared at the screen. Interesting.

She typed again and selected a new website. Rupert Bradley. There he was, more information following. RADA. Son of... Morwenna paused. Rupert seemed to be frowning in all of his photos; he clearly wanted to be seen as a serious actor. His mother was Arlene Santoro, a famous actor in the seventies and eighties, who'd appeared in a popular television series. Morwenna remembered it – she was the femme fatale. She read on. Rupert had performed a few minor roles on stage before Spriggan. There was little substance to his career so far. She'd try Ben.

Ben D'Arcy, RADA. The website contained lots of photos of him, some pouting, some extremely handsome, one of him, torso bare, in an aikido fighting position, holding knives. He was a versatile performer: he offered many regional accents, he'd do nudity, he could sing and dance. He was ambitious, keen to take on any role. He'd been in *Cats*, *Starlight Express*; he'd had minor roles in Shakespeare: *Titus Andronicus*, *Coriolanus*; he'd played Teddy Brewster in a stage version of *Arsenic and Old Lace*.

Morwenna was thoughtful for a moment, letting her theories develop and merge. Brenda moved a few inches to follow the beam of sunlight on the table, slumping next to her, purring rhythmically. It sounded like approval.

'Ström. Ah, I wonder...' Morwenna flicked back to the picture of Inga. It was a long shot but – there was a similarity between both women around the mouth. More than that. They carried themselves the same way... they had the same air of aloofness.

Morwenna's fingers tried the name Anna Ström. There was only one photo and it definitely wasn't Anna Carlyon – a completely different person, different hair and face. A coincidence. Then a thought occurred to her. She typed Mrs Anna Brownlow. There she was, younger, but it was definitely her. She'd been a volunteer at the theatre where her daughter was performing in St Albans. There was a group picture, Anna and a new sponsor she'd urged to help the theatre, Xander Driscoll. She appeared in a photo, receiving a cheque from Mr Driscoll, smiling at the camera, flanked by the theatre company, including Inga and... a familiar face. Morwenna paused, interested. There was the young man whom she'd seen in the restaurant – she was sure it was him.

Names of the assembled group appeared at the bottom of the photograph. She counted the cast and came to him, his face surly: of course. Karl...

Morwenna caught her breath. She typed both of his names into Google search and there he was on Facebook, hazel eyes, dark hair. It was definitely him. There wasn't much information – but from the Facebook page, she knew he lived in London.

'Here's your breakfast.' Lamorna placed baked beans on toast in front of her, just as there was a light rapping at the front door.

'Thanks, Mum.' Morwenna was still busy, typing, reading, puzzling.

'I'll get it,' Lamorna said. She was sprightly this morning. She sounded happy to be in company, her voice light as she called, 'Come in, Ruan. Breakfast will be on the plate dreckly. Morwenna's got hers – have a seat.'

Ruan followed her into the living room. He sat at the table next to Morwenna, taking in the dressing gown, the spilling hair. 'All right?'

'I am now... I was searching the Internet and I just found out some interesting things about the Spriggan actors' lives and what plays they've been in backalong,' Morwenna said, as Lamorna placed a plate on the table for Ruan. She changed the subject: she wouldn't share her new information with her mother. Lamorna seemed calmer now, happy even, after the trauma of the previous evening. Morwenna wouldn't rock the boat. She turned to Ruan. 'You never did say how the new technician got on last night.'

'He took to it like a duck to water.' Ruan smiled. 'We programmed the lighting board together before the show and he was very quick to pick up the changes. Milan and I were a bit worried at how easily he learned to set off the pyrotechnics. Just as Morgan le Fay made a spell, whoosh! Up went all the sparks and flames.' He paused, anxious. 'Are you both all right after the fire?'

He glanced at Lamorna. 'I thought we'd go down to Tregenna later, tidy up a bit, air the place out.'

'Oh, I'd like that, Ruan.' Lamorna placed a hand on his arm. 'I don't know what we'd do without you. I was worried about if the place would be all right, without me there. And that handsome Jim Hobbs said he'd come down and see how I was getting on. Nice chap – I like him. I'm surprised your friend Jane doesn't take up with him, Morwenna. What do you say?'

'Uh?' Morwenna wasn't listening. She'd been lost in thought, thinking about Anna Carlyon, the Spriggan actors, and the dark-haired man she now knew as Karl. She was putting her theories together, linking ideas, working out motives. She hadn't heard Lamorna or Ruan talking to her. 'How did you say young Tommy got on at the theatre?'

'You'll see later. It's the final night tonight,' Ruan said. 'Tommy's going to try it out on his own. Milan will be on standby. We'll be there, all of us. It's Elowen's last performance too.'

'Oh... of course.' Morwenna was remembering – thoughts were jumping inside her mind, playing leapfrog.

'Ruan's offered to take me up to Tregenna to tidy up. You haven't eaten a mouthful.' Lamorna grabbed Morwenna's wrist. 'Come on, you need your breakfast. I might ask Ruan to take me into Seal Bay and get some air freshener, some new cushions. You'll come with us, won't you? I'm so glad the fire missed my curtains – I'm very fond of them.'

'Mmm?' Morwenna allowed herself to be dragged from the theories forming in her mind. 'Oh, no, sorry, Mum – I don't think I'll have time. I'm off for a swim later and I need to pop into the Spriggan marquee. I want to see if Musa's there, if he's feeling better now.'

Ruan was tucking into beans on toast. 'He's seen a doctor – he said he'd got some meds.'

'Right.' Morwenna pressed her hands to her head, thinking again. 'We'll all meet up at Spriggan later to watch Elowen.'

'It'll be a packed house – the tickets are sold out, apparently,' Ruan said cheerily. 'Tam will be there, and just about everyone in Seal Bay.'

'Yes,' Morwenna said, still only half listening. 'That's good to know...'

'Eat up. Then you ought to go back to bed for an hour,' Lamorna said. 'You look tired out – and you haven't listened to a single thing I said.'

'Huh? Oh, no – I'll be fine after a swim.' She reached out and rubbed the cat's chin fondly. 'Won't I, Brenda?'

Brenda rolled on her back, her paws in the air. She stayed there a while, unmoving, one eye on Morwenna. Morwenna reached for her mug of cold tea and was dragged back to her thoughts. The cat stood up, tired of being ignored, stretched her back legs languidly and strolled to the laptop, flopping down purposefully on the keyboard. Immediately, the screen changed and the Facebook picture was replaced by another page.

Morwenna glanced at the photo of Anna shaking hands with Xander Driscoll, and wondered what to do next.

29

Morwenna waited next to her bicycle, shivering in her swimsuit and towel. Jane was late. There had been no texts to say that she was on her way, or that she'd been called into the office suddenly. It was unlike her not to be punctual. Morwenna glanced into the distance to see if Jane's car was approaching, but she couldn't recognise it amongst the traffic. In the distance, the Spriggan marquee seemed deserted. Morwenna wondered if Kenzie would have heard about the swim from Carole, if she'd join her, wanting to talk about her fling with Ruan. Morwenna wasn't sure if it was a fling or not. Ruan seemed to view Kenzie as someone who sat next to him in The Smugglers, drank too much and was happy to be escorted back to the guest house It wasn't Morwenna's idea of a relationship.

Talking of romance, she hadn't heard from Barnaby. She doubted he'd be working on a Saturday. He might ring her over the weekend to let her know when he'd be in Seal Bay. She wondered if he took other women out, if he had a throng of girlfriends. She asked herself how she'd feel about that and she was torn two ways. It would be nice to be the only one, to feel special. But London was full of wonderful restaurants, fabulous theatres and galleries and clubs. She couldn't imagine Barnaby not having a close circle of friends or regular dates. For a moment she imagined herself in the black tube dress sitting amongst his glamorous friends and was surprised to find herself undaunted, thinking that it might be good fun. She might enjoy a romantic weekend in London. But then again...

She glanced up the road again to see if Jane was on her way. A Korrik lorry spluttered by, several cars shuddered along, followed by a loud motorbike. The Saturday traffic was regular, but there was still no sign of Jane. Perhaps she would turn up tomorrow instead. The Sunday SWANs swim would be a lively affair – Louise had promised to come, Donald too, and the Grundy sisters. But Morwenna was keen to have a conversation with Jane today, just the two of them. There was something she wanted to run past her, to gauge her reaction to a theory that was buzzing in her brain. It would have to wait.

Morwenna tucked her bag and towel behind the bike, which was chained to the railings. As always, she assumed everything would be safe; most people in Seal Bay respected people's right to swim in the sea, especially in the off-season. She hurried to the lapping waves, feeling the immediate chill around her ankles, inhaling deeply, diving in, swimming strongly. The cold took her breath away, her skin tingling deliciously as she pushed forward into deep water, rolling on her back, staring up at marshmallow clouds. She watched the shift in patterns, the way a fluffy dragon cloud melted and became a sheep, a face with a pointed nose rounded into a cute cherub. Morwenna took another deep breath and let her thoughts form: Anna Carlyon, her husbands, her relationship with Daniel Kitto, with the Spriggan Theatre. Like the clouds forming and reforming above her, Morwenna let her ideas slide and merge. The jigsaw was coming together; it was almost completed.

She thought about the play, the last performance later, and she searched for a neat way to bring her suspicions to a safe conclusion. Ruan had said everyone would be there. He'd meant the audience, but Morwenna knew that the suspects would be in the marquee too. And now she was fairly sure who'd killed Daniel Kitto, how they had done it and what the motive was. She just had to prove it, and what better way than in front of an audience?

She heard someone yelling her name and turned to see Jane swimming towards her, spluttering water, her face wet and shining. 'I'm sorry I'm late. I've been working this morning, then on the phone talking to colleagues. I have some news.'

Morwenna kicked her legs, reaching out an arm, grabbing Jane's shoulder. 'Oh?'

'About the attack on your mum's house last night. I wanted to deal with it straight away. Jim Hobbs and I have been out this morning, interviewing people.'

'Where?'

'In the marquee. That's why I'm late. And Musa's dodgy tonic came back.' Jane blinked, wiping her face. 'Laced with just the right amount of arsenic. Slow poison.'

'Arsenic,' Morwenna repeated.

'Someone knew what they were doing. They wanted him out of the way.'

'He was surplus to Spriggan's requirements and he'd dug his heels in.'

'Who do you think is responsible?' Jane asked.

Morwenna wasn't ready to say. 'There are several names in the frame.'

'Jim and I talked to a few of the actors. Inga cried when we questioned her – she misses Daniel. Kenzie doesn't – she will happily tell everyone she had no respect for him. Apparently, he did the dirty on her mother years before. Ben put on an innocent face – he hasn't been told about the arsenic yet but we took his bottles for testing. We'll pick him up later when the results come through, if they are at all tampered with. Musa is lucky he's on the mend. And Rupert seemed to have nothing to say for himself at all. He was quite uninterested in the whole thing.'

'Ah,' Morwenna said.

'Off the record – it's not official police business anyway, so I can discuss it with you.' Jane was eager to share new information. 'You know that photo you gave me of Anna Carlyon and the young man in the restaurant? I had a hunch I knew him from somewhere.'

'And were you right?' Morwenna asked.

'I searched a few old records.' Jane gasped as a wave rushed over her head. 'A few years ago, there was a group of particularly nasty characters we knew had been up to no good, operating between Cornwall and London. We arrested a couple of them for dodgy stuff: drugs, extortion.'

'And?'

'He was linked to them. There wasn't anything we could pin on him, but he was very arrogant. I remember questioning him and he was particularly rude. It stayed with me, the way he laughed as if he was untouchable. I thought at the time that he was a slippery character.'

'Karl Brownlow,' Morwenna said simply.

'That's right.' Jane was amazed. 'How do you know?'

'Same as you – I looked at some old pictures,' Morwenna said. 'Do you think he's involved in Daniel's death?'

'I doubt it,' Jane said. 'He spends his time now between here and London, as so many of the people who own property here do. I suppose all he's guilty of is getting a free dinner courtesy of Anna, whatever their connection is.'

'Will you be at the performance tonight?' Morwenna asked.

'I will.' Jane shivered. 'Should we get out? I'm numb and my skin feels like sharks are chewing at it.'

'Yes, let's...' Morwenna smiled enigmatically. 'I've got what I came for.'

'Exercise and a damn good chilling?' Jane suggested.

'And clarity of thought,' Morwenna added. 'Come up to Harbour Cottages for hot chocolate and I'll tell you all about it. I think I know exactly who the killer is and I can prove it.'

'This had better be good, Morwenna,' Jane said, unconvinced.

'Oh, it is – and you'll be on hand to reel the murderer in. I promise you – you'll love it.'

* * *

Morwenna sidled into the Spriggan marquee late in the afternoon. The conversation she'd had with Jane had given her a chance to speak her thoughts aloud and it was surprising how plausible her theory had sounded. Now she was ready to put her plan into action. She watched as the actors finished their dress rehearsal. Tommy Buvač was sitting in front of a lighting board, sliding switches as the theatre was illuminated bright yellow, a deep ocean blue, then it changed to the emerald green of a forest and finally an indigo night sky filled with stars. He accompanied his lighting with sound effects, the hollow hoot of an owl, the haunting whisper of the sea. Behind him, his father smiled proudly and offered Morwenna a little wave.

She looked around. The actors hadn't noticed her. No one else had arrived. Ruan had taken Lamorna up to Tregenna Gardens.

She waited for the rehearsal to stop. A natural break came, and Kenzie tugged off the wig she wore as Morgan le Fay, tucking her hair into a black beanie and rushing across. 'Hi, Morwenna. Tommy's a great find, isn't he? And Ruan did so well too.'

'He did.'

'So where *is* Ruan today? I didn't see him in the pub last night.'

'He's performing his gallant knight act,' Morwenna said, examining Kenzie's face for a reaction. There was none, so she said, 'He's helping my mum. There was a little fire at her house last night.'

'Oh?' Kenzie didn't seem interested.

'He'll replace the fire blanket.'

'Old ladies and chip pans?' Kenzie smirked. 'He is coming tonight? I have a bottle of champagne chilling back at Carole's.'

Morwenna considered how the two facts might be connected and pushed the thought to the back of her mind. She said, 'He wouldn't miss it,' and watched Kenzie's face shine with delight. 'I need a quick word with Musa.'

Kenzie was opening a bar of chocolate, already wandering away. Morwenna caught Musa's eye and mouthed, 'How are you feeling?'

He hurried across, swigging water from a bottle. Morwenna was glad to see the ease in his movements. His face seemed healthier, without the beads of perspiration that had covered it last time.

'Hi, Morwenna. I'm a bit better.' He lowered his voice. 'The police were in this morning. They took Ben's entire stash of tonic away. I heard him saying he wouldn't hurt anyone. They've told him he's not to leave Seal Bay.'

'Do you think it's him?'

'I don't know.' Musa said. 'They gave me a hard time – as if I'd take arsenic on purpose! There's a theory going around that someone killed Daniel the same way. I'm not sure. The police wouldn't say. Kenzie thinks it's an outsider. She said that anyone could have wandered backstage, our security's so slack. Ben's spoken to me personally and apologised. He swore it wasn't him. He thinks Jesse might have had something to do with it and that makes sense, since he's in police custody.'

'Jesse was a chancer, a thief, someone who liked fast cars. That's all.'

'We all like fast cars,' Musa said ruefully. 'I wouldn't have stolen Daniel's car though. Is it true his funeral's been postponed while the police talk to the coroner?'

'There will be an inquest.' Morwenna said; Jane had told her over hot chocolate. 'I wanted to ask you, Musa...' She considered how to frame the question. 'Have you ever played Hamlet?'

'I always wanted to – all actors dream of it. I played Horatio once, his best friend.'

'So you know the play?'

'Yes.'

Musa seemed to wonder where this was going, so Morwenna quoted, '"The play's the thing wherein I'll catch the conscience of the king."'

'Hamlet's play within a play?'

'Exactly.'

'What are you getting at?'

'I have a bit of an idea.' Morwenna grasped his arm and led him to the tiered seating. They sat down and Morwenna glanced around. The actors were busy: Inga was on the phone, Rupert was changing his costume, Ben was drinking water from a bottle. Kenzie had disappeared. Milan and Tommy were still absorbed with the lighting board, moving ladders, angling spotlights.

Morwenna kept her voice low. 'At the end of *The Return of the Cornish King*, Morgan le Fay kills Uther Pendragon as he saves Arthur, right?'

'That's right.' Musa said. 'Then Merlin takes her on, in a battle of spells, sends her packing and Arthur and Guinevere take the throne.'

'Perfect. So...' Morwenna leaned her head towards Musa's. 'If we wrote some lines for your character to speak at the end of the play, just like Hamlet does, so that the guilty party will know they've been found out – it might force them into admitting their guilt because there's no other way out.'

'But what if they keep their cool?'

'In front of an entire audience – and with your acting talent? I think they might just crack. It's worth a shot...'

'Can you do that?'

'We can do it together now,' Morwenna said complicitly.

'I don't understand.' Musa was confused. 'In order to do that, we'd have to know who put arsenic in my bottle of tonic.'

'And they'd have to be the same person who made threats using Daniel's phone, who knocked me off my bike, attacked my mother's home and killed Daniel Kitto.'

'So do you know who did that?' Musa's eyes widened.

'I do. I've spoken to Jane Choy about it and she's agreed. The police will be poised outside and Jane will be in the audience to make the arrest after the show, and everyone will witness the moment of truth,' Morwenna whispered. 'I'm convinced this will put Daniel's killer in the spotlight. So – are you up for it?'

30

Morwenna stood in the entrance to the marquee, delighted that the last night of the play was bustling with so much excitement. The audience filled the theatre space quickly, buying knitted Spriggan hats from Susan and Barb. There were so many people perched in the tiered seating wearing brightly coloured elf knits, leaning forward eagerly, whispering quietly. Morwenna glanced round as she wriggled between Lamorna and Ruan. On the other side of Lamorna, a newly introduced Gill Bennett was whispering about Daniel Kitto. Morwenna heard her mother say, 'How do you know Daniel, then?'

Gill paused, then muttered, 'He was special to me.'

'Me too,' Lamorna replied quietly.

Next to Ruan, Becca Hawkins was looking around for the two actors she admired so much. Neither of them had asked her for a second date. Tamsin was behind the scenery, watching Elowen like a hawk as she dressed for her performance.

Morwenna scanned the audience. Jane was in the middle row with Jim Hobbs; Rick Tremayne shifted in his seat nearby. He was not in uniform, but he was alert and ready, acting on Morwenna's plan. The Buvač family sat in the row behind her, including Maya in mermaid costume, holding the tail beneath her arm. She'd be called on for a bow at the end, as would Tommy, who hovered offstage in the shadows, fixing several pyrotechnics in place. Morwenna spotted Damien Woon and Beverley and, two rows behind, Elowen's teacher, Imelda Parker. She waved cheerily to Louise and her husband, Steve, who were sharing a packet of sweets with Donald Stewart. Pam Truscott was seated right at the back, next to Julian and Pippa Pengellen and, on the other side of Pippa, Anna Carlyon was clutching a programme. They were deep in conversation.

Carole and Britney Taylor bustled in, faces ruddy from the wind, taking seats just behind Morwenna. Carole leaned forward and whispered, 'I've given up a takeaway pizza and a night in front of the TV with Vic for this. Britney wanted to see Elowen's last performance.'

Morwenna turned and whispered, 'It'll be good, believe me.'

She was looking forward to the show, especially because there wasn't an empty seat in the house. Things couldn't have worked out better. Most of Seal Bay would be able to hear Merlin's speech. She and Musa had prepared it together earlier, and Morwenna felt quite pleased with her efforts.

Then the house lights faded and a spotlight came up on a dark-haired mermaid gazing into a mirror. Someone in the audience was moved to breathe 'aww'. Elowen ignored it and continued to preen, then she spoke up. 'We Cornish mermaids are very happy to sit on a rock all day and comb our locks in the sunshine. But I'm going to stop what I do best dreckly, and welcome you to the last night of *The Return of the Cornish King* by The Spriggan Travelling Theatre Company. My grandma's a mermaid too, and you can all get yourselves down to the sea and join in the Seal Bay swim on Sunday mornings. Oh, and by the way, Mummy, can I have a dog?'

The audience rewarded her with hearty laughter. Becca leaned over to Morwenna, her eyes shining, and whispered, 'We practised that speech at home – but not the bit about the dog.'

Morwenna smiled and everyone clapped as Elowen flipped her tail, made a dive and rolled behind the wooden sea, waving an open hand in a cheeky goodbye. She looked towards the wings where Tommy's lighting desk sat; he was watching intently, taking out the sea-blue wash, bringing up the lighting for the first scene. She glanced at Ruan, who had a smile on his face. On the other side, a tear glistened on Lamorna's cheek. Then Rupert as Uther Pendragon, wearing a purple cloak, led Kenzie as Igraine on the stage and said tonelessly, 'O my queen, you and I have known many years on this earth and I fear we may, like summer flowers, soon shed life's petals.'

'But, husband, do not be afraid, for we have a son who will live in our place and tread boldly across the land of Cornweal. He will be King of all England. Merlin prophesied it when he was born.' Kenzie, frail in a pale dress, gave him her most adoring expression. 'And you and I will finally know the peace that comes with passing years.'

Lamorna hissed, 'What's she going on about, peace in passing years? My hip gives me constant grief.'

Morwenna pressed her hand and smiled, a signal to be patient; she was going to enjoy every moment of the play. Merlin bounded on, wearing a green velvet cloak with a voluminous hood, and Tommy pressed a button; a pyrotechnic cracked, sending green light in the air, and the audience gasped as one.

Musa said, 'Greetings, Uther Pendragon. You know me well as the seer of futures and the sayer of truth. But you must know now that I bring a grave warning. There is one amidst us who seeks to kill you and those you love, to turn good into evil and to rule Cornweal and the lands beyond in your place...'

Morwenna edged forward in her seat. She knew how close Musa's words came to the truth and she couldn't wait for the final explosive ending.

The play continued at a pace. Igraine passed away, blessing Cornweal in her final breath. Arthur courted Guinevere, battled against a dragon, which was a shapeshifting Kenzie in a long green cloak. Morgan le Fay captured Guinevere; she was rescued from the crashing waves by a brave Arthur, who had been brought back from near death by Merlin's strongest spell. The audience was entranced; a hush hung over the whole theatre.

It was almost the end of the play. Morgan le Fay had interrupted Arthur's coronation, and was hurling spells in the air. Pyrotechnics cracked, smoke billowed and dispersed. Then she whirled her cloak, spreading it wide, and cackled, 'You are a loathsome man, Uther, King of Cornweal, and long have I wished you dead. Now I turn to your son, Arthur, whom you have made King of all England. May your family be cursed hereafter...'

Morgan le Fay lurched towards Arthur, a stage dagger in her fist, and gave a blood-curdling scream. Rupert Bradley as Uther rushed forward, taking Arthur's place, grunting as the stage blade hit him full in the chest and an arc of blood spurted in the air. The audience gasped as he fell to his knees histrionically, a rose of stage blood spreading on his chest. He staggered up again, stumbling weakly across the stage, ready for his final soliloquy.

'I die – leaving behind all I love, my kingdom, my son Arthur, my heir... I go to meet my queen Igraine in the afterlife. But I have given you the best part of me, O Cornweal, home of my ancestors.' He lay on the floor, groaned a bit, stuck out his legs and lolled out a tongue, apparently dead. The audience held one breath to see what would happen.

Morwenna knew. She'd helped with the script.

'Wait.' Merlin threw out a wand-filled hand for attention. The other actors paused, expecting to hear the lines they had all rehearsed, but Musa drew himself tall and uttered, 'Morgan le Fay, you are a witch and you have slain the great Uther of Cornweal. Yet I say to everyone assembled—' he turned to address the audience '—you are not the most evil one here. But you will know of the truth, in the fullness of time. We will all know it.'

Kenzie stared at Musa. He was improvising, off text. She was a consummate professional, so she spoke up. 'What are you saying, Merlin? I have no idea what you speak of.'

He continued to talk directly to the audience. 'Watch closely, while I will reveal to you all, O honest people of Cornweal.' His face was serious with accusation. 'There is a traitor amongst us tonight. Perhaps more than one, by my magic.'

Someone in the audience laughed audibly as if the actor was making a joke. There was a nervous murmur from the tiered seats.

'I'll say it again. I am Merlin the mage, the untameable one. I have survived many years, though some have sought to poison me with their devilish potions.' He stared at each face on stage dramatically.

Morgan le Fay took a step backwards. Her face clouded. 'Not I, Merlin.'

'My wand twitches in my fingers – it tells me the evil one is not far away.' He looked around, his face gleeful. 'But who is the murderer, we must ask? Is it Morgan le Fay, Arthur, Guinevere or the brave Lancelot who has since departed, now a knight errant? One of them knows who killed the real Uther Pendragon, he who was our bold master and our teacher, who died in this very place less than two weeks since.'

'What?' Rupert sat up; the dead Uther was now bolt upright. 'What's going on, Musa?'

'I have no idea what your words mean.' Kenzie was still in role. 'Speak no more of this.'

'You cannot blame me,' Inga as Guinevere said, holding up her hands; she looked as if she'd fade away. 'For we are all loyal.'

'I don't get it,' Ben said. He was no longer Arthur. 'What are you doing?'

'Now it's time for me to reveal the one who poisons, who burns our homes and knocks us to the earth to break our bones.' Musa's voice rose in a spell. 'The wicked one is here with us now. And we must call for justice.'

He walked across the stage, standing amid the actors, speaking to the audience. He was now Musa, not Merlin. 'The police are here and they will make an arrest. PC Choy told me this evening who murdered Daniel Kitto, who tried to poison me, and I'll now reveal the name in a spell.'

He made his voice low, Merlin again. 'I bring you charm of life and death – to reveal the curse of the serpent's breath...' Musa lifted his wand and there was a loud crack and the bright yellow flash of a pyrotechnic. He continued, his voice hollow.

'So people of Cornweal, ye need to fear – the killer who is Guinevere.'

The gasp from members of the audience was echoed on stage. Ben D'Arcy turned to Musa. 'What are you doing?'

Rupert hissed, 'Will someone explain to me what's going on?'

Inga took two steps backwards, her face flushed and angry, pausing to gaze around the stage before she rushed off into the wings. Jane Choy sprang from her seat shouting an order to stop, followed by Jim Hobbs, quickly in pursuit. Rick Tremayne was on his feet, clattering after them, his voice commanding. There was a hubbub in the theatre, a shriek backstage; Inga was struggling to leave by the far exit but Jane had caught up with her.

More noise came from the auditorium. The house lights were bright now, the tiered area fully illuminated. People were talking loudly, amazed by what had just happened, asking questions, shuffling in their seats. Morwenna saw Anna Carlyon get up, squeeze past others, heading awkwardly down the steps towards the exit. By the time she reached the door, Morwenna had caught up with her. Anna pushed her away and rushed out. Morwenna followed her to the white BMW, and they both stopped.

A police car was waiting outside and Jane and Rick Tremayne were leading an unhappy Inga towards the vehicle. A blue light flashed and swirled. Morwenna heard Rick say, 'Ingrid Ström, you do not have to say anything, but it may harm your defence if you do not mention when questioned...'

Anna turned to Morwenna, her face distraught. 'They are taking her away.'

Morwenna nodded. 'What she did was wrong, Anna.'

'What happened just then, at the end of the play? The actor knew.' Anna gestured wildly towards the marquee. Then she pointed to Morwenna. 'How?'

'The jigsaw pieces fitted,' Morwenna said sadly.

'And – what about me?' Anna was trembling. She delved into her handbag for car keys. 'What will happen to me now?'

'You'll need to explain your part. What you did will come out.'

'I can't – I can't let this happen.' Anna grasped Morwenna's wrist. 'You're a mother – you must know how important it is to protect your family.'

'I do,' Morwenna admitted.

'Come with me.' Anna's grasp on her wrist tightened. 'Come with me to my home. I need to – to talk, to explain it to you. You owe me that.'

'How do I owe you anything?' Morwenna's voice was firm.

'You came round my house snooping – you asked questions. And what about that fiasco in The Marine Room? You were on to my daughter all the time, weren't you?'

'I just wondered—'

Anna was suddenly fierce. 'What happened on stage, all that stuff the actor said to the audience about people being poisoned, and then he turned it onto Inga. Were you behind that?'

Morwenna took a deep breath. 'Musa's health tonic was laced with arsenic, Anna. Daniel Kitto's too. But you know that, don't you?'

Anna met her eyes and Morwenna was surprised to see tears on her face. Her voice was desperate, but the grip on Morwenna's wrist was a vice. 'Please, I beg you. Come back to the house with me. Give me a chance to explain. I can tell you the truth. I can make you understand. You know how it is to love your child, to be prepared to do anything in the world for them.' She sniffed; more tears followed. 'Please, come with me. The police will pick me up soon and – and that will be it, the end of everything I've worked for, but I want the chance to explain.'

'Very well,' Morwenna said, pulling open the passenger door, sliding in. She knew it was unwise to go with Anna Carlyon but curiosity had got the better of her. Besides, the police wouldn't be far behind. And something made her feel a little sorry for Anna.

She was still wondering about her own actions as the engine roared to life. Morwenna slammed the passenger door.

Anna wiped her tears away with the back of her hand and drove away furiously into darkness.

31

Despite the intense darkness, Morwenna recognised the road that led to Knave-Go-By. The sea was a dark shadow to the right. The car hurtled along, bouncing over bumps in the road. Anna was probably breaking the speed limit, but she said nothing, simply glaring ahead, her hands clutching the steering wheel as if she might choke it. Morwenna decided she wouldn't speak either. Anna was concentrating – there was a frown line scored between her eyes, her mouth was slightly open, panting. Morwenna asked herself why she had come along – it probably wasn't her wisest decision – and began to plan escape routes. She knew the downstairs layout of the house; the road out of the front door to the headland led three ways, to the sea, to a field or back through the gates and onto the road. Her phone buzzed in her pocket; Morwenna thought she'd better not answer it, not yet. Anna was erratic, brittle, and Morwenna wondered when she'd crack.

The BMW careered through the tall gates, coming to a sharp stop, wheels veering to one side. Anna clambered out and hurried towards the door, her heels sinking into gravel. She waved an arm. 'Come on.'

Morwenna followed her inside, leaving the front door open, wondering if a police car would screech down the drive at any moment – if it did, she'd left them an easy entrance. Anna forged ahead, turning into the living room as if in a hurry. Morwenna stood in the doorway, and then sat down nervously on the leather sofa.

Anna took a breath, as if making a decision. 'I'll get us a strong coffee.'

'I usually drink tea,' Morwenna said, but Anna was on her way into the hall, her heels clicking downstairs to the kitchen. Morwenna wondered if she should follow her and observe her actions. She recalled with a sharp intake of breath that she'd photographed the brown envelope with the letters AS in the kitchen. She gazed around at the perfectly arranged cushions, the open fireplace with a black wood-burner, the mahogany chest. She stood up, choosing a wedding photo, and inspected the group. Anna and Will Carlyon were in the centre, the happy couple. Anna was smiling, flanked by guests. Daniel Kitto was in the back row wearing a silk suit and a cravat. But Morwenna was drawn to the two young people she'd tried to discern from the fuzzy pictures on her camera. They were distinct now, a dark-haired man in a sharp grey suit, an auburn-haired woman in a pale blue dress, standing side by side. They shared the same hazel eyes, brown mixed with amber and green. Morwenna knew only 18 per cent of the population had hazel eyes – she'd checked it in the library. They were brother and sister, Karl and Inga. She selected another photo at the back, a little girl in a ballet dress, her arms stretched upwards, her face angelic. It was clearly Inga Brownlow as a child. Morwenna felt momentarily sad; it was tragic that the mother's and daughter's lives had come to this. She had to admit, she was intrigued by what had led them from the happy people in the idyllic photographs to the lives they'd chosen.

There was a tinkling of cups. Anna carried a tray in, two coffees, a plate of biscuits. She placed the tray on a table and Morwenna reached for a china mug.

'No, the other one is yours,' Anna said sharply, then she forced a smile. 'I like mine bitter, but I put sugar in yours. I hope it's all right.'

Morwenna accepted the other delicate mug. She drank coffee occasionally. She rested it on her knee, relieved that Anna had kept her word and brought a tray of drinks – she'd half expected her to appear in the doorway with a dagger or a shotgun. She tried to keep her voice calm and wondered where to begin. The words, 'Anna, what made you become a serial poisoner?' wouldn't be the best place to start. So she said, 'That's a beautiful photograph of Inga when she was young, doing ballet.'

'She was very talented. She's always had a gift for performance. Singing, dancing, acting – that girl has it all. And she's stunning. She could have been so much.' Anna was clearly filled with regret. 'I promised I'd give her everything she needed. I promised both my children I'd help them to get on in the world.'

Morwenna agreed. 'You're a good mum.'

'I learned the hard way. My father came to this country with his parents in the forties.' She sighed, remembering. 'It all starts with the father.' She gave Morwenna a sharp look. 'I suppose your father was a wonderful man, a Cornish fisherman or something?'

'I never really knew him,' Morwenna replied. 'He was called Freddie Quick and he left when I was four years old.'

'My father married when he was twenty years old. He was a hard worker. We were a penniless family – I was the youngest. But he had two jobs, factory work, and we seldom saw him. When he was home, my mother would make us sit quietly. We weren't to disturb him because he worked so many hours. I remember him as an old man with a lined face, asleep in a chair, but he died when he was forty-two, so he wasn't really old at all.'

Morwenna thought she'd keep Anna talking. 'That must have been hard for you.'

'You've no idea. Five children and no income? We were always hungry, poor as urchins, dirty clothes. My mother used to cut our hair short because we were crawling with headlice. People avoided us in the street – we were the filthy Ström family from Limehouse. We were pariahs. I vowed I'd never let that happen to my children.'

Morwenna looked at the ceiling with a gold glass lightshade, the cream and blue tiles in the fireplace. 'This house is beautiful.'

Anna's expression was blank. 'I own everything now. You'd think that would be marvellous, but I live alone. I'm lost in this place. I take sleeping tablets every night. I'm so lonely I can't sleep.'

Morwenna felt sorry for her. 'That's awful.'

'I thought once I owned Korrik, it would bring me opportunity. It just brings money. I'm like Midas,' Anna admitted. 'Whatever I touch in life it turns to gold and then it becomes worthless.'

'So how did you get from poverty to – this?' Morwenna indicated the beautiful room, the panoramic French windows onto the patio.

'As soon as I could, I left home and trained as a nurse. I hoped I'd marry a rich doctor and live happily ever after.'

'Mr Brownlow?'

Anna gave a snort. 'Terry Brownlow was a hospital porter. I fell for his hazel eyes and his soft tongue. I was young and pregnant with Karl. It was a step up, I suppose. Then I had Inga.' She met Morwenna's eyes. 'I'd have done anything for those children. Karl was a naughty boy, but bright, fearless. Inga was the talented one. I pulled out all the stops for them, raised money for the theatre, used my influence so she could have the main roles, put her through a good education so she could get the best qualifications. And she was so driven and keen. Too driven.'

'You married an entrepreneur, Xander Driscoll?'

Anna nodded.

'What happened to Terry?'

Morwenna knew the answer before Anna said, 'He had a heart attack.'

'And Xander? And Will Carlyon?'

Anna nodded again. 'I kept taking another step up, then another. I needed to be richer, I had to pull strings. Inga was talented, but acting is such a difficult profession to succeed in.' Her hand shook as she sipped coffee from the china cup. She glanced towards Morwenna. 'Drink it up, before it's cold.'

Morwenna raised her mug as if she were thinking about taking a sip, then she said, 'So – why was it important to you to have control of Spriggan? Is that why Daniel Kitto died?'

'I wanted Inga to have her own company. I wanted her to be independent within the industry. It's a fickle world. She had a few roles: theatre; she was in a TV film. And she'd do anything for her career.' Anna looked sad. 'We both know that being invisible and poor is nothing more than disgrace. It's better to be dead than to be invisible.'

'She played Lorelei in *Burning Tarmac*, a drama about a dangerous driver who lured men to their deaths,' Morwenna said.

'How do you know that?'

'I saw the photo on her website. She was driving, wearing a black beanie, and I realised then that she was the person who ran into me in Daniel's yellow car. She's a very confident driver.'

'She did hours of training for that film.'

'I thought as much.'

'It was a flop. It led to nothing. Then Daniel put his company together and I persuaded him to take Inga on. He didn't take much persuading – she's talented and beautiful,' Anna said, her expression determined. 'We both knew if she could become company director of Spriggan, she'd be able to do just as she wished. But Daniel was about to change his will, to disband the company. So—'

'Inga put arsenic in his health tonic?'

'Ben D'Arcy's tonic. He's in love with Inga. She had him eating out of her hand, and Rupert, even Jesse Miles. Daniel worshipped her. Musa was difficult though.'

'Did Ben know she was doctoring his tonic?'

'Oh, he had no idea whatsoever. Inga's smart. I taught her well.' Anna's face creased and suddenly she began to cry. 'She'll go to prison. I've let her down.'

'She stole Daniel's phone, sent threatening messages, tried to set fire to my mother's house.'

'You interfered, Morwenna. You wouldn't be warned. You couldn't keep your nose out.' Anna's eyes narrowed. 'When I saw you at the restaurant, I wasn't sure what you were up to, but when you came here, I was certain you were snooping. And Inga knew: you were always looking round the marquee, asking questions. We put two and two together. But you wouldn't back off.' She indicated Morwenna's cup. 'You haven't touched your coffee.'

Morwenna ignored the final comment. 'So, tell me about your son. Tell me about Karl.'

'He's like me. He likes the nice things in life: money, power. He… dabbles.'

'In drugs?' Morwenna asked. 'I saw the big brown envelope in the kitchen, to Mum. Was that from Karl?'

'You have no proof of anything.'

'It had an A and an S on the front. At first I thought it was initials, but the 's' is small case…' Morwenna locked eyes with Anna. 'That's the chemical symbol for arsenic. And you gave it to Inga so that she could put it in the bottles of tonic.'

'My nursing background comes in useful.' Anna sipped again. 'And Karl has contacts. He can get his hands on anything – he's very versatile, my son.'

'Is that how your husbands died? Did you poison them all?' Morwenna asked.

'Drink up.' Anna drained her coffee. 'Or are you afraid I'll poison you too?'

Morwenna was thoughtful, watching her carefully as she put her empty mug back on the tray. Anna sat up straight, crossed her legs, now in charge, dignified. 'So, Morwenna, is there anything else you need to know?'

Morwenna shook her head. 'Don't you feel bad about what you've done? You've killed people, Daniel, others...'

Anna took a shuddering breath. 'Life's a rat race. It's a gamble too. And I wasn't going to spend it at the bottom of the dung heap. But you know, Morwenna, when you can end someone's life the way I have, a measured amount of arsenic in a cup of coffee, you realise it's nothing to be afraid of. It's just death. People struggle for a short while, close their eyes and – that's it, there's no more. A click of your fingers.'

Morwenna put her mug down as if she'd been burned. 'Did you poison my drink?'

'The first time you came here, yes, I put enough in so that your heart would fail, you'd fall off your bicycle on the way home and no one would pin it on me. It would be a shame, an older woman on a bicycle – the hills were too much for her now. But this time, no.' Anna reached down by the side of the sofa and picked up the Cornish-flag cardigan. She swayed a little. Perspiration beaded her brow. 'I'll give this knitted thing back to you. It's hideous. I'll never wear it.'

Morwenna took the cardigan. 'Are you sure?'

'I'm very sure. In fact, I'll never wear...' Anna tried to laugh but her expression changed. She blinked as if dizzy, then she groaned, a low sound of pain. Her eyes widened as if she was surprised by the amount of discomfort she felt, then she leaned forward and clutched her stomach. 'You know, I was pretty good at the discreet art of poisoning... I taught Inga well. The right measure in a... liquid... to make the poison take effect over... several... days. Or the perfect quantity in a drink to work instantly, to make a quick... exit.'

'Anna?' Morwenna stood up, alarmed. 'Anna, are you all right? What have you done?'

Anna swayed, panting lightly, her voice weak. 'Have you ever heard of Edward Black, the Tregonissey arsenic poisoner, who killed... his wife...? He was executed at Exeter Prison in 1922 by... hanging. But I'm not... going... to prison.'

'Have you taken something?' Morwenna knelt next to her. Her eyes were like glass, her brow a sheen of sweat.

'I've always been fond of cocktails.' Anna forced a grimace and groaned again. 'Arsenic is known as the king of poisons and the poison of... kings. Nero poisoned his... stepbrother Britannicus with it.'

'Can you drink some water? Should you try to be sick?' Morwenna asked quickly.

Anna moaned, closing her eyes, slumping forward. She was in intense pain. She fell to her knees, then on the floor, rolling on her back. 'In seventeenth-century Italy, a woman called Giulia turned her... make-up business... into a poison factory.' She rolled over, making a hollow heaving sound. Her mouth was wet with vomit. 'She sold Aqua Tofana... it was laced with arsenic, lead and...'

Morwenna tugged her phone out, dialling emergency services. She spoke quickly. 'Ambulance, please – and police. I'm at Knave-Go-By – out on the headland, outside Seal Bay – I think a woman has taken poison... She's breathing, yes, and awake, just. What can I do to help? I don't know, it might be arsenic or sleeping tablets...'

She turned quickly. Anna made a low heaving noise and was suddenly violently sick, shivering. She huddled into a ball on the carpet and didn't move. Morwenna spoke into the phone. 'Someone's on the way now? Thank you...'

She knelt next to Anna, whose face was damp, her mouth wet with spittle, breathing raggedly. Morwenna felt for a pulse. 'Anna, can you hear me?' She spoke gently. 'The ambulance will be here at any moment – can you look at me, Anna?'

Anna groaned; her eyelids flickered. Then Morwenna heard the distant whoop of sirens, the police, an ambulance. Help was coming.

32

Morwenna arrived home exhausted, well after midnight. She'd spent a long time with Rick Tremayne and Jim Hobbs, giving a statement about Anna's attempt on her own life. Dazed, she went straight to bed and slept badly, her phone lodged on the pillow, waking groggily as messages pinged in. Jane let her know that Inga had been charged with Daniel's murder and several other offences. Anna was in hospital, weak, receiving medication. Later, Jane texted again: Anna was responding to treatment, her system had been flushed out. She would probably have some kidney damage, she'd suffered a mild heart attack, but she'd survive to stand trial.

Earlier, Tamsin had sent photographs of Elowen and Maya on stage receiving audience acclaim at the end of the play – Morwenna had missed the final curtain call. There was a beautiful photo of Elowen the mermaid in Merlin's arms, cheering, and Tommy Buvač just behind the actors on stage, smiling proudly. Lamorna had texted five times between ten thirty and eleven fifteen, asking Morwenna if she was all right and what was happening and that Ruan had helped her buy some cushions and a new chair so, now her house was back to normal, she was going to bleddy well live in it. Oh, and Gill Bennett was a lovely woman, and she'd invited Lamorna round for Sunday lunch, so she wouldn't make the swim. As if she ever did, Morwenna thought – her mother always had an excuse. Ruan had messaged once. He'd catch up with her later, on Sunday afternoon. He had something he wanted to talk about. Morwenna answered all the texts and finally fell asleep at four o'clock, shattered.

The following morning the Cornish rain came down in stair rods as Morwenna sat at the breakfast table, her head in her hands. She'd go to the wild swim with the other SWANs after breakfast; the wet weather would make no difference. She wondered why she felt so tired, so totally fatigued. But she knew why. It wasn't just the lack of sleep. It was emotional exhaustion. The events of last night had taken it out of her. Swimming in the sea would either completely revitalise her or she wouldn't last five minutes, her muscles would turn to rubber and she'd have to clamber out, defeated. Brenda leaped on the table, pawing her hair, trying to scrounge toast. Morwenna gave her a tiny finger of butter and was rewarded with a loud purr.

It was still raining heavily as she stood shivering in her wetsuit on wet sand over an hour later. Despite Elowen's advertisement for the swimming group in the play last night, new swimmers stayed away; the cold rain had clearly put them off. Even Kenzie hadn't turned up; Morwenna wondered if she'd had a late night.

Louise, Susan, Barb and Donald surrounded her, bursting with questions – they had all witnessed Merlin's final magic spell on stage last night, and Guinevere's guilty run for freedom; Jane, Rick and Jim in pursuit, and they'd noticed Morwenna leave early. The grapevine in Seal Bay had been as effective as usual; rumours of Anna Carlyon's arrest were widespread. Morwenna found she was too tired to speak. Her hair was becoming damp, hanging in strands.

She muttered by way of explanation, 'Anna was Inga's mother.'

'But how ever did you find out?' Louise asked.

'And where did she get the poison?' Susan wanted to know.

'And how many people did she kill?' Barb added. 'I heard she murdered all her husbands.'

'And did she poison Daniel Kitto?' Donald said.

'I'll tell you in time,' Morwenna murmured. Her body ached and her head was still thumping. It was difficult to see straight, her eyes were so tired.

'Shall we get in the water?' a new voice suggested. Everyone turned to see Jane Choy, bright-eyed, full of energy. The swimmers turned to her eagerly.

'Will Inga go to prison for life?'

'Is Anna Carlyon a murderer?'

'Did she kidnap Morwenna and take her to that big house on the headland?'

'I heard Rick Tremayne pulled Morwenna in for questioning – that's not right.'

'Morwenna saved Anna Carlyon's life,' Jane said, throwing an arm around her friend, pulling her against her wetsuit. 'But now she needs a swim. Let's go in. We can talk about her heroics afterwards.'

'But what will happen to Spriggan theatre?' Susan wanted to know.

'We'll discuss it in the tearoom.' Jane used her best authoritarian tone. 'Come on, let's get in the sea.'

Morwenna allowed Jane to tug her along the sand. The sea was iron grey, corrugated. She felt the ice of the waves snap at her ankles, catching her breath as she was wrapped in the embrace of the ocean. It buffeted her and she pushed her arms as strongly as she could. Cold water slapped her face; she felt the gnaw of its teeth against her thighs. She shivered and allowed herself to be carried along. Loud squeals came from Barb and Susan a few yards away. Louise's head stuck above the waves; she was watching Morwenna carefully, checking that she was all right. Then Jane was swimming next to her.

'How are you feeling?'

'All right, I think.'

'Even Rick Tremayne said the girl done good.'

'Did he?' Morwenna was surprised.

'Yes, I was in the office earlier. He had a bit of a rant about you meddling in police business at first, but he had to admit, your input was invaluable.'

Morwenna groaned as a wave splashed in her eyes. 'I'm not the best of sleuths – I'm still learning. It makes me cross, the obvious clues I miss, the things I get wrong and the amount of time it takes for the penny to drop.'

'You're doing yourself an injustice. You're persistent, you have an incredible instinct – and you're brave,' Jane said, water shining on her face.

'Oh, I don't know.' Morwenna said. 'I'm just me.' She looked up into the rain as it plopped into her eyes. It pooled into the sea, deep droplets spattering. 'I feel a bit sorry for Anna.'

'She made choices,' Jane said gravely. 'And they weren't good ones.'

'No, they were all bad,' Morwenna agreed. She pushed away with strong arms, cutting through the sea; she needed a moment to herself. The image of Anna's wedding photo floated before her eyes, her smug expression, her new husband Will, smartly suited, and she wondered if Anna had ever known true love. The money and power she'd craved had been her undoing. She thought of Inga, and her brother, Karl, who'd supplied the arsenic. So many wasted lives.

No doubt Karl would be picked up by the police – Jane had the photo Morwenna took in the restaurant. Then she thought of Daniel Kitto, where it had all begun, his plans for retirement and a new life. It was all such a shame.

She stared towards the horizon, where stone-grey sea met silver-washed skies, and she thought of her own life, her family, friends. They were safe, alive, happy, and so was she. That counted for everything. She would focus on the people she loved. Morwenna turned back to shore; the others were already swimming back. They'd be cold. Morwenna was shivering. She was desperate to get dry, tug on her clothes, put on a brave face. At the moment, only one thing loomed large in her mind: a mug of scalding hot chocolate at the Proper Ansom Tearoom. With cream. And marshmallows.

* * *

The hour spent in the tearoom passed quickly; Morwenna stared into a steaming mug while the world whirled around her. Tamsin was busy serving drinks; several noisy visitors came in from the rain, emmets who'd just arrived for a holiday in sunny Cornwall and were dismayed by the dismal weather. Lamorna popped in on her way to Gill Bennett's house for lunch, kissing Morwenna on the top of her head tenderly. She muttered something about Daniel's post-mortem and his delayed funeral and was on her way. Elowen was a bundle of energy, playing a game of mermaids with Oggy Two, chattering about a visit to the trampoline park with Britney later. Morwenna heard Tamsin say, 'Give Grandma a bit of space today,' then she went back to staring into the mug. She heard voices, the doorbell clanging; she looked up occasionally as people came and went, calling out greetings.

But Anna Carlyon was still inside her head, saying she'd put enough poison in her tea, 'so that your heart would fail, you'd fall off your bicycle on the way home and no one would pin it on me...' The words looped in her mind like a stuck record and Morwenna shivered. Jane took pity on her, gave her a lift back to Harbour Cottages and promised to catch up soon. Morwenna hurried inside the house, out of the rain. She stood for a long time beneath a hot shower, pulled on her clothes, wrapping herself in the Cornish cardigan, and curled up on the sofa. Brenda leaped up to sit on her, pawing at the cardigan, nestling on her knee, her purr rhythmic and loud. Morwenna closed heavy eyelids and exhaled.

* * *

She must have slept for hours. She was woken by a rapping at the door. Brenda had gone; Morwenna could hear the sound of crunching from the kitchen, so the cat was snacking again. She wondered briefly if she was overfeeding her; Brenda had been all skin and bones when she'd rescued her from the library six months ago. She was a robust cat now, to say the least.

The knock came again and she heard the turn of a key. Ruan could let himself in. Morwenna eased her aching body out of the sofa and into the hall, padding in bare feet, her hair dishevelled, yawning. Ruan stood in front of her holding up the spare door key, a basket in his hands. He smiled, but it was not his usual easy grin. He said, 'I brought you some food. I don't suppose you've eaten?'

'What time is it?'

'Six thirty.'

Morwenna had had no idea it was so late. 'You'd better come in.'

Ruan led the way into the living room, depositing the basket on the table. 'I made a quiche, roasted potatoes, focaccia, and a green salad.'

'Focaccia?' Morwenna almost smiled. 'You're becoming a proper gourmet chef.' She recalled the bao buns he'd made for her months ago. He hadn't cooked for her since. 'This is nice, Ruan. Kind of you.'

'I took Elowen and Britney to Hippity Hoppers this afternoon. Carole's busy in the B & B. She's expecting new guests after the Spriggan crowd leave tomorrow.'

Morwenna saw a look pass across his face that was hard to read. She'd ignore it for now.

'I bet Elowen enjoyed herself.'

'She did. She trampolines like a mermaid apparently – as if she's swimming in the air. And she sings all the time, like a mermaid.' Ruan was unloading the basket. He showed her a bottle of Chianti. 'I brought this.'

'Lovely. What quiche is it?'

'Spinach and ricotta. I made it this morning before I took the girls out.'

Morwenna was impressed. 'We'd better sit down, then. I'll fetch plates and glasses.'

She dished up as Ruan poured wine. She wasn't sure yet if she was hungry or not. Ruan said, 'It's a shame you missed the curtain call last night. Elowen was on form. She kept bowing and bowing to the applause and the audience lapped it up. Musa had to pick her up to stop her showing off.'

'Ah.'

'I wouldn't be surprised if she ends up on the stage.'

Morwenna thought of Inga. 'It's a hard life, being an actor.'

'It is,' Ruan agreed and Morwenna assumed he was thinking of Kenzie.

She asked tentatively, 'What will happen to Spriggan now... now Daniel and Anna are out of the picture?'

Ruan sliced a piece of quiche. 'They'll carry on as a co-operative, I think. Several of the group have friends who are actors. They were talking about expanding. They'll need to fill Inga's role quickly before Padstow on Tuesday night. Tommy's been asked to go with them as the new techie.'

'He'll enjoy that.' Morwenna took a sip of wine, the sharpness staying on her tongue. 'Better than being on the fishing boats.'

'Fishing's not for everyone,' Ruan said.

Morwenna thought he looked handsome and allowed herself a moment's reflection. She'd always found him attractive. That hadn't ever been the problem between them. Then she said, 'It's nice, sharing dinner. Thanks, Ruan – I need this.'

'I thought so.' Ruan smiled. He was ever practical. There was a quiet time for a while, just the sound of munching. Then Ruan said, 'I wanted to talk to you about something.'

'Oh?' Morwenna remembered he'd texted that.

'About Kenzie.'

Morwenna put her fork down. 'Oh. Right.' She steeled herself: she knew what was coming. It had been on the cards for two weeks.

Ruan avoided her eyes. 'After the last night's performance, she invited me back to the B & B – for a drink.'

'I see.' Morwenna stared at a green leaf and wondered whether to eat it.

'So – I went.'

'Right.'

'She said she had a bottle of champagne in her room. I thought we'd have a drink together, celebrate the end of the show.' Ruan took a deep breath.

'Just you?' Morwenna asked tentatively.

'I guessed it might be just me there. And I was right.'

'So…' Morwenna wondered how to ask the question. Instead, she said, 'Was it nice? The champagne?'

'It was all right.' Ruan lifted his shoulders. That wasn't what he'd intended to talk about. 'When I got there, she was all dressed up, well, down.'

'Ah...'

'A black see-through thing.' Ruan met her gaze. 'I thought she might have something like that in mind. But I thought I could handle it.'

Morwenna imagined Kenzie the seductress in black lace, tugging Ruan onto the bed. She was Morgan le Fay again, all over him. He'd have been under her spell after the first gulp of Moët. She took a deep breath.

'Well, it was nice of you to tell me, Ruan, but what you do with your life is up to you. I mean, we're not together.' She swallowed more Chianti and started to ramble. 'And I've had a couple of dates with Barnaby, nothing serious of course, but you're a free agent, you can do as you wish—'

'I didn't sleep with her.'

Morwenna's mouth was open. 'Oh?'

'It wasn't right.'

'How do you mean?'

'I saw her in The Smugglers once or twice last week. I took her back to Carole's B & B because she asked me to – she'd drunk quite a lot. She hung on my arm all the time. I think she thought we were sort of going out together, that we were a couple.' Ruan shook his head, baffled. 'I never really kissed her. A peck on the cheek. But – well, I suppose I was curious, a bit.'

'How do you mean, curious?'

'She's young, attractive, vivacious – all those things, you know. And she seemed to like me a lot. So when she asked me to go round, I thought she'd have romance on her mind.'

Morwenna laughed at the euphemism. 'You mean sex?'

'I wasn't sure how I'd feel. So I went.' Ruan sounded ambivalent.

'I thought, well, you'd been dating Pam's brother. I knew it was all right – our lives are separate.'

He looked sad and Morwenna felt a pang of regret. 'But?'

'It wasn't for me,' Ruan said honestly. 'I told her I was very flattered and she was a lovely woman and any other man probably wouldn't hesitate but – I still had feelings for someone else.'

Morwenna looked away. 'Ruan…'

Ruan murmured, 'There it is. I'm not ready.'

'Yet.'

'Maybe.'

'The thing is…' Morwenna poked her fork in a potato '…to be honest, it's a bit like that with me and Barnaby. I'm not ready for a – a big relationship either. Maybe I never will be. Maybe it just takes time. I don't know.'

'Do you think we're both evolving?' Ruan asked.

'Possibly.'

His voice was low. 'Or maybe we're not over each other?'

Morwenna reached for her glass. 'Don't, Ruan…'

'I'm just saying.' He began to tuck into his quiche again. 'What will be will be.'

Morwenna stared at him. 'What are you suggesting?'

Ruan shrugged. 'We're Tam's parents, Elowen's grandparents. We share a past. We're friends. But no one can predict the future.'

'Right.'

'So, we'll just carry on as we are, take care of each other, see what happens.'

'See what happens.'

'And enjoy this dinner I made for us both. It's not every man who has a successful sleuth as his ex.'

'It makes sense.' Morwenna forced a grin. It did. 'All right, Ruan. We're fine as we are. We'll see where life takes us.'

Ruan lifted his glass. 'To friendship, then. And to us, to being whatever we will become.'

Morwenna raised her wine glass and said, *'Yeghes da.'*

'Yeghes da,' Ruan echoed and their eyes met.

He was right. The future was uncertain. What would be would be.

33

By Monday morning, Morwenna was feeling much better, full of the joys of spring. It was a bright day, the blue basin of the bay sparkled in sunlight at the bottom of the hill as she cycled to the library. Her spirits were lifting again; the month of May brought in the summer, the emmets visiting in droves with their different accents and their ready smiles. The beaches would be glorious and Seal Bay would be buzzing. She loved this time of year, cycling along the Cornish roads in a cardigan and a pair of stripy leggings. It would be shorts and T-shirts before too long. The thought made her smile. The tearoom would be busy; the business thriving throughout the summer meant extra work, no more swanning off sleuthing at least for a while, but Morwenna didn't mind. Warm days and balmy nights lay ahead.

The Spriggan Travelling Theatre Company had dismantled most of the marquee by the time she slowed down at the seafront. Tommy Buvač waved; he was packing boxes into the pickup trailer. Other members of the cast were lifting cases, moving costumes and lights. Musa noticed Morwenna and came over, holding out a hand for her to shake. 'It's goodbye, then, Morwenna. I won't forget Seal Bay.'

'I bet.' Morwenna offered a wry grin. 'I hope Padstow will be less eventful.'

'I'm sure it will. We have two more actors joining us later this afternoon. One's a friend of mine – she's taking over as Guinevere. The other's a director we've worked with before. Spriggan will really thrive with her at the helm.'

'I'm glad,' Morwenna said. 'And you have Tommy now.'

'He's a great find,' Musa agreed.

Morwenna examined his face. He looked well, but she had to ask. 'How are you feeling?'

'I'm OK.' Musa said. 'It's down to you, Morwenna. I shudder to think what might have happened...'

Morwenna put a hand up to stop him – it was best unsaid. Instead, she said, 'Jane tells me that Inga's been charged with Daniel's murder and attempted arson, as well as several other offences. Anna's been charged too...' She took a step closer to him. 'Musa, it would be nice if some of the Spriggan actors could come to Daniel's funeral. It's been put back a week or so. His daughter is organising the service and Mum's helping her.'

'I'll make sure we're all there to pay our respects,' Musa said quietly. 'I have your phone number. I'll text.'

She took his hand. 'All the best. We'll catch up then.'

'We will,' Musa said.

Morwenna was about to ride off when she heard a voice call her name. Kenzie, in a dark jacket, her hair tucked in a beanie, hurried across the beach.

'Morwenna – I wanted to say goodbye.' She clutched Morwenna in a spontaneous hug, bike and all. 'And to say thanks.'

'Thanks?'

'For the swimming and – and for just being so kind and supportive.'

'Right.' Morwenna wasn't sure she had been. 'Come swimming again next time you're this way.'

'I'd like that,' Kenzie said. She hesitated as if to say something, then she changed her mind and muttered, 'Stay safe. Follow your heart.'

'Oh, I always do.' Morwenna placed a foot on the pedal and took off, an arm in the air, waving.

She heard Kenzie call after her, 'I said your heart – not your head...'

Morwenna picked up speed, arriving at the library feeling too warm. She abandoned her bike in the corridor as she always did and rushed into the library. Jane was waiting, holding a tray with four mugs and a plate of biscuits. She grinned. 'Bang on time. Let me introduce our guest.'

Morwenna smiled a greeting at Donald Stewart, then her eyes slid to the man next to him and she extended a hand. 'You must be Pawly. Hello.'

Pawly Yelland shook it in his bear paw. 'Hello, Morwenna. I've heard so much about you.'

'Oh? Good, I hope.' Morwenna took in his broad shoulders, a thick thatch of slate-grey hair, sparkling eyes. He was probably in his fifties, muscular, jolly, in a 'Save the Earth' T-shirt and khaki shorts. She hadn't imagined a writer of historical books to look like an outdoors type. She said, 'I'm reading *Hidden Secrets of Seal Bay* at the moment. It's wonderful.'

'Thanks,' Pawly said. 'And I've been hearing all about you, how you help the police solve crimes. You must be a local treasure.'

Morwenna wasn't sure Rick Tremayne would agree. She said, 'Today, I'm just a librarian, standing in front of a writer, looking for a ghost.'

'Lady Elizabeth Pengellen,' Louise agreed.

'She's here with us now…' Donald did the thing he often did with his eyes, rolling them knowingly. 'I can feel her presence.'

Pawly glanced at Morwenna. 'What do you think?'

'That Lady Elizabeth killed herself at Pengellen Manor in 1859. It's a fact. I work with facts,' Morwenna said simply. She wouldn't mention the poison, not today.

'Right, good,' Pawly said enthusiastically. 'And do you believe she's here?'

'Not really, no.' Morwenna helped herself to a mug of tea. The bike ride had made her thirsty. She reminded herself to drink more water. 'She'd be more likely to haunt Pengellen Manor, if anywhere at all. That's where she died.'

'But she loved the library that the Pengellens built for Seal Bay. This is her refuge,' Louise insisted.

'She loves books,' Donald agreed. 'This place is her spiritual home.'

'The thing is,' Pawly explained, 'I'm keen to write a book about her. So I'll be here to do some research, invite some experts in and ask their opinions. I don't want to disturb your day-to-day library business, but I'd like to be a bit of a permanent fixture during the summer, and try to get to the bottom of this haunting business and Lady Elizabeth's backstory. What do you think of that?'

Louise's face flushed with excitement. 'Oh, I'd love that, Pawly.'

'You'd appear in my acknowledgements for the book, and I'd be very keen to draw on your expertise.' He turned to Morwenna. 'Would you be up for that?'

Morwenna was pleased. 'I don't see why not. It sounds interesting.'

'That's good,' Pawly began, but Donald rested a hand on his arm.

'Don't you think we should ask our resident ghost for her permission?' he murmured.

'Right,' Pawly said, humouring him. His eyes twinkled. 'I'll ask her.'

Louise and Donald watched him as he said matter-of-factly, 'Lady Elizabeth, may I come into the library and research your life?'

They waited. It might have been a slight creak over by the door. Or it might have been the wind.

Then Donald said, his voice deep, 'O speak to us, my lady – let your servants know your wishes...'

Morwenna pressed her lips together in an attempt to look serious. They waited even longer. Donald and Louise exchanged anxious gazes. Morwenna thought Pawly's eyes danced with mischief. Then the silence was broken with a loud blast of the *Mission Impossible* theme. It came from Morwenna's cardigan pocket. She tugged out her phone. 'Sorry – I'll just take this.'

She moved quickly into the hall, next to her bike, and said, 'Barnaby? Hello.'

'Hi, Morwenna.' Barnaby sounded eager to talk. 'How are you?'

'Fine.'

'Pam messaged me – she told me all about what's been happening in Seal Bay. Your hunch was correct about the Carlyon woman, then?'

'Sadly, yes,' Morwenna said.

'But you're all right, after everything that happened? Pam's given me the low-down.'

'I'm fine, thanks.' Morwenna was pleased to hear his concern. 'And thanks so much for your help, and your client who tested the tonic.'

'My pleasure...' Barnaby was about to speak, then he hesitated.

Morwenna said, 'How are you?'

'Busy. That's why I rang.'

'Oh?'

'I'm inundated with clients, and I'm having to schedule them for June and July, because I've just been invited to a conference in the States for a few weeks. I'm not sure when I'll be back. I might stay on to shadow a colleague.'

'Oh – that's nice,' Morwenna replied – she wasn't sure if she was being given the brush-off.

'It'll be beneficial for my business.'

'Ideal,' Morwenna said to fill the silence.

'But I'll be back in Seal Bay later in the summer. Maybe we can meet then, pick up where we left off, have dinner?'

'I owe you a pasty in The Smugglers,' Morwenna teased.

'Yes, I'll – ha, ha – I'll look forward to that.'

'Good.'

'Well, shall I text you?'

'All right. Send me some pictures of – the places you visit?' Morwenna suggested.

'Yes, indeed. Ah, so – take care of yourself, Morwenna. For now.'

'I will. Bye, Barnaby—' she began, but he was gone.

Morwenna stared at her phone and wondered what the call had meant. On the surface, he was going to the States for a surgeons' conference, staying on to learn new practices. That was fine. She wouldn't dig beneath the surface and overthink it – there was little point. She paused to think about their relationship. At the moment, they were friends who shared dinner. Little more. She was happy to keep it that way for the time being. Relationships were far too confusing.

She shoved the phone in her pocket and turned back to the library. Louise was talking excitedly about the ghost, asking Pawly if he liked wild swimming and would he join the SWANs on Sundays. Donald took over. He said he believed that Lady Elizabeth was a constant presence in the library and it should be acknowledged by everyone in Seal Bay once and for all.

Morwenna watched them for a moment, listening. She'd have a few moments to herself before she went back to join in the conversation. She gazed around, realising how much she loved the familiar old Victorian library. It was a second home, with its arched roof, books stacked on shelves, that warm musty smell of old tomes and crisp fresh pages. She heard Pawly Yelland say, 'I'm really looking forward to this project. Elizabeth Pengellen is a fascinating subject. Are we all on board?'

'I am. Definitely.' Morwenna sauntered towards him. 'Count me in. I can't wait to delve into the history of Lady Lizzie. Let's find out once and for all if there's really a ghost in our library, what she was like and what she got up to.'

The idea filled her with excitement; it would be just like sleuthing but hopefully a little safer. Summer was around the corner and, like a library packed with books, each day was a new page, a chance to start again. Daniel Kitto didn't have that chance now, nor did Inga, nor Anna Carlyon.

Morwenna took a deep breath. She'd never take that for granted. She'd concentrate on herself now, and on the people she cared about. She'd have so much fun.

That was what really mattered.

ACKNOWLEDGEMENTS

I have so many people to thank from the bottom of my heart.

Kiran, my agent. Sarah, my editor. Two of life's stars.

Everyone at Boldwood Books; the dream team. Fellow writers, bloggers, reviewers, editors, without whose support I would be invisible.

The writers of cosy crime at Boldwood and beyond: all the writers whose books I read avidly for research and pleasure. I continue to grow.

Friends, family, everyone I love.

Not forgetting the wonderful Solitary Writers and my fabulous neighbours.

My American family.

Tony and Kim. Liam, Maddie and Cait. Big G.

And huge thanks to my police consultants, James and Nina, and Kitty, the wild swimming expert. Their knowledge is invaluable.

To the people of Cornwall, who inspire my warm, wonderful characters.

And to you, my reader, I give my deepest thanks. A story without readers is a world without sunshine.

Sending warmest wishes, always. x

ABOUT THE AUTHOR

Judy Leigh is the bestselling author of *A Grand Old Time* and *Five French Hens* and the doyenne of the 'it's never too late' genre of women's fiction. She has lived all over the UK from Liverpool to Cornwall, but currently resides in Somerset.

Sign up to Judy Leigh's mailing list here for news, competitions and updates on future books.

Visit Judy's website: https://judyleigh.com

Follow Judy on social media:

- facebook.com/judyleighuk
- x.com/judyleighwriter
- instagram.com/judyrleigh
- bookbub.com/authors/judy-leigh

ALSO BY JUDY LEIGH

Five French Hens

The Old Girls' Network

Heading Over the Hill

Chasing the Sun

Lil's Bus Trip

The Golden Girls' Getaway

A Year of Mr Maybes

The Highland Hens

The Golden Oldies' Book Club

The Silver Ladies Do Lunch

The Vintage Village Bake Off

The Morwenna Mutton Mysteries Series

Foul Play at Seal Bay

Bloodshed on the Boards

Poison & Pens

POISON & PENS IS THE HOME OF
COZY MYSTERIES SO POUR YOURSELF
A CUP OF TEA & GET SLEUTHING!

DISCOVER PAGE-TURNING NOVELS FROM
YOUR FAVOURITE AUTHORS &
MEET NEW FRIENDS

JOIN OUR
FACEBOOK GROUP

BIT.LYPOISONANDPENSFB

SIGN UP TO OUR
NEWSLETTER

BIT.LY/POISONANDPENSNEWS

Boldwood

Boldwood Books is an award-winning fiction publishing company seeking out the best stories from around the world.

Find out more at www.boldwoodbooks.com

Join our reader community for brilliant books, competitions and offers!

Follow us
@BoldwoodBooks
@TheBoldBookClub

Sign up to our weekly deals newsletter

https://bit.ly/BoldwoodBNewsletter

Printed in Dunstable, United Kingdom